PENGUIN BOOKS
THE BOOK OF VOWS

Amit Majmudar is an internationally acclaimed novelist, poet and essayist, as well as a translator of the Bhagavad Gita (*Godsong*, PRHI, 2018). His work has won awards in both the United States and India. He works as a diagnostic and nuclear radiologist in Westerville, Ohio, where he lives with his wife and three children.

Celebrating 35 Years of
Penguin Random House India

PRAISE FOR THE AUTHOR

'This vibrant, vigorous reimagining of an ancient epic . . . [has] the feel and breath and urgency of lived life'—Namita Gokhale

'A lyrical kaleidoscope with many colours and prisms . . . An imaginative rendering demonstrating that as long as there are mountains and rivers on earth, this story will be popular . . . '—Bibek Debroy

'For those who like mythology and mytho-fiction, this book is a lovely read . . . The writing of the book . . . has a flow which is almost poetic'—*Times of India*

'. . . Majmudar's prose reads like verses, beautifully structured, using a fewer number of words to convey a complex range of emotions. What's more is that the entire story is presented to us like an epic drama playing out before our eyes . . . The experience can only be likened to witnessing a play in the theatre. Such is the mark of good writing; it leaves you not only with a story but an experience to remember'—*Financial Express*

ALSO BY THE SAME AUTHOR

Soar: A Novel

Sitayana

Godsong: A Verse Translation of the Bhagavad-Gita, with Commentary

The BOOK OF VOWS

THE MAHABHARATA TRILOGY
VOLUME 1

AMIT MAJMUDAR

PENGUIN BOOKS

An imprint of Penguin Random House

PENGUIN BOOKS

USA | Canada | UK | Ireland | Australia
New Zealand | India | South Africa | China | Singapore

Penguin Books is part of the Penguin Random House group of companies whose addresses can be found at global.penguinrandomhouse.com

Published by Penguin Random House India Pvt. Ltd
4th Floor, Capital Tower 1, MG Road,
Gurugram 122 002, Haryana, India

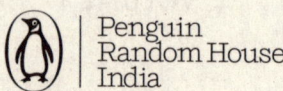

First published in Penguin Books by Penguin Random House India 2023

Copyright © Amit Majmudar 2023

All rights reserved

10 9 8 7 6 5 4 3 2 1

ISBN 9780143458302

This is a book of mythological fiction and contains the author's retellings of stories from cultural and religious lore, the sources and interpretations of which are varied and subjective in nature. The contents of this book do not purport to reflect the opinions or views of Penguin Random House or any of its officers. Nothing in this book is intended to cause offence or to hurt the sentiments of any individual, community, section of people, group or religion. Any liability arising from any action undertaken by any person by relying upon any part of this book is strictly disclaimed. The book contains some matters of sensitive nature, including references to sexual activity, sexuality and violence. Reader discretion is advised. The book is not recommended for anyone below the age of eighteen years.

This is a work of fiction. Names, characters, places and incidents are either the product of the author's imagination or are used fictitiously and any resemblance to any actual person, living or dead, events or locales is entirely coincidental.

For sale in the Indian Subcontinent only

Typeset in Adobe Garamond Pro by Manipal Technologies Limited, Manipal
Printed at Replika Press Pvt. Ltd, India

This book is sold subject to the condition that it shall not, by way of trade or otherwise, be lent, resold, hired out, or otherwise circulated without the publisher's prior consent in any form of binding or cover other than that in which it is published and without a similar condition including this condition being imposed on the subsequent purchaser.

www.penguin.co.in

'vixere fortas ante Agamemnona multi'
Many brave men lived before Agamemnon

—Horace

CONTENTS

Introduction ix
Prelude xvii

Sarga 1: Everything Begins with a Vow — 1
Sarga 2: The Perils of Marrying a River — 8
Sarga 3: The Fearsome Vow — 17
Sarga 4: A River in Spate — 30
Sarga 5: The Stained Battleaxe — 43
Sarga 6: 'The Bull of the Bharatas' — 56
Sarga 7: Blind Boy, Pale Boy, Visionary — 69
Sarga 8: Love of God — 77
Sarga 9: The Darling Darkling Changeling — 87
Sarga 10: Rivalries — 103
Sarga 11: Storytime for the Little Pandavas — 113
Sarga 12: The Bad Axle — 122
Sarga 13: From a Pail to the Palace — 139
Sarga 14: Sunrise of the Golden Boy — 152
Sarga 15: Ignition Her Beauty and Fire Her Womb — 164
Sarga 16: Deathtrap Vacation Home — 175

Sarga 17: Bheem in Love	185
Sarga 18: Wrestling on a Full Stomach	195
Sarga 19: For the Love of a Blue Lotus	204
Sarga 20: Dividing Infinity by Five	215
Sarga 21: Partitions	223
Sarga 22: Arjuna's Adventures in Exile	236
Sarga 23: Controlled Burn	259
Sarga 24: Tearing Along the Dotted Line	268
Sarga 25: Guests	278
Sarga 26: The Hundred Insults	290
Sarga 27: Skilled at a Game of Chance	301
Sarga 28: Raising the Stakes	310
Sarga 29: A Temple Is Sacked	320
Sarga 30: The Killing Vows	329

INTRODUCTION

WHAT IS THE MAHABHARATA?

Of India's two epic poems, one was seemingly designed to disseminate. The Ramayana has a love story, a clear hero and a clear villain, talking monkeys, victimhood transcended and victimization avenged and plenty of magical adventure. Puppets in Java and kings of Thailand took their names from it. Before the Gospels, the Ramayana was the most popular story on earth, and it spread because of its own appeal, without the help of missionary empires or a Gideon society. The story travelled so well in part because it resembles a fairy tale—its prince and princess separated and, after many brave deeds, reunited. And indeed it is believed to be the earlier of the two epics.

What about India's other epic poem, the Mahabharata? It travelled too—one of the earliest surviving Sanskrit manuscripts was found inside a cave along the northern Silk Road in present-day China; carbon dated to 130 CE, it contains a table of contents for the Mahabharata. This epic, which grew by accretion to the longest in the world, has a more forbidding design. The original text, which fills multiple volumes, seems meant to be accessed piecemeal and selectively, like the internet; meant to be read in segments, like genetic code, the DNA of a civilization.

The Mahabharata contains complexities, ambiguities, backstories, digressions, parables, treatises, dozens of characters who combine admirable and frustrating traits, interventions in the story by the poet who will go on to compose it and plenty of death on both sides. It hosts a complete version of the Ramayana, an incantatory list of the 1000 names of Vishnu and a philosophical dialogue that has since been elevated to the status of an independent scripture. This is no once-upon-a-time, no happily-ever-after. The Mahabharata is narrative art that has evolved far beyond the fairy tale. It makes the novel, even at its most 'epic' or experimental or capacious, at its most Tolstoian or Joycean or Proustian, seem reserved, small-scale, unambitious.

WHY WRITE A MAHABHARATA?

There are other things a poet or novelist could do with their limited time on earth. A novel with a contemporary setting is likelier to find an audience. Poems that find audiences are usually short and 'lyrical', focusing on personal experiences and emotions. I coach myself often enough to do what works, in prose and in verse—but the instant my fingers touch the keyboard, they disobey me. And so I ended up (re)writing the Mahabharata.

In the original epic, the frame story opens with a king holding a grand sacrifice. Vyasa, the epic's composer (as well as an important character in it, as you will see), shows up to present the epic poem for the first time. But it isn't Vyasa who recites it. Vyasa's pupil, Vaishampayana, has learned it from his teacher and recites it instead. Vyasa doesn't add a word. So, from the very beginning, the epic is *transmitted*. We do not hear from Vyasa. We hear from Vyasa's pupil. I, too, am Vyasa's pupil. I am a conduit of the story.

This transmission has a long tradition across cultures. The Bhagavad Gita, the famous dialogue-treatise-vision embedded in the Mahabharata, shows Krishna recounting the lineage of the wisdom he is sharing.

> This imperishable yoga
> I proclaimed to Vivasvat;
> Vivasvat explained it to Manu;
> Manu told it to Ishkvaku.
>
> Each one got it from another,
> And so the royal seers knew this.

Each one got it from another. The Gita itself has a frame story: a blind king's adviser, Sanjaya, has been blessed by Vyasa with the ability to see and hear the battlefield even though he is not there. In a faraway throne room with the blind king, Sanjaya reports on the battles in real time. So the Gita we have is not Krishna's own writing, nor Arjuna's account of what Krishna said to him. It is the transcription of a real-time account of a conversation occurring dozens of miles away, magically overheard. Add a translation to that passage, and you read *Godsong* at the end of multiple stages of transmission.

The epic in the Indian tradition that precedes the Mahabharata is the Ramayana, composed by the 'first poet', Valmiki. The first few chapters of the Ramayana also give us this theme of transmission. The Balakanda (Childhood Canto) begins with Valmiki asking the wandering, celestial sage Narada a question: 'Is there a man in the world today who is truly virtuous?' Narada responds by narrating to Valmiki a condensed version of the Ramayana. After that, Valmiki walks in the woods and sees a hunter kill two mating cranes. The curse that emerges from his lips is in the metre of his future epic. Marvelling at this metre, he decides to compose a full-length poem based on Narada's summary. When he is done, he asks himself another question: 'Who should perform it?' He settles on Rama's own sons, Lava and Kusha. So the first public recitation of the Ramayana is not performed by Valmiki, but by Valmiki's twin pupils.

It's not just the Indian tradition that insists on the separation between the story's origination and its actual performance. The Greek and Latin epics do this through the long-standing tradition of the 'invocation'. Homer's Iliad begins with a plea: 'Sing, Muse . . .' The poet is merely transcribing what the muse sings. It is significant that there is doubt and mystery regarding whether Homer and Vyasa were real people at all. Both traditions of scholarship speculate that Homer and Vyasa, if they did exist, played the role of a 'compiler', which is just another way of saying the transmission did not start with them—something Vyasa and Homer assert themselves at the very start of their respective epics.

Neither the Greek tragedians, nor Virgil and Dante, nor Shakespeare invented their own stories. Milton did not come up with the story of *Paradise Lost*, and Goethe did not invent the character of Faust. This should not be a surprise. A myth's source may well be some single mainspring, perhaps the human brain itself. Joseph Campbell once distilled the mythology of many different civilizations to a 'hero's journey' narrative. Kurt Vonnegut listed six basic plots; a 2004 book claimed to have discovered seven; there are other lists, too, but they all point to a larger pattern, which is that a good story has features that recur within and across cultures. The originality comes through, not in *what* is being told, but in *how*. Every story comes from somewhere; our lines have lineages. Originality is recombinant. A story resembles language itself: texts recombine pre-existing words, and words recombine twenty-six letters. A language resembles life itself: an individual recombines his or her parental DNA, and DNA recombines four nucleotides. That is the fundamental reason why I have written a Mahabharata, as taught to me by Vaishampayana, as taught to him by Vyasa. It is alive. It lives through me. It makes my writing live.

WHY READ THE MAHABHARATA?

I read the Mahabharata to renew my faith in the power of language. Warriors, using secret, charged incantations, arm their arrows like nuclear warheads, and ordinary wood and feather become capable of devastation; vows, curses, boons alter lives and histories, more binding than any paper treaty of modern times. The poet Vyasa, composer of the epic and grandfather of both sets of warring cousins, begets both—the lineage and the lines that record it.

I read the Mahabharata to transcend my sense of self and other. In this epic, neither side is demonized. Characters on both sides have flaws and virtues, shortcomings and excellence; the epic admits no simplistic good versus evil, with the good granted heaven and the evil sent to hell. That Heroic-age ethos has something to teach me in the age of propaganda and polarization. The first person the eldest Pandava sees in the heaven of warriors is the eldest Kaurava. Even the semi-divine characters are human and stuck making morally ambiguous decisions. Even the avatar.

I read the Mahabharata to understand my ancestors better—and not just my own ancestors. I understand how the ancient Greeks experienced the Iliad because I have known, since I was a child, how we experienced the Mahabharata and Ramayana. As I thought of Arjuna and Rama, so Socrates and Plato, as boys, thought of Hector and Odysseus; no doubt a Sumerian child listened, with identical fascination, to the adventures of Gilgamesh.

The epics defined a collective. They were well known but still exciting. Long before I knew Vyasa's massive poem, I knew picture books, songs, short prose versions and television series that retold stories from it. We loved these stories the way we loved our names and our families. The stories did not speak *to* us so much as *of* us. I felt the same thrill while hearing anecdotes about my grandfathers, who died before I was born. *That is who I come from.*

HOW TO READ THE MAHABHARATA

It is a historical anomaly that these epics have survived this long—and inside them, as if in a suit of armour, a religion. All the other ancient religions that identified with epic poems have been extinguished.

Yet the same patterns recur. Today, it seems to me that the modern West has reverted to a 'pagan' civilization, a development that began with the Renaissance and its copious mythological art. This has reached its apogee in the United States. The American insistence on freedom of religion replicates polytheistic Bharata's traditional plurality, which offered a safe haven to persecuted Zoroastrians, Jews and early Christians. At this point in its history, American culture largely ignores Biblical mythology in its mainstream cultural productions; the civilization that went to the moon and invented the internet has evolved and elevated its own epic cycle, *Star Wars*. It matches the Homeric cycle with its latter-day spawning of side stories and backstories, novels and comic books which proliferated even before Disney began filming sequels and spin-offs.

The Mahabharata is not an equivalent of the Iliad. The Iliad, like *A New Hope*, is a single episode in the long course of the conflict. Vyasa's epic is equivalent to the entire Homeric Cycle—the set of epics (by various forgotten poets like Stasinus and Actinus) that told the whole story of the Trojan War, from the Judgement of Paris to Odysseus's adventures after his return to Ithaca. It is the equivalent of the entire *Star Wars* series, spin-offs included. That is why it is so long.

How to read it, then? Every feast is divided into plates and every plate is cleared bite by bite. This book does that. I have distilled and recreated Vyasa's epic, the longest in existence, into a book that is shorter than the shortest volume of *Game of Thrones*. I have provided summaries that guide a reader through the next three or four *sargas* (chapters); these can serve as refreshers if the book is set down and returned to after a while. A division into three books provides another segmentation of the narrative—from small to medium to big bites. Three big bites and the poem's feast is in your belly. You have cleared the smorgasbord like wolf-bellied Bheem.

A NOTE ON THE SOURCES

The Mahabharata has been translated or retold in many ways prior to this trilogy. Some authors retell the epic plainly, focusing on the sequence of events. Such versions, often verging on mere summary, avoid linguistic artistry and narrative embellishment. Others novelize the epic, following the conventions and style, most commonly, of the West's 'fantasy' genre.

This trilogy, grounded in the original Sanskrit epic, attempts to *recreate* the ancient epic for a contemporary audience. What did experiencing an epic poem feel like? My main source has been Vyasa himself. I have accessed the 2009 Penguin Classics translation of the epic by John D. Smith and the 1997 Columbia University Press translation by Chakravarthi V. Narasimhan. Both of these are abridgements; even Smith's nearly 800-page version translates only 11 per cent of the original and summarizes the rest. I should also note that I watched B.R. Chopra's television series on Doordarshan as a boy in the late 1980s. That version made an early impression, and I still visualize some of those actors, in their brass *mukuts*, when I write the names of these characters.

Although I have followed Vyasa's work closely, no line of this prose translates any line in Vyasa's poem to my knowledge, because my other source has been my imagination. There are details and occasional stylistic touches here that are missing from other versions, including Vyasa's, because I made them up. My rule, when indulging my poetic licence, has always been to do no violence to the narrative itself. I have recreated, reimagined and retold, but I have not wrecked.

This trilogy, for all its pages, is not the work of a completist. I have not included some plodding equivalent of every single backstory, side story or learned discourse to be found in Vyasa. I would need thirty volumes and ten rebirths to cover all that material.

My aim has been to recreate the Mahabharata: the feel, though not the form, of its poetry and its fate-haunted, magical air. The first volume, *The Book of Vows,* follows the story from the earliest lineages to the catastrophic gambling match. The second volume is called *The Book of Discoveries* and takes you through the thirteen-year exile to the eve of war and the singing of the Bhagavad Gita. The third volume, *The Book of Killings*, covers the war at Kurukshetra and its aftermath. This natural, tripartite division of the Mahabharata allows each book to have a build-up and climax of its own. Read individually, each one is an artistic whole. Read together, they allow you to experience the main stories of the epic.

I am honoured to add this trilogy to the long lineage of Mahabharata versions out there. These exist in dozens of languages and in several different media—not just translations and retellings but paintings and sculptures, stage plays and puppet plays, animated films and television serials. I urge any reader of this book to continue their exploration to access this story in many different ways. There is no single, definitive version of the Mahabharata, not even Vyasa's. The epic tradition's exhilarating *openness*—open source, open access—is what makes books like this one possible. In that spirit of humility and gratitude, I present to you *The Book of Vows.*

PRELUDE

A princess makes love to the sun. An archer cross-dresses and teaches music to girls, telltale index-finger callus plucking sitar strings instead of a bowstring. An old man is so shot through with arrows, he tips over but doesn't touch the ground. He lies there six more months, waiting for the constellations to align their apertures. A princess makes love to the wind. A hundred foetuses incubate in jars of ghee. A prince, for the sake of his lovestruck father, vows never to marry or have a child. A wronged woman, with skin stained charcoal-black from the fire that birthed her, swears not to tie up her blue hair until her five husbands kill the men who wronged her. Arrows multiply mid-air, collide, explode, leave craters that pockmark the cheek of the earth. A princess makes love to the sky.

All these events fit together. All these events really happened. A God unscrews his elephant tusk, dips it in ink and writes . . .

SEQUENCE 1

HOW BHISHMA AND VYASA COME TO BE

I provide these summaries, which are full of spoilers, for anyone who doesn't already know who is who, and what happens in the Mahabharata. Audiences almost always experience epic poems with a sense of the story and characters beforehand. Homer wasn't introducing Achilles to his listeners; that's why the first book of the Iliad can just jump into a quarrel between two warriors without spending much time describing who Achilles and Agamemnon are. Indian children get to know their epics from their parents and grandparents, illustrated board books, cartoons and television shows; Arjun is a fairly common name for boys and Krishna has temples dedicated to him. The epics are in the cultural groundwater.

While these summaries of the action cannot substitute for cultural immersion, they can go some way towards acquainting a reader new to the epic with what to expect. In any case, summaries are nothing new: Milton's *Paradise Lost*, with a comparatively small cast of characters and a widely known and simple plot out of Genesis, added summaries before each book of his poem because readers requested them.

These summaries can serve as handy guides to revisit later on too, as characters reappear later. I have listed, at the end of each summary, the characters who show up again in major roles.

In this first sequence, we hear about the origins of the bloodline that will go on to fight the war. Yet the central figure, whose long life will be the through line for the entire epic, Bhishma, will father no one. The other figure who threads the whole epic is Vyasa, the poet who will go on to write the epic itself. This sequence tells the origin stories of both Bhishma and Vyasa.

The epic begins with Bhishma's father, King Shantanu of Hastinapur. Imagine him weak-chinned, puppy dog-eyed, quick to develop a crush. Shantanu's first love is the River Ganga in human form. She has taken human form to give birth to eight *Vasus* (celestial beings), cursed to mortal embodiment. She drowns each Vasu when he is born to release him from the curse, but to Shantanu's eyes, she is drowning his infant sons. He catches on and intervenes to save the eighth son.

This son is Devavrat. The river Goddess spirits their child away to be educated in the heavens.

Years later, King Shantanu falls in love with a fisherman's low-born daughter. The fisherman wants Shantanu to disinherit Devavrat and make the fisherman's eventual grandson the heir to the throne. Devavrat learns of this and secures his father's happiness by taking a fearsome vow never to marry or beget children. Ever after, his name is Fearsome: 'Bhishma'.

The new fisherwoman-queen has a past, too. Long ago, she ferried an ascetic over the river, slept with him on the boat and gave birth out of wedlock to a black-skinned child. That child is the prodigy, Vyasa.

Characters Who Will Show Up Again:

BHISHMA, the son of the King of Hastinapur and a Goddess, the River Ganga. He will go on to be a mentor and grandfather-figure to the warriors of the epic.

VYASA, the ascetic and poet. He will survive the civil war and write the Mahabharata.

SARGA 1

EVERYTHING BEGINS WITH A VOW

Everything begins with a vow.

Words were everything back then: honour, self-discipline, intensity, power. You said your will out loud: *I'm going to do this.* Once you said it, your will was out in the open. All the worlds and all the universes, all the Gods and all the Goddesses, all your ancestors and all your descendants compared what you said you would do to what you did. *Are you as good as your word, or aren't you?* You could break the vow, but you couldn't un-say it.

Here's one more vow, out in the open.

My name, for this birth at least, is Amit Majmudar, and I vow to tell you the bloody and mystical stories found in the bloodiest, most mystical epic of all time.

I vow to write the Mahabharata.

*

In the Himalayas, Ganga is a cold river, flowing through Shiva's hair. He's an ascetic God, his passions at absolute zero as she bears that iciness downstream. In the lowlands, she warms to her roll as a river. Pyres serve as space heaters for miles on either side.

Ashes from a pyre swirl across the *ghats* in a twister, unsteady, like someone trying to stand up without a skeleton. It's the residue of a once-living body. The cremation fire has shucked it of its *atman*, its self. Now, on legs still wobbly after a long sea voyage, it's trying to clothe another atman, but all that enters it is wind. Once the twister stumbles on to the river's surface, she mixes these fitful ashes into herself, like sugar into milk. She's saturated with the dead.

Downstream, she turns all those grave greys to gravid green. Life! Life to either side of her, reeds and rushes, kingfishers and sugarcane, tree frogs and neem trees. Neem trees: *Azadirachta indica*. An evergreen tree that sheds its leaves sometimes, in draught season. In that, it's like dharma, something immortal that seems to die every so often.

Those neem trees were in the same place three thousand years ago, just like the Ganga herself. A scent of some kind pulsed through those trees. I say *of some kind* because it wasn't the smell of the trees themselves, or the river beyond them, or any flower known to spring, or sandalwood incense or home cooking or recent rain, or a rosemary sprig ghosting my fingers here at home in Ohio, where I'm writing this. It was a beautiful scent—beautiful enough and unclassifiable enough to draw King Shantanu, chin up, eyes blissfully shut, sniff sniff sniffing through the trees.

Breathing had never felt so wonderful! He wouldn't have minded traipsing after that scent for the rest of his life. He could have followed it for weeks and never gotten hungry or thirsty. He couldn't classify it, but he loved it anyway; he loved it because he *remembered* it somehow. It gathered the happiest bits of his past births in a nosegay and took him back even as it drew him on.

When he found its source, though, he was baffled. A teenaged girl squatted on the riverbank, casually skinning lunch. The fish was still gasping, half its body raw and whitish-pink in the sun. Funny, he couldn't smell any fish smell at all.

'Is that really you? Or is that some magical fish that smells good when you skin it?'

The girl jabbed her curved knife at the silver scales. 'It's just a mahseer. The river's full of them.'

'Who are you?'

'A fisherman's daughter. I work that ferry boat right there.'

'Are you wearing perfume?'

'No.' She brought her arm to her nose, as if to check. 'That's just me. Do you want to go across the river?'

The girl had an effortless charm that would have won King Shantanu over even if he hadn't fallen in love with the scent of her. What was it he fell in love with, there on the riverbank? Was she really as good-looking or as lovely-voiced as Shantanu believed her to be? Her heady scent went right to Shantanu's head, and right to the head of everybody who ever met her. No one could see her or hear her objectively. They smelled the happiest moments of all their past lives, all at once. Satyavati may well have been the most beautiful woman in this whole story, since she alone made beauty secondary, if not irrelevant.

'Where's your father?' Shantanu asked her. 'I've got to ask him a question.'

Even though she was barely seventeen, Satyavati had a backstory King Shantanu would never learn.

She hadn't always smelled this good. In fact, she used to smell like a whole shoreline littered with dead carp at high noon. Her nickname across five villages was Matsyagandha, which meant, literally, Fish-stink. The ferry she operated didn't get much business.

She hadn't even told her father what had happened to her two years ago. The fisherman should have known better—what was he thinking, letting his teenaged daughter ferry strangers across a river, unsupervised? She was bound to encounter a randy old man sooner or later. Most people kept away from her fish stink, granted, but the sage Parasara had a cold that day. If he hadn't, the whole course of history and literature would have been different.

Satyavati's dirty old man happened to be one of the greatest wise men of his day. Parasara was literally dirty, having meditated for several months in the same place. Sparrows had nested in his topknot, and a monsoon mudslide still crusted his skin dark. His eyes were bloodshot. He didn't pay attention to the girl ferrying him across until he sneezed several times and blew his nose. When he brought his saffron shawl down from his face, he gagged on the revealed fish stink and registered the fisherman's daughter for the first time. In spite of the stink, he gasped with pleasure. He had spent so much energy these past months quelling his sexual desires that now, in his exhaustion, he couldn't control his response. The slender *apsara* in rags, with her lightly muscled arms working the oars and her knees just inches from his . . . Parasara hurriedly drew his shawl over his lap.

'What is that smell? Has some poison in the river killed off all the fish around here?'

'No, that's just me. They call me Fish-Stink around here.'

'A body like yours deserves to smell better.' Parasara wasn't the most tactful seducer; his fifty-some years had been spent in *samadhi* and Sanskrit grammar. 'You're more beautiful than any princess. I should be rowing *you* around.'

Satyavati, who had heard about old sages and their brutal lifelong curses, froze and handed him the oars. The great *yogi* rowed her to the middle of the river, then made his strokes lazy and light so the boat didn't progress. At last, he came out and asked for what he wanted.

Satyavati said, 'Out here? In the middle of a river?'

Parasara muttered two Sanskrit *slokas*. A thick fog hissed from the rushes on either bank, and darkness curtained them off. 'There. We're alone now.'

'But you yourself said I stink.' Satyavati looked around uneasily, drawing her arms across her chest. 'I'll just go home and wash up . . .'

'I'm giving you a boon. Do you know what a boon is? It's the opposite of a curse.' She nodded at him. 'Do you want one?'

Satyavati bit her lip and pondered for a moment. When else would she get this chance to better her lot? Luckier-born folks were always helping each other out, trading blessings and boons and medicinal verses. All people smelled of their trades—seed-sowers of sweat, swordsmiths of soot, priests of incense, warriors of horses. She was stuck with a fish-smell, and a bad case of it. Even the daughters of other fishermen stiffened in her company and found a way to stand upwind. 'What kind of boon?'

Parasara thought of a boon that would please them both. 'From now on, you'll smell better than any woman on earth, no matter when you soaped last or how much fish you eat.'

Satyavati sniffed her arm, and she smelled the happiest smells of all her past lives. How could she not have warmed, just a little, to this fearsome wonder-worker? 'I still can't,' she apologized. 'What about my future husband? He'll know on our wedding night that I've . . .'

'You'll seal back up,' said Parasara. Some sages, when they spend enough time in samadhi, start seeing the future. He might have been thinking of King Shantanu when he promised, 'Trust me, even after you have my baby, he'll never be able to tell.'

Even after you have my baby. That way of phrasing it made it sound like it had already happened. And in a sense it had, in the infinite repetitions of cyclic time. Everything we do, Satyavati thought, is just a rehearsal for the next time; everything we do is what we've already done. She felt those parallel past and future Satyavatis, in prior universes and universes still to come, synchronize and slide on to the floor of that little ferryboat, where the first drops of blood in this epic were shed.

A whole armada of Satyavatis, nine months later, rowed to a mid-river island and gave birth, each in her own respective *kalpa*, to a baby boy. The baby's skin was as dark as Parasara's skin had been, caked as the old sage was with fog-shadowed monsoon mud. She named her baby for the beautiful darkness of his skin. She named him Krishna.

No, no *that* Krishna. *This* Krishna, generations his elder, went on to become the greatest poet in human history, in part because he told the story of *that* Krishna, and in part because he wrote the bloodiest, most mystical epic ever.

He lived to meet that Krishna, and he wrote his poems under the name *Vyasa*. A God with the head of an elephant took dictation from him once. Unlike other epic poets, Vyasa's characters were his own lineal descendants. He was their first author in more ways than one.

I'll get to that backstory, too. This section is just the beginning, after all. Backstories are the best stories. You can see a whole war in embryo, its genetic code, its basic *raga*. Sage on a ferryboat or king on a riverside, it's always the same thing: desire, desire . . .

*

. . . Desire. What else could make King Shantanu sit cross-legged in a hut that stank of fish? He asked to keep the door open. Satyavati's father had just eaten a fish dinner. The floor, strewn with fish parts, needed sweeping. The shrewd fisherman selected a needle-thin fishbone off the floor and started picking his teeth.

'When the girl came home smelling that good,' he said philosophically, 'I figured she'd marry up one day. Never imagined it would be a palace, though.'

'It is. And you're welcome there.'

'I'm not sure I will like that. I've heard stories about how kings treat their second wives. What's the difference between a second wife and a concubine? It's the wife who gives you a son, an *heir*—that's the one you light incense to. She's your Goddess.'

'I promise I will treat Satyavati well.'

'Of course you will—she's a living stick of incense. What about her children? I have to think about my grandsons and great-grandsons. The way things are, they'll never grow up to be kings . . . unless . . .'

'Unless . . .'

'You have a son. From your first marriage.'

King Shantanu nodded.

'What's his name?'

'Devavrat,' whispered the king.

'Right. You can marry my sweet-smelling daughter, King Shantanu. Just cut your firstborn out of the succession.'

Satyavati wasn't the only one with a backstory. Shantanu, the lovestruck suitor, already had a son. And that backstory was far more scandalous than any secret of Satyavati's. The shrewd fisherman, like the rest of the kingdom, knew about the living son. But nobody knew *anything* about the eight drowned infants.

SARGA 2

THE PERILS OF MARRYING A RIVER

Every river is a woman, at least in Sanskrit. *Sarit* is feminine and *nadi* is feminine. Consider the braid in the flow to the small of her back, her descent from cooler elevations. A diamond city is merely her earring: her head tilts a little, listening to its secret, as she takes it off and sets it in the drawer of history. Every river is a woman.

Shantanu grew up on the bank of the river he married. His parents were pious, so pious they could hardly wait to abandon the material things of this world—which, in their case, were palaces and armies and the running of a kingdom. They ruled their kingdom reluctantly from meditative seats on the bare riverside clay. There they fasted through state dinners, obliging ministers and ambassadors to eat garlic-free food off palm leaves. The royal couple sold off war elephants to fund new temples. Neighbouring kings who bought the elephants turned them around and invaded. But the king and queen had endeared themselves to the Gods, who blessed them with energetic generals. All the invasions failed; they got the war elephants back, often with baby elephants in tow. Sternly, the royal couple ordered prisoners of war to assemble at once in their chains. The king harangued the wounded soldiers on the importance of detachment, yoga and deep breathing, then released them all to hobble home.

Shantanu's mother was the king's only wife, and Shantanu, his only child. This was a baffling decision at the time. Sound policy dictated many wives for a king and many heirs, to hedge against an unlucky mosquito bite or death by fever. The king, however, was beyond worldly considerations. He trusted Shantanu to grow up healthy. The prince played in the river muck and never washed his hands. He poked beetles the size of field mice and nibbled unfamiliar plants. His immunity was excellent. He grew up dark bronze and barefoot.

As he came of age, he came to the notice of the river herself. There was an age gap, of course, of a few million years, but what was that in the scope of a kalpa?

Shantanu's parents were thrilled when he reached the permitted age of kingship. They bequeathed him the kingdom and announced their early retirement.

'We'll be right up there,' said his father, pointing at a distant mountainside. Their downsized retirement home was a nook carpeted with antelope skins, just big enough for them to sit in lotus position, side by side, until they passed away naturally. 'You can come see us whenever you like, though we would prefer it if you stayed in the foothills.'

'Why?'

His father sighed with regret. 'Detachment, son. You'll understand soon enough. A knack for religion tends to run in the family.'

Shantanu had thought his parents' riverside royal court was normal. This wilful abandonment of the world—of *him*—struck him as cruel, and he lost, in an instant, what little love he'd had for philosophy. He looked to his mother in a panic. 'What if I need your advice?'

'We've left you all our ministers and advisors.'

'I mean with personal things. Like who to marry, or how to educate my own children—your grandchildren—or, or . . .'

'About that,' said the outgoing king. 'A beautiful young woman came by yesterday, asking about you.'

'About me?'

'Your name, your age—"Who's that boy," she said, "always swimming across the river?" She was so interested in you, I couldn't help but imagine her as a daughter-in-law.'

'We had the same idea, your father and I, at the same time,' said the queen. 'One look, and we knew.'

'What was her name?'

'We forgot to ask! Just imagine how lovely she is: your father and I are ascetics and we've trained our senses not to be impressed. My advice is, if she finds her way to you, go ahead and marry her.'

'Can I at least come get you on my wedding day?'

'We won't know you by then,' his mother said, stroking his cheek. 'Or so we hope.'

*

He visited his parents every month, waving at them from a distance. At first, his mother the queen would wave at him. Then she stopped, as though her arms were too heavy. Both his parents seemed to have taken on some of the greyish shade of their rocky nook, like chameleons attuned to their backdrop. Eventually, he could not make them out against the mountainside. He threw coins at a sherpa in the nearest village. Trussed and buckled to his new guide, Shantanu climbed the sheer face of the mountain to check on his parents. All he found were two parent-sized crags of weather-beaten rock, hammered out of recognition, it seemed, by ninety-nine monsoons. He garlanded each with marigolds and wept. Surrounding villages marvelled at the mad young king. They swore those crags had been there for generations.

For a year or so, Shantanu waited for this mysterious, divine-looking woman to find him. When his first beard peppered his cheeks and hormonal masala spiced his blood, he assumed that his parents had imagined the whole thing. He left orders with his foreign minister to strategize a marriage, then off he went on a hunt. He followed a trail far, far away from his starting point, and soon he was stalking the wetlands close to the river where he had grown up. He shot a deer at last, right through the heart. But instead of a dying leap or a tragic stagger, the animal straightened its neck and walked unperturbed behind some trees. When Shantanu followed it into the clearing, he found not a dead deer but a woman in a blue sari with hair to her ankles.

'Shantanu,' she said with delight and recognition. This was the same woman who had asked about him. It had to be, since he too, never asked her name, not even on their wedding night, which was just a week after he met her.

There were some irregularities, of course. The bride proposed to the groom within minutes of their first encounter. She wanted to get married right away, and she did not invite a single relative to the wedding ceremony. Strangest of all (since she had been the one to propose marriage in the first place), she set a condition.

'I will marry you,' she said gravely, 'as long as you vow never to question anything I do. If you question my actions, I will flow right out of your life and leave an empty bed behind me.'

She looked so good, he would have drowned himself in the river if she had asked it. Shantanu was never the domineering sort, and though she had no royal pedigree, he could tell he was marrying up.

After he made that vow and brought her to the palace, he braced himself for spending sprees and tantrums. At least his dear old mother wasn't around for her to fight with, he figured. To his surprise, his new bride was obedient, almost without a will of her own. She conformed to any situation, like water. Like water, she shifted the direction of her opinion whenever he put up resistance. She abased herself before him, always seeking the lowest point, his feet, which she washed three times a day. The basin would be empty when he set his feet in it. It would overflow as soon as he looked away.

Their first baby was born nine months into the marriage. A boy: he had fathered a male heir on his first try! His relatives were still hugging him outside the room when the new mother, looking fresh and not at all haggard with childbirth, gushed from the palace with the baby and returned empty-handed. His interior minister and several aunts wanted to plumb the whereabouts of the baby boy, but Shantanu shushed them.

The next day, at breakfast, he waited in silence. He asked no questions and she volunteered no answers. She ate her usual breakfast of water chestnuts.

'No music this morning, Shantanu?'

Marvelling at her, he clapped his hands, and the musicians arrived to play in raga Hemavati, her favourite.

After she made their third son vanish, he kept her in hiding during her pregnancies, so that others wouldn't question *him*. It was impossible to keep her pregnancies secret, even though her deliveries were fast and painless. When her water broke, the women's quarters flooded. The maids said they found small freshwater fish atwitch in the courtyard. The royal chronicles documented stillbirths, on Shantanu's orders—though the maids whispered how they had heard a baby crying. After delivering the fifth baby, the midwife committed suicide. Baby number six went the way of the five before him. It turned out that she didn't need a midwife to flush the newborn from her womb.

Shantanu paced the cold marble floor for what felt like nine months. His unquestionable wife was pregnant again. He shut everybody out of the women's quarters and waited. More than once, before the first pregnancy, he had suspected his own happiness—she was too beautiful and too easy to live with. There had to be a catch! He kept expecting her to badmouth his family or nag him. Infidelity at worst, he imagined. But this? Could it be? He could not pretend he didn't suspect it anymore. He felt nauseated and woozy on his feet. Just thinking of the word: *infanticide!* All at once, he felt horror, grief, remorse, disgust, estrangement and still, *still*, a stubborn, loathsome love.

The floor flooded, as usual. He waited for the splashes of her feet as she fled with the swaddled bundle.

This time, he followed her.

The moon kept its spotlight on her. Hunting was his favourite sport, so he was good at stalking unheard and unseen, even at night. He tracked her to the river where he had found her. There was nothing furtive in her walk, no criminal haste when she unwrapped Shantanu's seventh son. What was she doing? A cloud passed over the moon. He couldn't see. He squinted, taking a step forward. The cloud passed on and let through some pale light. He saw.

She held the human kitten underwater. Her lips were moving. Was she praying? No, she was counting, to make absolutely sure. When she stood up, her hands were empty.

*

Shantanu swore never to make love to her again. Every night for the next week, though, he fell asleep and dreamt he was making love to her. Had the lovemaking been a reality and the murder a dream? Soon she was puttering around the palace, one hand resting fondly on her eighth baby bump. More than once he almost did it—almost shouted: *What were you doing at the river? Did you kill them all that way? What kind of sick murderess are you?* But he remembered his vow—everything begins with a vow—and he held his tongue.

The sight seemed so unreal, in retrospect, that he spent his wife's whole third trimester convincing himself it had been a nightmare. He followed her again, neglecting his sandals like a sleepwalker.

The replay of events was exact, down to the phase of the moon. Maybe it was a nightmare, a recurring nightmare. Only this time he shouted, 'What are you *doing*?'

A question. She turned and shook her head in reproach and disappointment. How little she had asked of him! A little trust, a little time to herself—just enough to go drown a baby and stroll back. Her *own* baby, not someone else's. Even that he wouldn't grant her. The perils of incarnating as a woman, she supposed. She had heard that mortal women endured petty restrictions that Goddesses didn't. Well, now she knew it was true. And now *he* would know she had meant it when she set her condition. How could she bear his company, now that he imagined her a murderer? There was no way back to pillow talk and giggles, even if she explained. 'This was the last one,' she said in frustration. 'You just couldn't help yourself.'

'You've been drowning our babies? How could you?'

She tucked the baby's arm back into the swaddling, to keep him from scratching himself. 'I can't possibly drown this dear one, now that you've seen me,' she said regretfully. Celestial morality, she knew, didn't translate to the dirt world. What looked like mercy there could look like sin here, and vice versa. 'I should go now.'

Shantanu covered his mouth with both hands and sank to the riverbank. She realized she would have to explain herself in more detail, or the thought of those infanticides would haunt him to the point of insanity.

'Hear me out,' she said calmly. 'I'm not who you think I am. I am your lawful wife, that's not a lie. We could have grown old together, and my life here as your wife would still be a mask I tried on in the mirror and set aside. The way my mind processes time, I've done nothing more than smile as I walked past you, though to you it feels like a marriage and eight children. That's the real age gap when a Goddess weds a mortal man. The rates we age, I mean. Every river is a woman, and I am Ganga.

'It so happened that the eight Vasus, Indra's attendants, once visited the sage Vasishtha with their wives. One of the Vasus—Dyaus, with the sky-coloured eyes—stole the sage's wish-granting cow, Kamadhenu, at his wife's urging. The other seven helped him do it, the winds in his sky. They were just sneaking Kamadhenu out the front gate when the cow knocked over a watering can that Vasishtha used to slake his tulsi plants. A few minutes later, the sage cursed them: those eight celestial beings, accustomed to cruise the galaxies, would have to live out life sentences in human bodies. Prison bars made of ribs! The daily gut-punch of hunger! Solitary confinement! If it's bad enough for mortals like you, imagine what torture embodiment must be for a God, who has never known anything but immateriality. Incarnation is incarceration. A curse and a vow draw on the same fierce power of speech—they must be carried out—but I felt pity on those eight brothers condemned to Samsara. Together, we came up with a plan to break them out. I would become their mother and drown them. They would walk into the cell and walk back out. I helped seven back to freedom, but now you've stopped me—no doubt as Vasishtha wished, since this last baby is Dyaus himself, the ringleader of the theft. He will have to live out his sentence, it seems. I will train him to accomplish what your ninth son would have accomplished, if you had honuored your vow to me. If you had just waited. That destiny will be his now.'

Shantanu shook his head, bewildered at all these revelations and backstories. 'What destiny?' he murmured. He had understood very little of what she had told him; all he understood was the sharp, fresh cry of his newborn son in her arms. 'Is he hungry?' Shantanu said, still horrified with her. 'I can take him to the palace and find him a wet nurse, if you don't want to feed him. You killed seven. Seven! Let me have this *one*.'

She shook her head again, in resignation this time—and also to say *no*. Every woman is a river. Her hair shook loose and covered the baby in her arms just as she tipped backward into the suddenly turbulent flow. She swirled away instantly, like a blue inkwell poured over whitewater. Maybe it was an illusion of moonlight and tears, but the baby seemed to be swept upstream, towards Gangotri, the Ganga's Himalayan source. The river, like a widow composing her hair and make-up, resurfaced and resumed.

Shantanu splashed into the water and waded as far as he could before a swift undertow grabbed his ankles and pulled him to the bank again. He stood with mud between his toes, sobbing and dripping. A swirling arm of current pushed two mismatched sandals past him until they rested side by side on the bank—facing away from the river. *Put your feet in these*, she was saying, *and go home.*

SARGA 3

THE FEARSOME VOW

King Shantanu had his ministers find out how many drownings, including suicides, happened each year in the rivers of his kingdom. The number gave him some insight into how little she must have felt when she drowned the babies. Action worked differently for divine beings. On his long, glum walks along the Ganga, Shantanu arrived, by accident, at an understanding deeper than his own parents had ever reached. Certainly, he felt wiser than his officious, incense-waving Brahmins. Their Gods were all majesty and mercy, with no mention made of mindless grinding teeth.

Three hundred and seventeen drownings, he learned, just last year. A few dozen more, and she would have drowned one person a day. It must have been routine for her.

He imagined that last, eighth son, the one who had sailed north, against the current. Was he alive? She had said she wouldn't drown him . . . Shantanu imagined that boy growing. A palace gardener had a son that same year; he gave them a separate house on the palace grounds, situated so he could look at them from a window. He used the gardener's son as a reference. That is what a three-year-old looks like. That is how a six-year-old talks. That is how my nine-year-old boy must run, wherever he is.

Fifteen years later, his imagination seemed to project a fifteen-year-old youth on to a bare riverbed. Glassy-eyed fish, gagging on the air, slapped and thrashed on the mud. A slender boy stood before a dam and twirled his bow with great showmanship. Who had authorized a new dam there? A project like that should have been cleared with the king. Shantanu squinted to make it out for sure—it was a dam all right, but it was made of *arrows*, thatched thick and watertight in a wall twice the boy's height. How had he shot so many, so fast?

Shantanu shouted, 'Who are you?' And then, more quietly, almost meekly: 'Are you a God?'

The youth turned to the voice with alarm. He shot one last arrow at the base of his own dam, and it detonated against the riverbed with a thunderclap. The arrows scattered and the water came roaring through. The boy stood fast and stared fearlessly into King Shantanu's eyes as the river water engulfed him.

Shantanu did not leave the riverbank for hours after that. He kept staring at the spot where the radiant young archer had stood.

'That was him,' he said aloud to the serenely textured Ganga. 'You gave me a glimpse of him. What did you name him?'

A woman's voice, a familiar voice, sounded at his feet. 'Devavrat.'

The river shaped herself into a curvaceous body, which took on the look of prismatic flesh just as some more water swept aloft into a sari. This sari was red, the same one the Goddess had worn at their wedding. That, too, was a gift, an act of reconciliation.

Given the way her mind processed time, he speculated, maybe she thought of the past fifteen years as fifteen minutes. The sight of her was worth the wait by any reckoning.

Ganga reached down into the water and pulled the young archer to the surface. The water ran off him and his clothes, leaving him completely dry. Shantanu stared at his face and searched for himself and Ganga in the features. Ganga might claim the eyes and mouth, the loveliest parts of him, but his ears, nose and jaw came from his father. Did either of them have that dimple? It would be covered by a beard soon enough. Already there was the faintest fuzz on the boy's upper lip.

'I had to get him ready,' said Ganga. 'He's going to be the best king that Bharata has ever produced. Devavrat, say namaste to your father, King Shantanu.'

Devavrat joined his hands and lowered his eyes and said the word. His voice was unexpectedly deep, a fully grown man's.

Shantanu murmured, 'Half-divine . . . I believe it.'

Ganga, a dutiful mother, had spent the past several years shuttling her son from school to school both on earth and in the far reaches of space. The Seven Sages carved their ashrams into stars; they liked a strong light to read by. Ancient sages and even an immortal avatar had served as private tutors to Ganga's son. Shantanu gaped as she listed his credentials. Devavrat had learned political science from Brihaspati, theology from Vasishtha and weapon-wielding from Parashuram. Hastinapur's plodding scholars would do well to sit at this young man's feet.

'He is yours now,' said Ganga, 'yours and Hastinapur's—and one day, I have faith, he will belong to Bharata. Or rather, Bharata will belong to him.'

Shantanu barely paid attention to this prophecy. He had fallen to admiring the woman who was still his wife. 'Come back to the palace. Hastinapur misses you. I miss you.'

'Take my advice,' she said with a note of pity, 'and rinse me out of your memory.'

'I can't do that.'

'Remarrying will help,' she said, and patted him on the shoulder, a distant look in her eye, as though her mind were already on the delta.

Shantanu's sash grew dark at her touch and he rushed it to his cheek. It felt cool and wet, like a kiss. With immaculate tact,

Devavrat looked away. His mother dropped into her element without a splash. His father, tearful, cupped his son's face in both hands. The father tiptoed, the son stooped and the kiss made it to Devavrat's forehead, disturbing the grain of *tilak* rice still stuck there from morning prayers.

'Come along, my boy,' he said proudly. 'I want to show you your city.'

*

Hope thrills any city when it drafts a six-foot-seven champion-to-be. Hastinapur heard it had gotten the pick of princes and the citizens were eager to see their prospect. The next day, on short notice, King Shantanu declared a kingdom-wide holiday and arranged a chariot parade. Hastinapur's towering athlete of a prince stepped out to a balcony. Marigolds, dew-dropped with milk, fell like confetti from the clear sky. Devavrat turned one between his fingers. None of this frenzy infected him. He knew he hadn't brought home a single ring yet, not one double-handled golden cup. The city was not so level-headed. The prince bit into a green apple in public, and green apples, ever after, were 'Devavrat apples', triple the price.

For the next two years, he learned the intricacies of Hastinpur's economy and border defences. All he encountered were smiling generals and beaming aunts. He had seen neither sadness nor yearning in his celestial classrooms. *Dukha* was an abstract word to him, like *integral*.

So it was a first for Devavrat when he found his father, the king, red-eyed, blowing his nose and recovering from a long, private cry. His first thought was that his father might have bitten into a ghost pepper and failed to handle the spice. 'What's happened, Father?'

King Shantanu lifted his heavy head, straggly-haired around the sides and balding on the top, the horizontal line from his recently cast-down crown still pink on his brow. Earlier that afternoon, the king had dismissed his musicians and smashed his *shatranj* pieces. Only two things can make you lose interest in what you have: transcendence of desire or a desire for something else. The king spoke with a voice drained of joy.

'You wouldn't understand, Devavrat. You got to live with your mother for years. Everyone loves you. Soon, royal families from here to Gandhara will be throwing their daughters at you. But me? My parents abandoned me in favour of samadhi. They loved me less than their tulsi plant. I loved one woman, but she turned out to be a river Goddess and flowed away. And now, at long last, I fall in love with a fisherman's daughter. A low-born, common girl! And I can't have *her*, either? I must have done something hateful in a past life to be denied love.'

'You have my love. A son's love.'

'Those eyes you're looking at me with, the mouth you say you love me with—Devavrat, you're a demi-*deva*. You love me the way your mother loved me, with detachment.'

'Detachedly is how the celestials love—that much you're right about, Father. It's why my mother found it so easy to leave us both. I love her detachedly, too, with the deva half of me. I've never missed her. But you? I love you with my human half. With attachment. Tell me about this fisherman's daughter. I would love to have a human mother, here in the palace . . . Why can't you marry her? She should be honoured and so should her father.'

Shantanu, throwing his arms around his magnificent son, sobbingly told him the whole story. Devavrat walked him to his chamber and told him to lie down and nap. The aging king was soon snoring. The son tucked the father in and drove his own chariot to the river. He made sure that he brought a small entourage in tow—both to make an impression on the fisherman and to have witnesses for what he planned to do.

*

The fisherman's wife came in breathless, desperately trying to wave the fish smell out of the windows. 'He's here! The new prince—the son of Ganga!'

The fisherman did not stir from his seat. 'If a river's his mother, he shouldn't have a problem with how we smell. It will remind him of home.' Then he whistled his daughter over. 'I've never seen one bait catch two fish before,' he said, shaking his head. 'You sure know how to hook them, don't you? Second member of the royal family to come sniffing after you in a week.'

'I swear, Papa, I've never met Prince Devavrat before.'

'Promiscuous little flirt! I ought to marry you off as soon as I can, before you disgrace me.'

Satyavati blushed, thinking of the mid-river island and her illegitimate son Vyasa. Chakora birds were already teaching him to speak to the moon, good training for the future poet. She crossed her arms defensively under her full bosom (she still rowed out three times a day to breastfeed her toddler) and went to the window. Seven giant chariots had pulled up to their hut.

'Go hide yourselves away,' the fisherman said to his daughter and wife. 'Let me handle this negotiation, man to man.'

Devavrat wasted no time with formalities or introductions. He strode into the hut, ducking low to avoid bumping his head on the doorframe, and joined his hands. 'You're Satyavati's father?'

'That's right.'

'My father says you don't want me to inherit the throne.'

'I set that condition, yes, for my daughter's hand in marriage. He declined, so I declined.'

'I'll give up the throne if you let your daughter marry my father. Have her pack her things. I'll take her back to the palace with me.'

'Wait, wait, my handsome prince. Slow down. I'm an old fisherman. I don't move this fast.' The fisherman shook his head. 'I fling my nets and pull them back in. I'm patient. I haven't studied history with the sage Angiras, like you, but I'm downstream from gossip and I know a bit about palace intrigues. You may well renounce the throne, but twenty years from now, your sons will wonder why your self-denial denies *them*. They will quarrel with my grandsons. Any sons of *yours*—one-quarter divine, and that's assuming you marry a human woman—why, they'll clobber my grandsons! Like dead mahseer littering a poisoned shore. If I say yes, I'll be setting up the extinction of my line. Can you think of a way to ensure that doesn't happen, Prince Devavrat? I want peace. I want to ward off civil war.'

The name *Devavrat* yokes two words together. It means *God-vow*. To make a vow his God and obey that God's command: his name encoded his destiny.

Devavrat paced the hut for several minutes. The fisherman yawned and observed the prince's anguish. Outside, to the horror of the courtiers, nature itself began to disrupt. The sky bruised in three places. Thirteen vultures, their bodies in a motionless circle overhead, kept their wings perfectly still, suspended uncannily on steady intangible winds. And Devavrat hadn't even made his decision yet.

Just then, Satyavati stepped up and peeked at him through the back door of that small hut. He saw her face and caught a whiff of her; though he had little experience of desire, he knew instantly that there would be no talking his father out of this love.

Devavrat walked his father's future father-in-law out among the chariots so the courtiers could witness his vow. His arms struggled to rise over his head, and the harder he strained, the louder the ongoing thunder sounded. A fault line opened somewhere with the sound of a glacier calving. His palms felt like two magnets with their north poles forced flush. The earth shook as his hands clapped together over his head, and he announced, at the top of his lungs, a vow of celibacy. '*Never will I marry, never will I know a woman, never will I dream of a woman, never will I be a king, never will I father a king.*' These five 'nevers' cut off his bloodline.

The sky went silent and all the strange omens cleared up. Creation knew there was nothing to protest anymore. The vow had been voiced.

*

Devavrat, forcibly altering his own fate, was altering history too. Why else had his mother, Ganga, shuttled him from class to class among the celestials? They were preparing Devavrat to rule—not just his father's kingdom, but *all* kingdoms, from the Saraswati to the Ganga, from the Himalayas through the Deccan, across the Vindhyas, over Rama's Bridge, down to Lanka . . .

He was supposed to take the throne. He was supposed to marry a dark-skinned princess from the southernmost kingdom of Bharata. That royal couple was scheduled to start the Gangavamshi lineage—one hegemonic Gangetic dynasty to unite all the quarrelsome groups of what was not yet called India.

Under King Devavrat I, the Vedas were to be written down for the first time, and the dharma was to take on an aggressive, expansive form. In that other timeline, Devavrat was to found a new caste of *kshatrishis*, which anyone could join. These 'warrior-seers' would devote themselves to studying—and mastering and manipulating—the physical world of Maya. Thanks to their keen minds, the benevolent Ganga would turn paddlewheels and convert her water into steam under pressure. That steam would power *mahayantras*, 'great machines' larger than any war elephant.

Infinitely articulated, spraying Agni, spreading enormous iron wings and flying Garuda-like over the Himalayas and oceans, these mahayantras would render King Devavrat I invincible. His first round of conquests would spread the dharma north-west to the mountains, southeast to the island chains. His Brahmins, in that alternate, more Dharmic timeline, fostered the worship of all the Gods, but the Mother Goddess most of all—in the form of Ganga, the king's own mother.

King Devavrat I would be called *Bhishma*, 'Fearsome.' In the history that happened, he still ended up with that name, thanks to the courtiers who witnessed his fearsome vow. His defeated enemies were supposed to give him that title.

Clever medicines and surgical techniques, too, were to have flourished in the capital city of the Gangaputra Empire, Gangotri. Devavrat would have lived well over a hundred years, a full life sentence for the condemned Vasu. That Vasu was Dyaus, alias Prabhasa, *Light*: and light his descendants would bring to all the peoples of the world, who had never heard of the Vedas or the dharma.

History books in heaven already recounted the conquests of King Devavrat IX among the Yavanas, and the expansion of the empire under Queen Gangotri I to the snowy Arctic. Queen Gangotri III was to commission the *Varunarmada*, an immense group of sailing islands that would discover new continents beyond the expanse of the Mahasagar, the Great Ocean.

After making landfall, the Gangetic Navy would find thousands of small, half-naked tribes, with no mahayantras of their own, utterly vulnerable to imported diseases. But Ayurvedic medical science would have progressed by that time. The Gangaputras would have protected those tribes against infection with turmeric capsules and needles in the arm. They would have learned the

Gods and Goddesses of these peoples—and added them to their own, near-infinite pantheon. Meeting new Gods would be no different than discovering new star systems in the cosmos, which temples of astronomy back home in Gangotri were doing all the time, naming them for Goddesses and poets.

In time, the Gangaputras who marched west would meet the Gangaputras who sailed east. Equidistant from their sacred river, they would embrace and laugh and chat in Sanskrit along the very seam of the earth. They would share the names of the Gods and Goddesses they had found in their wars of enlightenment. *Look at what this dharma has done*, they would marvel. *Everyone's home river is sacred. They don't have to name her Ganga if they don't want to. Every river is someone's mother—let them love her as they please.* They would build temples all along the equator and illuminate them from within, constantly maintaining fires inside square-mile mandalas. Every year, at the hour of King Devavrat I's death, all the followers of the dharma around the world would chant one long *aum*, and the sound would carry through space like a gust of solar wind until it reached Devavrat in heaven, in his original shining form. Delighting in the sound, he would peer out across the galaxies. The earth, he would see, was still at peace, under the one multifarious dharma. He would raise his palm to bless it, and saffron-clad astronomers in *yojana*-high temple *shikharas* would register, on their sensitive instruments, a pulse of light.

SEQUENCE 2

HOW BHISHMA AND VYASA SECURE THE LINEAGE

Bhishma's stepbrother turns out to be a weakling, so Bhishma kidnaps three princesses to serve as his stepbrother's brides. This is the sin that, decades later, will lead to his downfall.

One of these three sisters, Amba, turns out to have been in love with someone already; Bhishma lets her return to him, but her lover doesn't take her back. Amba demands that Bhishma marry her, but Bhishma refuses because of his vow.

Outraged at this double rejection, Amba appeals to Parashuram. (Fun fact: Parashuram is the only character to have a cameo in both the Mahabharata and Ramayana. Parashuram, or 'Axe-Rama,' is actually—like Prince Rama and Krishna—an avatar of Vishnu . . . During his heyday, he got carried away slaughtering his enemies. Tainted by all that killing, but still an avatar, he cannot be reborn or sent to hell, but he can't be admitted to heaven, either—and so, indigestible by time, he is cursed to live forever.) Parashuram lives as a warrior-ascetic, forever practising martial arts, and he agrees to champion Princess Amba's cause. Bhishma fights him to a draw. Amba, thwarted again, will now have to seek Shiva's help in getting vengeance against Bhishma.

Meanwhile, Bhishma's stepbrother falls sick and dies without issue. Bhishma's stepmother, the queen who was once a fisherman's daughter, hits on a shrewd idea about how to carry on her line: she will have her illegitimate son, the poet Vyasa, sleep with the two remaining princesses.

The opportunity is worth putting asceticism on hold. Vyasa agrees. But he has been out in the wilderness so long, he looks disgusting.

One princess shuts her eyes to avoid having to look at Vyasa. Her son, Vyasa prophesies, will come out blind. This son is Dhritarashtra, the father of the hundred Kauravas. The other princess goes pale at the sight of Vyasa, and the son she has by him comes out pale too: this is Pandu, the father of the five Pandavas. These are the two branches of the lineage that will fight the Mahabharata's civil war. In one of literature's earliest metafictional devices, Vyasa, their eventual chronicler, has fathered them both.

Vyasa also fathers a third child before he leaves, this one with a palace maid, who loves him for his poetic prowess. So this son is blessed by his father with visionary wisdom; his name, Vidura, means *wise*.

Characters Who Will Show Up Again:

AMBA, the wronged princess who will seek her vengeance and, with karmic inexorability, lead to Bhishma's downfall decades hence.
DHRITARASHTRA, the blind king, father of the hundred Kauravas.

PANDU, the pale prince, father of the five Pandavas.

VIDURA, the half-brother of the royals, son of Vyasa and a maid. Brainy and bookish, blessed by his genius father to inherit his paternal traits. Vidura will be respected for his wisdom for decades to come—but when his half-brothers' children work themselves up for war, his counsels will be powerless to stop it.

SARGA 4

A RIVER IN SPATE

You should pray love never hits you like wrath or thirst. You should pray love takes centuries to shape you, as the patient river does her canyon. Love is best when it passes through you, the same love stringing all the pearls you have been and will be. Monogamy across rebirths! No one prays for that kind of love, do they? Most pray for a forest fire without a firebreak. They daydream of the body lashed to a steel post in the sand. As the hurricane makes landfall, they writhe and shout into the roaring wind, *Pick me!*

Far fewer—ascetics, mostly, and the occasional fearsome prince—pray and strive for no love at all. They plant a Shiva *lingam* of polished black ice at the South Pole of their minds. There they welcome the absolute zero into their bloodstream. A vow of celibacy exiles you from your own body.

King Devavrat I was destined, originally, to have three hundred wives and nine hundred children. His name as a Vasu, Dyaus, meant sky, and rain is what the king was destined to do. Bhishma never married, never made love, never fathered any children. All that seminal energy, denied any outlet, built up behind the dam of his vow. He began to change.

Hastinapur noticed it within days of his vow. They rioted on his behalf, demanding that King Shantanu reinstate their favourite prince. They grabbed and rattled the palace gates, and thousands chanted '*No one cares how good you smell! Satyavati, go to hell!*' and '*Fry your fish and have your fling! Give us Devavrat for king!*'

Shantanu clutched his thinning hair and stared at the grim profile of young Bhishma.

'You can do it,' he said, pressing his tearful eyes to Bhishma's cold hand. 'Carry out a coup. Imprison us somewhere, me and Satyavati. We'll be happy together, as long as we can share a cell.'

Jail the king and break your vow! Bhishma, we're your subjects now!

'The generals will back you, Devavrat. The people obviously want it. It's only right.'

Bhishma snatched his hand away and strode to the balcony. The rioters screamed and whistled with joy.

Bhishma flooded the city with sound, outshouting thousands, striking them silent with the shockwave of his voice.

'*My choice. My life. My vow.*'

He unsheathed a jewelled dagger and held it at his own throat. Gasps. A few cries of *No!* The startled crying of a baby, somewhere in the crowd.

'*Go. Home. Now.*'

The scolded city threw no more tantrums after that.

*

The aging king and his teenaged queen spent all their hours in the bedroom, or at the table or on the boat. Bhishma embraced the administration of the kingdom. That took his mind off his own dammed-up virility. Rarely did he ventured to the king's private palace wing for a stamp of the royal signet ring. Satyavati's feral shouts of pleasure disturbed the Himalayas reflected on the still pool of his mind. Bhishma dispatched swift riders north-east to fetch snow for his bath.

Once, on the boat, Satyavati put Shantanu to sleep as best she knew how. She ordered the boat to dock on her mid-river island. There she brought little Vyasa aboard. She covered him in sandal paste and made some marks on his forehead, approximations of what she'd seen on Brahmin mendicants. Then she dropped him off at a riverside ashram. Every so often, she sent a discreet servant to check up on the temple foundling. Soon she got reports he had mastered writing and reading, and she asked for a writing sample. Six weeks later, while she was pregnant with her first Kuru prince, Vyasa sent her fifty sheets of birch bark. Satyavati could not read; to her, the letters looked like the footprints of birds. She dared not trust a court Brahmin to read it to her, as she didn't know what was in it. So she burned Vyasa's first epic poem, which described a war in the far future and foretold the extinction of the Kuru line.

She wouldn't have believed it if she'd read it—since she herself was perpetuating the Kurus with a healthy baby boy. King Shantanu held a newborn in his arms for the first time. Gratefully he beamed at Devavrat, whom he had never held this way. (Shantanu alone never called him *Bhishma*.) He called his first son over and spoke in a whisper to let Bhishma's baby stepbrother sleep.

'I told you how my parents—your grandparents—were a very devout couple. They gained powers, abilities . . . Before they left, they granted me a boon. It's mine, but I want to pass it on. I want to give it to you.'

'What boon is that?'

Shantanu cleared his throat and spoke quietly but formally, so the Gods could hear. 'I grant you the boon that you can choose the time of your death.'

Bhishma shook his head. 'That's a precious boon. Keep it. You're a father now.'

'I could die at any time, and I wouldn't mind.' He smiled. 'I am happy.'

The baby laughed, and so musically that Shantanu knew exactly what his name should be: Chitrangada, same as the king of the Gandharvas. A year later, Satyavati gave him another son, Vichitravirya. And then, unceremoniously, after binge-eating puran poli, Shantanu died in his sleep. Satyavati's sons were still too young to shoulder their father under his shroud and flowers, so fearsome Bhishma led the procession up the mountain.

The flames hadn't gone out before Hastinapur started getting restive again. The army and the people didn't want the 'fishwife' or the 'fishwife's sons' running the country. Why not persuade Bhishma to substitute some proper penance for his vow? Maybe he could fund some spectacular *yagna*, with horses and a big public feast? And then imprison, or ideally drown, the fishwife and her guppies? Such measures were commonplace in disputed successions.

Bhishma was presented these proposals as murmured questions; no general or minister dared present them as advice. Bhishma responded by installing Chitrangada on the throne the next afternoon. He ruled as a regent for a while. When the boy's voice cracked, Bhishma bowed and backed away from the throne.

*

The Gandharvas were a race of heavenly six-fingered geniuses. They were the hereditary musicians at Indra's court.

The newly crowned King Chitrangada took his birth name seriously and read, in esoteric texts, how the Gandharvas had once been a warlike race. Gandharvas were immortals, so it wasn't a fair fight. (Immortal Devas never invaded earthly kingdoms, preferring to besiege individual hearts.) Indra, to preserve peace in the cosmos, redirected their interest from bowstrings to sitar-strings, from war-drums to tablas. The Gandharvas had been revered musicians ever since, all their innate aggression routed into competitive riffs.

Shantanu's second firstborn gave Hastinapur's armies a musical rearrangement. Officers worked their way up the ranks based on their knowledge of ragas. Every archer was issued a bowstring of a specific note, every chariot fitted with windchimes, every elephant given lessons in trumpeting. Chitrangada and his orchestra of generals extemporized music on the eve of battle and their *akshauhinis*, their battle formations, listened closely. Chitrangada blew his conch shell, and the same raga rose from hectares of heroes. Opposing infantrymen were terrorized and charmed in equal measure. Their death cries kept time.

The music was loud enough to reach Indraloka and interrupt the *original* Chitrangada, the Gandharva himself, at his rehearsals. Maybe he was reminded of his youthful campaigns, of his army's cookfires scattered among the floating meteors. He asked the eternally wandering sage, Narada, about this space-faring music. Narada always carried the freshest gossip from all four arms of the galaxy.

'That? That is King Chitrangada, playing his war music.'

'But King Chitrangada is standing right here in front of you!'

'Not you,' said Narada. 'The *famous* one.'

Naturally, the Gandharva king raged with jealousy after that comment. Did Narada phrase it that way on purpose? He was notorious for setting off conflicts with off-the-cuff remarks and strategically dropped secrets. Whether or not he meant to, the old sage goaded the Gandharva to get his army back together.

The armoured musicians rocketed to earth, where the Gandharva king sent a challenge to the 'tone-deaf impostor.' What a *jugalbandi* followed! A real battle of the bands: thousands of mortals on one side faced off against thousands of immortals. Who would prove the singing masters of whom? In their desperation, Hastinapur's foot soldiers stripped the bells from temples and clanged their heavenly invaders on their bald skulls.

Indra had gone into a black mood without his court musicians. Watching his apsaras spin and jingle their anklets gave him no pleasure. A dance to no music isn't really a dance. So he descended in a cloud and threw a lightning tantrum.

'Squash this squabble now!' he roared. 'You two Chitrangadas have ruined my evening entertainment over a personal quarrel. Divas! Fight each other one on one, and the victor can keep the name.'

When the Gandharva brought out an eighteen-string bow, the man unveiled a twenty-one-string bow, and the armies gasped. Each sitarcher stood behind his instrument and played with both hands, furiously loading and loosing arrows, every string sounding a different note. One by one, though, the Gandharva's precision arrows snapped the strings of his opponent's bow. When the last string broke, Shantanu's son stood exposed. He cast aside the empty C of his bow and improvised a mournful *alap*. Indra, too, fell to admiring, wondering what masterful music this might be a prologue to. The Gandharva king waited for the mortal to pause and take a breath; he knew his rival did not enjoy the infinite lung capacity of an infinite being. Through that gasping aperture of silence, Chitrangada shot Chitrangada through his mortal, muscled heart. The Gandharva returned, vindicated, to centre stage on Indraloka, the most prestigious gig of all. He played the God his most cheerful love songs.

Hastinapur, meanwhile, sang dirges for a childless king. The memory of what should have been stays strong in any thwarted people. Before the citizens could fantasize again about a King Devavrat I, Bhishma installed Shantanu's second son on the vacant throne.

*

King Vichitravirya, unlike his brother, had little interest in warfare. He did like music, though, and colourful sashes, and sometimes Bhishma caught him dancing in the twilight, a sash in either hand, to the surprise of the musicians. They kept glancing at Bhishma, worried he would roar them out of the palace. The adolescent king had called the tune, so they played, and Vichitravirya tickled his uncle's face, now with the crimson silk, now with the purple.

'Our king needs a queen,' declared Bhishma one morning.

Redolent Satyavati glanced at her son, who slouched casually on his throne. 'I hear the king of Kashi is holding a *swayamvara* for his three daughters.'

Swayamvara. A compound word, joining *self* and *groom*. Letting the princess take her pick was the new, enlightened way of doing things.

'Why should I wait like a dog for a treat?' complained Vichitravirya. 'I'm one of the richest kings out there. Those princesses should make a pilgrimage to *me*.'

'That's not how it works. This is the new way.' Bhishma shook his head at Vichitravirya's indifference. The boy had no respect.

'What was the old way?'

'When Sita was young, King Janaka offered her to any man who could string the Bow of Shiva.'

'Was that a hard bow to string, Uncle Bhishma?'

'It belonged to Shiva himself. What do you think? Setting a feat was an improvement on what came before it. It used to be a business transaction between kings, or a knowing nod between royal dowagers. In most cases, it still is.'

'But that's still better than what the ancients did, before Janaka's day,' said Satyavati. 'Bridal raids.'

'How barbaric!'

'The ancients were barbaric,' Bhishma said grimly, 'but they were *men*. The swayamvara is how it's done now, so I suggest we get some carriages ready.'

'Why are Kashi's princesses so special, that they get to choose me or reject me?'

'I hear they're very lovely,' Satyavati said leadingly. 'Maybe you should go there just to see.'

'How far is it to Kashi?'

'About eighty yojanas.'

'That would take hours, Uncle Bhishma. Besides, they wouldn't pick me anyway.'

'You'd have three chances in Kashi. I could train you. Build your legs, straighten your spine. We'd have a special suit of armour made. You like nice clothes, don't you?'

Vichitravirya waved his hand. 'I do wish my brother hadn't died childless. There wouldn't be so much pressure on me to marry.'

Satyavati made eye contact with Bhishma and shook her head gently. Her son got off the throne and strolled off to tend to his flowers. When they were alone, Satyavati sighed. 'He is a strange boy. He goes his own way. There will be no persuading him.'

Bhishma ground his teeth. She could see his jaw muscles moving under his beard. 'Hastinapur needs heirs,' he said, 'which means *he* needs a wife.'

'Or three,' whispered Satyavati.

'Or three.'

*

Amba, Ambika, Ambalika: theme, variation, fugue, three names with an alliterative link, genetically consonant. The names themselves were sisters. Their height went up by an inch side by side by side as they stood: Amba, Ambika, Ambalika.

Kashi's three princesses wore bridal red and dowry gold, and then more gold because gold pairs best with gold. Chains of filigree dangled between nose ring and tiara. Necklaces covered their chests like breastplates. Armoured this heavily, they might have been waiting for battle, not marriage. Shackle-thick bangles made their arms ache, but they kept the lotus garlands level, as they had been instructed. The priests chanting their verses droned to a stop.

Sixty royal bachelors fidgeted in a semicircle. Two of the princesses, Ambika and Ambalika, looked from face to face, still trying to decide. Only Amba held eye contact with a single prince in the crowd, Prince Shalva. She winked at him. Shalva smiled and glanced a little smugly at the hopefuls to either side of him. Amba was the eldest sister, so she would go first. He was going to be singled out from all these lesser men.

'And now,' said the court's chief Brahmin, 'may the key choose her lock, the hen choose her cock; may Rati choose her Kama, Sita choose her Rama.'

Amba felt an aquifer of laughter under her breath. She brought the garland up and tilted her head down a little just to hide her joy. Shalva bit his lip and elbowed his neighbours a bit to give himself room. The other princes had heard rumours of this epic flirtation—pigeons carrying letters; the border town he invaded on her birthday, just to rename it Ambapur; a new temple to Amba's namesake Goddess, already three-quarters finished, stonemasons and sculptors working on three hours of sleep; a secret ring exchange.

Her choice was a secret from no one, but she took her time, walking along the row very slowly, savouring Shalva's impatience from the corner of her eye. She sighed dramatically as she contemplated a portly competitor to his right, strolled on, paused and tilted her head to inspect a mustached thirty-something . . .

Shalva knew she was teasing him and he planned to get her back later that afternoon. This called for a retaliatory prank. Maybe a lizard in her slipper? Even her outrage was delicious. His girl drew blood when she kissed angrily.

Amba backtracked until she was level with Shalva. She tilted her chin, sizing him up. Everyone thought they knew what was going to happen next. Everyone was wrong.

*

An arrow with a Sanskrit warhead blew the twenty-foot-high bronze gates off their hinges. People rush to their roofs and terraces when the Ganga floods: more than one prince and minister, unthinkingly, sensing a river in spate, clambered on to chairs as if for safety's sake.

Amba watched in shock, immobilized as in a dream, as flash-flood Bhishma crested his own chariot, landed in mid-sprint and crashed into her. She screamed and kicked against his riptide arms. His wild undone hair filled her mouth and made her gag. She spun—*was* spun—several times in the air, unless it was in the water, and her head hit something hard. She forced her clenched eyes open, slack and agasp in the prince's muscular rapids.

Bhishma stood on the platform. He gazed out at the assembly the way a hurricane gazes inland. This row of blinking princelings were to him just shacks along a boardwalk, shutters flapping in the gale.

He looked down at the three girls, Amba, Ambika, Ambalika, leashed to his fist by their jasmine-flecked braids.

'I claim these brides for the King of Hastinapur,' he boomed. 'Keep your distance, and you won't get hurt.'

This was not a common crowd. These were Kshatriya princes, birth-proud. There were no shouts of protest, no boos or heckles—just the synchronous, metallic swish of dozens of swords drawn from dozens of sheaths. Bhishma still had one arm free to draw his own. Meanwhile, he swung his human loot up and around, like a day labourer shouldering a sack.

Amba's younger sisters clutched their hair close to their scalps, to relieve the pull. Moments later they clung, with both arms and both legs, to Bhishma's magnificently scarred and straining torso. They had never been this flush with a man before, and they ran their hands along his back and shoulders until they found handholds among his ridges.

Amba, however, was unimpressed with his sweaty, hairy back, this brutal and retrograde bride-raider. She wanted to break free and get to her beloved Shalva for protection. Bhishma, she knew, had to make his escape quickly—not even he could withstand so many enemies in an enclosed space—so he would leave her and settle for two. Amba bit the cinder block of his trapezius, scratched his skin, pulled his flowing black hair. Bhishma seemed indifferent to her. He mowed the thicket of blades with broad sweeps. A whistle triggered his trained steeds to kick the closest princes and veer the chariot this way and that, like a mace on wheels. Amba, growing desperate, jerked her head, trying to rip the braid off her own scalp.

Whenever a princeling took a stand against Bhishma, he seemed to divide, like flowing water around a jut of rock, and reappear behind the obstacle. Bhishma was careful not to kill, only disarm and stun—he had no interest in creating blood feuds between the Kurus and other royal families. His sword struck sparks as he smacked smaller swords out of weaker hands.

Bhishma felt these female softnesses against his back as he scooped and swept them, shouldered and hauled them to his chariot. He tossed them there as if on to a bed, and they lay wide-eyed before him in their loosened bridal dresses and loosened braids. The sensation, the delight surged into his body and flowed, not down to his lower *chakras*, but out through his sword arm, whose muscles swelled before the eyes of the men blocking his way, engorged veins river-blue along his forearm.

The chariot ground its axles and bowled straight through the crowd. For a while, he was clear of the palace and the outraged

Kshatriyas—but then, at his elbow, an archer materialized, riding hands free on a desperate horse.

'Shalva!'

Bhishma glanced at the tearful joy of Amba—and back at the young prince loading his bow. The celibate warrior's impossibly lengthening arm, once he tilted his impossibly long torso, cut Shalva's bowstring. Shalva flung the bow at Bhishma, who jerked his head out of the way. Shalva had already drawn his sword. Amba, on the other side of Bhishma, tried to help her true love. Her hands were too small to get all the way around Bhishma's bull neck, and the bump on his throat was a rock, but she got some purchase on his trachea and squeezed, trusting the cartilage was just as fragile there as anyone else's.

Throttled by the girl, Bhishma matched swords with the boy—and he came closer to drawing blood than he had with any other fighter so far, simply because of this complication with the girl. Soon he grew impatient tapping blades—the hellcat's grip was really cutting off his air exchange—so he did the efficient, unchivalrous thing and cut the saddle's leather at the buckle. Shalva, feeling the saddle tilt and slide, slipped from the stirrups and let the seat tumble from the gallop. He leapt, like a circus performer, so he had one foot on the back and one foot on the mane, balancing. When he dropped down again, riding bareback, he brought his sword around—and felt it fly, almost immediately, out of his hand. Next he pulled out a dagger, ready to lunge, but Bhishma had had enough. He veered his chariot into the flank of Shalva's horse. The rider hit the ground hard and rolled, and when he came to a bloody rest, his right collarbone tented the skin, and his right leg lay under him at an angle that made it look like another body's.

Bhishma pulled Amba off him and kept his foot on her braid the whole way home to Hastinapur. She lay on the floor of the chariot, crying, her mind tortured by the image of Shalva falling from his horse.

When they arrived at the palace, Amba did not stir from the chariot floor. Ambika and Ambalika stood up and tucked stray locks behind their ears. Ambalika spoke up. 'You could have stood at the swayamvara beside the other princes. Who knows? You might have come away with a bride by gentler means.'

'Or even two brides,' added Ambika.

Bhishma had dismounted. He patted his horses on the neck and gave one a kiss. *Good girls,* he whispered. *Beautiful girls.*

SARGA 5

THE STAINED BATTLEAXE

Bhishma dropped off his prisoners of war with their wardens, an all-female battalion, armed with kohl and combs. He was just leaving when he heard a sharp shout. *No!* It was the eldest sister, Amba.

'I am not submitting to this. Bridal raids have been illegal since Shri Rama's day. It was one of the first customs he outlawed! Look it up!'

'Shri Rama was king in Ayodhya. This is Hastinapur.'

'That horseman you toppled to the ground—that was supposed to be my husband. Prince Shalva. He's still alive—I saw him moving. I vowed to marry him.'

Bhishma flinched at this word, *vowed*. He made eye contact with the incensed princess for the first time. There he saw a determination much like his own. He nodded and murmured, 'Hastinapur respects a vow.'

'So send me back to him, right now. Give me a horse, and I will ride to him myself.'

'On these roads?' Bhishma marvelled at the young woman's courage; if he hadn't been celibate, he thought, he would have liked to have married a true warrior-princess like this. Shalva was lucky. 'I'll arrange an armed escort and a carriage. Come with me.'

Amba insisted on riding her own horse because the carriage would rattle along too slowly. Bhishma gave in to all her requests, down to the canteen and dagger. She arrived, at midnight, smeared with the dust of the road, bright as the turmeric-rosewater paste that aunts anoint a bride with on the day before her wedding. Her hair was bound up in a fierce topknot, and the bruises from Bhishma's manhandling made her look war-haggard, war-weary—but in that war, the victor.

Shalva, cocooned in bandages, his leg in a cast, stared at her from his cot. She rushed to embrace him but had to stop short lest she jostle his rib fractures. So she knelt and kissed his hand.

The hand withdrew from under her lips.

'Go back to him,' said Shalva. 'The man who won you.'

'He didn't win me. *You* won me, a year ago, with that serenade you wrote me.'

Shalva shook his head. 'You're his now. You were in his power. Who knows what he did?'

Amba stood up in horror. 'This is exactly what Rama did to Sita. This is it. She stays pure as fire for eleven months and two weeks in Lanka, and when he sets her free, the first thing he does is reproach her, cast suspicion on her.'

'So there's good precedent, then.'

'She was gone eleven months and two weeks. I was barely gone a day!'

'A lot can happen in a day, Amba. We both know that. A lot that can't be recovered can be lost.'

'I've been on the road for almost all that time! Kashi to Hastinapur, Hastinapur to here!'

'And what happened in Hastinapur?'

'A fresh change of horses, Shalva! It was a stop on my way back to you!'

Shalva raised a hand. 'It's too late. Even if I knew he hadn't touched you, I couldn't possibly take you as a *gift* from someone. I'm a Kshatriya. I have my pride.'

'Your pride? What about your love?'

Shalva rang a bell, and a lieutenant appeared at the door. 'Escort this wandering madwoman out.' It took more than the one lieutenant to do it.

The next morning, she burst into the full royal assembly, howling Bhishma's name. Now she looked like the madwoman Shalva had said she was, the topknot dishevelled across her face, and the bridal kohl in twin black rivers down her cheeks. Her lips were cracked and bloody. She pointed at the resplendent celibate prince. 'You!'

The courtiers murmured at this most scandalous intrusion. Bhishma said respectfully, 'We feed the mendicants around the back.' Some twitched and muttered, others writhed and hollered; holy men wandered Bharata in those days, as they do now, and Bhishma assumed Amba was such a man. 'Our royal kitchen serves the charity meals at noon. I'm sure one of our courtiers can show you there.'

Amba parted the curtain of her hair. Her head was tilted down, but not in feminine modesty; her eyes glared up at him from under her eyebrows. 'I am no beggar Brahmin. I am Princess Amba, the woman you won as your wife.'

The courtiers burst out laughing. Bhishma raised a hand to silence them. 'Did you go astray on your way to Prince Shalva?'

'I made a detour all the way to Hastinapur. You should know, you dragged me the whole way. Now he won't take me back. He says I belong to you because you won me, through the ancient Kshatriya custom. So here I am. Marry me.'

'You may not have heard of my vow, but—'

'I've heard of it. I made a vow, too. But now I can't fulfil that one, so you can't fulfil yours, either.'

'It's Prince Shalva who's breaking a vow to marry you. That's no reason for me to break mine, young lady. See yourself out.'

Amba, sensing soldiers approach from the wings like bailiffs, drew the dagger Bhishma himself had issued her. She sprinted at him. The court erupted into shouts, but Bhishma caught the snake-strike of her wrist just in time, the steel fang poised at his pulsing jugular.

*

Amba, exiled from Hastinapur, grew even more embittered as she walked the lonely roads. She did not go back to Kashi, though her gentle father would have taken her back. She didn't want a soft bed and wealthy spinsterhood, or a marriage to someone else after the gossip cycle moved on.

She wanted to destroy Bhishma.

The problem was his strength. How could she find someone to champion her against a hurricane of knives?

There was only one man on earth stronger than Bhishma, one man Bhishma simply *couldn't* kill, and that was Parashuram, denied death. So to Parashuram's ashram she went. On his private spice island, the air was sharp with cloves.

Parashuram had been young Devavrat's teacher in the arts of war and weaponry. Ganga had wanted the best teacher for her son. There was only one choice: the feral-eyed Brahmin who had slaughtered the Kshatriyas twenty-one times.

Parashuram was an avatar of Vishnu, but he was older than Rama would have been. Rama had long ago returned to his Source, but Parashuram, unlike any other avatar, was shut out from the God who emanated him. Cut off, like a gangrenous hand. He had taken up violence to defend the dharma, but he had gone too far.

Parashuram's father and mother had lived in a hut with their five sons. The family had only one source of wealth, a single cow who fed them all. The boys milked her for just as much as they needed. Her name was Kamadhenu.

In those days, the Kshatriya caste had multiplied and run amok. Their mandate was to uphold order, by force if need be.

In practice, they used force whenever they wanted something and upheld desire as the one true dharma. A king on a hunt, hearing that a poor local Brahmin kept an infinitely gift-giving cow, went to the hut and asked for lunch. He kept asking for more and more elaborate dishes, and Parashuram's mother, trying to be a good hostess, went behind the hut and piled hay before Kamadhenu. As usual, Kamadhenu snuffled in the hay a bit, then swished her tail; and there, under the hay, was the wished-for dish.

At the end of the feast, the king asked Parashuram's parents how they had prepared such royal dishes on command, at such short notice. The innocent old Brahmin took the king to see Kamadhenu. The king asked for a demonstration and clapped his hands with delight when the hay revealed a rod of ice. The king untied the cow and walked her to the gate, and the family of five followed him in perplexity.

'One question,' said the avaricious king, 'is bothering me. Why don't you use this magic to build yourself a nicer house? Look at this hovel! I'm going to use her to put a new wing on my palace.'

'I ask for what we need and nothing more,' said Parashuram's father. 'She's how I feed my family. I can't give her up.'

The king smashed him across the mouth with the rod of ice and tossed it on the ground. 'Come and take her back from me. If you can.' And with that, he walked the wish-fulfilling cow away.

He didn't get far. Parashuram brought home the cow, which went out a white heifer and came back brindled red.

Parashuram's father, Jamadagni, embraced Parashuram's mother, but not out of joy. He set some hay before Kamadhenu and made a wish. From the hay he brought out an axe.

'Go cut down twenty-one trees,' he ordered his son, 'and build a pyre of their wood.'

Parashuram, a respectful son, went to his task. It took him until dinnertime. At dusk, he passed three men on horseback, going the other way.

When he got back to the hut, Parashuram found his mother kneeling in blood. She beat her chest twenty-one times; twenty-one times she called her husband's name.

The pyre his father had sent his son to build had been meant for Jamadagni himself. He had known the sons of the murdered king would make sure their father's killer lost a father, too.

Parashuram alone had the stomach to wash his father's corpse and prepare it for the cremation. He counted twenty-one stab wounds on the old man's body.

The only justice in those days was justice's lookalike, justice's fetch, signalling the death of justice. The Kshatriyas called it vengeance, while Parashuram called it karma in this lifetime. He took a vow—everything begins with a vow—to slaughter the Kshatriyas twenty-one times before he turned twenty-one years old. Culling the warrior caste would restore balance to the society. That was what he did.

He deforested that caste with his axe. The long, repetitive battles, one versus one hundred thousand, sent him into samadhi, or something like it. He called it *hanti-yoga*, the yoga of killing. When all the killing was done, Parashuram stitched his slashed body with silk thread and decided he was ready to go home to heaven. For he had learned, along the way, his true Vishnu-nature.

The yakshas guarding the gravel path to heaven crossed their spears. 'You got carried away,' said one gruffly. 'You're unclean now.'

There is more than one heaven in the cosmos—one for each God and Goddess—so Parashuram went from door to door, begging admission for the I, the iota of Vishnu he was. Each heaven's gatekeepers turned him away like priests keeping a temple free of stray dogs.

So he went to hell, ruled over by King Yama, who received the filthiest of sinners. At Parashuram's approach, the guardian yakshas lowered a crossbar made of bones across the highway.

'Since when has hell barred anyone entry?'

'Standing orders from King Yama,' said a yaksha.

'I only want a place to rest,' said Parashuram. 'I have been campaigning for years. I ask no special treatment. He can give me whatever torment murderers get.'

'Standing orders.'

'What does the God of Death have to fear from me?'

They were functionaries, not authorized to think or answer, only to block his entry. He did not doubt he could fight them and win, but to what end? If the God of Death would not touch him, he had no choice but to live on, earth-bound, body-bound.

What he did resembled living, but it really wasn't. Gray hairs on the chin meant Yama lifted your face to inspect you for the kill and decided, *not yet*. Stooped posture meant Yama had clambered atop your back to pluck the hairs from the top of your head. Yama breathed on you while you slept, and your face went all mud-cracked with wrinkles. None of this happened to Parashuram because Yama would not touch him for fear of pollution. So he neither aged nor died, like an inanimate object. He remained as instantaneous as thought, and so, at the speed of thought, he moved.

It did not take him long, after Amba's appeal, to find Bhishma. The celibate prince, having married off Vichitravirya to the two sisters from Kashi, had given himself a week to meditate on his mother's banks. He had not left behind his weapons, since he had just publicly insulted (and trounced) several hundred of the most powerful men in Bharata.

Parashuram's voice chilled him. It sounded unbearably close and loud, *inside* his head.

'A bridal raid, Devavrat? In the grand old style?'

Bhishma's eyes fluttered open. He stood and turned to his old guru. He joined his hands and bowed his head.

'That's not why I taught you the use of weapons.'

'I take it Princess Amba has found her cause a champion.'

'You brought back the worst of the old Kshatriya customs.'

'Just once, beloved Guru. I did what I had to. The boy had no interest.'

'I suppose the traits are passed down.' Parashuram tightened and tested his bowstring. 'I taught the half of you that came from your Goddess mother. I couldn't help but teach the Kshatriya-half of you as well.'

'You hate us, I know. But this is what I am. Half and half.'

'If you knew how your ancestors behaved back then, you would hate them too. Bridal raids were the least of it. But I am not the one who writes these histories.'

'You slaughtered them twenty-one times.'

'The wolf pack thinned the herd, so I thinned the wolf pack. The violence I did, I did for dharma's sake.' Parashuram hoisted his bow and spun it. 'Then as now.'

'What do you think you will accomplish by fighting me? Do you think I will break my vow?'

'I don't expect you to break your vow. I will break it for you. I will take you captive, so you are no longer in control. And I will marry you to Amba. I am a Brahmin, after all. I'll officiate.'

'But why, Master Parashuram? What does her falling out with her fiancé have to do with dharma? Go to Shalva! Hold your axe to his neck, order him seven times around the marriage fire. Leave me to myself.'

'I'm not just here on her behalf. The dharma needs you to marry and govern and father heirs, Devavrat. You have built a dam across your bloodline. You have blocked history's river from its natural course. I am going to break that dam. There isn't just life energy in a man, there's death energy, all pent up. I should know. The people a man is supposed to father, the people a man is supposed to kill. The numbers are calculated elsewhere. We just fill the quota. Your death energy is supposed to be directed outward: global conquest, the dharma everywhere, ice masons carving a temple the height of Mount Meru at the South Pole... If it doesn't go outward, it will go inward. Civil war, Devavrat! All of Bharata involved. The pyres will muffle the sun and famine will follow. The dead won't fit as smoke in the sky, much less as names in a book.'

Bhishma brought his bow forward. 'No one decides for me.'

And so he went to war one on one against the avatar who had trained him in the art of war. Master versus apprentice, guru versus novice. As Parashuram knew, even fifteen-year-old Devavrat had been a danger. Ganga's genetics gave him the agility of water, the ability of water to absorb and disperse a blow. Nor had Bhishma neglected his training in the intervening years—he always had surplus energy to get out. Now was the test.

Parashuram fired first. Bhishma took off, running at an angle. *Don't stand still.* Parashuram's own precepts echoed in his memory as the arrow curved in the air. *Don't wait for your enemy's arrow to miss, knock it out of the sky.* Bhishma fired at the arrow. His arrow blindsided his master's in mid-air.

Bhishma was ready for the shockwave. The impact domed outward, and both he and Parashuram ran up the expanding curve of pressure, facing each other again hundreds of feet off the ground. They had been murmuring spells to prime their next arrows the whole way up: such rapid Sanskrit looked like prayer.

Another point-blank arrow-impact. The blast, far off the ground, expanded in a sphere, and Bhishma and Parashuram were both caught against the southern half of it. They slammed to the earth. Bhishma sat up in a crater of his own making, then leapt to the lip of it, looking for his teacher.

Parashuram was waiting with his axe. 'I never imagined a Kshatriya would take so much convincing to spill his seed in a girl.'

'I am no ordinary Kshatriya. You know that.'

'And a pretty girl at that. Amba is a beauty . . . As you saw for yourself. Your heart skipped a beat when I said her name just now.'

'They call me Fearsome for a reason. I am at war with myself.'

'And with me.'

Parashuram rushed at Bhishma, who drew his sword and got it up just in time against the murderous lumberjack. His blade scraped sparks off the axe. Every swing of Parashuram's muscular torso made the white thread he wore turn red and redder. That Brahmin's thread, soaked with the blood of Kshatriyas, remembered ancient bloodbaths. Its colour change was salivation at the whiff of a hot meal.

Bhishma was not so easy to dice. His sword stopped, scraped, sparked the axe blade, hundreds of times. Soon they were both exhausted. Parashuram relented and staggered back. His hair had come undone and he paused to bind it up. Bhishma, grateful for the respite, rested the tip of his nicked sword on the earth.

'All you're doing is sharpening my axe,' said Parashuram, 'and sparking forest fires.' He jerked his head at the conflagration that silhouetted him.

Bhishma squinted and raised an arm against the heat. When he lowered it, Parashuram's arrow-hand fanned ten. That was a trick young Devavrat had never mastered. Their feathered fletches shivered in the fiery whirlwind.

'Go get your bow, boy.'

Bhishma raced to his chariot, knowing Parashuram would not fire until he had a bow in his hand. So he ran around to the back of his chariot, using it as a barrier, before he sprang up, snatched the weapon and crouched again. The barrage began immediately. The first few shots tore the chariot from its harnesses. The horses shrieked as Bhishma felt himself shoved—impact, impact, impact—towards the water. Riverbank mud accumulated all around him. A final salvo flung the horseless chariot-car into the Ganga, with Bhishma half-unconscious in the water around it.

The mother intervened to help her son. Four frothing, thousand-gallon stallions shaped themselves and threaded their necks through the torn harnesses. The chariot-car righted and Bhishma found himself carried, on a surge, into it. He fired back as his mother guided him back to shore, and this time, Parashuram had to hopscotch among the tops of fiery trees as they fell.

The two archers began trading even more violent warheads, armed with ever more dangerous mantras. Hoofed animals and birds fled the forest fires, people and dogs fled the villages. At last it was dinnertime, and the great Brahmin called a halt to the day's fighting. The guru led his pupil to a spot in the blackened forest, where he had buried some plump root vegetables and herbs, now thoroughly cooked and steaming where he broke them open. They shared the meal, and Parashuram corrected his student's swordsmanship. They agreed to resume the fight at dawn, with maces. That was the end of the first day.

*

Twenty more days passed in combat with various weapons systems, most commonly—and most destructively—the mantra-studded arrow. King Vichitravirya watched it daily from a terrace with his two new wives. Smoke rose in the distance, and the occasional deflected arrow spiralled into the sky and exploded. The royal observers snacked on roasted chickpeas, drank rice wine and never quite got around to consummating the marriage.

'Aren't you worried about your uncle?' asked Ambalika.

'Not really,' Vichitravirya shrugged. 'Uncle can't kill Parashuram, since death won't touch the crazy old Brahmin. But Parashuram *won't* kill Uncle, since he wants to force him to marry your sister—and besides, Uncle has a boon to choose the day and hour he dies. So they're both using non-lethal force, and this is all one boom and dazzle display for us to enjoy.'

It was not quite so enjoyable for the people closer to the epicentre. By the tenth day, even Hastinapur suffered the fallout as its marble columns webbed through with cracks. By the fifteenth, fissures had opened in the streets.

At sundown on the twenty-first day, a twelve-kingdom joint delegation arrived at the battle site. The haggard duelists sat sharing a boiled beet in silence. Blood red juice stained their lips and beards.

Bhishma had gone deaf from all the up-close explosions. (He would not recover his hearing for two months, and that, too, only after flushing his ears with Ganga water twice a day.) The delegation had to speak with Parashuram. Further escalation, they pled, would crack the ground in half. All the cities and rivers of the earth would empty into space. What would become of temples, murtis, incense sticks? They would float through space like debris and fall, eventually, into the incinerating eye of Surya. What would become of the dharma then?

Parashuram gazed with grudging love at his soot-smeared student with blood still spilling from his ear canals, his hand still in spasm from clutching his bow. He could speak to the deafened Bhishma because he could throw his voice to a place inside his head.

'It is a draw, then. We have bludgeoned each other enough.'
Bhishma nodded.
'I advise you to wed the girl, Devavrat. She will love you as fiercely as she hates you now. But if you don't, she will hate you even harder.'
Bhishma shook his head.
'You will hear from her again. I am not the most powerful being on earth to whom she can appeal. There is one greater than me.'

Bhishma looked into Parashuram's eyes and shook his head.

'Oh but there is, my boy, there is. He sits atop Mount Kailasa. And should he choose to help her, no vow or boon will protect you.'

'Shiva!' Bhishma shouted. It was the overloud voice of a man who cannot hear himself. 'Shiva!'

'And she will not ask of him what she asked of me. She does not want to be your bride, not anymore. She wants to be your killer.'

SARGA 6

'THE BULL OF THE BHARATAS'

Ambika and Ambalika did not conceive for years, even though they spent hours every day with their husband. Bhishma could hear them in the bedchamber even though he wasn't eavesdropping. Plenty of giggling, plenty of gossip. The girls tried on saris, and the young king gave them advice on how to tuck the pleats. In the mornings, the king and his two queens gardened together and praised each other's lotuses.

The celibate Bhishma had never loved or made love, but he had seen enough of Shantanu and Satyavati, breakfasting knee to knee, to know what lovers who had made love looked like. And this wasn't that.

The king's occasional coughs interrupted the giggles and gossip. What had seemed a chest cold one year ago had never gone away. Vichitravirya's two adoring wives laid wet towels on his feverish forehead. They allowed none of the maids to slip a spoon between their darling's chapped lips. Even Satyavati had her visiting hour.

He recovered, and they giggled again; he relapsed, and they moped.

Bhishma saw nothing of Vichitravirya for months, just the two princesses of Kashi breathlessly shuttling in and out. Bhishma sent in a squad of Ayurvedic doctors.

'The king is losing weight,' they reported.

More time passed. 'They're coddling him,' Bhishma snarled one morning. 'Of course he's going to lose weight, if all he does is lie about among women and sip turmeric-water. He needs to swing an iron club over his head! He needs to ride a horse!'

These tough cures had always worked for Bhishma. He barged into the royal bedroom to shake some manliness into his stepbrother. He stopped short at the threshold. The blood heat of a slit-open animal throbbed from the bed. Vichitravirya's eyes looked bulbous against his sunken face. They blinked weakly at Bhishma, like the flexing of moths on a wall, two beats before dream sleep. Everyone else had seen the king's transformation day by day, by degrees. Bhishma saw the contrast all at once: those ropy veins and fanned tendons on the backs of the king's hands; this mouth, the rip in a cocoon. Bhishma gasped. The man was dying.

And die he did, six weeks later in the stink of fever sweat, his sister wives now sister widows. Childless.

*

Hastinapur's riot to restore Bhishma to the line of succession, Amba's ferocious demand to marry him, Parashuram's twenty-one-day holy war to force him back into getting and begetting . . . These were all attacks on Bhishma's fearsome vow. They were all the doing of History, which wanted to reset and return to its proper sequence of events: The coronation of King Devavrat, the royal wedding of north and south, the first auspicious coconut broken on the first mahayantra's chassis. Queen Satyavati's plea was one more form of pressure on Bhishma to relent. The dharma made her its mouthpiece.

'Vichitravirya was sick for so long,' she said, clutching Bhishma's scarred hand, 'and he was so young when he married them... Bhishma, those girls are your brides anyway, by rights—you're the one who won them! I can send out scouts to bring back Amba, wherever she might be. You should marry all three.'

'You're watering granite and waiting for marigolds.'

'Stop thinking of yourself for once. Think of Hastinapur. What would your father want you to do? A vow is words! That's all a vow is!'

'Can words be unsaid?'

'You've already shown you can keep it. You've proven your power. Now prove you have the power to *break* it. Think of marrying these widows as an austerity. Prove your ascetic self-denial by denying yourself the pleasure of upholding your vow.'

'Please, Mother Satyavati. You're twisting things in your desperation. A married ascetic?'

'Then don't marry them. Just give them sons—once would be enough with each, since you've stored up so much over the years.'

'Never.'

'Do it now and we can say they are Vichitravirya's sons. We can say he fathered them just before he died.'

'Never.' He shuddered at the thought of the stud horse led to the whinnying stables.

'If not you, who else? Do you want the Kuru line to go extinct?'

'Fetch a Brahmin to do the job. Not some paunchy, happily married pandit—I mean an austere one, a wanderer who has restrained himself for just as long as I have.'

Satyavati looked into the distance, and her eyes blinked thoughtfully. An idea had occurred to her.

'Remember, my dear Queen Mother,' said Bhishma, 'all the kings in Bharata are half-Brahmin anyway.'

'How so?'

'That was the fallout from Parashuram's twenty-one massacres. He killed all the Kshatriya men but none of the women. So the Kshatriya war widows went looking for fathers to continue their dynasties. They passed the farms and held their noses at the manure stink; passed the markets and plugged their ears at the crass calls to buy this, buy that. They ended up at the ashrams.'

'The ashrams . . .' Satyavati echoed. She thought of her own mud-caked Brahmin. Of fog around a ferryboat, and a mid-river island. 'Devavrat, let me tell you a story.'

*

A month later, Satyavati took Ambika aside and said, 'Vichitravirya had a secret half-brother. Tonight, he will be your secret husband. Take off this widow-white sari and wear something bride-red.'

Ambika had come of age and entered her twenties without the satisfaction of a man. She knew the Kurus to be bull-necked, thick-wristed men. The feel of Bhishma's naked back, the afternoon of her abduction, had never left her memory. It kept her company. Who could that 'secret half-brother' be but Bhishma? The fearsome one had made an exception for her; she was certain. He had felt what she had felt, all those years before.

The door opened and shut, and the candle flames trembled. An odour pervaded the room. What *was* that? She sat up in alarm and saw Vichitravirya's stepbrother, Satyavati's secret son.

Krishna Dvaipayana Vyasa.

Shrewd Queen Satyavati did not intend for her father's work to go to waste. The fisherman had hooked the throne to his bloodline like bait to his fishing-pole. Too bad his grandson had been averse to skinny-dipping between a woman's thighs, averse to the oyster with no shell, its cloistered pearl. That was Shantanu's droopy-necked nature manifesting. What did water do but shape itself to circumstance? The fisherman's daughter thought of her options. She had another son, didn't she? Vyasa would be willing to swim upstream. Vyasa's father—the Brahmin who had bulled her long ago in the boat—*that* had been a man, his seminal floodwaters dammed up for years. He had taken her like an escaped convict hungry for his first woman. Vyasa, lost in poetry as his father had been in samadhi, must have inherited that randy streak. She could exploit that. He wouldn't say no. Parents routinely gave the lowest urge of a child their blessing. They even made a party of it: what else was a wedding? Given his bookish seclusion, Vyasa might well be too innocent to think it shameful, no shyer than a stud horse led to the mare, going to it in a state of nature. The only obstacle would be her own ability to say it, request it, command it. It would come down to her tone. Uneasiness in her would lead to uneasiness in him. She had decided to discuss the proposal matter-of-factly, no bobbing a knee or dropping her gaze, no erms or ahems. Here is your mother's problem. Here is how you can help.

As for Vyasa, he had no particular wish to mount and seed these mares. He had been hard at work on a new metre, measuring the joints between short and long syllables just so, like a carpenter building a table. The master poet acknowledged one master, and that was his mother. When she asked him to do this task, he agreed—and he came as he was. Did he bother to shower? Did he bother to shave? That was not what his mother had asked of him.

So the stud horse came to the stall smelling worse than unswept stables. His reddish hair was so tangly, things crawled up in there and died before they found their way out. Also contributing to his odour: the unscraped tongue in his sleep-stale mouth, last night's garlic, armpits never violated by soap or water, urine stains from marathon meditation sessions, dung-flecked feet from a journey on foot, and a beetle bite on his thigh whose pus he simply didn't notice.

Still, it wasn't the occult signs chalked on his slate-black forehead, or the stink root fungus growing from his navel, or the scorpion that skittered on to his foot and back up his dhoti, or his third nipple, or the captive asps braided into his beard, or the bright pink fissure in his lower lip that made Ambika shut her eyes. It was how his lazy right eye rolled about a bit, like a ball compass, then ticked level with his left, and stared into hers.

Ambika could not bear the intensity of that gaze. She did not know how to read, so *being* read unsettled her twice over. Vyasa could not look at anything with both eyes, living or non-living, without reading and transcribing it into his memory, a phrase to be used later. That was why his right eye was lazy; it allowed him to function and go about his day without turning it into literature. His night with Ambika was literature.

Amba's sisters had experimented with themselves before, and many a lady-in-waiting had blushed and gabbed. Ambika did not know Vyasa long enough to hear his mastery of language, and even if she had gotten acquainted before he bulled her, she was too shallow to admire him. She never imagined her first and only experience would be with such a dishevelled spectacle. Why a holy man? What possible use could a spindly, twitchy, mangy scholar be to a royal dynasty? Was this what Hastinapur wanted in the bloodline? Well, it would have to be borne, since there was no gainsaying the Queen Mother. Maybe, Ambika calculated, she could have Bhishma in her imagination. It would be no different than what she did at night, fantasizing with the help of her fingers. Ambika shut her eyes. Vyasa, reflexively, mirrored her with his inner eye, shutting his third one; his other two stayed open, memorizing her form in case he needed, in the future, to write love poetry.

When he emerged a half-hour later, Satyavati was waiting for him. 'Vyasa, my dear boy, you didn't bathe? Or at least perfume yourself? Even Shiva cleaned himself up for Parvati. No matter.

Tell me what you see with that third eye you've drawn on your forehead. What will Ambika's son be like?'

> The sun who crowns, the crown that dawns
> Out of the amniotic sea
> Will be a light, but see no light
> Because she shut her eyes at me.

'Vyasa, you know I cannot construe your riddling verses.'

'The boy will be virtuous and strong and utterly blind from birth. She shut her eyes and willed not to see me. She will pass that down like an eye colour.'

The next night, Satyavati briefed Ambalika. The princess was already trembling, for her sister had told her about the horrific creature.

'He is obedient in some things and stubborn in others,' Satyavati explained. 'I have persuaded him to perpetuate the Kuru line, but I can't persuade him to get a haircut. No matter how monstrous his appearance, you have to keep your eyes open.'

Ambalika nodded and let herself be closed in the bedchamber. She paced back and forth, planning to hold her breath for as long as she could. Vyasa showed up again, and she choked back her gasp. Ambika's description hadn't conveyed half of the poet's ugliness!

Still, it wasn't the occult signs chalked on his slate-black forehead, or the stink root fungus growing from his navel, or the scorpion that skittered on to his foot and back up his dhoti, or his third nipple, or the captive asps braided into his beard, or the bright pink fissure in his lower lip that made her blanch. It was how his lazy right eye rolled about a bit, like a ball compass, then ticked level with his left, and stared into hers.

Ambalika could not look away from the beast she had been fed to. Horrified, she blanched and contrasted so intensely with his skin that she nearly left him snow-blind. The whiteness passed into him through his eyes, down his *kundalini* channels, chakra to chakra lower and lower until, still inside him, his seed turned to gelatinous chalk.

When he emerged a half-hour later, Satyavati was waiting for him. 'Vyasa, my dear boy, did she keep her eyes open for you or didn't she? I thought so! No hitches this time, I trust? Tell me, what will Ambalika's son be like?'

> The son who crowns will be a moon
> Frosting the amniotic sea,
> His back, a peeling burn by noon
> Because his mother blanched at me.

'Vyasa, you know I cannot construe your riddling verses.'

'The boy is going to be virtuous and strong and as pale as I am dark. She kept her eyes open, but the blood so drained from her, I lost sight of her body against the bedsheet.'

Satyavati was less concerned about this problem after she spoke with the Ayurvedic doctors. If the boy did have to do battle under raw sky, they assured her, there were herbal ointments they could smear on his exposed skin. Much of him would be covered by armour. Even his boyhood would likely be normal. Playtime might require an umbrella man, sufficiently spry to sprint behind a five-year-old. They would make it work.

The blind grandson-to-be, though, bothered Satyavati, and she wondered whether she ought to re-seed the botched patch. She convinced Vyasa to stay one last night and browbeat Ambika into trying again. The princess of Kashi grew exasperated with her mother-in-law treating her like a flowerpot in which to grow her dynastic ambitions. She told Satyavati she would do it one last time—and then poured a pomegranate's worth of rubies into her maid's lap.

'Suffer this for me,' she said, 'and there will be more.'

The maid's name was Parishrami, and unlike the flighty princesses of Kashi, she knew how to read even though no one had taught her. More than once she had answered her mistress in the sloka metre, unwittingly, when promising to scrub a sink or wash a sari. And as for the poet Vyasa, she had met him and prepared his room. She thought he smelled like poetry, and she saw through his gnat-flecked, ash-dusted exterior to a sharp jaw and delicate ears. Vyasa had a habit of standing on his head and composing out loud. What sounded like cryptic mutterings to other people had made Parishrami feel like she was lucid dreaming.

When the time came, she didn't snuff out all the lamps the way Ambika had instructed her to do. She lay fit and naked on the bed and explained to Vyasa, in the *trishtubh* meter, how the princess had delegated this duty to the maid, and how the maid would have volunteered anyway. Vyasa had never been desired before, and under his black skin, he blushed. Being desired felt even better than being read! He laid on his back and Parishrami showed him what lovemaking felt like when the woman wanted it too. This night was different than the other two nights. He didn't emerge a half-hour later. He didn't emerge a full hour later. He didn't come out until close to noon the next day. Sweat had washed all the occult signs off his forehead.

Satyavati heard the door open and rushed over to find Vyasa holding the maid's hand. 'She doesn't work here anymore,' he said. 'I want you to give her a few rooms in the palace, and servants of her own. She is going to give birth to the wisest boy in all of Bharata. He'll see clearly everything that Ambika's son cannot. Make sure his brothers listen to his advice, and they will avoid the worst of what's to come.'

Satyavati, fondest of her firstborn as she was, did not grow angry at this. This third grandson, by the maid, would help the other two princes. Focused on that calculation, she ignored the dark hint of catastrophe in her son's parting words. She hugged him to her bosom and kissed his matted hair as only a mother could, since she was bothered by his stink even less than Parishrami.

Vyasa, soon to be a father of three, joined his hands in *namaskar* to his mother and wandered off to the Himalayas, with no need or nostalgia for the sex, food and soft pillows he had just enjoyed. All he really loved was language. He was already extemporizing the first fifty or so thousand lines of the Mahabharata, happy and prolific as ever.

SEQUENCE 3

THE PARENTS OF THE RIVAL SETS OF COUSINS

The three sons of Vyasa grow up. Following young Vidura's advice, Bhishma approaches other kingdoms for brides for the two royal princes.

Dhritarashtra marries Gandhari, whose kingdom corresponds to modern-day Afghanistan (and, centuries later, after Alexander's conquests, became the source of Greco-Indian fusion art). Gandhari's brother is Shakuni, a cunning gambler. He becomes very important later on.

Pandu marries Kunti. Kunti has quite the backstory; she, too, had a secret baby in her teens. Granted a boon to invoke any God she wanted to father her children, Kunti tested it out and invoked Surya, the Sun God. She abandoned that half-solar son, Karna. Karna has been blessed by his father with golden earrings and a golden suit of armour, sealed to his skin, growing with his body, impenetrable. Half-royal, half-divine, Karna will grow up poor.

Pandu suffers a curse that prevents him from making love ever again. Kunti consoles him by revealing the boon she got when she was a girl. She invokes a different God to father each of the five Pandavas.

Kunti's brother, quite symmetrically, is just as important as Gandhari's to the plot. Kunti's brother is Vasudeva—and Vasudeva is the father of Krishna. Sarga 9, 'The Darling Darkling Changeling', recounts the tragic backstory leading up to Krishna's birth. Here, for a third time, in yet another example of the epic's architectural symmetries, the wife's brother has an outsized role: Vasudeva's brother-in-law imprisons him shortly after his wedding, and Krishna is born in a prison.

Characters Who Will Show Up Again:

GANDHARI, mother of the Kauravas, the blind king Dhritarashtra's wife.

SHAKUNI, her brother. Favouring his own sister's sons (the future Kauravas), he will arrange the Game of Dice in which the Pandavas lose everything.

KUNTI, the mother of the Pandavas and Karna.

KARNA, the son of the Sun God, scandalously born to Kunti out of wedlock. Raised in poverty, he will grow up to become Arjuna's equal in archery.

KRISHNA, the son of Kunti's brother. Needless to say, he will have a major role in the epic to come. The coming sargas, though, will deal mostly with the Pandavas and Kauravas; Krishna will reappear much later, as a well-wisher, adviser, cousin and friend of the five Pandavas.

SARGA 7

BLIND BOY, PALE BOY, VISIONARY

Three brothers, close to each other in age, carrying Vyasa's epic blood in them: the eldest prince, Dhritarashtra, blind; the second-born, Pandu, always game to hunt; the third-born, Vidura, a chambermaid's son, the slightest and brightest.

It was the perfect setup for palace intrigue, for brother to backstab brother. So it might have played out in other kingdoms, under other guidance, but in Hastinapur, Bhishma governed. The city couldn't have him as king, but it did get him as regent until the boys came of age.

Bhishma raised them right, passing on all the arts and sciences, skills and insights he had gotten in his own youth, sitting at the feet of the Seven Sages. He didn't leave them to the lax discipline of palace tutors, as he had done his stepbrothers. The three boys were always at his side in the throne room. Early on, he distilled his celestial lessons into maxims. One maxim, in fact. Statecraft? Love your brothers. Theology? Love your brothers. Poetry, ethics, philosophy, dharma? Love your brothers. Mathematics, a little more involved, dusted Bhishma's fingers white with chalk—but 'three over three equals one' was one more way of saying: love your brothers.

Love each other they did, to the astonishment of court historians and diplomatic observers. To their disappointment, there was harmony, no story to be told. 'The blind prince has been told the pale prince should rule in his stead, even though the blind prince is older,' the ambassador from Gandhara wrote home. 'For some reason, he embraced his brother Pandu and, hard as this is to believe, agreed.'

Kashi's ambassador kept a close eye on the sole son who wasn't born of a Kashi princess. He was always monitoring this potential usurper. Yet he ended up thinking Vidura the greatest of the three. 'In the morning, he catches the smallest errors in ministerial presentations,' the ambassador wrote home to Kashi, 'and then, in the afternoon, he rides and shoots with his pale half-brother, no less an athlete. Thanks to his skin, as dark as Vyasa's, he can stay out far longer in the sun than Pandu. In the evening, while his brothers relax before the musicians, he hurries off to hear lectures from visiting holy men or to study obscure sutras. Bhishma respects him as an equal in matters of governance—just this week, with the whole court assembled, he asked the youngest's advice on finding a match for the eldest . . .'

*

Vidura had already thought out the ideal matches for his brothers. Surrounded by courtiers, though, he said he would consider the question, then moved the day's business along to the next topic. It would have been tactless for him to answer. Dhritarashtra would have been humiliated if his youngest brother had dictated the marriage, though that kindly, tentative smile suggested he didn't *feel* the humiliation of it. Vidura, very gently, told Bhishma afterwards not to ask such a thing in public when it came to Pandu. They could discuss it privately.

'I will do as you say, Vidura my boy. You're wise even when it comes to how to ask a question. But tell me, who will be a good wife to Dhritarashtra? Do you see any candidates?'

See. Bhishma knew that Vidura had inherited, from his poet father, an uncanny mindsight. What else could it be called but that? His exterior eyes went glassy, and he surveyed things far away as if they were right in front of him; he could eavesdrop, too, on conversations near and far, past and present and (he was still working on this) future. For a few moments, he checked his work, scanning the kingdoms of the Angas, the Madras, the Pauravas and Kekeyas and Sauviras . . . and finally, far to the north-west, the white-peaked and green-eyed city of Gandhara.

'There is a princess, far to the north-west. Her father named her for his kingdom: Gandhari. There is no better wife for my brother, no better queen for the dynasty, since she is destined to have one hundred sons and one daughter.'

'How can you possibly know that?'

'It was a boon from Shiva, which he gave her when she was a little girl . . .'

*

Gandhari was born with a caul. Midwives say that a caul is a layer of skin left over from the dead body the soul left behind in its past life. It clings to the atman as it crosses the finish line, like the ribbon plastered to the runner's chest. Children born with a caul risk remembering their past lives. Gandhari gazed into a mirror for the first time and saw, through her own light eyes, straight to the bottom of the pool of her being. There, inside herself, she recognized a holy woman, a devotee of Shiva, the wandering singer she had been in her past life.

Before she turned seven, she fell to practising austerities. She gave her dolls away and played with a *mala* of rudraksha seeds.

Her parents were shocked to find their little girl standing on one leg, her hands clasped over her head, humming aum.

Shiva had never been propitiated by so small a girl, so he found his way to her. 'You again,' he said fondly. 'You have been dedicating yourself to me for your past hundred births, and you get younger and younger every time. You have never been a wife, never been a mother or grandmother, all because of me! I am an ascetic, but I am married to Parvati, and I have sons of my own. Stay behind and live in the world for this life, my dear! I bless you with a son for every birth you devoted to me, and a daughter for this life, so you can taste that too. One hundred and one children! And a strong husband, and a vast palace.' Shiva took the mala from the little girl and broke the string. The rudraksha seeds bounced on the palace floor and scattered, and little Gandhari snapped out of her asceticism—though she never lost her piety or her devotion to Shiva. She remembered her past life only vaguely, as she might a dream, and in time, she forgot it entirely.

*

Once the request made it to Gandhara, nestled in its slopes, Gandhari's father accepted right away. He knew there was no greater family than the Kurus, and besides, with Bhishma doing the asking, what was he inviting if he refused? The prince in question, Dhritarashtra, was blind, he had heard. Hastinapur would grow indignant if he called that a dealbreaker.

He called his son, Shakuni, to join him in telling her the news. The princess was less likely to act out with her brother around. They had reason to be wary of her. All those past lives worshipping Shiva had rubbed off on Gandhari, and she had taken on some of the unpredictable irascibility of Kailasa's master. She had grown up expecting, like most modern girls, to have a swayamvara where she could search the faces for the most Shiva-dark and Shiva-dishevelled of the princes. A messenger was already galloping east, carrying the king's *Yes* in his gunny sack. This arranged marriage might not go over well.

Gandhari's brother was a dashing young man back then. Decades of alcohol hadn't yet yellowed Shakuni's eyes and softened his jowls. It was easy to lose track of how much he drank while gambling, and he was *always* gambling. That was Shakuni's great white shark of a vice. All his other evils swam among its teeth, like so many sycophant suckerfish. The cosmos struck him as one vast casino, the planets just mystical spherical dice, rolled once by their creator and rolling ever since. Each life was a turn at the velvet. If you were lucky, you had a pretty girl to kiss your fist before you threw six and six—though everyone's dice clattered and stopped and showed perfectly blank white sides, eventually. Here as in every gambling den, chance was king, and the house always won in the end. You strolled home as poor as you strolled in.

Gandhari heard the two men out and asked, 'What do you know of Prince Dhritarashtra?'

'We know he is . . . blind,' said her father. 'He comes from a famous family.'

'And that is all?'

'That can be a good thing, my dear daughter. If he tries to beat you, you can slip away from his blows.'

'And when you play dice with him,' reflected Shakuni, 'he'll rely on *you* to read him the numbers.'

'What could be better, Gandhari, than having a blind husband? Many a woman would love to lead her man submissively about the palace. You're likely to get your way in everything, they'll be so grateful to you for marrying him. Since he's a Kuru, he's probably built like a bull. They all are, in that lineage—it's the blood of their fisherman forefather, who pulled in nets for a living.'

'You've found out nothing about him, other than his blindness?'

Her father shrugged.

'And you've already accepted on my behalf?'

He nodded, with a glance at Shakuni.

'Sister,' said Shakuni, 'diplomacy isn't chess. You can't stare at the squares and meditate on your next move. Quickness is a kind of luck.'

Gandhari went to her drawer without a word and drew out a silk sash. She folded it with care and laid it across her eyes. 'There,' she said, tightening the knot. 'I have no ascendancy over Prince Dhritarashtra now.'

She stood taller, prouder than before. She had taken on his disability as if it were a superpower.

'What are you trying to prove?'

She felt her way to a chair and sat down mutely. Realizing his mistake, her father sent a second messenger after the first and recalled him. Then he ordered envoys to seven kingdoms—Hastinapur and its closest neighbours—to gather information about his daughter's prospective match. He had them report directly to her. A wave of her hand dismissed the breadth of his shoulders and the circumference of his forearms. She gave to praise and censure an equally sceptical ear.

In Hastinapur, Bhishma grew impatient and indignant as the months went by. Vidura calmed him. 'Let Gandhara find out everything they can about my dear brother,' he said. 'They already know he is blind, and if that is no obstacle, then everything else they find out will delight them. Didn't I buy the testimony of a dozen tongues before I proposed Gandhari's name to you? Give it time.'

Vidura, as usual, was right. The messenger arrived first with the letter, and close behind him, Princess Gandhari, Prince Shakuni and their attendants. To Bhishma's astonishment, Gandhari had a blindfold on. When she knelt to touch his feet in reverence, he knelt to face her and whispered, 'My dear, that won't be necessary.'

'I swore that one day I would marry my equal,' she said. Her ring fingertip touched one muffled eye, the next, and then, in the centre of her forehead, the third. 'My husband and I are equals now.'

When Dhritarashtra heard how his bride-to-be had chosen to join him in his darkness, he wept for a full hour, so many tears that he sent them to her in a small bottle. Before the wedding ceremony, she mixed his tears with red powder and painted a blood-red line down the part in her hair—the first time *sindoor* was ever applied. It became a custom among brides ever after. On their wedding night, he offered to take off her blindfold with the rest of her clothes, so she could see his face just once and know that he was handsome. Gandhari kept the blindfold on and felt his face as he felt hers. In that chamber with no candle, she whispered, *I know what I need to know.*

*

'Vidura, you really found us a jewel in Gandhari. You asked me to bring this up next time in confidence, so let's talk about it now, while our relatives and cousins lie there and snore, having stuffed themselves after Dhritarashtra's wedding feast. I would say it is time to look for Pandu's match.'

'I've already studied the subject, Grandfather Bhishma. I knew you would ask sooner or later.'

'Do you have a name yet?'

'I do. Have you heard of a princess by the name of Pritha?'

Bhishma and Vidura discussed this prospective match in private—or so they thought. Outside their room, however, crouched the one guest who had not eaten himself into a stupor. Ever-alert, ever-conniving Shakuni learned of the plan to marry Pandu and Pritha just as it was being formulated. As his excitement at this inside knowledge grew, his gambler's hands grew restless.

He knew his dice would make a clicking sound that might give away his eavesdropping, so he flipped a coin instead, guessing heads or tails, playing against himself for want of an opponent.

Ah, but there would be an opponent, wouldn't there? He had marvelled at Hastinapur's wealth, and it bothered him that his sister Gandhari couldn't see it and wouldn't be queen of it—instead, this Princess Pritha would get to enjoy it, and her sons would get to inherit it. *Heads.* Hearing of his sister's soon-to-be rival on the very day of her wedding (didn't these schemers have the decency to wait a *day*?), Shakuni began hating the Pandavas years before they were born. He made no plans to harm them just then. *Heads.* What he did with the dice, years later, was a move in a game that began that night, when he had his belly full of Hastinapur's food. *Heads.* There would be a time, he told himself. There would be an opportunity. Shakuni sent the coin spinning six feet into the air and caught it between his thumb and forefinger. Heads, Shakuni's and Shakuni's, both sides: Turning the coin in the light, he twice admired his own silver profile, which smiled as he was smiling now—and as he and his future nephews would smile, he vowed, in the future.

SARGA 8

LOVE OF GOD

Wandering sages were not all alike. For every cross-eyed muttering Vyasa, there was a randy Parasara, ogling the girl as she worked the oars. They weren't even all dirty; Narada muni kept himself clean-shaven, with a frizz-free topknot the size of his fist, and no matter how many yojanas he travelled, he smelled like he'd just had a jasmine-littered tub bath. The Seven Sages, who wandered the cosmos in (and as) stars, smelled of tulsi and hydrogen fusion.

The sage Durvasas was yet another sort of barefoot Brahmin. He had the sublime irritability of an open, metaphysical cut. Exceedingly permeable, exceedingly sensitive, Durvasas let everything in: temple bells clanging on the yonder side of the galaxy, Himalayan wildflowers, the scent of ghee spooned into a sacred fire . . . and an uneven stitch in the mat he sat on, and brats scrapping two streets over, and a fat man's chewing noises in the audience at a wedding. Such things worse than irked him. They eclipsed the face of Brahman. Why wouldn't he lash out, if a badly prepared cup of turmeric milk cost him existence, consciousness, bliss?

So Durvasas became known for his short temper and his long-winded curses. When he showed up at a palace and asked for charity, servants tendered their resignations. It just wasn't worth the risk! You could spill something on him and—*Just as you made me wet, so you shall be made wettest of all!*—end up reborn as a fish. An orange roughy could live for a hundred and fifty years. Who had that kind of time?

One day, in the kingdom of Kunti, word spread in the royal kitchens and servants' quarters that the godly grump Durvasas was coming to terrorize them for a week. The king, Kuntibhoja, could not order the gates closed fast enough. The fourteen-year-old princess, Pritha, offered to take care of the sage. Kuntibhoja warned her of the danger. Just because she was royalty didn't mean that Durvasas wouldn't give her a tongue-lashing, or worse, an outright curse if she displeased him.

Pritha insisted, and within a day of the sage's arrival, she was teaching Durvasas how to say 'Thank you' and 'If it's not too much trouble'. Her lessons introduced him to the vast dance of people in society. Human interaction was as intricate as any Vedic ritual. The holy curmudgeon found himself disarmed by his hostess's sweetness. He was no Parasara, fortunately; he was far from harbouring any desire for her. Instead, she gave him a vision of an entirely different life course for himself. What if he had become a prosperous doctor or a minister at court? Wouldn't he have ended up exactly like this in his retirement, with a granddaughter like Pritha to wait on him, to chide him, to show him everything he'd been doing wrong? He couldn't muster any anger, not even when she delayed his nightcap of turmeric milk. In fact, he thought back to some of his past curses, and he wondered whether they had been justified.

Every day he stayed in King Kuntibhoja's palace, he liked Pritha more. The more he liked her, the sweeter his nature got. In time, the palace saw the old sage at a game of hopscotch, jumping from square to chalked square while the princess clapped her hands and encouraged him. When it was her turn, Durvasas tilted his head in adoration, and he thought, as many a grandfather has thought, 'What husband will ever be worthy of this little one? Whoever it is, he better value what he has, for this delight of a girl deserves nothing but happiness.'

How could he help himself? He peeked into her future. There, he saw her marrying Prince Pandu of the Kuru line. Not a bad match, Durvasas thought, as far as the family is concerned. He was surprised at Pandu's skin (though it made sense, since *Pandu*, literally, meant pale), and he wondered, looking at those light eyes, if Pritha's groom was an albino. He studied Pandu's future to see how he would treat his bride. He would become king without any struggle with his blind elder brother, who would give up the throne willingly. Kalinga, Anga, Magadha—only victories for Pritha's husband, and no serious war wounds. All well, so far. Here was Pandu in his marriage get-up again, next to another girl . . . He was going to take another wife, a princess from the Madra Kingdom. Durvasas did not hold that against Pandu. Two wives was a modest tally for a king. Events got misty beyond that. He was already looking over a decade into the future.

But what was this? Pandu was going on a hunt. Durvasas used all his yogic power to peer at this next event. He wouldn't be seeing it if it weren't something momentous. His visionary eyes asquint, he saw Pandu loading his arrow. Over there, a deer and his doe were mating. That was a sacrilegious thing to do, killing two creatures while they made love—hadn't Pandu heard the story of Valmiki and the origin of poetry? The First Poet had cursed a Nishada hunter who had killed a pair of copulating cranes and through that excess of emotion had discovered metre; metre made it possible to write the Ramayana, the consummate story of lovers parted and parted again. Physical union between beast and beast was just as holy as the metaphysical union between self and Brahman. The language called one thing sex and the other, yoga, but joining was joining. And now Pandu sundered the two deer at that very moment. Maybe he couldn't see they were mating through the trees.

While Durvasas watched in horror, Pandu's arrow passed through the two dear ones. As they bled, they reverted to their true forms: the sage Kindama and his wife, naked and surprised in the act. After years of celibacy and *stotras*, the couple had begged Shiva—Pashupati, Lord of the Animals—to teach them the obscure tantric art of erotic metamorphosis. The sage and his wife, to make up for their austere twenties and thirties, had decided to tour together the bodies of beasts and birds and bugs. They wanted to discover which species derived the greatest pleasure from sex, and this afternoon, they had been testing out deer and doe.

Kindama, shot through, affixed to his shrieking wife by the arrow, shouted over his shoulder at Pandu. Hastinapur's king argued his innocence, which only incensed the dying Kindama. What happened next was familiar to Durvasas. Would he have done anything different himself?

'The next time you try to make love to your wife,' said Kindama through agonal gasps, 'I curse you to drop dead.'

Durvasas gasped just as deeply as Kindama would gasp, all those years later. The moment Pandu tried to make a mother of Pritha, he would make her a widow. Didn't that beastly sage realize a curse hurt more people than just the person it was laid on? 'Kindama, *think*, damn you—think of his loved ones!' Durvasas cried out.

Pritha rushed a chair over and lowered him into it.

'I'm perfectly all right, my poor, poor girl,' he murmured. 'Don't worry about me.'

'You stared into the distance and started gasping.'

'Into the distance, yes . . . A bow shot into the future.'

Pritha called across the courtyard for a doctor.

'No need,' Durvasas assured her, patting his forehead with his dhoti.

'Dada,' she said, 'there is no shame in accepting help when you're not feeling well.'

Dada! A title that honoured him more than *king* or *rishi*. No wonder men dwelt in the world and started families and businesses.

Durvasas looked at her with pity and affection. 'I'll let the doctor examine me, if it makes you feel better. Listen, Pritha. I want to thank you. No one has ever spoken so forthrightly with me since I was a little boy. Even your chiding is sweet to me. Maybe you were my mother in a past life. I want to grant you a boon. I've always laid curses, my whole career.'

'If I had your powers, I would grant boons to everyone I came across. I would make everyone joyful.'

Durvasas laughed. 'That's why the Gods only grant such powers to bitter old codgers like me. They don't want to break the system of karma and comeuppance. No doubt I'll be granting more boons in the coming years, though. I feel I couldn't bear to lay a curse, not today, not even if someone threw buffalo bones in my mandala . . . Your boon is this, Pritha. Remember this verse:

Through love, unite, through yoga, join
Both sides of mirror, moon and coin.
Become the Om within the ovum.
Give me this God so I may love him.

Just say that verse, then say the name of the God you want to father your child.'

'To father my child?' Pritha raised her eyebrows in astonishment. 'That's a strange boon, Dada! I doubt my future husband would approve.'

'I told you, I have so little practice granting boons, my first one was bound to be a little awkward. It's like someone's first poem or first joke. But now that you have the boon, keep it in reserve. Who knows, darling Pritha? You may need it someday . . .'

*

If a boy of Pritha's age were given the power to call any Goddess he wished to his bed, he would have invoked a different one every six hours or so, and spent the rest of his life cycling through the pantheon (excluding Kali, of course). Durvasas knew that and would have never given that boon to a male. The old man understood many things, Gods, men, the Vedas, maya, karma and all that; what he didn't understand was women. He assumed that Pritha, because she was a girl, couldn't possibly feel *lust* the way a boy did, couldn't possibly be tempted to experiment before marriage.

The fact that she set the boon on her lap and waited two whole years testifies to her reserve and self-control. Sometimes she would say two of the lines, but not all four. Then she said three of the lines and pressed her thighs and lips together, delighting in this secretive mischief. Then she tiptoed deep into the fourth line but stopped short at *love him*, biting her lip as she imagined being clasped by Vishnu's four arms, or maybe even invoking Shiva Nataraja and finishing like the universe itself in a sphere of fire . . .

Sphere of fire. Wasn't the Sun, by definition, the hottest of the Gods? No one's embrace could be warmer. Would Surya's kisses blister? Would his skin be char-black or athletic bronze or a distant and alien gold? Would he let her walk his surface? Would he erupt in a solar flare?

She went all the way, at last, to the end of the verse before whispering *Surya*. The *su* sound brought her lips forward in a pucker. The *ya* relaxed her all over and segued into a sigh, *ahhhh* . . . And he came.

She sat up in bed and swept the sheet up over her bare legs. He was sitting on the windowsill in a cloak of cashmere night. She wanted to look at his face, but her eyes kept dropping as if she were looking directly at the sun—though in this case, it was because of shame. 'You can go,' she whispered.

No, I can't.

'I changed my mind.'

I would expect that. Change is what minds do. But not words.

Vow, curse, boon: all words, in the end. You said words, and they stayed words. No unsaying them. Pritha had said the words. The God had arrived.

And what a God he was! He closed the curtains behind him and let the cloak slip. His skin was the colour of noon's glint on faraway waves. She had to shade her eyes against him at first, but the more her pupils dilated, the better her eyes adjusted. Soon she could make out the sharp cut lines of his torso and the sunspot of his navel. The copper coins on his chest looked on the verge of liquefaction but never quite melted. The heat shimmer around him got mixed up with the blur of tears in her eyes. He moved very, very slowly, as the sun always does. She was crying by the time he reached her. Instinctively, as though awakened, she rose from bed and stood before him, head down, feet turned slightly in, shivering in his heat.

Are you afraid?

'Will you burn me?'

Only if you want me to. There are ways to make it feel good.

'Don't. Just—just do what a husband would do. Nothing more. I'm human. I won't be able to . . ..'

I'll take it slow.

'No. Please be quick. What if someone comes?'

I can put off the dawn for as long as we need.

His black hair floated off his skull in every direction, as if he were under the sea, which, because it was night, he was. She dared to touch it. Her hand vanished into that pure shadow. It was cooler in there. Surya set himself down on his knees. Pritha turned her face to the sky and opened her mouth in ecstasy, and out of her throat shot a steady silent scream of light.

*

The suntan from that one night did not fade for decades. Even after she married Pandu, even after he collected Kindama's curse and retired with his two wives to the ascetic forest, the colour stayed on her, like a full-body love bite that bruised bronze. Other than that, though, Surya left no trace. *Don't worry,* he had told her as he left. *Nothing penetrated you but light.*

No traces... except for the baby boy, of course. She tucked him into a wicker basket and placed him in the arms of his first wet nurse, the Ganga. Pritha worried he might drown if his little boat capsized, soldered as he was to so much metal. The baby sunrose from the sea of her, golden like his father; only the son's gold was literal gold: armour and an earring, birthday gifts from Surya to his son, forged in the fiercest solar smithy. If the baby *did* drown, she reasoned, at least he would sink to the bottom and not wash up somewhere public. The baby, like his father, would leave no trace.

The unwed teenaged mother had been burned once. She did not experiment again. It was easy to move on from that memory after she married. In Hastinapur, to mark her origin as well as her separation from it, she started going by the name of Kunti. She felt like that curious girl, 'Pritha', was someone else.

Kunti never told Pandu about her boon (much less how she had tried it out) until she found her childless, celibate husband watering the tulsi plants with his tears. He begged her to let a Brahmin sage couple with her, the way his mother had coupled with Vyasa—a mere transaction, seed in a furrow.

'Why ask a Brahmin to father our princes,' she said quietly, 'when we can recruit a God?'

Pandu assented immediately and prepared the bed of kusha grass with his own hands. No murti's pedestal received half as much care from a devotee. Pandu had seen how one divine parent could translate into a Bhishma. Pritha's boon would fortify the Kuru line with a demigod—hopefully, several demigods. And though they weren't his, they would bear his name: the Pandavas.

*

Kunti ended up enjoying three trysts with supernatural beauty. Yama, to quell her trembling, encouraged her to think of him under his other name. *Call me Dharma,* he said, *and my lips won't feel so cold.* He was even paler than Pandu, but his skin left her body with a dusting of ash. Some of it collected in her navel, and she dipped her pinky and touched it to her tongue. Sweet. She waited nine months after her meeting with Yama to invoke Vayu, Wind, and nine months after that to invoke Indra, Sky. Two and a half years later, she was the mother of three sons. In her later life, she would invoke her three divine lovers again—bodilessly, through the boon of memory. Kunti alone of all women, mortal or immortal, could reminisce about her intimacies with more than one God. Vayu swept her off her feet. Indra laid her on her back and hovered over her, unreachable even when inside her. Death was an icicle. He let out a cry and melted. Vayu's hand in hers felt as thrilling as breath on her neck. She rested her ear on Indra's chest and heard, instead of a heartbeat, a lion-like satisfied purr, the thunder in Sindh. Yama insisted, even though she was his only for one night, that they walk seven times around a burning straw. His other name was Dharma; everything had to be proper, official, right. So, for that one night, she took off Pandu's ring and slipped on Yama's. The ring was a smoke ring set with a twenty-four-carat spark. Wind perfumed himself with sea air. She wanted him to linger afterwards for a few moments, just so she could hug him goodbye. *I'm not the sort,* he apologized over his shoulder as he headed for her open window, *to settle down long term.* Indra's weight was rain weight, ten thousand fingertips tapping her chest and thighs. Death was an arrow, piercing her. His eyes rolled back in his head as he deliquesced. He did not fall asleep until she closed his eyelids for him, and he stayed asleep no matter what she tried, until she bit his earlobe. Vayu, the most energetic lover of the three, left her blue silk sheets in a whirlpool on the floor. The pleasure the sky gave her came and came again in bright white flashes behind her eyes. Death came for her, and she came for Death. She never slept better.

SARGA 9

THE DARLING DARKLING CHANGELING

When the Pandavas and Kauravas came into the world, so did the war between them, though it would gestate for a while yet. Decades later, it would crown and take its birth, ripping the world open. Bloody, messy, howling—its birth canal, a plain not yet known as *Kurukshetra*. The Gods, too, knew what was coming, Vishnu most keenly, since he was the one who oversaw the turning of the Wheel. Every so often, the hissing pistons and clicking clockwise gears at the heart of the world grew hot and gave off sinister smoke, and their divine mechanic, answering history's unholy incense, had to descend to the engine room and give the sides of things a kick. To do that, he needed a foot with bones in it, a leg with muscle on it and everything else that made a body. So he took one on, and that was an avatar, an incarnation. He triangulated his own birth precisely, time and place and lineage. The Pandavas could not rely on their father's side of the family, obviously; that way lay the blind king and his hundred sons, foredoomed to fall out with them. Vishnu had to take birth in their mother's family, Queen Kunti's family. Four-armed Vishnu surveyed her family tree, counting all her many relatives on his forty fingers, until he settled on the perfect candidate: Kunti's brother. The symmetry in this choice pleased the God: After all, Duryodhan's mother's brother, dice-delighted Shakuni, was going to bring the Great War into the world. He would end up being that *adharma*'s father in a sense. Let Arjuna's mother's brother, then, father the avatar who would help re-establish dharma. Let Vasudeva be the father of Krishna.

*

Pritha had not grown up with her brother. While still in cloth diapers, she had been gifted to her father's best friend. King Kuntibhoja lacked a daughter; his own had died of fever at age two, and he had grieved for years. That daughter's name, too, had been Pritha. Kuntibhoja cherished this gift, this miraculous restoration of the lost daughter with a daughter of the same age and name.

Back in Yadava country, where Pritha came from, her elder brother grew up to be soft-spoken, noble, free of vice and envy (the opposite of green-eyed Shakuni). Though raised in separate places, brother and sister met several times a year to celebrate festivals like Holi, Diwali and Uttarayan together. Vasudeva deserved the best things in life—but the world was on the eve of the Kali Yuga, and reality was already starting to worsen, to warp, to war.

Vasudeva married a princess named Devaki. Her cousin, the wealthy King Kamsa of Mathura, made sure the wedding was the biggest anyone could remember—partly out of love for his family, partly out of a need to show off, as these things always go. Kamsa paid for a quarter-mile-long dinner buffet, shouted requests at the band and danced extravagantly, and gave Devaki a tower of silk sarees. Horns announced it when he gave Vasudeva two heart-sized rubies—'because I heard red was your favourite colour'. No common chauffeur drove the carriage that bore the bride and bridegroom to their new home. Kamsa himself tapped the driver on the shoulder, took the reins and the cap and made a gallant bow to the newly-weds. Relatives and well-wishers cheered, and Devaki beamed at her garrulous, mildly soused cousin as he drove them off. Kamsa sang folk songs she hadn't known he knew, and he pointed out the beauties of their childhood kingdom like a tour guide, saying, 'This mountain, Vasudeva, is worth remembering, and worth a hike someday!' or 'Next time, you should take a boat ride on that lake!'

They were rolling along when Kamsa stopped mid-song. Devaki thought he was clearing his throat or getting a sip of water from the canteen at his side.

But Kamsa had heard a voice. It wasn't the first time. The voices had started about a year ago; he heard them rarely, as he drifted off to sleep. Who knew what they whispered while he snored? Now, for the first time, he was hearing one in broad daylight.

Kamsa! Oy, Kamsa!

His head jerked his head suspiciously to the left.

Kamsa!

The voice was coming from above. Startled, Kamsa brought the carriage to a halt. 'Who are you? What do you want?'

The newly-weds thought they were being waylaid by bandits. The back of the carriage was packed with wedding gifts and jewellery. Vasudeva was unarmed, but even a band of forty thieves would be crazy to clash with Kamsa, who had drawn his sword.

And was pointing it, for some reason, at the sky.

Kamsa, you idiot! The voice came from the heavens, but it was mocking, guttural, demonic, amused. *Giving them a ride home . . . what a little singing fool you are! That couple's going to be the death of you.*

Kamsa squinted at clouds that seemed to redden overhead. 'What?'

He's going to put her to work in the bedroom, man. He looks all pious, but inside, he's a horny bastard, trust me. She's going to spit out sons. And her eighth one? Her eighth is going to kill *you, Kamsa!*

Kamsa jumped off his seat, ran a few steps in different directions, then flung his sword at the sky. It flipped and flashed in the sunlight. When it doubled back, it seemed to seek him. A shriek and leap saved him as it gouged the grass, upright and shivering exactly where he had been standing. He pulled it out and verified, with his pinky, the inexplicable fresh blood on the blade. Touching it to his tongue convinced him it was his. Several blood vessels popped in his eyes. Red-eyed, demonic-looking, he sprinted to the carriage and dragged Devaki out by the braid.

His arm was in the air when Vasudeva fell at his feet. 'What are you doing? Kamsa, please! What's going on?'

'You heard it, same as me!'

'Heard *what*?' Devaki writhed, her hands on her thick braid. The jasmine flowers adorning it had shredded on to her shoulders and Kamsa's feet. 'Kamsa, let go!'

Kamsa seemed confused for a moment. He told them what the sky had told him. They hadn't heard it, or *claimed* they hadn't.

'Our eighth son?' Vasudeva said incredulously. 'We mean to raise our children to honour all their elders. We'll take special care with our eighth, Kamsa. I promise you.'

'These prophecies have a way of working themselves out.'

'We'll stop at seven. We won't *have* an eighth.'

'I can't risk it.'

'We'll stop at six. You can send her a midwife. The midwife can report to you.'

'No. You're fated for eight, you'll have eight. You'll try for six, but the sixth pregnancy will spit out triplets and the last one out will kill me.'

'Five—'

'The only way to counteract this prophecy is to cut off the timeline. Cut off the bloodline. And the only way to do that is to cut off . . . .' He shook his head in disbelief at what he was doing. The sword rose on its own.

'Wait! Kamsa! *I'll take a vow*.'

Kamsa lowered the sword. A vow, also a thing made of speech, was just as powerful as a spoken prophecy—an opposing arrow to knock time's arrow off its course. 'I'm listening.'

'I vow to hand our newborn sons over to you, so you can do with them what you please.'

Kamsa let go of his cousin's braid. She lay on her back and stared in shock at the empty sky. He stepped over her as he returned to the carriage. Vasudeva eased his new bride off the ground. Kamsa resumed his chauffeuring, resumed his cheerful song—interrupting it every so often to snarl at the voices, now innumerable, that heckled his dim-witted mercy and guffawed to discover he had spared Devaki's life.

*

A menacingly quiet Kamsa returned to his father's kingdom. A year later, when Vasudeva came with his firstborn son, he came to a monstered Mathura, where Kamsa had overthrown and imprisoned his father the king. He had shredded his father's roster of court officials too. Only yes-men lived to collect their pensions.

The beast in the crown sniffed the morsel set before him. Baby-smell has an effect on men no less than women. Even the voices in Kamsa's head made cooing noises.

'Take him back to Devaki, and give her my best wishes,' he said, handing the swaddled baby to his brother-in-law. 'The voice in the sky warned me about your eighth, not your first.'

Vasudeva bowed and hurried home to Devaki, staying not one more day in Mathura than he had to—mustn't risk the psychotic king hearing a new voice!

Kamsa did hear a new voice, but it wasn't in his head. The wandering sage Narada, as karma would have it, happened to have wandered into Mathura that week. Did Narada say what he said with a mind to make Kamsa lose his? Slick and ubiquitous Narada, always advancing a storyline: 'I say, Kamsa, do miscarriages count?'

'What do you mean?'

'Well, if she *conceives*, but the miscarriage happens right away, and if that happens a few times—is baby one really baby one? Or is he, by *that* count, baby three? Confusing, wouldn't you say? Or is it just me? I'm no good at math.'

The sky in Kamsa's skull crowded with voices now, like a sky usurped by chirps before a storm. He paced; he stuck his finger in his ear and jiggled it roughly; he monologued into the mirror. A white dwarf star of doubt dilated to a red giant of panic.

By the end of the month, the young parents and their newborn were locked in a Mathura prison. Vasudeva and Devaki wore shin-high shackles. The chain was three strides long. Kamsa got the idea to shackle the baby, too, to a bar of the jail cell, lest some attempt be made to smuggle it out. He even had one specially made, a chain as thin as a necklace's. When he came to click it on the pudgy ankle, though, he had a change of heart and swung his nephew smartly against the wall.

*

What did it do to their blood, their genes, her soil, his seed, to see their infant sons die that way? Each one brained, then bundled in sackcloth for disposal, his first time swaddled and his last. Did the second, third, fourth one, conceived in horror, inherit horror? What was the damage, and was that damage heritable? Did a new understanding of evil get passed down, like a new eye colour or some rare anaemia? Vasudeva and his wife had to watch six of their newborns get murdered—knuckles clipping ankles, smashed against a jail cell wall, shrivelled grey-pink bodies still flecked with birth-curd vernix. Each new bloodstain looked to Vasudeva and Devaki like a butterfly, like two men shouting chin to chin, like a supernova. No one came to wash it off.

Fate forced the imprisoned couple to couple. The tally the stars had set was eight, and eight she would have to bear. Her beauty grew inexorably in that cell. No lipstick of red lac could compare to the reddening of her lips, chewed anxiously as each delivery approached. Vasudeva wished he could resist her. He ploughed and sowed though he knew the same crow would come gore the fruit. She sobbed into her husband's neck, though the bloodstains on the wall were watching, and occasionally the jailer too. They made love like two castaways making a fire against the darkness. Two or three times a day, she was free.

*

Shantanu made a vow and lasted seven infanticides before he broke it. Vasudeva made a vow and lasted seven infanticides before he broke it. The sons they saved by breaking their vows grew up to be gifts to the world. World-conquering Devavrat, vow-bound, vow-stymied, became self-conquering Bhishma. Vasudeva's son would place no such check on himself or the good he could do. He would grow up to be a flaunter of rules, a master of words whom words could never master. All because his father broke his vow and kept his eighth son from his wife's brother.

The seventh had been a late miscarriage, or so it seemed. They had wondered whether that son would count. The bits and blood that puddled between Devaki's shackled legs had no resemblance to a baby. Miraculously, unknown to either of them, Vasudeva's other wife, Rohini, smuggled to safety in the countryside, domed with a sudden pregnancy and delivered: foetus and placenta, implanted and expelled, all in one night. This newborn boy was so white-skinned that Rohini, shocked and shucked in her blood-soaked bed, thought he had bled out entirely and searched him for a wound. But now he began crying: was he an albino? Had Soma, the God of the Moon, inseminated her with moonlight? Rohini, baffled, overjoyed, wept to see Vasudeva's features in the boy. Had her imprisoned husband made love to her in a mutual dream? How could this happen?

This mystery was no mystery to Vishnu, who had arranged that switch of wombs. He never incarnated without Shesha, the divine snake that served as his bed on the Sea of Milk. They went everywhere together, in the heavenly sphere and on the earthly one. Infinity—and infinity's remainder. Rama had his Shesha in a younger brother, Lakshman; Krishna had his in an older brother, Balarama.

*

Vasudeva wasn't sure if the eighth would be the blessed accursed, the tyrannicide-to-be, the cause and redeemer of his seven brothers' deaths. Vasudeva had to deliver Devaki in prison because a midwife might have gossiped. King Kamsa did not permit scissors in the cell, either. Vasudeva had to cut the umbilical cord with his bare teeth; what filled his mouth was not blood, as with the other sons, but Ganga water. *This is the one.* The knot tied itself with barely any help from his fingers. When he stood, he heard a clunk.

Devaki, haggard but lovely, sat up in alarm. 'What was that?'
'My leg shackle fell off.'

The Darling Darkling Changeling

They looked at each other, and then at the baby. In the uncanny silence (the newborn was breathing and aimlessly rubbing his own face, but not crying), all they could hear was . . . snoring?

Vasudeva tried to glimpse their jailer through the cell bars. His forehead touched them, and a section opened freely, on a hinge.

The open cell door, his shackle mysteriously coming unfastened, the guards all drugged with poppies: this much could have been conspiracy. Kamsa had enemies scattered throughout the countryside, Yadu refugees disguised as farmhands, biding their time. Vasudeva smuggling his eighth son to a specific house in the country may have been part of the plan, too—particularly since that house had seen a delivery that very night, of a girl. A wicker basket lay at the feet of one of the snoring guards, complete with a blanket for swaddling. Who could possibly arrange so loud a storm, so dark a night for cover?

The Yamuna river was the sole variable that didn't cooperate. Vasudeva arrived at its banks and found it roaring past him. Or more accurately, *her* roaring past him.

Yamuna, too, was a Goddess. She was the God of Death's kid sister. Legend had it that she was a mirror-river. Her original body of water flowed in hell, where she spent her days polishing skulls instead of stones. Yamuna's brother Yama had always been fond of her, and he coached her in the blood sport he was the reigning champion of. He clocked her time until she drowned schoolboys thirteen seconds faster than the Ganga. She dried up, too, at record speed whenever her famished brother wished to dine on famine victims. Not the most reasonable river to meet on a night of spontaneous monsoon, with an infant in your care.

Vasudeva's sister had entrusted her own wicker basket infant to the whim of the current, but she never faced the Yamuna in spate. Vasudeva knew that if his foot slipped or if the basket slipped his grip, it would be death for him and for his son. There would be no reaching the rushes downstream in the calm of dawn—and no kindly and childless charioteer to treasure the basket and adopt the baby. Death for Devaki, too, no doubt, if Kamsa showed up tomorrow morning and found neither Vasudeva nor the infant there. And after that, death for every newborn in Kamsa's jurisdiction, as he extinguished every possible candidate. Yamuna, with two brisk drownings, could send a week of hot meals to her brother.

Vasudeva had no inkling whom he bore to safety. If the hair on his nape had risen, the rain had long since drubbed them back down. Yet he prayed to Vishnu. Not even his own ears could hear his lips in that downpour, but Vishnu was closer to his lips than a hand's span. Vishnu was in his breath itself, and in the words that comprised the prayer to him. Wicker basket propped atop his head, Vasudeva waded into that breath-bereaving river. His bony legs, emaciated by years of prison food, wobbled at the knees and straightened. Cords of riptide looped his ankles—and unravelled.

The mud should have made him slip. Instead it vacuum-sealed each step in place. The Yamuna, flash-flooding as he entered, was several times deeper than Vasudeva was tall. He felt the riverbed the whole way across. He never sank deeper than the divot above his lip, and the bottom of the basket never brushed an eddy.

When he arrived in Vrindavan at the house of Nanda and Yashoda, he unwrapped and swapped his newborn and theirs. Theirs was a daughter, and he wondered whether Kamsa would notice, whether the couple would notice when they awoke—for they, too, were sleeping soundly through the flashing, peepal-thrashing storm. Three times the draggle-haired and dripping Vasudeva sneezed out loud, but no one woke up, not even the newborn farmer's daughter he placed in the basket. Now he had to carry her back to the prison, he realized. To prison, and a changeling death. Tears mingled with the rain on his cheeks. The paranoid beast Kamsa would have to be fed one child; the girl would die, Vasudeva told himself, to prevent a massacre. Yet guilt stopped his hands more than once, and he pounded his chest and head in anguish at what he was doing—swaddling this sleeping girl with lethal tenderness. It was for the best that, in the darkness, he could not see her face. The lightning held off to make it easier on him.

The next morning, the farmer and his wife marvelled to find a son where they had left a daughter. The baby had been born in the storm's darkness, and the midwife, abashed, said she might well have made a mistake. Nanda, though he kept this to himself, wondered if the Gods had pitied his disappointment and miracled his daughter into a son. Five cows had been earmarked for donation, but he gifted the local temple fifteen cows in thanks. The new parents and all the villagers marvelled at the beautiful bluish-blackness of the baby's skin. The storm rain, beating down on him when Vasudeva raised the wicker basket overhead, had bruised him all over a stormcloud's hue, a stormcloud's blackish-blue. They were all so in love with his dark complexion, they named him for it. *Krishna.*

SEQUENCE 4

THE BIRTH AND CHILDHOOD OF THE RIVAL COUSINS

Kunti invokes three Gods for three sons, then a pair of celestial twins for her sister-wife. Kunti's three sons are Yudhishtir, Bheem and Arjuna. The sister-wife's twins are Nakula, known for his handsomeness, and Sahadev, known for his wisdom. Together, they are the five Pandavas ('sons of Pandu', though technically they are not really Pandu's sons). Kunti is widowed when Pandu, seized with passion, triggers the curse and dies.

Gandhari, with Vyasa's help at the delivery, bears one hundred sons. The eldest is Duryodhan. His father, the blind king Dhritarashtra, ignores evil omens and Vidura's advice; he refuses to expose the baby.

The childhood of the princes are a contrast: Kunti tells her Pandavas a story of Bharata, their ancestor. The Kauravas, meanwhile, are a rough-and-tumble mob of brothers. Among them, Duryodhan is dominant. The two sets of cousins are rivals from the start, but Duryodhan and Bheem have a special animosity towards one another. That animosity will play out on the battlefield decades later—but even now, while they're still boys, Duryodhan tries to kill Bheem on more than one occasion.

Characters Who Will Show Up Again:

This is the section of the epic where the main fighters of the coming war are introduced—two sets of cousins, five on one side, one hundred on the other. The boys in these chapters will go to war when they grow up. 'Pandavas and Kauravas' are shorthand for irreconcilable, bloody rivalry in Indian languages, just as 'Hatfields and McCoys' are in American English and 'Montagues and Capulets' are in British English.

THE PANDAVAS:

Yudhishtir, the eldest and most pious. A love of gambling, as time will tell, is his only moral weakness.

Bheem, a physical giant with a massive appetite (hence his epithet 'wolf-belly').

Arjuna, destined to become his age's greatest archer, rivalled only by Karna. These are the three 'main' Pandavas, considering the coming action of the epic—all three are Kunti's sons, fathered by various Gods. Her sister-wife's twin sons are:

Nakula, known for his good looks and mastery of medicine.

Sahadev, known for his wisdom and horse-taming skills.

THE KAURAVAS:

Duryodhan, the eldest, with a murderous streak that shows up early.

Dushasana, the second eldest, is his loyal sidekick.

There are ninety-eight other Kauravas, who for the most part follow Duryodhan's lead.

SARGA 10

RIVALRIES

After his accidental Brahmin-killing, Pandu, his head hanging low with the weight of the curse, left Hastinapur. His two wives, Kunti and Madri, followed him into the ascetic forest. This left Dhritarashtra on the throne with white-bearded Bhishma for his eyes and dark-skinned Vidura for his brain.

Kunti's belly, when she was pregnant with Surya's son, had throbbed with heat. A line darkens down the belly on expecting mothers. With Surya's son, that line looked like a thumb had smeared not ash but gold dust. Now that she was bearing Yama's child, the thick line lay kohl-black, and her belly was cold to the touch. The midwife feared the baby had already died—but Pandu's palm on Kunti's clammy tummy felt a kick.

Gandhari started showing at the same time as Kunti. This delighted Bhishma, but he had no inkling how much pressure it put on the two mothers-to-be. Though they weren't around each other—Gandhari in a palace, Kunti in a forest hut—the parallel gestations became a race. The messengers they sent to each other with gifts and tips also served as spies.

Their progress, though, was deceptive. Gandhari, according to the letter of her boon, was destined to have a hundred babies.

Her pregnancy became a huge dome very early. No one expected her to have her babies all at once. Five weeks pregnant with one hundred foetuses, Gandhari *looked* like she was just as far along as Kunti, five months pregnant with one.

Soon enough, Gandhari got word that Kunti had delivered a son. Something, she feared, must be wrong with her pregnancy. The nine-month mark came and went. Gandhari kept growing larger. Blindfolded, she couldn't see her body or the midwife's face, and that was a good thing, since her belly grew enormous and oddly lumpy, as though she had swallowed a whole watermelon patch without chewing. Eventually, she couldn't even stir from her bed. Dhritarashtra came to massage her, but he could scarcely tell her swollen feet from the pillows.

One day, in a fit of frustration, Gandhari snarled at her midwife. 'How many months has it been? Twenty? I'm three times the size of any expecting mom I've ever seen. Can't these Brahmins give me something to make me spit it out? What good is their Ayurveda? What do we pay them for? I don't want to give birth to a full-grown man. I have ninety-nine more sons to beget. At this rate, I'll be a hundred years old myself before I'm done!'

Sweetsop, leadwort, bitter gourd, ashwagandha, milkweed: the doctors refused to prescribe her anything. When it came to pregnancy, every accelerant was a potential abortifacient. No one wanted to risk the blame for a stillbirth.

Gandhari went into contractions the same afternoon they sent word they couldn't help her.

The midwife stared at the queen's domed belly. A natural dark line divided the dome into hemispheres, but she pointed in shock at a purple subcontinent on the right. 'What is that?'

'I didn't see anything.'

'Did you fall?'

Gandhari turned to face her midwife, and in spite of the blindfold, the midwife could *feel* the rage in the queen's eyes. 'I didn't see anything!'

Well past midnight, the panicking midwife found the sleeping Bhishma. He followed her and found his bare feet splashing on the marble floor as he approached the women's wing. Shantanu had done something similar decades before, when Ganga's water had broken. Gandhari's water was not that copious, just a hundred times normal.

Bhishma hesitated before entering the bedchamber, but the midwife pulled him in, assuring him that Gandhari had been covered with a blanket and hidden away behind a screen.

A red glow filled the room. On the floor, in a pool of blood, was an immense pomegranate without a rind. Every seed of that pomegranate was a translucent sac with a salamander-sized human inside it. Where the red light came from, Bhishma could not imagine, but it throbbed bright and dimmed, throbbed bright and dimmed, in keeping with some alien three-phased pulse. White fibres, tendon-thick, threaded these sacs. These were the one hundred Kauravas, born premature. Bhishma covered his mouth with his sash and stumbled out of the chamber. The Ayurvedic doctors who inspected the monstrosity could not, in spite of their best efforts, find a role for turmeric here. Bhishma went straight to Vidura, who went straight to the highest authority of all, the author. 'Where is Vyasa?'

Right there in Hastinapur, as it turned out, waiting for his grandchildren to be born. The birth of Yudhishthir had pleased Vyasa, but he knew of the arrangement between Pandu's wife and Yama; Yudhishthir had none of his blood. The blind Dhritarashtra, though, had fathered his own sons, and Vyasa was eager to meet his hundred grandsons.

Bhishma's messengers fetched him from the temple of Saraswati. When Vyasa saw his grandsons in a salmon-egg clump on the floor, he shouted, 'Gandhari, what have you done?'

Gandhari shouted from behind her screen, 'I saw nothing!'

Vyasa shook his head in disgust. Her tone of voice told him everything. A vision flashed before him of Gandhari, in that very room, striking her own womb with her fist over and over until the gush. Many would wonder, in years to come, how the Kauravas ended up so obsessed with besting their five Pandava cousins—after all, their blind father had placed his hand on Pandu's shoulder and let him lead. Who knew, they speculated, what resentment the blind brother kept hidden his whole life? The real spirit of rivalry, Vyasa knew, came from the mountain-stock beauty with the blindfolded green eyes.

'Go to the kitchen and fetch me a hundred jars,' demanded Vyasa. 'And wake up the cooks! I need those hundred jars full of ghee by this morning.'

His orders set the whole palace in a frenzy. The incubators were ready before dawn—which was for the best, since the glow from the clump had been failing, and the foetuses twitched less and less often.

Vyasa did not trust the doctors with such delicate transplantations. To keep from popping any membranes, he trimmed his corkscrew fingernails with his teeth. A sprinkle of cold water made the foetuses less sticky. One foetus, one jar; one foetus, one jar. The worried grandfather knew their names before they were named, and he whispered each name as he closed the jar: Duryodhan, Dushasan, Vikarna . . . and ninety-five more, without a single mix-up . . . until he got to the youngest two, Kundhaasy and Virajas.

Months later, they began to hatch from their jars in the order Vyasa had transferred them. Duryodhan was first. His tiny fist punched a hole in his clay cocoon. The ghee leaked out, and his furious cry sounded in the hollow.

On the same day, Kunti delivered her next semidivine son, the one fathered by the God of Wind: Bheem. The two newborn cousins engaged in an epic cry-off. Each one heard the other across a distance of many yojanas and strove to be the louder male. That was how early they started competing.

*

The blind king had Duryodhan brought to him in the throne room. He wanted the first time he held his firstborn son to be on the throne he had regained from his sighted brother Pandu.

At his request, a few Brahmins—three of the sort that sell predictions about the future; three more of an aggressive, lawyerish bent—accompanied the midwife. Vidura stayed close by, unannounced. He wanted to know what was said, given this mix of soothsayers and quarrelsome pundits.

Dhritarashtra kissed baby Duryodhan on his forehead, on his little hands, and on the soft spot atop his head.

'Little one, how I wish I could see you!' he whispered. And then, in a voice not much louder, he said to the Brahmins, 'I know Yudhishthir, Pandu's boy, is the eldest prince in the line. I am not challenging that. But after him? Will this baby boy become king one day? Is there a case to make him second in line?'

The lost vulture that swept into the throne room should have been omen enough. Dhritarashtra heard wingbeats as its prodigious bulk knocked over a courtier's empty chair. Though he couldn't see the hundred torches lining the throne room that the vulture extinguished in its panic, the blind king could feel the room go colder. All the stray dogs in Hastinapur chose that moment to start barking at each other, a war of all versus all, a territorial frenzy.

'Well? What is your verdict?'

All six Brahmins were terrified. They didn't want to say anything that would displease the king and jeopardize their fees, but they could not ignore this unequivocal signal from the universe. Vidura strode out of the darkness. He clapped his hands as though scattering chickens. 'Go on! Get out of here! Go!'

The Brahmins, afraid of this powerful voice, ran from the darkness as if from a fire. The vulture swooped a foot above the father and son, then chased the Brahmins all the way down the hall and out of the palace. This helped Vidura. He didn't want anyone to overhear what he said next.

'Dhritarashtra, we need to expose this baby on a snowy mountainside right away. I'll take care of it. I'll stand watch until he turns to ice. But we can't let him live.'

'What are you doing here, Vidura? I did not invite you. This is a private moment between a father and his boy.'

'The omens aren't subtle ones. Even those money-minded pandits could see what that vulture indicated. This baby is going to cause the snuffing-out of the Kuru line. Get rid of him, and you can save the other ninety-nine who are still in their jars. You know the proverb. "Give up one member for the sake of the family, one family for the sake of the village, one village for the sake of the kingdom, one kingdom for the sake of the world." This is what the old sages were talking about. This is it.'

Vidura held out his hands to receive the danger to the dynasty. But Dhritarashtra, his face twisted in disgust, clutched baby Duryodhan to his chest. He had no trouble dead reckoning his way out; he used to visit that room often, back in the days when his younger brother was king, in the dead of night.

*

A third royal wife was shut out from all that conceiving and delivering: Pandu's second wife, Madri.

She tried to redeem her time reading palm-leaf manuscripts of ancient sutras. The night of the great storm that battered baby Krishna, the floor of Pandu's forest hut sloshed with three inches of rainwater. Madri imagined flooding this hut with her own amniotic fluid, just as Ganga had flooded the palace. What a joy motherhood must be! Not just the begetting, though she did miss sleeping in Pandu's bed, but the *having*. Would she never see hints of her own features on a toddler's face? Only Kunti's?

No, no, she told herself, don't be jealous of Kunti—you should be happy for your sister-wife—but it's no moral shortcoming to be sad for yourself, is it? Madri tore out a Sanskrit-etched palm leaf and folded a little boat. It sailed a modest cargo of hope from her room.

Worst for Madri were the nights that Kunti invoked her Gods. In that little two-room hut, how could she keep from eavesdropping? Pandu, avoiding the sage's curse, had taken to sleeping alone in one of those rooms, locked from outside. Lust, leashed all day, he feared, might sleepwalk him into the abyss. So Madri had to sleep under the stars that night and hear *everything*.

Wasn't Madri's fate worse than widowhood, in a way? To know her husband was *there*, and endure the tantalization? The nights when Kunti got to enjoy a celestial lover felt to Madri like a Night of Brahma: twelve million years of insomnia.

When Kunti woke up, she sang back at the sparrows. Madri noticed every minor dishevelment of her hair, every mysterious bruise on her neck.

*

After Kunti conceived her third Pandava—Indra's gift: Arjuna—Madri emptied a cup of ginger water and built up the courage to address her husband. Two yearnings battled it out in her, but she could only express one.

'Kunti is a mother three times over,' she whispered to Pandu, 'and all I get is a pet parakeet.'

What she also wanted to say: *Kunti is three times a lover. All I get to do are cat-cows.*

Pandu had no scruples welcoming more divine blood into the Kuru line. After all, he dared not satisfy Madri's wish on pain of death. Madri was easily the fullest-hipped woman in Kuru history, a body just begging to bear sons. Nothing dizzied a hero with desire back then like a big girl. Three rolls of fat down the sides was the very ladder to heaven. Pandu was just as hot for Madri as Madri was for any man at all. A pregnancy for Madri might quell Pandu's own torment at seeing but never seeding his voluptuous wife.

Pandu cajoled Kunti to use her boon on Madri's behalf. Kunti had already declined Pandu's request for a fourth son, this one by Skanda, the War God. Kunti didn't want the future to think her a nymphomaniac, recruiting a whole pantheon to bull her. To make up for that refusal, she gave in to this latest request. Besides, Kunti had secured the firstborn, secondborn and thirdborn spots. If ever there should be a succession dispute, Madri's son would be a distant fourth on the list. (Even a sister-queen as envy-free as Kunti made such dynastic calculations.)

That night, she laid Madri on the cot and said the first three lines under her breath, so Madri could not hear them. Madri, at the press of Kunti's hand, recited only the fourth line, as Kunti had taught her. And then she invoked her lover of choice: 'The Ashvins!'

Kunti hurried out of the hut as the divine twins, answering this house call, parked their chariot in the air. The Ashvins were Gods of medicine and horses: so they had a firm knowledge of female anatomy, and possessed the long faces, long torsos and long necks of horses and everything else of horses that was long. The religiously astute and sex-starved Madri had invoked the two most knowing, best-endowed lovers at one go. Being twins, they strove to outdo each other even in this. For two straight nights, Madri took part in a joyful, cathartic ruckus. It took her two weeks of twice-daily baths to stop smelling like an unswept stable. Soon, she turned out to be pregnant with twins.

Nakula and Sahadeva were the last of the Pandavas. Pandu implored Kunti for one more invocation on Madri's behalf, to give them each an auspicious brood, three and three. Kunti refused to use her boon for Madri again. What if Madri invoked the eight Vasus (technically seven, given that Light was locked away in Bhishma's body), or the eleven Rudras, or the twelve Adityas or the twenty-seven Maruts? She would become a mother of multiples, second only to Gandhari. Pandu, knowing it was her boon to use or not, acquiesced. In a hut full of cradles and toys and princes, he had no right to complain.

*

Except about Kindama's curse. Even as he entered middle age, and his temples and chin got white hair, and his niggling yoga-twinges never went away, Pandu got no rest from lust.

Madri made it no easier. Since her pregnancy, she had grown fuller everywhere. When he hugged her good night, he carried the memory of her softness to his cot. In his dreams, his bony ascetic body vanished between her breasts.

One night, though, Madri forgot to lock her husband's door, and he woke up early, furious with desire. He must have chanted the Gayatri mantra three hundred times before he burst into the room where his wives were sleeping. *Cool it, Pandu*, he thought. *Think of Kindama, bleeding out. The curse is still on you!* Pacing outside in the cold night and cool dawn failed to help him.

Around this time, Madri emerged and went to bathe in a nearby river. From between some rushes, he watched the water caress her curves.

Back during her tryst with the Ashvins, she had sobbed with gratitude and confessed her loneliness and they had taught her, with their own expert fingers, how a woman could treat that ailment. Thinking herself alone, Madri tried to give herself peace for the rest of the day. It was hard to meditate otherwise, and her mind wandered during prayers. She allowed herself the occasional moan as she conjured her mirror-image lovers. Maddened by the vision and voice of Madri, Pandu charged out of his hiding place. Powerfully towering, the equal of any equine lover, he mounted Madri and made a mare of her at long last. Within a minute, he arched his back—not in climax, but in sharp back pain, as though shot from behind. He rolled off Madri and splashed in the river. Screaming, crying, she kept him from getting swept downstream.

At the funeral, she handed Kunti her swaddled and capped twins. 'It was my fault,' she whispered. 'I can't tell you how, Kunti, but the guilt for what happened is mine. Take care of them.'

Kunti had no time to reason with her sister-widow. Madri, her hands free of her baby boys, backed away from them right into her husband's pyre. Bhishma in his white dhoti lunged to save her, but he clutched only ashes and heat. The hair on his arms, eyebrows and beard were singed. Madri's body had ignited all at once. Two shades of smoke braided skyward from the pyre.

SARGA 11

STORYTIME FOR THE LITTLE PANDAVAS

'Let's hear a story, Ma!'

'Which story would you like, Yudhishtir?'

'There must be a story about our ancestors you could tell us,' said the most mature of her sons. 'It's always good to hear about our elders.'

'Why listen to stuff from old chronicles if we don't have to?' frowned Bheem. 'Give us something exciting from the Ramayana, Ma. Give us Hanuman.'

Big-bodied Bheem was always keen on Hanuman stories. Hanuman, too, was a son of the Wind, Bheem's stepbrother. Both had inherited their father's forest-swaying, mountain-reshaping strength.

Arjuna shook his head. 'We haven't had an animal fable in over a week. There are plenty of stories with monkeys in them, Bheem, if you have to have a monkey.'

Three of Kunti's little Pandavas went back and forth for a bit, debating the merits of sundry sorts of stories—history, epic and fable, though they didn't think in those terms. Kunti shushed them and asked the quietly conferring twins about their preference. The twins always voted together and tended to settle such questions. 'Give us one about the ancestors,' they said, 'but go back so far that everything's in it—a famous hero, a magical animal and things that really happened.'

How wise a solution this was! Kunti thought back to what she knew of the Kuru line. King Shantanu's story was a bit grown-up for such little boys, and besides, there was a river in female form, but not much in the way of animal magic. Kunti reached back all the way to King Bharata, the founder of the dynasty. Could she adjust the chronicles a little?

'I think I know one—' she began, but just then, about two dozen boys burst into that modest courtyard. They were Kauravas, and they were battering each other with wooden swords. The five Pandavas watched that frenzy calmly, as if these were young orangutans quarrelling up in the trees. The widow and her boys waited a while, but when the Kauravas settled down to a fistfight, they left. Kunti knew better than to grind down her voice shouting at the Kauravas to stop giving each other bloody noses.

The widow had left the forest and returned to Hastinapur with her brood. Living in the palace again, she taught numbers and stories to the five boys who bore Pandu's name. As usual, it was hard to make herself heard. Her hundred nephews made every wing of the palace their crowded playground, or wrestling ring, or snack room, or all three. Kunti took her boys to the temple room, since that was the only place the hundred cousins would never overrun. The Kauravas tried to spend as little time there as possible. Incense made them antsy.

In that seclusion, under the shadow of a four-armed marble Vishnu, Kunti told her sons the story of Bharata.

*

He was called Sarvadaman back then, a boy of six or seven or eight or so, just like any of the boys before her. That name meant *tamer-of-all*, and the name fit. He had the same mysterious power as Shiva, Lord of the Animals. Hummingbirds sipped from the corner of his mouth. A grown tigress pawed and tumbled him as if he were a cub from her litter.

His mother, Shakuntala, raised him to know his lineage. The old ascetic Kanva, whose ashram he grew up in, wasn't his grandfather, first of all. She was the daughter, not of Kanva, but of a far more powerful seer: Vishwamitra, a soldier who became a holy man. His trajectory was the opposite of Parashuram's, but his endpoint—power that offended heaven—was the same. Indra, God of Sky and Thunder, feared Vishwamitra's exultant voice. *Aum!* shouted Vishwamitra, every time he acquired a new power. The power of going weightless. The power of shrinking to a mustard-seed, the power of swelling to mountainous size. The power of pervasion, so he could flash his flesh to any spot on earth. And finally, most offensive of all, the power that let him control the weather. *Aum! Aum! Aum!* he shouted each time, nothing serene about it. It was a war-cry. Indra refused to tolerate this.

So he sent a heavenly dancer, Menaka, down to Sarvadaman's powerful grandfather. Here Kunti had to elide a few details. The boys were not yet of an age to know how Menaka told Indra to gust her *choli* up over her legs, how she blushed and acted like it wasn't planned. Kunti didn't say what happened after Vishwamitra fell for Menaka—just that Vishwamitra squandered his powers.

'Did she steal his powers and take them back to heaven?' asked Arjuna.

'Maybe he'd taken a vow not to marry,' speculated Bheem, 'like our own Grandfather Bhishma.'

Kunti glossed over how Vishwamitra and Menaka did not marry. She went straight to Menaka giving birth to a beautiful daughter—and, flighty artiste that she was, abandoning the baby and returning to her troupe in heaven. The birds protected that little baby girl. The wolves shuffled off, still hungry, sneezing on feathers and nursing talon scratches.

Kanva, on a philosophical forest walk, found her in a bird's nest cradle. Vigilant birds circled above her in a tower, all species of birds, flying clockwise. This tower dispersed at his approach, squawking and trilling and hooting. White drops spattered the forest, a brief excited cloudburst. Kanva adopted her and named her *bird girl:* Shakuntala.

*

Kanva's ashram lay in the realm of a king named Dushyant, and this king, on one of his hunting expeditions, tore past the ashram in his chariot. (Kunti made sure to dwell on the hunt a bit, for Arjuna's sake—he had, even at that young age, an interest in anything involving a bow and arrow.) A couple of Kanva's fellow ascetics came out to protest the hunt. They claimed the deer came under the ashram's protection, and Dushyant, who knew that killing a sacred animal was a sure way to incur a curse, relented. Offering his respects and apologies, he got out of his chariot to refill his canteen.

Kanva was off hanging upside down from a banyan tree, one of his ascetic practices. The blood rushed to his head, and it helped him think. Shakuntala was home to receive Dushyant, to make the modest fuss that could be made in a humble hermitage like that. Dushyant fell in love right away, and he convinced Shakuntala to marry him in the way Gandharvas marry.

'How do Gandharvas marry?' Nakula and Sahadev asked together.

Kunti flushed. These old stories had no sense that children might be listening! You started a story and found yourself veering this way and that to skirt lechery and earthiness and all sorts of behaviour that would be improper today. Gandharvas married by making love, and they divorced by getting off the cot—musicians were a disreputable sort, even in heaven. 'Gandharvas marry for . . . love,' she said evasively. 'Without their parents' permission. So that is what Shakuntala did—but she set a condition.'

'What condition was that?' Yudhishthir, the most pious of her boys, loved stories with vows, curses, boons, conditions—anything where a character had to follow his word. That was why he revered Bhishma so much, and why he himself, at this young age, had already sworn a vow never to tell a lie.

'She insisted that, if she bore a son, he must inherit King Dushyant's throne. Otherwise, she wouldn't marry the king.'

'Did he agree?'

'He did, and they, ahem, *married* each other right there, before Kanva could make it back. King Dushyant went back to his kingdom, telling her to visit him with their son when he was about seven or eight years old.'

'And that boy was Sarvadaman, right?' Bheem's stomach gurgled; his interest waned, which meant his hunger waxed. 'Is a monkey going to show up?'

Nakula and Sahadev nodded. 'Where's the magic?'

Kunti realized she had to add some details. The story picked up with Shakuntala showing up Hastinapur seven years later, her boy in tow, dharma-wheel birthmarks on either one of his palms—and the king refusing to acknowledge them. But the way it happened simply wouldn't do.

So she thought fast, and she looked at her fingers, which still had white lines where she once wore Pandu's rings. Long ago she had slipped those off and packed them away, but the rings of pallor—*Pandu*, pale—never browned after all these years.

King Dushyant, she extemporized, gave Shakuntala . . . his ring! A *magical* ring with a magical stone in it that he would recognize no matter what, even if he died and was reborn in another body. Shakuntala never took off the ring for seven years, not even when she bathed her baby boy.

Whenever she fetched water, she tapped a clay pot with her ring as she walked back from the well. On one such errand, she was tapping a rhythm and singing to herself, and she disturbed an important guest at Kanva's ashram. A famous Brahmin was visiting—a famously irascible Brahmin named . . . *Durvasas*.

Kunti (she went by Pritha back then) smiled at her memory of the sweet old man and his penchant for curses. He had given Pritha a boon, but no doubt he would have laid a curse on Shakuntala if she disturbed his meditation. And that is what he did. He cursed her son's father to forget her.

Troubled by the curse, Shakuntala fetched Sarvadaman and headed to Hastinapur. All was not lost; she still had the ring. The ring would counteract the curse.

On the way to the river, she had to cross a river in a ferry, one that matched the boat that young Satyavati used to row. Kunti thought of the times she herself had ridden in boats as a girl, and she imagined Shakuntala trailing her hand in the water. It would have soothed her unease at the Brahmin's curse.

In Hastinapur, standing with her son before the throne, Shakuntala brought her hand forward to show the ring. But the magical ring was gone!

The little Pandavas gasped.

'All that was left on her finger,' said Kunti, showing her own widow's hand, 'was a thin circle of pale skin, where the ring used to sit!'

King Dushyant, she explained to her little Pandavas, had lost his memory of Shakuntala. He had never seen Sarvadaman before. And the ring had slipped off her finger, so he could not recognize that either. The son's profile echoed the father's, but a kingly nose didn't certify princely blood. Dushyant denied ever meeting Shakuntala, much less marrying her, and the more tearfully she insisted, the angrier he got. From his perspective, she was accusing him of something he hadn't done—and trying to slip her bastard son into the royal family. In public! In the throne room! His reputation chipped a little with every plea she made. The longer people looked at the boy, too, the more they started to wonder. Dushyant ordered the vagrant woman and her whelp kicked out of the city.

Kunti had to bring back the ring, she knew. To please her little Pandavas, magic would have to save the day. The ferry made her think of Satyavati, and Satyavati made her think of Satyavati's father, the fisherman.

So a fisherman, maybe Queen Satyavati's great-great-grandfather, went fishing in Kunti's story. He caught a fish, skinned the fish, slit the fish open—and found a royal signet ring in its belly. With a hoot and hallo, he rowed back to shore. Should he sell it? No, too risky—any city jeweller would report it stolen. Should he build a fire and melt it in a crucible? Best to return it, his wife advised. King Dushyant would give him a reward.

To Hastinapur, then, the fisherman went, bearing the magical ring on his finger and wondering what it must be like to be a king and own so many rings you could lose one in a fish's belly and never bother looking for it.

In Hastinapur's assembly hall, though guards and courtiers held their noses, King Dushyant rushed off his throne to embrace the fisherman. At the sight of that ring, even from twenty feet away, all the memories of Shakuntala came back, and Dushyant rued his mistake.

The fisherman expected a reward—but received not one coin for his daylong journey. King Dushyant, shoving him aside, ran out and gave orders to ready his chariot. More than once, between shouts at the stable boys to hurry up, Dushyant pressed the ring to his lips and tearful eyes. He forgot the fisherman entirely, and so did the court, abuzz with this revelation.

The fisherman seethed. These elites were ignoring him, even though *he'd* brought the king that sentimental trinket. On his way home, the opulence he'd seen began to bother him. Why should a king and a king's children enjoy high ceilings and red sherbet and silk dhotis, while *he,* a hardworking man, stank of fish all day? The only pearls he got to wear were pustules where the fishhooks gouged his thumbs.

His resentment never left him. His soul ended up in a fisherman's body again, decades later. It was *his* daughter with whom King Shantanu fell in love. A glance at the rings on Shantanu's hands made him recall what he had coveted, all those births ago. So he drove his bargain and demanded that Satyavati's son become the heir of Hastinapur. That demand led to Devavrat's fearsome vow, and Devavrat's fearsome vow led, generations later, to everything else.

King Dushyant recognized his lost love—and recognized her son, too, legally and permanently. What was later named 'India' named itself for King Dushyant's new heir: 'Bharata' was the name that Dushyant gave to Shakuntala's son. Bharata, when he came of age, tamed all the kingdoms, just as he'd tamed all the animals. He merged all those lineages into one greater dynasty, his own.

'And you five boys,' said Kunti proudly, 'are the latest flowers of that dynasty.'

'And how about our hundred cousins?' Bheem said, glancing over his shoulder at the batch that had just whistled and sniggered and run away. 'Them, too?'

'Yes, Bheem. Your cousins, too. You are all part of the same great lineage. The heirs of Bharata.'

*

Neither Kunti, nor Kunti's sons, nor Gandhari, nor Gandhari's sons knew what was coming. Generations after Bharata, on the eve of the Kali Yuga, all those kingdoms were going to unite again, only in two halves this time, to fight a great—*maha*—war. In time, when Vyasa himself would come to write the epic poem of that war between his two sets of grandsons, he would name it for the greatness and the greatest ancestor: *Mahabharata*.

SARGA 12

THE BAD AXLE

The Ashvin-fathered twins, yoked like two horses pulling the same chariot, thought as one. The twins were a braid. Though that did not keep them from spats, their poking, bickering, whispered altercations hushed as soon as someone else came close. Private jokes, private fallouts, private reconciliations: they did not have to stand or sit next to one another for everyone, even the other three Pandavas, to sense an enclave for two. Quieter than the Kauravas, overshadowed (literally) by Bheem, less eager to answer in class than Yudhishtir, deft with a bow but not showily so, the twin sons of the twin Ashvins loved brushing horses. The stables were their playroom.

The horses sensed nephews in Nakula and Sahadev. The twins needed no equestrian lessons. They grew up doing handstands at a trot, like sons of the steppe. Who needed a saddle? Horse care led naturally to medical knowhow. A turmeric-soaked rag wiped away an infected hoof fissure. When a horse's knee looked like a parasite-bulge in a bole, ginger-shreds in the feed bag shrank the swelling. Ayurveda taught them ashwagandha, *horse smell*, preparation and use. From there, they expanded the pharmacopeia—ajwain seeds for a fiery digestive, rock salt for headache. They were the first Kuru princes to acquaint themselves with death. Yama was Yudhishtir's father, but the twins met him first when they knelt next to a grandmother mare, rasping on her side in the grass. A pale colt, baffling the veterinarians, withered away with no wound and no fever. The twins, aged ten, read why in the black hole of its stilled eye.

*

Every shot was a trickshot with Arjuna, or felt like one. Sandals, shaken off in thoughtless haste, landed side by side, neatly, with their toes aligned against the wall. After prayers in the mountaintop temple, his feet pulse-shuffled evenly down steps with a masculine, dancerly grace. A strong wind might tempt him to toss a sash that twisted and fluttered and ribboned on to his shoulders at the foot of the staircase. The Kauravas could tell he was playing with them. Maybe this was why none of the Kauravas took up a poisonous personal rivalry with Kunti's third son. (Karna, who took that mad risk, knew Arjuna only by hearsay, and never witnessed his wink-and-a-miracle ways.)

Chalk left no dust on Arjuna's fingers. Nothing he drank dribbled, and nothing he bit shed crumbs. He and his brothers were all five fathered by Gods, but only Arjuna wore his divinity on the outside, casually, unthinkingly, exactly as a God would, leaving no prints behind him as he sprinted, no ripples where he dove. Where was he not at his ease? The bullseye was his birthright, and so was the adoration of aunts. The six-spoked mole on his right heel, a horoscope-making pundit told Kunti, was dharma's wheel. The planets aligned just so over his cradle, their orbits concentric, like a shooting-range target or the rings of a tree.

Arjuna could flick a stray fly out of the air without taking his eye off the stag he stalked. At the instant he let go of the nocked arrow, world and wind stopped moving, ensuring his aim was true. Or so it seemed to everyone who competed against him. His eldest brother Yudhishtir preferred games of chance; Arjuna preferred games of skill. According to Arjuna, skill didn't give chance a chance.

The brothers and cousins who marvelled at his natural physical grace never considered how hard he practised. What they perceived as uncannily beautiful movement was just his body spilling up the ruts of rote transcendence. Arjuna knew the secret of genius. Serendipity is hard-won, hard-won the luck of hand and eye. Felicity comes on the fiftieth try.

*

Bheem, the biggest of the boys, did not think of himself as bigger, much less better. He was the right and most fitting size for a boy; everyone else was too small, unluckily runty. So he was frequently heard encouraging his brothers and cousins to eat more. He wanted them to catch up so he could have a wrestling match that challenged him. What did he care about bigger or smaller? It was all maya anyway. He just happened to have a whole lot more maya on him than the other guys.

Bheem's tendency was to guard, not bash, the little ones around him. The Pandavas treated him well and never learned what his fist looked like from the front. The Kauravas, though, could not bear that Bheemalayan mountain. So they harried and heckled him—and ran off crying when he snarled and stomped them. Naturally, they forgot their own provocations. To hear the Kauravas tell it, Bheem bullied them with his bulk, which he had done nothing to earn but eat. When confronted by his teachers with the complaints, Bheem only shrugged. Maybe he *was* a bully. Maya was illusory and so was his body, and so were theirs. Illusion, after a punch from illusion, pinched illusion's nostrils to stop the illusion of blood. Illusion dragged illusion by the topknot howling through the mud.

*

'Pious Yudhishtir.' That was what everyone called Kunti's eldest son, his elders and his cousins alike. He made a point of always chanting the loudest, his voice distinct in the teacher's ear. His straight-backed lotus position and fiercely crinkled-shut eyes caught the notice of the Gods as well as the people around him. He liked his reputation for piety, and the more he fostered that perception, the more he lived it up to it. Did you hear? Pious Yudhishtir took an oath never to tell a lie.

The physical world seemed to hold the same lofty opinion of him. When he trained in a chariot, he never had a bumpy ride, since the wheels stayed an inch off the track. It gave him an unfair advantage in races and manoeuvres. All his roads were paved with air.

Yet pious Yudhishtir harboured a secret fascination with that counter-god, Chance. Hours of perfectly pronounced stotras, the cynical side of him knew, could not keep someone from getting paralysed for life in a fall from a horse. A moment's inattention, or a lightning strike, or a fever in mosquito season—where was karma then? Piety couldn't see you through. With the lust of a faithful husband for a forbidden hussy, pious Yudhishtir lusted after games of chance. Dice thrilled him far more than weapons or Vedic fire sticks. The way they clicked, tumbled and decided the winner and loser at random—how profound it was! Innate prowess, training, the favour of the Gods—powerless!

Palace tutors, pressed about gambling, claimed the superstructure of cosmic justice was revealed in that moment. Each player's karma weighed into the decision that only *seemed* to be chance. Yudhishtir wondered, though, whether a dice throw or coin toss might pause that whole system for a split second. A state of exception! A rent in the karmic network! At a throw of the dice, Yudhishtir got to gaze, lovingly, illicitly, into the dark eyes of lady chaos.

The Kauravas knew the goody-goody's one weakness, but Yudhishtir refused to feel ashamed. Was it as bad as Duryodhan's anger problem, or Dushasana's habit of leering at maids and washerwomen? Yudhishtir's love of gaming kept him, in spite of his piety, affable and approachable, excellent qualities for a king of men. Gaming was fun and made *him* fun. Why resist it? It was harmless. Right?

*

Gandhari's experience of motherhood was considerably more hectic than Kunti's. A ghee-filled clay cocoon had ruptured every few weeks, and in the noisy springtime, every few days. The lack of an age gap led to bigger gulfs—rivalry, bullying, fistfights, cliques. Gandhari and Dhritarashtra were hardly equipped to hold those rude and sturdy boys to account. They called this or that one close and felt his face to figure out which son to (gently, apologetically) scold. More often than not, their fingers misidentified the son in question, calling Vivitsu Vikata, or Srutavan Srutanta, or Durmarsha Durmadha. It didn't help that Vyasa, proposing names for each ghee-slick hatchling, had indulged his love of alliteration.

The eldest of the hundred was Duryodhan. His original name was 'Suyodhan', *Good Axle*—but 'Duryodhan' sounded intimidatingly dangerous, the *Bad Axle* threatening to overturn the chariot. The eldest Kaurava preferred that nickname from a young age. Besides, it connected him alliteratively with the next eldest Kaurava, the one who held whichever boy Duryodhan was punching: Dushasana. Dushasana had tipped over his clay incubator just a month after Duryodhan. His over-large skull crowned at the jar's mouth and got stuck there. Vyasa had shattered the jar with a hammer and raised the second Kaurava to the light.

Gandhari never had storytime with her Kauravas. Overhearing Kunti, Gandhari had made an effort to imitate her, but she couldn't shout loud enough. She didn't pray with her sons, and she didn't cook for them. Most days, she fled to her bedchamber and stuffed cotton balls in her ears. Between that and the blindfold, she was two-fifths of the way to conquering her senses, like her cherished Shiva.

Dhritarashtra was too mild-mannered and too fond to discipline those boys. Their math tutors, hired a dozen at a time, lasted a few weeks before fleeing in tears and terror, sometimes with bruises as souvenirs of Hastinapur. Only their weapons instructors lasted, and among those, only the ones with combat experience.

In an environment like that, Duryodhan adapted. He was the eldest, and he had inherited his father's ape-armed strength more thoroughly than any other Kaurava. Amidst that lawlessness, he, inevitably, became the law. Unsupervised, unseen, the Kauravas cowered under no one else's gaze.

Duryodhan's power didn't derive from threats and beatdowns. When Anuvindha needed some broken ribs, he broke the necessary ribs. But that was a rare event; the Kauravas gathered to watch that sacred rite. Nothing else could shush them like that, except maybe a frown from Grandfather Bhishma. The object of Duryodhan's violence seemed graced by it, privileged, set apart.

The real power lay in patronage. Duryodhan sat under a tree like a rural thakur, hearing out the feuds among his peasantry, delivering judgements, penalties and awards. He never made his brothers grovel, and they never made the mistake of challenging him. Where else could a brother show a black eye and demand justice? Who else could order the stolen toy returned—and see the order through? Dushasana, secondborn and second in command, enforced Duryodhan's regime. Though they seemed ungoverned and ungovernable to everyone else, the cacophanous Kauravas had an intricate law code, an honour system and a master who commanded their loyalty. Their law, their system and their master were Duryodhan, Duryodhan and Duryodhan.

Who could say whether pious Yudhishthir, if he'd come of age inside that mob, might not have developed more like his opposite number? The Pandavas had a balance in their home life between ruckus and respite. Their mother's warm attention evened out the hours when they held their own against their cousins. Unschooled by high-minded Kunti, the Pandavas would have been mere brawlers; untested by the Kauravas, pushovers.

The Kauravas had a half-brother. King Dhritarashtra's blind hands had fluttered here and there during Gandhari's overlong pregnancy. In no time, they found a housemaid. He learned her name just before he fathered Yuyutsu. But he had never felt her face.

The Kauravas had one sister, too, Dussala. Naturally she picked up the slang and swear words of her brothers, but only by overhearing them—they weren't allowed to swear *at* her. On Duryodhan's orders, Dussala's hundred brothers taught her to box and kick, bludgeon a man with a rolling-pin, and scratch out his eyes with a comb. 'I pity your husband, if ever he raises his hand against you,' said Duryodhan proudly. 'A week before you circle the fire, I'll have him watch you train. He'll behave after that!'

*

The Pandavas and Kauravas played together all day, except for the time the Pandavas spent with Kunti. The Kauravas lost to Arjuna at slingshot contests, archery contests and even at how many skips they could get from their stones. In a foot race? Nakula and Sahadev galloped neck and neck, with forty or so Kauravas galumphing after. Things were humiliating enough without Bheem.

Did Bheem want to hurt them, terrorize them, make them pee their dhotis? Loud-mouthed and rowdy was just how Bheem played. In his boyhood, he actually liked his cousins, and he assumed their screams were screams of delight when he thumped splashing into the pool, beating his giant, jiggly chest. 'Where are you at, my Kauravas, my krill? The whale is here! Gulp gulp gulp!' He scooped five Kauravas under one arm, five under the other and spun them around. Was he paying close enough attention to see that their faces were underwater? Finished roughhousing, he shouted, 'Whale spout!' and threw all ten Kauravas high into the air. They landed on the grass beside the pool, gasping for air and coughing up water.

The Kauravas tried to hold eating contests in secret, but Bheem, led by his appetite as if by a dog on a taut leash, always showed up and out-ate them all. Arm-wrestling matches were painful. He took them on two at a time, dislocated their shoulders, then popped each ball back in its joint socket with a 'There you go! Just like new!' They scowled at him, rubbing their arms as he swaggered off. He liked to sneak up behind snacking Kauravas and belch out swallowed air. Luckless Jalagandha lost the hearing in his left ear for a week. These belches, coming from deep in his wolf's belly, could be heard downtown at noon.

No hate motivated Bheem when he dragged four Kauravas by the hair, shouting, 'Check it out! The chariot's pulling the horses!' No hate when he called his brothers over to inspect the full-body grass stains on these crying Kauravas. No hate when, on haircut day, he ran down the line of barber's chairs, slapping sixteen Kauravas on the freshly shaven napes of their necks . . . and knocking three of them unconscious.

Once, he saw three Kauravas climb up a tree to pick some apples. He ran over. 'You know there's a quicker way, right?' Five Bheem-sized shakes of the tree, and all the apples pattered to the ground. 'Well, *these* are the rottenest apples *I've* ever seen!' Bheem was pointing at the three Kauravas who had fallen with the apples. They groaned and cursed with the agony of broken ribs. One of the Kauravas shaken out of that tree was Duryodhan.

*

In Duryodhan, there was hate—and plenty of it. The apple-tree incident was only the latest in a string of humiliations Bheem didn't even notice. The big-boned Pandava didn't target that particular cousin. If anything, Bheem's seeming indifference made Duryodhan hate him even more. Duryodhan couldn't bear to be regarded as just another Kaurava weakling, undistinguished and indistinguishable. That insult was an imagined one: the five Pandavas knew Duryodhan was the strongest, bravest, most athletic of the Kauravas. Even if he had known that, it wouldn't have mattered. He had insults aplenty to nurse. Like his broken left rib.

A broken rib is no great injury; it heals and leaves a knuckle in the bone. For weeks, though, it hurts to breathe. So every breath reminded him of Bheem, of Bheem, of Bheem.

*

'Fell from a tree, did you?' By chance, Gandhari's brother Shakuni happened to be visiting his sister then. 'Be careful, my dear nephew.'

'I didn't fall.'

'No? What happened?' Shakuni had seen everything from a window, but he gave an exaggerated gasp of indignation as

The Bad Axle

Duryodhan told him the story. 'So tell me, nephew, are you going to do your dharma?'

'My dharma?'

'A Kshatriya,' said Shakuni, 'slays his foes. Or that's what I hear in the ballads back home. Is it different here in Hastinapur?'

'Dharma there is dharma here. Bheem is my cousin.'

'If someone's abusing his strength to torment your brothers, you, my boy, ought to do your dharma.'

'A Kshatriya,' Duryodhan said tentatively, 'slays his foes.'

Shakuni smiled. 'I forgot to tell you! I've arranged for an outing tomorrow for all you princes. To the banks of the Ganga. Slides, boats and a big lunch under a big tent. A whole day of water games. Go tell your brothers the good news.' His smile collapsed, and he looked into Duryodhan's eyes, dead serious. 'Go tell Bheem.'

*

The water slides were made of giant gheeleaves, so called because they secreted a greasy film that made for a swift whoop of a descent. Each gheeleaf, as big as an elephant-ear, hung from long ropes braided out of creepers. They were strong enough to hold even Bheem's weight. These ropes were also used for mooring the paddle boats.

King Shakuni's green-eyed Gandharan servants staffed the games and slides. One of them pointed out a pile of green rope to Duryodhan. 'The good thing about those ropes,' he said, 'is that we can throw them into the water afterwards, and in a few hours, they go soft, and unbraid, and float apart. His Majesty, your uncle, likes them.' The servant paused. 'No traces.'

Duryodhan went to where a dozen of his brothers had gathered. Another Gandharan servant was showing off a snake. 'This lady is so poisonous—the females are always more deadly—

that I have to milk her fangs every two days, just to relieve her. I collect her venom in this cup because it would burn the grass or make the river dangerous to drink. Even a drop or two in your khichdi would send you along to your next life! A bite directly from her fangs would be even worse, if she should be let out of her cage.'

'What's her name?' asked Vikarna.

The snake handler looked at Duryodhan. 'Her name is Dharma.'

All morning and most of the afternoon, the Kauravas and Pandavas played in the sun and water. Bheem played harder than everyone else because he had the whole hundred of his cousins to splash, dunk and half-drown. The water that arced from his mouth could batter a Kaurava in conversation thirty feet away. A tent was set up with hot snacks, a square with ten stations on each side. King Shakuni was so generous! Bheem sampled everything three times, one plate in either hand, cutting in line as he pleased. Between the exhaustion and the food, he felt an afternoon nap coming on. For that, he needed some quiet. Far from those one hundred and four chatty and quarrelsome princes, Bheem found a banyan grove overhanging a pond. The dangling shoots were a cinch to tie. Soon he snored away in a hammock over the water.

Duryodhan tiptoed up with the green ropes. A snoring Bheem was hard to disturb. It took some dexterity for Duryodhan to truss his cousin, as he was hanging from the banyan shoots himself. The Kaurava was a natural gymnast, even at that young age displaying a murderous masculine grace. Satisfied with his crisscrosses and knots, Duryodhan knifed the banyan hammock free.

Bheem's splash drenched his would-be killer, who watched from above. Bheem, still half asleep, struggled against the ropes as though he were tossing in his sleep, sinking all the while. A crocodile slid into the water to investigate this meaty feast of a boy. A noseful of water finally bothered Bheem enough to grunt and snap the ropes. This he did just in time to thrash the ill-timed crocodile. The dead beast floated belly up. Bheem crawled on to the crocodile's pale leathery underside and continued his nap.

Duryodhan regrouped and returned, proceeding banyan-shoot by banyan-shoot. This time, far more slowly: he had the snake's cage, hooked to his left great toe. Dharma, he knew, was another name for Yama. The snake would do the job.

At last, after great effort, he hung directly above Bheem. Sliding up the cage door, he poured the snake on to Bheem's belly. Then he trapezed away to watch. The snake could not flee off that crocodile-raft, and Bheem's thunderous digestion-gurgles alarmed her. She rose and struck! And struck, and struck. Her fangs couldn't pierce Bheem's thick skin. On the third attempted bite, her bruised fangs snapped like twigs, and snake blood mixed with snake venom spilled on to Bheem's belly. On anyone else's bare skin, this fluid would have burned and bubbled. Bheem felt a tickle. His eyelids fluttered, and he looked down at his guest. A casual fist crushed the deadly snake's head. He flung the limp length of it away—unwittingly right at Duryodhan, who had to swallow a startled shout. Bheem went back to sleep. The Kaurava prince went back to the tent.

Dinner was being served by then, an even bigger spread than before. Duryodhan ordered his uncle's servants to heap up five plates for Bheem. The smell of the food called Bheem, and he showed up for the feast as expected. He drank his dal straight from the bowl, did the same with his bright orange mango puree and dealt with his buttermilk most savagely. That covered all three of the dishes over which Duryodhan had tilted the steel cup of snake's venom. He watched in eager fascination as Bheem proceeded to wolf down every other dish and sweet. When would he clutch his throat? When would he sweat, retch, go cross-eyed, tip over?

Bheem began to beat against his stomach. Duryodhan smiled with anticipation. It was happening! Bheem kept beating, now with both fists, a frenzied drumroll. Finally he opened his mouth. What came out was not a scream of agony. It was a satisfied earthquake of a burp that made the right half of the tent come down. Fifty Kauravas, kicking their own plates, struggled to find their way out from under the canvas and tent-poles—among them Duryodhan, also swearing in frustration, but not for the same reason as his brothers.

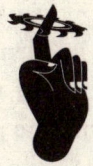

SEQUENCE 5

THE EDUCATION AND MARRIAGE OF THE PANDAVAS

Bhishma recruits a poor Brahmin, Drona, to train the princes in the arts of war. With Drona comes his son, Asvatthama—a strange child, born with a mysterious jewel embedded in his forehead. Asvatthama grows jealous of his father's love for his star student, Arjuna.

At a royal exhibition, where the princes show off their skills, an unexpected visitor challenges Arjuna. The youth wears golden armour: it is Karna, Queen Kunti's illegitimate son by the Sun God, the unknown half-brother of the Pandavas.

Karna tricked Parashuram into training him, and Parashuram laid a curse on him. (That curse will lead to catastrophe decades later, on the battlefield.)

Rules prevent Karna (a non-royal) from fighting Arjuna (a royal), but Duryodhan, wanting to see Arjuna bested, gifts the commoner a kingdom on the spot. A friendship has been formed. That friendship will play into which side Karna supports when the war starts—not his half-brothers, but Duryodhan, who befriended him. An emergency sundown (perhaps Surya, protecting his son) prevents the fight from happening.

Drona, their guru, set a condition before agreeing to train the princes: Once they are grown, they will have to avenge themselves on an old rival of his, the king of Panchala, who slighted him when they were younger. The Kauravas fail at this task, but the Pandavas succeed.

The king of Panchala, incidentally, has a daughter and son, both born of sacred fire. They will have a major role—the daughter, Panchali, will become the polyandrous wife of the five Pandavas.

Characters Who Will Show Up Again:

DRONA, a poor Brahmin, beholden to the throne of Hastinapur for keeping his family from starving. The military teacher of both sets of princes.

ASVATTHAMA, his son, born with a jewel in his forehead. Jealous of Arjuna.

PANCHALI, alias Draupadi, the fire-born daughter of the king of Panchala, future wife of the Pandavas. Those two names refer to her kingdom of origin and her father. Her original first name is actually *Krishnaa*, the female form of 'Krishna', and she has a mysterious, sisterly connection to Krishna, in addition to sharing his black skin.

DHRISTADYUMNA, her fire-born brother. You have probably noticed that there are a lot of characters whose names start with 'D' so far: Dhritarashtra, Duryodhan, Dushasana . . . In most cases, the 'D' characters are on the side of the Kauravas. Panchali's brother Dhristadyumna is the exception to this rule. A casual eye can turn the name 'Dhristadyumna' into 'Dhritarashtra', so in the text, I consistently refer to 'blind King Dhritarashtra' to keep that from happening; and instead of 'Draupadi' or 'Krishnaa', I use the name Panchali to refer to her.

SARGA 13

FROM A PAIL TO THE PALACE

Bheem had a habit of interrupting the games the Kauravas were playing, too. One day, he swaggered over and grabbed a bat.

'It isn't your turn, Bheem!'

'You're right. It's *your* turn to see how far that ball can go.'

The Pandava twins were taking part in this game. Bheem knocked the ball far beyond the palace wall. The Kauravas ran after it, but long-striding Nakula and Sahadev pulled ahead. Nakula cut in front of Sahadev, lowered his shoulders and let Sahadev push off so he could hurdle the wall. Sahadev watched the ball bounce down a Hastinapur street and plunk into a well. The other players found their way there soon enough. A crowd of princes murmured around the well.

Bheem showed up too, and spat in the well. He was amused. 'What luck!' he marvelled. 'I couldn't do that again if I tried.'

Nakula and Sahadev began quarrelling with their brother. Arjuna and Yudhishthir arrived by the well, too, and so did Duryodhan, called there by his brothers. Once the eldest Kaurava showed up and started talking, Bheem's mood changed. The fight looked like it might escalate.

'All this fuss over a ball? I'm happy to send any one of you,' Bheem said, glaring at Duryodhan, 'down there to fetch it! Any volunteers?'

Just then, a man in a beggar's rags, but with the forehead-markings of a Brahmin, strolled by and peeked down the well. 'What fell in?'

His voice was quiet—but commanding enough to lay a hush on these scrapping princes. Arjuna told him what had happened.

'Easy enough,' said the priest in rags. 'Fetch me about ten of those reeds from the roadside, will you?'

Arjuna, sensing this man deserved respect, did what he was asked. The stranger bent and tested the reeds, then used the longest one to make a neat bow. He did this with a few threads from his threadbare rags. Twang! It was ready. Now he pitched a pebble down there and observed the ripples and bobs. From his makeshift bow, the rest of the reeds *thwipped, thwipped, thwipped* into the darkness. A thin tower of reeds, splitting each other end to end, waved from the stone rim of the well. The man slid it out, and at the end of it was the ball. 'There you go, boys,' he whispered, and went on his way.

The encounter left the princes murmuring in awe for a good hour. The whole palace noticed the Kauravas quieter than usual. Grandfather Bhishma asked Arjuna what had happened, and Arjuna described the feat with the reeds.

'A beggar, you say?'

'But with the white thread across his chest.'

'There's only one place he could have learned that trick, and that's Mount Mahendra.' Bhishma steepled his fingers, closed his eyes and nodded. 'That Brahmin has studied with Parashuram, just as I did, long ago. Could you recognize him if you saw him again, Arjuna?'

'Of course.'

'Let's go for a walk, my boy. I want this man to teach my Kuru princes.'

*

That penniless stranger was the son of the seer Bharadwaj. Bharadwaj used to practise the esoteric art of semen blocking. Self-disciplined until it hurt, he shunted tantric energy from the base camp of his spine right up to the snowy peak of his spirit. There he could meditate atop the Mount Kailasa of his Self.

That was in theory. In practice, semen blocking involved cold baths, mentally shouting down your arousals and three-yojana walks to ground the excess charge in your pelvis.

On one such walk, Bharadwaj glimpsed an apsara on the riverbank. Or that was the story he told his colleagues. Ever since Vishwamitra, pleading temptation-by-celestial-dancer was the honourable way to concede defeat. Maybe she was just a washerwoman whipping the rocks with a wet sheet. Maybe she was a girl in a ferry boat.

The seer had enough self-control not to approach her. He ran home to his hut, hands crossed over his shame, cross-eyed with lust. He knelt over a copper bucket because he had heard a story in which Shiva's seed fell to earth and formed not one but six babies. Once he got his own lust out, he dropped beside that bucket and slept for two days straight.

In this bucket, he brewed his week's supply of *soma*. Lately, he had been lax about rinsing it out. So mystical herbs and spells still laced it.

Over the past decade, the fapless Brahmin's seminal vesicles had swollen to the size of lychees. His spilled seed—a quart's worth—congealed and gestated. By the time he woke up, a salamander-sized slip of a foetus swam down there, complete with ink-drop eyes and winking heart. 'Bucket boy, bucket boy,' murmured the new father in alarm, 'how can I dump you out now?'

A fresh gallon of soma, sprinkles of tulsi, incense-ash, sandalwood oil, Ganga water, powdered almonds, turmeric, his own saliva . . . It was all experimentation, since none of the Vedas had a rite or recipe to brew a baby. When he saw eyelids and fingernails, the Brahmin called a midwife, who cut and tied the cord. What other name could belong to this motherless boy? *Bucket* in Sanskrit is *Drona*.

*

It was easy to convince Drona to train the Pandavas and Kauravas. He had never been offered money before. Drona had no money; never sought it, never understood it. Still, he could kill a man with a coin. The occult power of money made him uneasy. It drove grown men crazy. The brightest coins had the blackest auras.

'In the scriptures,' he said uneasily, 'Brahmins get paid in cows, don't they?'

'You'll be living in the palace,' Bhishma said patiently. He had last been in a house this small when he bargained for Satyavati's hand. The fisherman's hut was a palace compared to this. 'I can give you cows if you want, but where would you keep them?'

A scrawny boy emerged from behind his father's bony leg. This was Drona's only son. Arjuna looked in the Brahmin boy's eyes, which narrowed at him. Maybe it was the boy's freshly shaven head, maybe that head's unlikely size, maybe the black gemstone set inside his forehead like a third eye—but this boy looked feral, hostile, alien. The razor that shaved him had been old and rusty. A dozen spots of blood bloomed on his naked scalp.

'This is Asvatthama.' Drona patted the boy's head, not noticing it sweated blood. 'Can I bring him with me?'

Arjuna, instinctively, wished Bhishma would say no. But Bhishma welcomed the boy into the palace and promised Drona that Asvatthama would dine at the same table as the princes.

Drona arrived the next morning, Asvatthama in tow, but he did not surrender his little bundle (all his possessions fit inside a towel) when Bhishma came out to greet him.

'I have one last request before I accept this position.'

The Pandavas and Kauravas, on Bhishma's orders, stood stiffly, their hands joined. They respected the stranger who had retrieved their ball—and considered him slightly magical. Some of the Kauravas tittered and nudged each other when they saw the Brahmin runt with the nine-faceted black gem stuck in his forehead. But Duryodhan shushed them. He sensed the same strangeness in the boy that Arjuna had sensed—but he wanted that weird energy on his side. *I'll seat that beggar's son at my elbow for a few meals*, he thought to himself. *He'll be useful someday.*

'In the old days,' Drona said, 'every guru got to ask one gift after he finished training his pupil. I don't want money. Room and board will be enough. But I have one . . . task I will ask of you. After I have made you warriors.'

Bhishma turned to the Kuru princes. 'That's not for me to promise.'

The Pandavas and Kauravas murmured amongst themselves. This open-ended request—that odd pause before he said the word *task*—and that odd-looking hairless Brahmin boy at his side . . .

'I'll do it,' said Arjuna, stepping forward. 'Train us, Guru Drona. Whatever the task turns out to be, I'll do it.'

*

From Asvatthama's perspective, his father had one son, *him*, for the first ten years of his life. They had grown up poor but happy. Drona used to smear wheat flour and water on Asvatthama's lips to make the other kids think he'd been drinking real milk. It didn't matter. He was his father's one and only son, won from Shiva by a decade's devotion. One day, they left the hut for a palace. The price: now his father had over a hundred sons. He went down the line, adjusting a shoulder, widening a stance with a tap of his foot on either shin. Asvatthama would have given up the palace to get his father's exclusive attention back. What was so great about living in a palace, anyway? Real milk was overrated.

In a few months, his father Drona went back to having one son. Only that son wasn't Asvatthama. It was Arjuna.

Arjuna would have been Drona's favourite on natural talent alone. The Gods had built him for archery: his thumb was as long as his index finger, his wingspan longer than his height, his shoulders broader than everyone but Bheem's.

On top of physique, though, Arjuna had ambition. One night, after a long day's training, the five Pandavas ate together with their mother, away from the Kaurava mess-hall and its food fights. A storm was on its way, and the wind blew out all the candles and slammed the shutters.

Everyone stopped eating but Bheem. 'Why would darkness stop me? My hand can always find my mouth. It's got a lot of practice!'

That got Arjuna thinking. He thought of the way his blind uncle strode the halls of the palace, no less confidently than a sighted man; how his blindfolded aunt could centre her necklaces without a mirror, simply by sensing the lie of the chain. Arjuna tried eating like Bheem, in the total darkness. 'Practise,' he whispered under his breath.

The storm didn't stop him from night shooting. The new moon added a challenge. Eventually even using the stars felt like cheating. At last he graduated to the blindfold. One glance at the target, tie the blindfold, spin until dizzy. Bullseye.

Beyond ambition, though, he had the love. Of archery, of excellence, of self-surpassing. Wasn't that the method of yoga—surpassing yourself until you arrived at Brahman? An intellectual with no interest in money-making, Drona knew what it was like to love abstractions and impossible, self-assigned goals: samadhi, the Fourth State, nirvana. Arjuna's love of sending a feather-fletched, finely weighted arrow through the air; of imagining a thread-thin trajectory and threading it; of ignoring infinite space in favour of a single point and piercing it, from a distance, with another point . . . Drona loved that love in Arjuna.

Duryodhan loved the war sciences too, but he loved the power they promised, not the sciences themselves. This held true for most of the fleet-footed, ambidextrous Kauravas—though there were about ten who were lazy, and another ten who were slug-brained. The Pandavas had the benefit of divine genes, so they started at a higher skill level than their cousins. The Kauravas got with grit what graced the Pandavas. Yudhishthir was diligent, the first to raise his hand, eager to please. Nakula and Sahadev wasted time debating whose bullseye was more dead centre. Bheem broke equipment. The only weapon that held up was the mace, and Arjuna, at the top at everything else, acknowledged Bheem's superiority with that.

Duryodhan thought the mace a stupid weapon. After watching his most hated cousin swing that brass onion—and take such pride in his prowess—Duryodhan practised extra every evening. He saw daydreams of besting Bheem with Bheem's weapon of choice, of setting his foot on the knocked-out giant's stove-in chest.

*

As Drona's reputation grew, neighbouring kingdoms tried to lure him away. Bhishma never kept an offer from reaching Drona. The master regarded his pupils as works in progress, and he could not bear to abandon Arjuna three quivers short of mastery.

Sometimes a pupil approached Drona on his own, hoping to join class alongside the Kuru princes. One such prospect was a Nishada boy named Ekalavya. The Nishadas were a wild tribe from the east, known to be preternaturally fierce warriors.

'You can't possibly start at this late date,' Drona demurred. The unkempt, squat boy was covered in Kali tattoos and had a pierced eyebrow. 'The princes are months ahead of you.'

Ekalavya bowed. 'Test me, Guru Drona.'

Drona sighed deeply, surprised at this tribal boy's politeness. He pointed out a sparrow and said, 'Eye,' and Ekalavya loaded his arrow with a hectic, amateurish shuffle. But moments later, he fetched the dead sparrow and set it at Drona's feet, panting and smiling, like a proud Labrador.

'Who is your father, boy?'

'Hiranyadhanush, chief of the Bheels. He's the one who taught me how to hunt.'

Drona shook his head. 'That name sounds familiar.'

'He's famous! He's a general over in Magadha.'

'Right. He serves King Jarasandha.' Drona was relieved. 'That's a rival kingdom, kid. I couldn't possibly train you. You might use those skills against Hastinapur one day.'

'I promise not to! Sir, I'll swear to serve Hastinapur's king all my life, even if it's against my own father. I promise.'

'Run along, boy.'

'I'll take a vow. I'll make it official.'

'I'm sure Magadha has plenty of fine teachers . . .'

'None like you!'

Drona turned away. He had reasons not to train Ekalavya; the boy's coarse Sanskrit and pierced eyebrow were only two of many. He had his reservations about teaching a forest tribesman. Just because the boy's father was a general didn't make either of them true Kshatriyas. In Drona's worldview, everyone had a pre-set role, and they were born to it. Drona never questioned that order; he had never known a world that didn't have that order; and while he could imagine a world without that order, such a world struck him as helter-skelter, its intergenerational links broken, in the process of dissolving. Priests taught war, and warriors made war. A wild boy from the wilderness, with no lineage, had no place in Drona's school.

The Kuru princes agreed. As Ekalavya left, he heard snickers from scattered Kauravas. Out of earshot of Drona, the heckling became overt. *How come he's not wearing feathers?* A few sat on the wall and flung garbage at him. *Ooga-booga!* They mimicked his bowlegged gait and jeered at his moleskin moccasins. *You don't need a guru to shoot squirrels for dinner. Remember your place.*

Ekalavya went off to the forest, his ancestral element. Out of Drona's muddy footprints, river clay and forest creepers, he fashioned a statue, an idol of Drona. Pebbles were his eyes. Snake-slough served as the white Brahmin thread across his chest.

One day, Drona took his princes into the forest to practise archery on squirrels and hummingbirds. Some of the Kauravas kept a pet dog. This dog got wind of Ekalavya spying on the class and trotted over. Before the dog could give his position away, Ekalavya shot his throat full of arrows.

The dog—silenced, but mysteriously not in pain—returned to the princes with a bouquet of twenty fletches emerging from his mouth. The Kauravas shouted in distress at the sight of their cherished dog. Arjuna rushed over, too, but his concern was different. 'Who pulled off *that* trick?'

The mute dog led them to the tree where Ekalavya had perched. The boy seemed unfazed by the growing mob of outraged Kauravas. In fact, he seemed to be snacking.

Arjuna shoved through his cousins and confronted Ekalavya. 'You shut that dog up before he could bark?'

'Sure did,' said Ekalavya, and spat out the shell of a sunflower seed.

'Who's your guru?'

'Same as yours.'

'Drona?'

'That's right.'

The mob dissolved into murmurs. Arjuna ran back to where Drona was supervising a batch of Kauravas. The guru rushed over and recognized the tribal boy at once. Ekalavya hopped off the tree and pressed his forehead reverently to Drona's feet.

'I never trained you,' said Drona, shaking his head.

'But you did,' insisted Ekalavya. 'Follow me.'

The guru soon stood face to face with the crudely made statue of himself. The Nishada boy, he realized, was a self-taught genius, ripened in isolation, idiosyncratic. There was no way these conventionally schooled princes could compete. Even Arjuna had taken on the refinements—and hence, the limitations—of formal training. It didn't matter that Arjuna's guru-pupil lineage placed him at just one remove from Parashuram. Ekalavya had developed on his own into something that—in Magadha's service—would pick off Kuru princes like bottles off a fence.

'I'm your guru, am I? Well, there was never a guru who didn't get his guru's gift.'

'Ask me for anything, Guru Drona.'

'I want your thumb.'

*

Well after midnight, back in Hastinapur, Drona discovered Arjuna weeping off by himself.

'You have nothing to fear, Arjuna. No archer without a thumb will ever pose a risk to you.'

'How did he *do* that? He didn't even hurt the dog. Could Parashuram do that?'

'Best not to think about it.'

'Guru Drona, he was *better* than me. Never trained under anyone except that . . . that mound of clay. And he was *better*.'

'Think of how many warriors are out there. Beyond the Himalayas, beyond the Saraswati river . . . Thousands, perhaps millions of warriors, who speak no Sanskrit and have never heard of Rama or Indra. There will always be someone out there who is more skilled than you.'

'No.' Arjuna wiped away his tears. 'No. I'm going to train even harder. I can't let there be *anyone*. Bow and arrow? Me. Only me. The best in the world. The best ever.'

*

Ekalavya gave up his thumb with a smile, went the story. It was a deranged, madhouse smile, a smile of disbelief at the way of the world, a smile of disgust at his pain. Drona, he intuited, felt no guilt extracting this thumb. And he was right: Ekalavya had eavesdropped on the guru's lessons, stealing from the guru; now Drona simply stole back, in the form of that skilled thumb, what Ekalavya had stolen from him. The Kuru princes were gleeful and—though they would never admit it—relieved. Their smugness, their contempt, their elite births: Ekalavya had imagined he might overcome these things by skill. They would see what he could do, and they would say forget the old restrictions and taboos, forget the old slots where people never really were a perfect fit, Manu and the ancestors never imagined anyone could be quite like you, Ekalavya! Join us, let us welcome you into the company of princes, a master archer among master archers, now that you have earned entry, the way the atman earns entry in Brahman. Merit should be rewarded in society as it is in the ashram. Patient yoga and self-discipline and concentration should receive their reward.

Instead? A rust-flecked knife drawn from his gator-skin belt, his thumb stump pattering blood on the earth. The guru he had revered in mud-murti form extended his naked hand and received the stiff slug. The fingernail had drained white. And then they all walked away, chatting of other things. He tied his own tourniquet.

That was not the end of Ekalavya's career. He still knew what he taught himself. Within hours of the stump crusting over, he began training again. He simply flipped the image for every move he remembered, re-teaching himself in a mirror so that right-handed Ekalavya became left-handed Ekalavya. He shaped himself a clay thumb to keep the amputation from throwing off his mind. Constant adjustments and workarounds became second nature. Every few years, he tested his skill level on stray dogs, trying to silence their barking with his arrows, as he had done as a boy. His shots beheaded the first two. But the third one lived.

In two decades, he was fully lethal again. He helped his father attack an ally of Hastinapur: Krishna's city, the city of Mathura. Krishna knew that Ekalavya, when the great war came, would choose the Kauravas over the Pandavas. For Ekalavya knew what Drona's own son knew: Drona loved Arjuna most of all. It wasn't caste indignation, it wasn't fear of Ekalavya using his skill against Hastinapur. Those were all excuses, or secondary causes. Drona had taken Ekalavya's thumb out of love for Arjuna. And Ekalavya would swallow his hatred of the Kauravas to have his vengeance on the favoured prince who had cost him his thumb.

So Krishna would set out to kill Ekalavya, all those years later—also out of love for Arjuna, and to secure his ascendancy on that future battlefield. Yet Krishna knew the injustice that had been done to the boy. So he raised his hand before their one-on-one fight began and promised him justice. Ekalavya would not just be reborn a prince. He would be reborn as the prince who would kill Drona. Ekalavya smiled the same smile he had smiled at Drona, and he shook his head, saying that was no justice at all. Justice would mean a future in which every self-taught Ekalavya would best every guru-coddled Arjuna, and be *allowed* to best him, no bar to his art, no bias against his bow: universal delight in brilliance, regardless of birth. Ekalavya, still smiling Ekalavya's smile, bit his clay thumb off and spat it on the ground between himself and the avatar. Then he strung his bow.

SARGA 14

SUNRISE OF THE GOLDEN BOY

A year later, at the Royal Exhibition, Duryodhan got his chance to fight Bheem one on one with the mace. The exhibition was as much Drona's as his students': their skill would prove his skill. Eventually, he knew, his fame would spread to Panchala. Because of a long-ago slight, *that* was the kingdom he wanted abuzz with his name.

    Blind king Dhritarashtra authorized the funds for a new arena on the outskirts of Hastinapur. The city showed up to watch the show. What a show it was! Synchronized archery: thirty Kauravas sent beribboned arrows in patterns through the sky. Spear throws burst balloons full of flashing glitter or sliced the cord that tied shut a cage full of doves. Ten princes shot at the freed doves, ten more shot the arrows before they hit home. The Pandava twins performed horseback feats that would have broken anybody else's neck. After them came the chariots, racing the arena's oval. Through the dust of their own wheels, the princes shot flying targets out of the air. That was Yudhishthir's best event.

    The mace fight had not been cleared with Drona. He preferred to have the princes, in sets of twenty, go through stylized moves with the mace—an interlude of skill display between set pieces, with music. A personal battle might cause an injury and change the mood of the afternoon. But what could he do when Bheem and Duryodhan, agreeing on nothing else, agreed to tap mace-heads and thump their chests in challenge?

Drona had just realized what was happening when money started changing hands in the bleachers. Hastinapur always had a gambling habit, and now the men and women were screaming at each other. 'Twenty on Big Boy, in three rounds!' 'I'll bet this ring on the Kaurava—he's solid muscle!'

Meanwhile, Bheem had taken a look from Duryodhan amiss, and he flung aside his padded leather vest.

'Bare-chested fight!' he shouted at his cousin. 'This is it, Duryodhan!'

Duryodhan went as pale as his late Uncle Pandu to hear this added challenge—for he knew that Bheem had a good three inches of fat and another five of muscle, while he had far less natural padding. Bheem grinned at the reaction and twirled the giant mace in one hand, as if it were just some street acrobat's baton.

In the bleachers, meanwhile, the excitement had given way to shoves and curses. The crowd, which had been docile during the recent spectacles, got so hot-headed about this face-off, you would think they had been following the rivalry for years.

Bheem turned in astonishment—his mace had disappeared. Drona had snatched it away. Now he approached Duryodhan, who made a show of obedience and handed over his own. The Kaurava prince was relieved to give up the weapon. He realized he wasn't ready to fight Bheem yet, in spite of all his practice. His own fear was a revelation. Duryodhan decided he would commission an iron figure, cast to Bheem's proportions. Practising on that iron Bheem would be like sprinting at high altitude, with weights tied to his arms and legs. Battering iron would make him likelier to shatter bone, when the opportunity came.

Drona, knocking the maces together to shush the crowd, boomed: 'And now for the star of the show: Prince Arjuna!'

Almost everyone clapped and cheered. The only exceptions were Duryodhan and Asvatthama, who glanced at each other and rolled their eyes.

In the royal balcony, Kunti waved her hands at her boy. Arjuna bowed piously in the direction of his elders, then touched Drona's feet. Hundreds of trial runs had left him free of anxiety. First he shot an arrow through the holes of twelve axe heads, lined up by stable-boys who scurried clear. Then Drona placed an apple on his own head, and Arjuna sent an arrow through it. The citizens, delighted, returned to their seats and forgot their recent gambling frenzy. Arjuna shot twelve arrows at two hundred feet into a hollowed-out cow's horn that swung from a rope. Drona picked a blue morpho from a glass jar and set her free; Arjuna dipped an arrow in red paint, broke off the arrowhead and sent the naked shaft *between* the flapping wings. The butterfly, caught with a net and shown around the arena, was revealed to be sporting a fresh red line along the topside of either wing. It was otherwise unscathed.

Kunti beamed at her son. Grandfather Bhishma leaned over to tell her that even Parashuram didn't have that kind of accuracy.

These were just introductory tricks. Arjuna brought out whistling wonder-weapons made of Sanskrit and teak. One shot skywards and turned into a conflagration that burned on nothing but air. The next weapon caused a whoosh of wind that spread the fire. People started screaming because they feared the wooden arena would burn, and they felt the scorching heat. The third weapon he shot became furiously pressured water and doused the whole thing. The meeting hissed and crackled, and harmless steam floated into the sky and dispersed.

Hastinapur cheered. Everyone got to their feet, including Bhishma and Kunti. Dhritarashtra and Gandhari, who had given ear to a breathless and impartial commentary, rose as well and applauded their nephew. The king murmured to Gandhari, 'He's popular, isn't he?'

'Just like his father,' she answered.

When the applause died down, the arena heard an unusual sound.

'What's that?' Drona said to no one in particular.

Metal slamming metal . . . strange.

The princes turned to the sound. Overhead, the clouds burned away, and the sun seemed to intensify its heat. Arjuna broke out in a sweat, his cheeks burning. Princes and citizens alike squinted and raised the visor of a hand.

The main gate of the arena flew open, as if with an imperious kick. In the royal balcony, Kunti got to her feet.

A young man in golden armour strode into the arena. Silence, except for a few stray gasps. One of those was Kunti's, just before she collapsed.

Bhishma knelt at her side in alarm. Was it heat stroke? He grabbed a servant's palm-frond to fan her. Her eyelids fluttered. 'My son! My son!' Everyone thought she was speaking of Arjuna. She wasn't.

*

Recall the son that Kunti, testing out her boon, conceived with the Sun God. He sailed a river in a wicker basket, vernixed with golden armour, earlobes pierced with simple golden earrings. Kunti had been trying to forget him for years. Marriage, three divine lovers, three semi-divine sons, widowhood: a lot had transpired since that adolescent fling. But a woman never forgets her first. Especially if her first results in a baby. She took one look at Karna and knew. The armour, malleable magical gold, had stretched with the growth of his torso. The earrings, too, had kept pace.

Kunti recognized Surya's jawline. Did her Pandavas recognize, on Karna's face, their mother's eyebrows and lips? The resemblance, she thought, was so obvious! Kunti flushed. Everyone in this arena must already *know*. Why hadn't Hastinapur turned to point at her?

The city was rapt by the drama in the arena. The flashy newcomer swaggered up to Drona. Kunti's first son bowed with joined hands—but there was aggression, almost contempt in it. When that formality was over, he thrust his chest at Arjuna and abruptly unshouldered his bow. The younger archer flinched and stepped back a little, his hand floating instinctively to his quiver, then floating down again.

Karna grinned to see it. Three arrowheads eclipsed his Sanskrit-murmuring lips.

The first arrow hit an atmospheric pressure change and burst into a pond of fire, suspended in the air. The second arrow whooshed the fire up into a teetering fire tornado. The third arrow pierced this tornado through its tapered end, reducing it to harmless steam. Karna's display had been identical, at the level of physics, to Arjuna's. If anything, it was more aesthetic. If a panel of judges had been present, they might have regretted the perfect score they gave Arjuna.

No one watched with more awe and delight than Duryodhan. Even Bhishma, whom nothing threatened (he had the gift of choosing his time of death, after all), frowned with puzzlement and suspicion. Kunti feared for Arjuna. Arjuna himself looked grave. That gravity concealed the lump in his throat, the same feeling he'd gotten from seeing Ekalavya's archery. The Pandavas looked threatened and uncertain of themselves, as though a rift had split the earth where Karna stood.

But Duryodhan? Duryodhan clasped his hands over his heart the way he did as a toddler, when Grandfather Bhishma spun a top for the first time. The spectacle of Karna's prowess made him rejoice. Duryodhan had pondered Ekalavya's thumb many times—if only he had recruited Ekalavya, made a vassal of him and had him humiliate Arjuna some time in the future! Too late to co-opt that thumbless genius, but here was another one, another chance. Duryodhan shouted 'Yes!' and 'Ha!' as Karna's arrows corkscrewed and whistled skyward. Arjuna and Bheem had seemed insuperable obstacles, unbeatable rivals, proof of a Pandava ascendancy that would see Yudhishtir to the throne and Duryodhan married to some minor princess. Why fear any of them now? Finally, someone who could best them all.

As the mist and steam dispersed, as scattered applause rose from the crowd, Duryodhan strode over to the newcomer. He embraced Karna and gave him two firm claps on his shoulder. Karna, stunned to be touched, staggered back a step—but ninety-nine Kauravas, following their eldest brother's lead, cheered and swarmed Arjuna's rival. They almost hoisted him on to their shoulders, but Karna raised his hand and kept his distance.

'I'm not done!' he shouted. 'This isn't the end! I thank you kind princes for your friendliness—'

'Our friendship. Our *friendship*.'

'I want a one-on-one battle. Me versus Arjuna.'

Arjuna shook off his shock with a snarl. 'You want to fight me? Who are you, anyway? Who invited you? State your name!'

'Don't ask for my name, bitch. All you need to know, you *saw*.'

'Who invited you in here? Go sit in the stands and I'll show you how it's done. I haven't shown half of what I've got.'

'What's wrong, Arjuna?' Duryodhan asked mockingly. 'Can't handle a challenger? He'll blow your head off while your guru looks on.'

Just as when Duryodhan and Bheem scorpion-circled each other, the arena grew boisterous with bets and bookies. This was high entertainment. Kunti felt faint again, but Vidura intervened with a sprinkle of tulsi water, and she revived. She had raised Arjuna for years. Why did she feel such a draw to Karna, the son she hadn't seen since she was a teen—and then only for a day? Bhishma, thinking she feared for Arjuna, rose from his chair and joined the Pandavas on the field. He said nothing, but his presence heartened them more than ninety-five brothers would have.

Drona had already broken up a mace challenge between cousins. Where was he now? Quiet, and off to the side. A secret had him chewing his lip. Drona *knew* Karna; he had even trained the boy, briefly, on the side. Intrigued by that golden armour, Drona had assessed the boy's talent to see whether he posed a threat to Arjuna. The shining athlete was clearly another Ekalavya in the making, born with an exoskeleton, hence even harder to kill. Drona had dropped his all-too-promising student without telling the palace.

Karna had sought another guru. And Drona knew *exactly* who that guru was.

Drona did not dare stop this fight, since the heavens were showing an interest. Clouds gathered over half the sky, the shadow-border stopping halfway across the field. This protected Arjuna and the Pandavas against the intensifying sun that illuminated Karna and the Kauravas. Karna's father, Surya, and Arjuna's father, Indra, were watching: the Sun God and the God of Rain and Thunder. No wonder rainbows tangled in the sky at uncanny angles.

Arjuna turned to Drona for permission to engage. Drona glanced at the sky, swallowed and nodded. Kripa, a fellow guru of the military arts, sensed the hesitation in his colleague. He stepped forward and announced the matchup. 'Prince Arjuna of Hastinapur, son of Pandu, son of Kunti, a Kshatriya born in the Kuru lineage, will fight his challenger in single combat . . . Now *you*, young man, announce your parentage for us, and your royal house. Then we can get started.'

Karna scowled. 'What does that matter? How I fight will announce who taught me. I am Karna. That's all the lineage anybody needs to know.'

The elderly Brahmin shook his head. 'There are rules about who can fight whom. Like fights like. It was a rule instituted long ago to keep Kshatriyas from fighting people whose dharma wasn't warfare. Say who you are, so the prince here can assess if he can fight you.'

The arena was silent, waiting for Karna's announcement. The booming voice that had bludgeoned Arjuna had fled. He cleared his throat and looked around at the stands. Even his armour seemed dimmer than before, more brass than gold.

'He's right! What does that old rule matter?' Duryodhan threw his arm around Karna in solidarity. 'This man has the shoulders, the swagger, the skill of a Kshatriya. If warfare isn't his dharma, why did nature build him like this? I'm not letting Arjuna weasel out of a fair fight. Birth didn't do right by Karna, but I will. I have kingdoms, mine by birthright, gifted to me by karma. What I was gifted, I regift, right now, to him. All hail Karna, King of Anga!'

The Kauravas cheered. The crowds, not wanting to lose out on another fight, roared and stomped their support. Duryodhan ran to the balcony. Bhishma's tasselled and lotus-decorated chair was empty, so Duryodhan, up with a pull-up and clamber, down with a leap, fetched it for Karna and sat him down. As he did this, he shouted, 'Get the Brahmins out here! And bring some sacred water!' Thirty or so Kauravas made it happen. Duryodhan grabbed a fan from a rich woman's servant in the stands. With great pride, he fanned King Karna through his consecration. A few hymns, some flower petals and a sprinkle of sacred water on his head—and Karna was a king. The sacred water hid his tears.

When Karna had entered the arena, he had felt, for the first time, the weight of *gazes*. A gaze had seemed such a weightless thing before that! In the few instances he had been looked at, that is—for in spite of his (dust-dimmed) golden body armour, and the earring concealed by his straggly and lice-laced black curls, no one ever really noticed the charioteer's son on the street. Maybe that was his unknown ancestry at work: no one looked directly at the sun, either. Today, in the arena, he became the focus of thousands of people. The collected eyebeams pushed on his body from every direction until he could scarcely breathe. How did Arjuna and the other princes ignore it? The ambient pressure matched the feeling of being two yojanas underwater, or standing on a planet with stronger gravity. Royalty experienced it from birth. Their ribcages were accustomed to it; they could breathe. As the crown of Anga descended on his head, the burden lifted. He was royalty now. His crying stopped on its own. He took a deep, satisfying breath; other people were looking at him, but their gazes were weightless again.

Doubt jabbed his inflating self-image with a needle. Were these princes mocking him? Was the arena about to break into guffaws? Check Duryodhan's face, check the faces of the supposedly friendly Kauravas—Karna looked from face to face in suspicion and muted panic and fear—were they toying with him? Was he the butt of a prank right now? Did real-life princes play crown-the-pauper? Duryodhan's smile—admittedly tactical—and Arjuna's scowl both seemed genuine. Could Karna trust this abrupt coronation? Did he even know where Anga was? How could he on the spot be crowned king of a place he had never visited? Glory, ascendancy, power had always seemed rigged to Karna, entirely an accident of who you knew and where you were born, and now he knew it for a fact. Yet he felt no disenchantment, only the joy of shedding his insecurities. If you can get it, take it: there are no impostors. Everyone is faking it. Statecraft is stagecraft. Lionization starts with a lie.

'What do you want in return for this?' he asked. 'Set me any task, ask for anything I have.'

Duryodhan kept fanning him. 'Just your friendship. That's all.'

'It's yours.'

The last Sanskrit sloka wended its way to a rhythmical end. In the silence that followed, everyone heard a shuffle and tap, shuffle and tap, interspersed with grunts and wheezes. Karna must have recognized that mix of sounds because his shoulders slumped a little, his thrust-forward jaw retreated, and his eyes softened as he rose from the chair.

An old man with a cane had entered through the main arena gate, the same one Karna had blown wide open when he made his entrance. The old man's clothes were frumpled, and more than one tooth seemed to be missing.

'That's my boy,' muttered the man, almost to himself, 'there he is.' Seeing Karna approach, he waved his hand. 'Don't mind me, kiddo. I'll be over here. Is it true what I heard? The good folks here are making you a king?'

This poor, elderly man—who had lifted a baby from a wicker basket, years ago—relaxed into a roadside idler's squat. His joints crackled, and the crackles echoed.

Karna followed him down, on one knee. He longed for a shawl to hide this treasure of a man.

'Did you show off your tricks yet, son?'

'Dad . . .'

'Big day for you. So nice to see you finally get your due. You're better than all of them.'

The crowd had identified the old man. Bheem saw some citizens talking and nodding, and he jogged over to them for details. Bheem's belly-laugh hushed the crowd.

'A carriage-driver? Really?' Bheem pointed at the old man. 'You're a driver, are you?'

Karna's father nodded pleasantly. 'I am now! I used to pull a tonga on my bare feet for oh, twenty years. Really did a job on these knees. Saved up, bought a carriage and a nag. The nag, she does my running for me. I just tickle her along with the whip.'

Bheem glanced at the Pandavas, then turned back to Karna with a contemptuous smile. 'Sorry, your Majesty, "King Karna". Bloodlines are bloodlines. Why don't you go home with your father and learn the whip and reins? Maybe we can get you a job in the army. You can be my charioteer one day!'

Hastinapur's reaction to Bheem was mixed: half laughter, half indignation.

Duryodhan clapped his powerful hands twice to shush them all. 'He'll be a warrior! And his father will be chief of the charioteers! What do we know about where we came from? A river runs underground for who knows how long before it sees the sun for the first time. We call that spot the source, but is it *really*? Heroes are like that. *People* are like that. Right? Do I know who I was before I was born in the body of a Kuru prince? Do I know who *he* was in a past life? We all come from someplace else, and where that is, nobody remembers. Just look at him! You can bet he was royal in a past life. And he's royal in this one, too, because I just made him king of Anga, didn't I? So treat him like the king he is'—at this, Duryodhan turned to Arjuna—'and fight him as an equal.'

The arena got to its feet, and this time, it was all of one voice. Duryodhan was never so popular as at that moment. Did he believe what he had said? Maybe yes, maybe no; it felt good while he was saying it. Duryodhan never would have exalted this commoner's son if doing so hadn't humiliated a Pandava and made him a powerful ally. Floating on the applause, he joined his hands before the crowd, like an actor.

The fight never happened. Surya was late to the other side of the world, and his departure darkened the sky as fast as an eclipse. Servants hurried over with newly lit torches, but the Kauravas needed none because Karna's golden armour flamed against the night. Karna's father, the humble carriage-driver, felt himself rise on the shoulders of two Kauravas. Clustering around him, they called him by new titles, 'chief charioteer' and 'master of the horse'. Duryodhan put an arm around Karna and walked him out of the arena, basking in the crowd's chants of Karna's name and his own.

In a quieter corner of the stadium, Kunti praised her sons for their performances. Arjuna bowed to touch Kunti's feet in reverence. His shadow warped and flickered in the torchlight. She raised her hand to bless him, but she gazed over his bending figure—to the youth in golden armour leaving the arena, shining by his own light.

SARGA 15

IGNITION HER BEAUTY AND FIRE HER WOMB

The next morning, Drona reminded the princes of the condition he had set. 'It's time for your guru to collect his gift. Ekalayva gave me his thumb. You have to complete a task for me.'

Arjuna had been the one to agree to do it, but all the Pandavas and Kauravas gathered close. 'Tell us what it is,' said Arjuna. 'Even if you ask us to scale Mount Kailasa, we'll do it.'

'Nothing so dangerous as that. I want you to attack the kingdom of Panchala and bring me King Drupada, bound at the wrists and blindfolded. You will find me at sundown, day after tomorrow, in the hut where I lived before I came to the palace. Tell King Drupada nothing of who you are, who sent you or where you are taking him. Just force him to his knees in my hut, and I'll consider myself paid in full.'

The princes wondered what King Drupada had done to Drona, but it wasn't their place to glean gossip. The Pandavas turned their thoughts to strategy. Yudhishtir meditated how to coordinate with Duryodhan, since the Kauravas would accept only one of their own as commander. The objective would be to surprise the palace and capture the king. Seeing King Drupada headlocked in Bheem's cavernous armpit, Panchala's army would stand down. Nakula and Sahadev prepared medical kits. Arjuna raided the map room and guided Bheem, who heaved mounds of earth and rocks to create a scale map of Panchala's terrain.

Around dinnertime, they got a surprise of their own. Their hundred cousins, along with the new 'honorary Kaurava' Karna, had left seven hours earlier. Woollen tire-sleeves hushed their chariots through the palace's back gate. Duryodhan figured he was invincible with Karna beside him—why give the Pandavas even a twentieth share of the glory?

King Drupada's army puzzled over these hundred and one teenagers. Three regiments rounded up the over-hasty expedition, and all the showmanship of the prior afternoon evaporated. They were no match for experienced soldiers, and they hadn't even scouted the city's defences. King Drupada sent a letter to Hastinapur, asking what he should do with the blind king's hundred sons, who were clogging up his prison. Were they drunk or were they just reckless? In any case, Panchala wasn't a kingdom that would tolerate boys playing with weapons. Someone could have gotten hurt.

King Drupada's messenger met the Pandavas riding the other way. Bheem lifted the messenger, removed the letter and let the messenger drop. 'No need to distress Uncle and Aunty,' he told his brothers, ripping up the letter. 'But I know my first stop in Panchala.'

Duryodhan and all the Kauravas endured the humiliations both of prison and of prison-break. Their liberator was a smirking, chuckling Bheem. 'Look sharp, you little jailbirds! Grab some weapons and meet us at the palace! We're taking the kingdom!'

*

Drona, back in his slum shack after years, made no effort to tidy the place up to receive a royal guest. No point in sweeping a dirt floor. He left the fly-studded cobwebs as they were.

Arjuna and his brothers brought their guru his gift an hour early. The only sign they had penetrated a city, thrashed a royal bodyguard and scattered an army in pursuit was the dust of the road on their cheeks and arms. Arjuna's only injury was a sore thumb from firing so many arrows. The blindfolded, wrist-trussed king did not struggle when hands on his shoulders forced him to kneel.

Drona had told Arjuna what to ask the blindfolded Drupada. With the hooded eyelids and level smile of a yogi in bliss, Drona savoured his triumph.

'Where do you think you are? And who is it you bow before?' Arjuna demanded.

King Drupada brought his bound hands up in supplication. 'I watched you, you elegant warrior, with your four brothers-in-arms, and I knew right away that you were celestial beings. Only Gandharvas could move with such musical lethality. Like you were dancing with your weapons. You've got to be Chitraratha, and the big fellow must be your drummer, given how deft he was with the mace. Which tells me that you must have brought me to Indraloka—I can smell incense and tulsi and sandalwood . . . I must have done something wonderful in a past life to be kidnapped this way by heaven! Unless I've done something wrong in this life, which made Indra send you down to drag me here. Is this you, Indra? Is it you I'm bowing to? Take off my blindfold so I can see you once before you strike me with the *vajra*.'

Drona laughed bitterly and snatched off King Drupada's blindfold. 'So I'm Indra now, am I? When ten years ago, I was a poor priest not worth your time!'

'Drona!' Drupada tried to leap to his feet in indignation, but Arjuna touched his shoulder with a single finger, and the king stayed on his knees. 'You're behind this? You sent those Gandharvas to shred my bodyguards?'

'Those were princes of Hastinapur. I trained them. This one is my star student—introduce yourself.'

Arjuna untucked the sash that covered his face. 'Prince Arjuna, son of Pandu. I am sorry we had to meet this way, King Drupada.'

'Don't call this captive a king, Arjuna. He's kneeling before a mere schoolteacher in a moth-eaten dhoti, an old mantra-mumbler.' Drona rose to his feet and crossed his arms. 'No wonder my five princes bested you. You always *were* a klutz.'

'I just needed a little extra help back then.'

'You sure did, from *me*. Our teachers had you squatting in the corner every day, holding your earlobes, until I taught you the basics. "This is how you string a bow, Drupada." "This is how you stack your hands on a mace grip." But *you* were the rich prince, and I was the poor priest.'

'What's this, Drona? A Brahmin resenting differences in birth? Go to the Shudras in the fields and see if they shed a tear for you.'

'You swore you were my friend. You offered me half your kingdom.'

'We were kids.'

'Half your kingdom!'

'You should've said yes, if you're so materialistic.'

'Me? Materialistic? I only came to your fancy palace, all those years later, because I had a son, and I needed to feed him. Three cows. I asked for three cows.'

'And I gave them to you, didn't I?'

'Your doormen wouldn't let me through!'

'You were wearing rags. You stank. And not of incense, either.'

'Three cows. That's all.'

'I gave them to you.'

'And made me feel like a beggar.'

'That's what you were doing, Drona! You were begging!'

Arjuna had never seen his guru so frustrated and hurt. This wasn't anger; Arjuna had seen Drona's anger. Drona and Drupada had both reverted to boyhood, when they studied warcraft at the same school—Drona, no doubt, an Arjuna among those students, but realmless; Drupada, from the sound of it, a slow learner, but soon to inherit and rule.

'I wasn't begging,' Drona said, his chest heaving and his fists clenched. 'I was asking a friend for a favour. And you thought that was ridiculous. "How can a king and a pauper be friends?" Those were your exact words. Well, now look at you, Drupada. You've got nothing just like I had nothing. You're in a hovel now, not a palace. Are we friends again? Are we?'

Drupada looked down in shame—at his past behaviour or his present condition, Arjuna couldn't tell.

'I'm your enemy, aren't I, Drupada? Because I just won. Your kingdom made you proud, so I took your kingdom away. Still, I have some good news for you: you may see an enemy in me, but I see a friend in you. The same friend who offered me half his kingdom. So I'm going to take you up on that offer. I'm going to give you back half your kingdom. That will be South Panchala. North Panchala, where all the richest rice paddies are, that's going to have a different king in charge. My bloodline. King Asvatthama. He doesn't need your crown jewels. He was born with a gem in his head, the blessed, blessed boy. A king now! We might as well be friends again, Drupada. Because from now on, we're neighbours.'

*

Drupada accepted the terms and became King Drupada again. To the southern rump of his realm he slouched home. His maps ever after looked discoloured, blotched with leprosy, Drona's intolerable partition.

What could he do? Launch a war on 'King' Asvatthama? News of a border skirmish would get to Drona, then pass from Drona to that balletic bowman, Arjuna. What the dispossessed king needed was an Arjuna of his own. Why not Arjuna himself? A father-in-law demanded more allegiance than a guru, but the king of 'South Panchala' (grotesque country, like a walking waist and legs!) had no daughter to tempt him with. Even if Arjuna joined his family, the pupil would never condemn the guru, much less kill him. Drupada needed a son with Arjuna's prowess to cultivate like a poison tree.

The guru and the king had one thing in common: neither was willing to wait for karma to work. They wanted vengeance in *this* lifetime, so they could see and savour it. Everything begins with a vow, but King Drupada wanted to end things once and for all. So he had to opt for the one word-weapon more fearsome than a vow.

Sacrifice. A fire sanctified the centre of a mystical mandala. Words, rice, ghee, tulsi leaves, everything went into the fire. Fire had many more names than just Agni. Purifier, Godmouth, Bearer Away. Drupada purified his mind of everything but vengeance. He thought his vengeful thoughts and flung them, like so many grains of rice, into the burning mouth of Agni. The fire bore it away. Whatever burns enters a wormhole and crosses the cosmos. Whatever burns goes into the ear canals of the Gods and comes out through the birth canal of time, full grown.

Drupada's Brahmins warned him: *There will be no going back.* Drupada's Brahmins begged him: *Nobody's done this sacrifice in centuries—we get warned about it when we start our training.*

This specific sacrifice did an end run around biology. The Sanskrit overleaped nature. Nine months gestation, twenty years of training—Drupada would have been an old man before he got his own back. He needed Drona's assassin and Arjuna's temptress *now*. So he branded thousands of cows with the names of his chief Brahmins. As their financial worries eased, so did their scruples. They built the mandala. They started the fire. They spoke the Sanskrit in unfamiliar metres, unnatural inflections.

The square mandala measured twenty feet on each side. The fire itself roared ten feet high. Drupada and the Brahmins dripped with sweat as they chanted.

A silhouette, recognizably human, darkened that block of solid blaze. Out of the fire, not one hair singed, stepped a full-grown man in full-body armour. The metal on his body and his monstrous six-foot-tall bow, glowed orange. This man had the same stature and V-shaped torso as Arjuna—an Arjuna of his own.

'A son!' cried Drupada, his eyes big with bloodlust, his earlobes and beard dripping with sweat. His rocking, swaying Brahmins kept going. King Drupada dared not touch this son yet, fresh from the furnace. 'It's real,' he whispered incredulously. Some small part of Drupada had been sceptical the old Vedic rites could create life. 'It's *real*.'

That's what the Vedic fire was: A breach in reality, allowing imagination through. The Vedas were poetry. That's what opened the portal for Drupada's son, Drona's future assassin, Ekalavya's reincarnation: a prince of Panchala, soon to be named Dhristadyumna.

Drupada was still marvelling when another figure stepped out of the fire. She was wearing a saree made of coarse, ascetic cotton. As for the shape of her silhouette, there was no comparing the twin sin waves of her bust, waist and hips. No woman alive could match her curves, only shadow puppets and temple sculptures.

Her skin was the black of a black panther's pupils. Her hair was the blue of a blue lotus glimpsed by that panther at five past midnight. The fire still burned, but gone was any smell of smoke. Instead, everywhere, the breath of blue lotuses, as if the mandala were a cool pond littered with them. Her eyes flashed open and her lips parted in a smile. The whites of her eyes and her teeth shone white. Simply by glancing down at the Brahmins, she interrupted their recitation. While the men all joined their hands in awe, the woman tied her wavy, navy-blue curls behind her in a ponytail. Then she turned to the fire, cupped some in her black-palmed hand and sipped it.

Drupada knew right away what her name must be. The blackness of her skin demanded it: *Krishnaa*, the feminine form of a word for *black*, her beauty a visual synonym for that other black Goddess, Kali. Over time, Krishnaa would attract other names. Her father Drupada gave her a name that made sure everybody know whose daughter she was: *Draupadi*. Yet another name boasted of where she came from, Panchala, the kingdom that had hosted her incubating fire: *Panchali*.

SEQUENCE 6

THE ADVENTURES OF THE PANDAVAS

The Kauravas entrap the Pandavas and their mother inside a flammable house and set it alight. The Pandavas escape but realize their lives are in danger.

They go into hiding. Bheem, in the forest, meets a giantess named Hidimba who is just his size. She is a *rakshasa*, a monstrous and magical being, and Bheem's half-rakshasa son comes out lovably strange-looking. His name is Ghatotkach, and he and his human father love each other very much. Though Bheem leaves his son behind with his mother, Ghatotkach will rush to fight alongside his father in the war.

They encounter Vyasa, who guides them to a village. Bheem frees the village of a gluttonous predator. One thing leads to another: that village is on the route to Panchala, where the king is holding a contest for the hand of his daughter, Panchali.

Krishna, as always mysteriously connected to Panchali, is present for the contest. So is Balarama, Krishna's brother.

Arjuna beats the golden-armoured Karna for Panchali's hand—another incident in the growing rivalry between Arjuna and Karna, which matches the long-standing rivalry between Bheem and Duryodhan.

Characters Who Will Show Up Again:

GHATOTKACH, Bheem's beloved, magical son by a giant *rakshasi*.

BALARAMA, black-skinned Krishna's white-skinned brother. Though extremely strong and skilled, he will not fight in the war on either side because he is Duryodhan's teacher and has a soft spot for him.

SARGA 16

DEATHTRAP VACATION HOME

After the victory in Panchala, Yudhishtir did a circuit of Hastinapur's temples. There was nothing political about this. Genuinely believing the sermons and precepts, he genuinely wanted to give thanks. No city street, in those days, had seen a prince stroll by in a simple, undyed garment, or stop to buy an apple. Yudhishtir won hearts the moment he crunched down and chewed. Add to that how he waited in line with the hoi polloi for darshan, how he raised a namaste to a throng of pilgrims, how he stood on the temple steps and gave a short account of the conquest of Panchala—and in commoner's Prakrit, too, not princely Sanskrit . . . Within a week, he was the most popular public figure since his ancestor Bharata, founder of the line.

Duryodhan found his father during his yoga hour, doing a salutation to the sun he'd never seen.

'Yudhishtir is plotting in public,' stormed the blind king's eldest son, '*with* the public!' He listed Yudhishtir's offences, but the king only shrugged his enormous shoulders.

'Suyodhan,' he said (for he still called Duryodhan by his birth name), 'you must know by now, that's just your cousin's personality. He is always visiting temples.'

'Can't you see what's he going to do with this popularity? He's going to muscle me out of the succession. Cut off your bloodline.'

'If the people do really like him . . .'

'What? You can't let *people* decide who's in charge of them. Imagine what a disaster that would be. Whimsy would be king, and hysteria would be queen. They'd throw their ruler out every four years and elevate someone else. Whoever lied to them most prettily. Whoever put on a show of piety and Prakrit. You need to exile Yudhishtir.'

'On what grounds? And why?'

'So I can give out gifts and hold games and win my citizens back to the rightful heir.' Duryodhan felt no contradiction between these words and what he had said seconds before. His memory was agile like that. In the same way, Duryodhan had forgotten that he had ever tried to kill his cousin Bheem. His memory switched it to a prank— Bheem was soaking wet and stomping around, wasn't that funny? This was a talent Duryodhan was born with, and a real advantage. He could reshape any encounter into one in which he was innocent and the other fellow unreasonably aggressive; he could be honestly hypocritical. A malleable memory made for a malleable conscience. 'All I need is a year, Father. One year to capture their love.'

'What have the Pandavas done to deserve exile? I can't treat Pandu's boys unfairly like that.' The blind king paused. 'People would talk. Bhishma would reproach me, Suyodhan.'

'Bhishma's vow is to protect the throne of Hastinapur. That throne, for now, is yours. You could declare war on them, and he'd rage and sob, but he'd buckle his armour.'

'Vidura, though . . .'

'He's on your payroll. Where else can he go?'

Dhritarashtra's blind eyes seemed to be searching the floor. Satyavati, Amba and Ambalika had passed away years before, after retreating to the forest. Who else was around, from the old days, to chide him? 'What about Vyasa?' he whispered.

'Vyasa is a poet. He watches the drama, he doesn't script it.'

'Kunti. I couldn't do that to Kunti.'

'She can go with them. You don't have to make it a punishment. Exile them—*invite* them—to Varanavarta.'

'That's a nice place,' Dhritarashtra said, with a weak smile. 'I've heard nice things about it.'

'And so have they. They will love staying there.' Duryodhan patted his father's hand. 'I'll even arrange for their lodging.'

*

Varanavarta had the broadest avenues, the tallest doorframes the highest ceilings in all of Bharata. Or so some Kauravas told big-bodied Bheem.

A few others told pious Yudhishtir that the city had a temple every few blocks. It would take a year to ring a bell in each one! Nakula and Sahadev heard all about its hospitals. Varanavarta's surgeons cut flesh to drive screws into bones, like carpenters; they knew how to stop a heart and throw stitches in it. Arjuna got a description of its shooting ranges.

No Kaurava had chatted up a Pandava before. When the brothers got into bed that night, Bheem asked the question all five were thinking. 'Why have they been selling us this city all day?'

'If they invite us on a trip there,' Yudhishtir said bluntly, 'it's a trap, and we're not going.'

The Kauravas were too shrewd to do the asking. Next morning, when all the cousins sat in the royal assembly hall, Duryodhan touched his blind father's hand to remind him.

'Yudhishtir?' queried King Dhritarashtra airily. 'Where are you, my dear boy?'

'Here, Your Majesty.'

'Have you done any traveling since . . . since that holiday in Panchala?'

'I have stayed right here in Hastinapur, sir.'

'Going out among the people. Seeing the city.'

'That's right. Temples, mostly.'

'You must be tired of the same streets and the same people. Have you heard anything good about Varanavarta?'

Yudhisthir, recall, had taken a vow *never* to tell a lie. So the way his uncle's question was phrased, he had to answer: 'Yes, sir.' But he added, slowly, and just as truthfully: 'Things *so* good I had trouble believing them.'

'I would like you to visit the city. Stay there a while with your brothers and your mother. You'll enjoy it.'

Yudhishtir hadn't taken a vow never to talk back or express displeasure, but his pious nature wouldn't allow him to contradict his blind uncle. He joined his hands and bowed his head. 'As you wish, Uncle.'

'And by *a while*,' the blind king added, 'I mean a full year. You can leave by the end of the week.'

Vidura, looking grief-stricken, found Yudhishthir after the assembly. Kauravas flecked the palace like june bugs; he could speak freely nowhere. Here at least, among the milling ministers, he had covering noise. His speech was winding, but Yudhishtir followed enough to know a tangle was there to unwind.

'Mice always keep one tunnel in reserve,' said Vidura, 'in case the house gets . . . inhospitable.'

'Inhospitable *how*, Uncle Vidura?'

'What's the morsel, and what's the bait? The table is hinged. Two of the legs are solid wood and two are coiled springs.'

Yudhisthir nodded at this mousetrap of a riddle.

'In four things, mice can see their doom: the torch, the bane, the trap, the broom—safe travels, my boy, and safe return. But above all . . . a safe *stay*, once you get there.' Vidura clasped Yudhishtir's hand. The prince discovered a half-coin had been pressed into his palm. It was deliberately notched, cut with the igh Bheem had to tiptoe to touch them . . . Any bigger, and they would have to call it the Lac Palace.

Nakula and Sahadev had the keenest noses of the brothers, and after Purochan left, they tilted their chins up and sniffed. 'Brother,' said one twin, 'do you smell ghee?'

Ghee was the most commonly used fuel back then—but it was used for so many things, from cooking to religious rites, that a whiff meant nothing on its own.

'Not just ghee,' said the other twin, 'but dry grass and peanut oil.'

'And rotten eggs.'

'Or something insufferably sulfuric. Is it all one odour or many odours at once?'

'Hard to make out through the mask of shellac.' Was this the expected smell of a newly built house? A breeze came through the window and it whisked the clues away, unless their noses got used to the odour.

Still, the twins picked up that peculiar mix of smells every so often over the next few days. So did the other Pandavas, especially when the noon heat baked the slats and rafters.

Purochan visited them every day to show them the sights around Varanavarta. He was either their tour guide or their jailor.

One evening, after Purochan had dropped them off at the Lac House, the Pandavas heard a knock. Yudhishtir opened the door.

'The man who sent me is a friend to mice.'

The visitor took out a notched half-coin. Yudhishtir took out the half-coin Vidura had slipped him. The two halves fit perfectly, and the coin showed the smiling profile of King Pandu. The Pandavas gathered close. They loved these rare coins that bore their father's profile; their uncle had removed them from circulation years ago.

'If you will excuse the noise and mess,' said the visitor, 'I will get to work.'

Deathtrap Vacation Home

A whistle and two brisk claps, and a crew of three entered the Lac House, shovels tilted on their shoulders. They paced the main room, consulted in murmurs and nodded. The first shovel cracked the floor.

The Pandavas and Kunti went for a twilight walk in the forest. Bheem walked ahead, giant hands clasped behind him, head down. He was in a bad mood, and not just because of the interrupted dinner. He felt like doing bad things to bad men.

Back at the Lac House, Vidura's crew excavated an escape tunnel for whenever this wooden house, resin-primed by Duryodhan's design, went up in flames.

Bheem stopped and swivelled on his heel. To his family's surprise, he was smiling. 'That's a new house, right? Let's throw a housewarming party.'

*

Purochan was the only one Bheem wanted to burn alive. Did he ask Yudhishthir's permission? Big brother would counsel mercy, and Bheem didn't need ethics getting in the way of justice. Purochan's mule-cart, parked outside the Lac House the day of the party, held a flint blade and a checked slate: tools for starting a fire. The mule revealed them by pulling away a mouthful of hay.

'So tonight is the night, my friend,' Bheem muttered, patting the mule on the head. 'It was Duryodhan who sent him, wasn't it? Who else?'

Tonight made sense, from Purochan's perspective: Kunti and her sons would have full stomachs and a late night. Their sleep would be deep.

Palming the fire-starting tools, Bheem conceived his plan.

The party had a Bheem-sized smorgasbord, cooked by the man himself. Bheem, who ate more and more often than anyone else in the palace, had long ago started fixing his own midnight meals so the cooks could rest up for his breakfast. He had set his own pots boiling.

Purochan, who knew the Pandavas did not drink, had stocked the Lac House's pantry full of casks and wineskins. These he had charged to Duryodhan's account, and he helped himself regularly to the unused stash. Bheem knew this and set out all the drinks. 'It'll all be gone by midnight tonight,' he said loudly, for Purochan's benefit. 'Whoever wants to drink it, better drink up *now*.'

Rumours of liquor coaxed most of Varanavarta to the party. The Lac House, its doors open, hosted over a hundred ministers, physicians and common citizens, no one barred. Purochan started drinking early. Before sundown, he was drunk. Come nightfall, he was snoring, and the guests had to step over him.

Around this time, a Nishada woman and her five sons got word of the party. She brought her brood into the Lac House, and the six of them tramped about the rooms, calling to each other loudly at this or that find. They played with Arjuna's bow and arrows they tried on Sahadev's sash and Nakula's slippers and they paraded in all sorts of ill-fitting martial attire. Free liquor only loudened their barbaric brogue.

Yudhishtir signalled to Bheem to remove these insolent guests. Bheem was about to oblige when the drunk Nishada matriarch danced by with a cask in one hand and Kunti's comb in the other. She drew it through her leaf-littered gray hair. Bheem stayed his first, violent impulse and let her continue. Soon he rolled an entire keg into his own room and poured this garrulous family cup after cup. The disruption they caused went quiet. They, too, were asleep now, the same as Purochan. Bheem shut the door on them.

The Lac House had emptied of guests. Kunti closed the gate, and Bheem's four brothers turned back. Bheem pulled Purochan into the kitchen and waved his family indoors again. 'Tonight is the night!' he hissed, and pulled his mother and Yudhishtir to the escape tunnel's door.

'The night for what?'

'They're going to burn this house and us inside it. There's no time. Help her, Yudhisthir, or she'll break her hip. Mother, there's no time to explain, just go!'

Yudhishtir, his arm around Kunti, crouched and led her down the dark passageway, ribbed with teak beams. Nakula and Sahadev followed, and Bheem had already fetched Arjuna's bow and quiver—he knew Arjuna would have gone back to get them. He shouted at them to keep running, but the tunnel went dark as he slammed the hatch. Briskly he distributed the snoring Nishadas, each one to a room, the matriarch in Kunti's room, the fattest son in his own, and so on. Then he struck the flint and struck the flint and struck the—

Fire! Fire, everywhere: the deathtrap Lac House had been waiting impatiently for just this moment. All four walls and the ceiling flared all at once. Smoke-choked, blindfolded by the blaze, Bheem stumbled over furniture that ignited at his touch. A rafter slammed his shoulder, and he shrugged it aside as if a Kaurava had jumped him. On his hands and knees, he found his way to the escape hatch, swung it open, and dove.

Vidura's workmen had failed to account for Bheem's size. His broad shoulders dislodged the teak rafters as he crawled, wormed, grunted. The tunnel collapsed behind him and over him. The earth itself heated up because the first part of the tunnel ran under the Lac House. Bheem baked in an underground oven. Twisting and jerking, he broke through at last—into a night on fire.

The Lac House had gone up so spectacularly, it had set off a full-blown forest fire. Through the cracking trees, the leaping fires and the smoke, Bheem made out his family. Their silhouettes coughed, wandered and reached for each other. He could make out Kunti, for she was small, and she had Yudhishtir faithfully beside her. There was Arjuna, hugging his bow and quiver to his chest to keep them from the snatching flames. The twins had gotten separated and searched for each other more desperately than they searched for safety.

Eyes stinging with tears, Bheem roared at the forest fire and charged. One by one, he scooped his family members off the ground. A twin perched on either shoulder, Yudhishtir and Arjuna under either arm, Kunti clinging to his front like a seven-year-old daughter, Bheem trampled some flames under his feet and hurdled others outright, soaring over a burning log or flame-filled ravine. At last, he made it to an open field and a bridge across a river, and though Kunti and his brothers begged him to spare his back and legs, Bheem kept rampaging onward, like a wild elephant, until, amid the sparser trees on a hillside, he could look back and see the whole burning forest no bigger than a cookfire on a plain.

Bheem knelt to ease his mother and four brothers to the ground. The twins massaged his shoulders and Kunti, weeping, kissed his forehead. 'Get some sleep,' he whispered to the five people he loved most in the world. He kept watch for the rest of the night.

SARGA 17

BHEEM IN LOVE

Bheem stayed awake easily. Only his body felt the night. An Arctic sun lingered in his skull. He thought about the trajectory of his mother and brothers: from the luxury of the palace, to the luxury of the Lac House, to sleeping on the ground without a sheet.

Sahadev rose and sat next to him. 'Thank you for saving our lives. And thank you for making us "dead" in the process.'

'You know who burned to death in that house?'

'Six people: Kunti, the five Pandavas and Purochan, the man who built it. Very tragic.'

Bheem nodded. It was easy to think of the twins as identical, in keeping with their appearance, but Sahadev had a wisdom and tact that reminded Bheem less of Sahadev's twin and more of Vidura. 'No doubt our uncle the king and our hundred cousins will grieve our passing.'

'Our uncle more sincerely than our cousins. But it's not so bad for that mother and her five sons. Their ashes will be kept in a golden urn and poured into the Ganga, with all the rites.'

'How do you think they will be reborn?'

'As soldiers in the army of King Yudhishtir the First.'

'Does he know? Does our mother?'

'They were too far ahead of us in the tunnel to hear when I whispered my suspicion to Nakula. Arjuna, though, was right behind me.'

'What did he say?'

'That you were saving our lives by making it seem we had died. We slipped this mousetrap. We might not have slipped the next.'

Bheem stared forlornly at Kunti. 'How will I tell Ma? Yudhishtir will think I'm a murderer.'

'A Nishada woman and her five sons fell asleep in the Lac House. When the house burned, they burned. That is what I will tell him.'

'He took a vow to always tell the truth.'

'But not a vow to always hear it. Besides, I will be telling him the truth. Just with a detail or two left out.'

'It will be hard to travel under assumed identities if he insists on saying his real name.'

Sahadev smiled. 'He has more than one name. Ma calls him the son of Dharma sometimes. So he'll go by the name of Dharmaputra.'

'Go to sleep, Sahadev, and dream up a name for me.'

'Hanuman carried a mountain and jumped the sea to save someone he loved. You jumped the fire, carrying four loved ones to this mountain. We should call you Pavanaputra: Son of the Wind.'

Sahadev crawled to a spot on the ground next to his twin and soon was snoring. Bheem himself, calmed by Sahadev's wise and soothing words, might have fallen asleep, too, if a pretty predator hadn't come sniffing.

Springing to his feet, he found himself eye to eye with a woman. This was an unfamiliar thing of late for Bheem. Not since puberty had he made eye contact without gazing down.

'Why do you smell like smoke?' the woman asked.

'We escaped a fire.' Bheem cursed his breathy giddiness around this big-boned, Bheem-sized beauty. He had already spilled the secret of their flight from the Lac House! 'There was a forest fire back there. What are you doing out alone? It's dangerous in the forest at night.'

'Oh, this is when we hunt,' she said casually.

The nape of his neck went prickly and hot. 'Let's talk over here,' he said, leading her away from his sleeping family. He also wanted to get a good look at her by moonlight. 'What's your name?'

'Hidimba.' When his eyes searched hers, he stirred a flutter in her chest, not her hungry stomach. 'What's yours?'

Bheem saw tigress irises: amber, reflective, with vertical eye slits. 'No wonder you found our scent. You're a rakshasi.'

'Just my eyes,' she whimpered, hurt. 'I wasn't born with fangs or claws or anything. That would be my brother. Look at my hands. They're just like yours.'

'Your brother?'

'He sent me here to . . . He's the one who scented you.'

'To hunt us? To kill us and take us home to cook?'

'No. I would never cook you, I swear. We only eat raw meat.'

'Why didn't he come himself?'

'My brother is lazy. He says lionesses do most of the hunting. But I don't want to put you inside my belly, not there. I've never seen a handsomer man in my life. You never told me your name.'

'Bheem,' he whispered. The fleshly peril, the forbidden mate, that body that seemed built to bear his weight—he felt no fear, only desire. *That's your real name, idiot!* 'Bheemasena,' he said, trying to correct himself but instead giving his full name. *Might as well give her your parentage and title while you're at it.* A true rakshasi, she had made no secret of what she wanted. The forthrightness of her lust stoked his own. And he was just a hundred feet from his mother and brothers—what a shameful, delectable thing he was feeling!

Her right hand (and it was a human hand, fingernails painted black but curved, not pointed) gripped his shoulder, the muscular slant of his trapezius, his thick neck. Her throat gave an admiring purr. For over an hour, the well-matched pair talked quietly of their favourite seasons, favourite birds, favourite Hanuman stories, favourite childhood memories . . . Bheem steered her away from the topic of favourite foods. They had drifted very close indeed when a snarl came through the nearby trees.

'Hidimba? What are you doing?'

She sprang back and lowered her head. It was her brother. Bheem caught the smell of rotten meat on the rakshasa's breath, even from that distance.

'You should've had their bodies flayed and their meat in strips by now. I want to get the jerky drying in the sun starting at dawn, just before bedtime. Now go and get to work, woman.'

She looked at Bheem. Her hand ventured out to stroke his pinky.

'Listen, night-stalker,' growled Bheem. 'My mother and my brothers are sleeping over there. So keep your voice down. I don't want to have to rip out your throat.'

This was the crucial test: either Hidimba, on hearing him threaten her brother, would join her brother's assault on him, or she would let her brother and new boyfriend knock skulls like rams in springtime.

A rakshasa less lazy about hunting would have eviscerated Bheem in seconds. Bheem had the nickname 'Wolfbelly', but wolf-*clawed* he wasn't. Hidimba's brother had let his reflexes grow sluggish, his claws grow dull, his muscles grow pale with lacework fat. Bheem was as well-matched with the brother as he was with the sister. Inflicting and exiting headlocks like hands washing each other in the dark, Bheem and Hidimba's brother fought for half an hour. Hidimba looked on, unable to hope for either to win, unable to intervene. Bheem, still concerned about his family's sleep, dragged his adversary away by the hair, the ankle, the dislocated arm. When he twisted a wrist or bit some neck flab (in existential wrestling, no moves are disbarred), Bheem made sure to slap a hand over the rakshasa's mouth, risking the teeth to tamp the howl. He swallowed his own oomphs and arrghs, too, but Arjuna, the lightest sleeper, sat up at the thud and rustles of Bheem getting slammed into a peepal tree.

Arjuna drew his arrow and targeted Hidimba. 'I don't want to shoot a woman,' he said. 'Lie face down on the ground, claws retracted, and don't get up until I give you permission.'

'That's my brother,' she choked.

'That's my brother, too.'

'Bheem! Yes, I know!'

This puzzled Arjuna. He did not let his guard down around Hidimba, but he shouted past her. 'Bheem! Throw him clear so I can get a clean shot.'

'Arjuna, you're supposed to be asleep!'

'Let me kill that thing for you.'

'It's fine! I'm winning! Go back to sleep.'

Bheem's other brothers had gathered behind Arjuna. Kunti tiptoed over to pat the shoulder of a sobbing Hidimba.

'Everybody's up now, Bheem! Let me do this!'

Bheem, no longer constrained by the need to be quiet, roar-snarled at the rakshasa and charged anew. Now he had no scruples about tearing up a tree. The roots snapped their taut cables. Branches cracked and echoed as Bheem pounded his adversary flat, two extra smacks at the end, like a shoe in the hand making sure of the spider. When he tossed the tree aside he saw, in the brightening dawn, that this wasn't just Hidimba's brother but her beardless fraternal twin, their profiles almost identical; identical, too, their eyes: amber, with vertical eye slits, still reflecting the light, though their own lights had been snuffed.

*

Kunti had never imagined a son of hers marrying a rakshasi, and her eyebrows shot up when Hidimba asked her son's hand in marriage.

The hope on Bheem's face changed Kunti's mind instantly. She reminded herself how he had saved the line of Pandu twice in six hours, once from the forest fire's mouth, once from a rakshasa's. How ungrateful to refuse him anything! Hadn't he been born with a bigger appetite than any other prince, Pandava or Kaurava? What held for one appetite, held for the other. Hidimba's cheek reached Bheem's shoulder, just as Kunti's had once reached Pandu's. Best to let Bheem snatch joy from smoking ruins.

Kunti raised her hand, palm out, to bless them. The couple bent reverently to touch her feet.

'How do we find someone to officiate?' Bheem asked anxiously. 'We can hardly expect to find a Brahmin out here, unless Narada cruises by on a cloud.'

'Do you remember the story of Shakuntala? I told it to you long ago.'

'The mother of Bharata.'

'Right. She and King Dushyant had a Gandharva marriage ceremony.'

'I remember you saying they married for love. That's what we're doing, just like Gandharvas. But there still has to be a priest.'

'No, no priest needed. No ceremony, no dinner, no guests. Just the bride and groom.'

Hidimba smiled and lunged to touch Kunti's feet again. 'I know all about this sort of wedding ceremony!' Kunti flushed as Hidimba straightened and gave her, and then each of her new brothers-in-law, a smothering bosomy bear hug. Grabbing the wrist of her perplexed husband, she tugged him into the forest.

Entering the hut she had shared with her brother, the dwelling of the rakshasa he had just killed, Bheem grew uneasy. It wasn't just the slaughterhouse smell, no less off-putting than the fishmarket smell in Satyavati's hut. What about Hidimba's grief? She had just seen her brother bludgeoned to death with a tree, but here she was, sweeping her brother's clothes off the cot and pulling Bheem on to her.

'Is it too soon? It's only been an hour since . . .'

'My love,' she whispered, her eyes filling with tears, 'I didn't find you soon enough.'

Bheem stroked her cheek and realized in a flash: there was only one cot here . . . What lives these rakshasas lived! It was a curse to be born a rakshasa, but twice the curse to be born a rakshasa's daughter or niece or sister, always in his power in a one-room hut with one cot. Bheem kissed Hidimba's mouth so hard, he wiped away all her memories of ever being kissed before. The blood from their crushed lips mingled and, when she swallowed it, cleansed her. Every part he touched, he made virginal again. His body changed hers, an autumnal spring deflowering what he coaxed to blossom.

*

Kunti and her sons saw a patch of green forest shake on a distant mountain every half hour or so. That was where the two lovers slapped their hulking bodies together like wine-crazed elephants.

Conscientious even on his honeymoon, Bheem came back that evening and built his family a house. He was clearly in a hurry, but the work proved sturdy. Out of earshot of Kunti and Yudhishtir, his brothers teased him about the bruises on his neck, the parallel scratches on his back. 'Did you fight off a panther on the way over, Bheem? Or was it . . . a rakshasi?' He shook his head bashfully and said nothing. When the teak house withstood Bheem slamming its front door and jumping three times on its roof, he declared it ready—then rushed home to his napping bride.

Two weeks later, Bheem and Hidimba showed up with what looked like a five-year-old rakshasa boy. The child had pointy ears, copper-coloured lips and a totally hairless body, not even eyebrows. Only his thick limbs and neck and his enormous belly made him seem like he could be Bheem's son.

'Go on, boy! Touch your grandmother's feet!' Bheem beamed as his son did what his father had trained him to do. (That gesture of reverence wasn't known among rakshasas: three failed deer hunts, and they ate a grandparent rather than go hungry.)

Kunti blessed the boy, at once fascinated and repelled by him. 'What's his name?'

'I've named him Ghatotkach,' said Bheem proudly. 'It means *bald pot* because, well, look at his head, right? He's only three days old, and he's already walking!'

'He looks . . . a lot older than that, Bheem.'

'Doesn't he? That's one of the great things about rakshasa babies. They come out full grown. No messing around with diapers and such. Right, sweetheart?'

'That's right. And rakshasa mothers,' added Hidimba, 'conceive and deliver on the same day.'

Yudhishtir patted Ghatotkach on his bald head. The fat, wheat-coloured boy gave a throaty gurgle. His eyes squinnied with satisfaction. With a twitch of his pointy ears, he threw his arms around Yudhisthir's leg and hugged it so hard, the foot felt pins and needles.

If Bheem had gone back into the forest with his new wife and son, Kunti and the other Pandavas would have anguished over this development. Hidimba, they would have said, had hoodwinked big-hearted Bheem into adopting her son from a former relationship. But before they left, two things happened. First, Hidimba shared a dream she'd had immediately before she'd woken up from her afternoon nap and given birth. Indra, she said, or else some other God with rain-coloured eyes, had spoken a riddle: *No womb but it's a conduit, no love but by design. Your son will keep the Sun's son from incinerating mine.* None of the Pandavas could suss out the sense of these words. Kunti knew Karna's parentage and Arjuna's, and she feared their rivalry in the arena would one day redux on a battlefield somewhere. She gazed on Ghatotkach with adoration after that, knowing he was destined to save Arjuna in some way, and when she hurried off to cook up some sweets, she warned Bheem not to hog them, since they were for her grandson.

Just then, one more incident favoured Bheem's paternity. Little Ghatotkach got hold of a log. Like his father, the mace champion, he swung it with both hands and felled so many trees that Bheem used the wood to build an addition to the house. The new family of three stayed there whenever they visited Grandma's house—as Ghatotkach, who learned to speak at a week old, frequently nagged them to do.

Kunti and her sons lived this way in exile and secrecy for some time, and though they enjoyed no power or wealth, they were happy. Arjuna's bow kept them from going hungry, and the twins treated the occasional dysentery with herbs. Bheem, for his part, enjoyed domesticity off in the misty and Veda-unvisited hills.

One year after their wedding night, Hidimba told Bheem that she would raise their boy on her own. She released Bheem from every obligation. She would expect nothing from him when he returned to the royal life, as a man of his prowess surely would one day, save for a promise to call on Ghatotkach if ever he needed a bodyguard or a soldier. What had Bheem done to get put out of the house? Nothing at all. This, she consoled her sobbing husband, was the rakshasa way: all rakshasas ended their marriages at one year. It kept the memory sweet.

Bheem, his shoulders shaking, could not bear dwelling in that part of the forest anymore. Nor were the local deer and fruit trees numerous enough to satisfy his caloric needs. Yudhishtir led his family out into the wilderness again, not knowing where they would eat or where they would sleep.

   Luckily for them, they encountered a bedraggled mendicant in the forest. Because he knew where their story was going, he knew where they had to go. They recognized him right away, and even Kunti fell at his feet to get his blessing. It was Vyasa.

SARGA 18

WRESTLING ON A FULL STOMACH

Kunti knew best how to talk to him. 'Where have you been wandering, Vyasa?'

'In sunset declensions, conjugations of roebuck and doe.'

'And what have you been doing all this while?'

'Pounding my head against the ceiling of my speech. The roof of my mouth has been aching.'

'And have you broken through?'

'My own skull, yes, to find it a pomegranate full of teeth.'

The Pandavas marvelled at this strange dialogue between their elders. Was this how people spoke, back in ancient times? Only Grandfather Bhishma was older than Vyasa, but Bhishma, living in the palace and dealing with the world, had tracked his speech to each new generation. Or was it that Vyasa, spending his life in poetry, had reached a point where he could only speak in riddles, metaphors, images, oddities?

'Is where you're coming from, Vyasa, where we should go?'

'A unicycle of a village, teetering. A village with just One Wheel: Ekachakra.'

'Why just one wheel?'

'Because the other three were stolen. It is a sad, a grisly story, but you will find out, in time.'

'How do we get there?'

'By letting the toes of one foot leapfrog the heel of its rival.'

'Why should we go there, Vyasa?'

Vyasa gazed with pity at Kunti's princes, whose ragged clothes, though washed many times since the Lac House, were still lacklustre with ash. 'Because the villagers are kind to beggars.'

*

And so Vyasa brought it about that a queen and five princes of Hastinapur lived, for months, on alms. This was the education he wanted them to have, the misery he wanted them not to see, but to taste. No king who had torn a stranger's two-days-cold roti could berate a starving subject for not working hard enough, or turn away a holy rover as a freeloader, or hoard grain in a bad season. Yudhishtir, the eldest, learned the lesson best, since he was in charge of dividing all the day's takings in half, giving half to wolf-bellied Bheem, then dividing the other half in five shares.

A Brahmin family took them in, believing a family so poor and pious could only be one of their own. Because they were living with Brahmins, in the guise of Brahmins, they had a further constraint—which was that they couldn't eat meat. Bheem's belly, long accustomed to Hidimba's hot meals (he had taught her to roast meat on a fire before eating it), kept everyone up at night with its girthquake. *Ekachakra* meant One Wheel, but it could just as well have meant One Meal. Arjuna tried to sneak outside the village and hunt—he was lethal even with a slingshot—but mysteriously, all the game in his radius vanished. Even the sparrows and squirrels hid. He thought back to Vyasa's lilting phrase, 'conjugations of roebuck and doe'.

Had Vyasa arranged this ascetic diet? Because Arjuna and his brothers never concentrated so hard as they did during those vegetarian months. In that Brahmin's hovel, the Pandavas memorized entire Upanishads on the first try. Yudhishtir started catching errors of pronunciation in his Vedic recitations. The twins explained that their brains were getting more blood flow because their bodies had nothing but Sanskrit to digest. Arjuna's eyesight improved past its original perfection. He accessed the acuity of birds of prey. From then on, he decided, he would always go into battle on an empty stomach. If he ever lived as a Kshatriya again.

*

Kunti knew that Vyasa had sent them to Ekachakra for some reason. She kept searching for that reason, but no matter how alert and fast-thinking her hunger made her, she couldn't figure it out. Still, she had faith in her mysterious genius of a father-in-law. In Ekachakra, she and her sons were syllables in his sloka, precisely placed. When she relaxed her vigilance, the meaning became clear. For she overheard their host family talking through some kind of crisis. There were only two rooms in that modest house. Bheem had just gotten back from collecting alms so Kunti waved him close, and they eavesdropped together.

The husband—slight of build, stooped from a lifelong study of commentaries—consoled his sobbing wife. Their toddler was banging on the ground with a toy mace that Bheem had carved for him. The newborn slept.

'Baka made it clear that I didn't have enough meat on me,' said the husband. 'He has demanded both of us.'

'It's not fair. The price has always been one body.'

'How can we bargain with a demon? We knew our family's time was coming.'

'I know, my love. I just fooled myself into thinking we had more time.'

'This is how all people live—ignoring that they're going to die. The only difference is here in Ekachakra, we know *when*. We loved, we had kids, we read books, we went for walks . . . hasn't it been a good life?'

'It has. I know.'

'We shouldn't be greedy. We have been happier than most. Except for money, we've had everything.'

'But our babies . . .'

'How can we leave them orphans? Our guests are poor holy beggars, just like us. We can't leave them such a burden. Or anyone else. And in time, they, too, will be called up anyway. We are all food for Baka. Let's all die together, in the same stomach. I wish I'd managed to fatten myself in time. I'm sorry, my love.'

'It's not your fault. It's Baka's.'

'If only I'd been able to put on weight . . . There was just no food. And I'm a skinny person, sweetie. I wish I'd been enough to satisfy him.'

The toddler slammed his toy mace. 'I'm Vayuputra!' That was the name that Bheem had assumed. 'Death to Baka! Bam! Bam! Bam!'

The doomed family sob-giggled at his antics. Kunti and Bheem looked at each other in alarm. She did not knock; she simply opened the door with her son in tow. 'Tell us about this Baka,' she demanded. 'We are going to help.'

Their host told them the horrifying plight of that village. Every solstice, Ekachakra had to provide one villager, two buffaloes and a cart heaped with *subzi*, fresh naan and all sorts of other food—in buckets, not bowls. Who demanded this meal? The demon Baka, who claimed it was payment for 'protection', though the only threat he protected them from was himself. Baka, a night-stalking rakshasa (no relation to Hidimba), took a midnight census, peeking in on the sleeping villagers; the next morning, he provided a ten-year schedule of which family would feed him at which solstice. He didn't even send the carts back intact. Splinters from their smashing picked the gristle from his teeth. The skinny priest, who had begged radishes and rabbit-food his whole life, would have left Baka hungry. So the rakshasa had sent a note demanding the couple.

Kunti did not have to check with Bheem before offering to send him in the Brahmin's stead.

'I could not possibly surrender you to suffer what we've been scheduled to suffer. You're our guests! It's our karma, not yours, that drives us to this end.'

Bheem guffawed. 'My friend, you study this for a living, and you still think of karma like this? If a man takes a swing at you and you don't duck, your karma's why your jaw broke. If he takes a swing at you and you *do* duck, what happened to your karma? Turns out you weren't fated to have your jaw broken, after all. In fact, if you go ahead and take a swing at *him*, it turns out *he* was the one karmically predestined to spit blood and teeth on the ground. You see what I'm saying? You don't know your destiny until you fight back.'

The Brahmin got several years' worth of teaching from Bheem, who had learned his wisdom by growing up among the Kauravas. 'You would be going to your death. You realize that, right?'

Kunti ran her fingers fondly through Bheem's hair. 'This big, rowdy boy of mine? He'll be fine.'

Bheem had already left with the food cart and the buffaloes by the time the other Pandavas returned. Yudhisthir sat down in shock at his mother's decision to send Bheem to the slaughter. 'Think about how much weight he's lost! He's going into that fight unarmed and out of practice. You should have sent all five of us. You should have let Arjuna fetch his bow and quiver from the banyan tree where he stashed them. We're helpless without Bheem.'

The other brothers were less comfortable reproaching their mother, but they shared Yudhishtir's worries. Kunti talked him down with the voice that quelled his tantrums. Bheem, she repeated, would be fine.

Bheem, just then, was *better* than fine. The cart, sloshing with buckets of food, delighted his nose with spicy and buttery scents. As he clicked the buffaloes along, he peeked under lid after lid. At the spot where Baka traditionally ate his victims, a mandrake-stubby field littered with bones and vultures, Bheem parked the cart and started eating Baka's lunch. Naan after naan he folded tight and chewed, each one a single morsel. Buckets of dal glugged down his throat. His belches made the buffaloes skittish, so he untied them and patted their flanks and sent them on their way. Back to the feast!

Three rice balls crashed meteorically into his mouth just as Baka showed up and roared in his ear. 'That's my food!'

Bheem did not flinch or even glance at Baka. But he did raise his right buttock to let out a fart. It sputtered for several seconds, then took on a high-pitched lilt just as it ended.

'Where,' Baka boomed, 'are my buffaloes?'

Bheem calmly reached past Baka for a pitcher of ghee. 'Bottoms up . . .'

'That's it, you gluttonous thief! I'm going to eat *you!*'

Bheem raised his hand. 'Wait a second.'

Baka looked on, frozen with indignation. His mouth hung open to reveal his filed-sharp incisors.

Bheem pounded his belly to loosen things, then belched. 'I hadn't eaten a proper meal in weeks. The chicken was a little undercooked, but everything else was splendid. Thank you, Baka. Now bus my table! I want to take this cart home nice and clean.'

Baka roared again. Bheem turned, unimpressed, to the twisted, enormous mouth. He saw an unexpectedly well-dressed rakshasa, with combed hair, manicured claws and a dainty earring in his right ear. Like Hidimba's lazy brother, Baka had gotten out of practice—he had given up stalking prey in favour of periodic extortion. No doubt he victimized several villages on a rolling basis. Ekachakra was only one of his kitchens.

'What are you even doing here?' Baka anguished, banging his fist on the cart. 'You aren't the fellow on the schedule!'

'I'm his houseguest.'

'You've got a meaty pair of haunches on you, but you won't be enough, now that you've emptied my buckets.'

'Why not? It's all in my belly, isn't it?'

'It's not the same. I'll have to go eat your host and his wife as well, just to make it worth the trip.'

Bheem licked his fingers. 'You're not going to eat anything,' he said (lick, lick, lick), 'but on the upside, you'll never be hungry again. Because I'm going to kill you.'

Baka flared his fingernail claws and narrowed his light green feline eyes. 'And how do you plan to do that?'

'With this.' Bheem held up, between his thumb and forefinger, the toy mace he had carved for his host's three-year-old. Bheem had borrowed it before he left, for good luck, he said. Now he held it before Baka's flared nostrils, and the rakshasa stared at it with cross-eyed contempt. The toy mace swung down into Bheem's palm, and his fingers closed around the handle. The mace's onion-shaped head stuck out below his closed fist. Before Baka could slash, Bheem slammed the little mace-head on Baka's temple. The thin bone cracked, and rakshasa's brain started filling up with blood. This slowed his reactions, which were not as quick as Bheem's anyway. Leaping on to the cart, Bheem twisted Baka's arms so they popped from their sockets, the claws dangling useless at his sides. The toy mace burst Baka's eyeballs. Bheem's fist was fast and perfunctory, as though pounding two stamps flat. The bloody eye-jelly oozed over Baka's cheeks. His mouth opened, but he couldn't see where to bite. Quick punches with the mace knocked Baka's own filed incisors into his mouth. A tug of the rakshasa's topknot jerked the head back so Baka swallowed them. Now they worked their way agonizingly through his stomach, lacerating the bowels as they went. He might as well have swallowed hot nails. Baka writhed on the ground at Bheem's feet, clutching his belly as his own teeth ripped his bowels. That murderous belly inflated, fit to explode. Baka's navel, which had been a deep hole, popped out: a tiny, shiny dome. Bheem brought the mace's nub down on it—then stepped back as blood, bile and noxious bowel gas geysered a foot off the ground.

When Baka was done dying (it took over half an hour for his agonies to end), Bheem heaved the corpse on to the cart. Ekachakra cheered his return. Every family who had lost someone on a solstice spat on the corpse. A vote struck down the motion to cremate, so the corpse was wheeled back to the bone-strewn field and left there. That night the jackals and buzzards ate well.

*

Precisely placed, like syllables in a sloka: Ekachakra was also on the route between Panchala and the self-shifting sandcastle-shrines of the Ganges delta. Pilgrims from that part of Bharata, with the sacred sand still whitening their calves, passed through Ekachakra on their way to a major celebration. The Pandavas had been busy begging for alms and had not heard the news.

'It's the swayamvara of King Drupada's daughter,' said one of the travellers. 'You've heard of Panchali, haven't you? It's taken some time but her skin has finally cooled off from her birth fire, so she can be touched by a husband now. All the bachelor princes are headed there.'

'Is it a swayamvara where she garlands her favourite,' asked Yudhishtir, 'or is it one where there's a challenge?'

'I expect there will be a challenge,' said Kunti. 'When there are a dozen or so princes, a princess can get a good look. But with the numbers that will go to Panchali's swayamvara? The garland will wither in her hands before she can read all those eyes.'

'We want to go there,' said the pilgrims, 'because we have a suspicion she's a Goddess in disguise, and we've placed bets on which one. She came out smelling of blue lotuses, and who sits in a lotus but Saraswati?'

Another pilgrim shook his head. 'All the Goddesses sit in lotuses. If she came *out* of a fire, she must be the Goddess who went *into* one, that is, Sati. They say she is as black as black beryl, and Sati is just one more form of Kali.'

A third scoffed. 'Fools! All the Goddesses are the same Goddess. If she's an incarnation of one, she's an incarnation of all.'

Kunti sensed these fellows could debate theology for hours. A mother of grown men, Kunti thought of matchmaking. 'Would you mind,' she asked the travellers, 'if my sons and I travelled with you to Panchala? Goddess or not, Panchali's swayamvara will be worth attending. I do so love the scent of blue lotuses . . .'

SARGA 19

FOR THE LOVE OF A BLUE LOTUS

You could get swept up by a tornado and fight that tornado to the ground again. You could lift a mountain on your pinky finger to shelter your whole village against an enraged rain God, you could retrieve your ball from a pond and dance on the head of the snake demon who (like a curmudgeonly neighbour) refused to give it back. You could collect a few, no, a few dozen, no, a few thousand girlfriends in the forest of Vrindavan, you could even have a scandalous affair with a married woman, your love life so energetic the rumours said you literally *multiplied yourself* to dance with all the girls at the same time on the same night. You could stride into a city, throw its brawniest wrestlers over your shoulder, leap up into a stadium's royal box seat and dash your tyrannical uncle head first to the ground while the city cheered. You could set your imprisoned parents free, the mother who gave birth to half a dozen before you and saw them murdered, the father who smuggled you out to the countryside in a storm.

You could do *all* those things, Krishna knew, and the only thing people would whisper about was the blackness of your skin.

Since when did darkness learn how to blaze? The people wondered, too, about the black beauty whose swayamvara they had gathered for: Panchali was the only person with skin the same colour. Dhristadyumna, her fire-born fraternal twin, didn't have it. Krishna and Panchali—Krishna and Krish*naa*—had to be siblings, or else visitors from the same mystical continent, the same mystical planet. Everyone knew that Panchali called Krishna 'brother' whenever they met. She had recognized him the first time they met, their conversation already stocked with inside jokes. Messages passed between them with just a word or a grin. There was some backstory between them, but even though Krishna had a reputation as a tomcat, not even the nastiest gossips speculated they were anything but brother and sister.

Sure enough, Krishna attended her swayamvara, but he stood in the crowd as a spectator, not a candidate. Next to him stood a man of the same stature, with the same features, only as white as Krishna was dark. He had the bloodshot eyes of a heavy drinker and the arms of a prizefighter. This was Balarama. He had grown up in the same countryside as Krishna, the son of Rohini—Vasudeva's second wife, who had fled when Kamsa had jailed her husband and Devaki. Krishna, at the time he and Balarama became buddies as close as brothers, did not know he was Balarama's stepbrother. Village grandmothers speculated that Balarama was illegitimate. How could Vasudeva have fathered him while in jail, dozens of yojanas away? The boy discovered alcohol early, pondering his own birth. Years later, under Krishna's supervision, palace pandits correlated Devaki's miscarriage in Mathura with Rohini's delivery in exile, without any preceding sign, of a baby two months premature. Obviously, the royal commission concluded, the Gods had transplanted the fetus from Devaki's womb to Rohini's. Prematurity would explain Balarama's white skin, too: he was undercooked. Officially, Krishna and Balarama were brothers, both sons of Devaki and Vasudeva; Balarama had escaped Kamsa through a different womb. No one had dared challenge the story, at least not to either brother's face.

'Is that a statue under all that drapery, Krishna?'

'I doubt it, Balarama. I'm guessing that's the challenge.'

'There's Panchali's brother, Prince Dhristadyumna.'

'He's going to do the announcing, I think.'

'You know what the sky said when he was born? He's going to kill Guru Drona, the chief of weapons at Hastinapur.'

'That's why King Drupada built his fire sacrifice. To get revenge.'

'Does Drona know?'

'He does. He has even been training Dhristadyumna.'

'What? Why?' Balarama shook his head. 'To make friends with the young prince, I guess. To win his mercy.'

'I doubt it. Dhristadyumna has never made any secret of his birth prophecy. Drona knows the prophecy will play out eventually. He just doesn't want to be slain by someone with inferior training. There's no shame in being killed by a pupil one remove from Parashuram . . .'

Drona's future killer stepped to the centre of the open-air stadium, next to the mysteriously draped structure. In his right hand he held a bow as tall as himself—without a string.

'Princes of Bharata! Welcome to my sister's swayamvara! You are all so handsome, so well-dressed, so wealthy, so athletic that no woman could possibly choose among you. So my father the king has decreed that Panchala's precious princess will go to the sharpest shooter, the best bowman, the apex of archers.'

A tug of the drapery revealed the challenge: a flagpole emerging from a pool of water. At the top of the flagpole was a contraption.

'Five spokes up there, and at the end of each, a brass fish. In each brass fish, an eye made of black beryl. Their reflections chase each other in this pool of water. Princes! String this bow of Himalayan ironwood, shoot all five fish through their eyes by looking only at their reflections—and then come lower your head before the girl with the garland.'

The scent of blue lotuses came from either Panchali or the garland she held. Having emerged at the far end of the stadium, she took her seat beside King Drupada and gazed imperiously at the assembled Kshatriya royals. Not one of them could hold eye contact with her, not one of them could look away. Full of lust, full of rivalry, the crowd of Kshatriyas started to churn. Princes shoved princes, first to get a better look at her, then in retaliation, then in rage. Soon the brass fish weren't the only ones with black eyes.

Panchali's brother tried hard to maintain order among those approaching the bow. Volunteers went up with varying degrees of swagger and shuffle. Forget about gouging out a fisheye, they couldn't even get the ironwood bow to take the string. The bow had a mind of its own and seemed to thrash these princes and send them on their way. Pieces of armour and dislodged jewels littered the stadium floor, as well as ceremonial daggers that had never sunk in anything but the smithy's bucket and the showroom's sheath. Every prince who went back humiliated lashed out at someone who smirked at him, and the brutish Kshatriyas started scrapping again. When a prince made a particular fool of himself—face red, back thrown out, limping clear—Panchali and Krishna, across the stadium, winked at each other. The novelty of ongoing squabbles and trash-talking soon wore off.

Balarama yawned. Krishna nudged him. 'Do you see those beggarly-looking Brahmins over there?'

'I do, Krishna. Do you mean those five who are standing apart?'

'I think those are the Pandavas.'

'What? They died horribly a year back, didn't they? In a tragic fire.'

'Rumour has it they escaped. I believe it. Look: that hulking fellow stands two feet taller than the tallest prince here. The two to his left look like twins. The one to his right wears calluses on both thumbs that only ambidextrous archers earn.'

'And the one with the tilak?'

'He got up early to do his prayers this morning. You'll notice none of the other Brahmins did that.'

'So that would be Yudhishtir.'

'Exactly.'

'It's an interesting theory, Krishna. But why would they be here?'

'Karma.' Krishna grinned. 'Or Kama.'

'Even heroes like the Pandavas can't fight them both. But who's that prince approaching the bow, in the golden armour and earring?'

'Karna.'

Krishna watched Karna's powerful musculature bulge and ridge as he crushed the ironwood bow into more of a C shape. Krishna's gaze went level, cold. The chatty, convivial brother of moments before was gone. His eyes met Panchali's. An understanding passed between them. Panchali turned to one of her ladies-in-waiting and hid her lips with her hand.

The notch tantalized the string in Karna's hand. Just a hair's breadth, a smidgen more! All the other princes had forgotten their quarrels and watched in an awed hush. As Karna's core tensed, as he readied for one last, full-body contraction to string the bow, Panchali whispered her whisper. What did she say to distract Karna? *Oh, not this son of a driver—how is he even* here . . . No one heard for sure, and even the women in her retinue, much later, said she hadn't said a word. But Karna's head turned, and the bow scooted out of his control and slammed the dust. He stood holding the string, forlorn as a boy with a snapped kite. Flushed pink—with embarrassment, not exertion—he covered his face as he walked back to his seat.

The princes murmured and looked away. They did not dare challenge or mock Karna, since a challenge to Karna wouldn't stop at big words and little shoves. Their heads turned as one to the tatterdemalion saffron-clad pilgrims watching from the cheap seats. They scooted and tilted their knees as one of them—the same Brahmin that Krishna had suggested was Arjuna—made his way down to the stadium floor. He swung himself over the wall and, though the drop was twice his height, landed weightlessly on his bare feet.

'Just look at his gait,' said Krishna to his brother. 'Have you ever seen a priest walk like that to water his tulsi plants?'

'That's a panther after prey.'

They watched Arjuna walk around the bow with joined hands. That changed Balarama's mind.

'Awfully pious of him,' commented Krishna's brother. 'He may be a Brahmin after all.'

Krishna shook his head. 'Mastery reveres the tool. Haven't you heard a poet praise his language? If he strings it, we'll know for sure. That bow will never bow to some ghee-and-guavas *sutra*-student.'

The princes, Kshatriyas all, were in an uproar. So were the Brahmins themselves. The days of Parashuram were long gone. What was he thinking? This interloper, both groups worried, would humiliate them. The Brahmins saw Arjuna's rags and topknot and feared he wouldn't string it. The Kshatriyas, instinctively sensing a threat, feared he would.

What Karna almost accomplished deliberately, laboriously and in stages, Arjuna did in one movement, as if thinking about doing a thing were the enemy of doing it. He knelt and bowed again, a vision of humility, of total submission to his craft—as he fired towards the sky five arrows in succession. The disc with the fish clattered to the ground. Arjuna lifted it, turned it towards Panchali and King Drupada so they could verify his success, then tossed it indifferently at the mute, shocked princes.

Panchali laughed and, after a glance at grinning Krishna, descended the steps like sparkles down a fuse. Arjuna bowed a third time, this time to receive her garland. Her blue lotuses spread their petals wide at the touch of his skin, and at that surge of scent, the rioting started. Panchali took Arjuna by the hand and hurried him out of the stadium. Meanwhile, the princes tumbled, hooted and harrumphed their way to King Drupada.

Panchali's father was overjoyed at this outcome. Rumours had given him hope the Pandavas had survived. It seemed his advertisements for the swayamvara had found the Pandavas in hiding! Karna had given him a scare. After Arjuna's reported death, the 'King of Anga' had been discussed as the world's best archer. If Karna couldn't string the bow but that lean, muscular 'Brahmin' could—well, that young man was almost certainly Arjuna, and if not Arjuna, then some God in disguise.

The Kshatriya princes, though, wanted blood. The old king joined his hands and tried to speak, but he couldn't soothe their egos if they couldn't hear him. Drupada, they shouted, had rigged the challenge—that Brahmin was a plant, Panchali's groom had been decided beforehand—the event was just a ploy to bring revenue into Panchala, a hundred princes buying food and drink for their whole retinues—and the price-gouging on the mangoes, by the way, was atrocious! All of which was why the city deserved to be sacked.

Balarama kept their kinsmen, the Yadavas, back from the fracas. Krishna, meanwhile, kept an eye on the four men he suspected were Pandavas. The giant was talking and gesturing to the twins and Yudhishtir, who snuck out of the stadium. The giant—Bheem; there could be no doubt, now that he was standing up—took the steps three at a time and entered the fray, flinging princes aside by the nape of the neck. A two-pinky whistle called Arjuna back into the stadium, armed with the bow he had just strung, as well as a quiver of arrows he had filched from the stadium's guardhouse. Sprinting fleet-footed to Bheem's whistle, Arjuna revealed himself to be Arjuna.

Bheem escorted Drupada, and, on the way, he uprooted one of the decorative trees that gave shade to the spectators. This would serve as his mace. Drupada's son Dhristadyumna joined him. The teams had formed.

In the stadium, then, as if it were a sport and not a battle, the warriors took shots, drove down the field, guarded each other and racked up foul after bloody personal foul.

Karna was loading his bow when he heard a thunderclap. His bowstring had been shot through. The bow, straightened in his hand, still thrummed, and the thrum tickled the bones of his hand. To send an arrow through a bowstring at a hundred feet requires something more than precision. A taut bowstring stores the archer's strength. That strength gets paid out with each shot he fires. Cutting a bowstring wounds the archer at the source of his archery. The 'Brahmin' in the blue lotus garland had done this. The eye beside his bow, still shut, opened.

'I can string my bow again and exchange missiles with you,' boomed Karna. 'It's a matter of seconds for me.'

'Then do it.'

'I want to know who it is I'm fighting. Confess, stranger.'

'Every living thing has a self. Each self is divinity, disguised in a form.'

'Spare me the theology lesson. Who are you, really?'

'*Aham Brahmasmi*. I am Brahman.' Arjuna loaded his next arrow and pulled its fletch to his ear. 'Now string your bow and load your arrow. I'll wait.'

Karna ducked as a Bheem-batted princeling soared towards the fences. 'Brahmin or Brahman,' he said with a sceptical shake of his head, 'you're best left alone, on the off chance you're Indra, slumming it on this ball of mud. A trip well worth it, if so. You've won the most beautiful woman this planet has to offer. I did come close—but no matter. I'm not one of these rich kids; I'm used to not getting my way. Today's outcome doesn't hurt me one bit.'

The pain and disappointment in his eyes suggested otherwise. 'Congratulations.'

Karna tilted his bow on his shoulder and strolled through the fracas. On his way out of the stadium, he passed Panchali and the other princesses, who watched the battle anxiously from the gateway. Whatever she had whispered while he strung the bow, he forgot in that instant. An astronomer's smile at the transit of Venus, detached and delighted, passed over his face. He might have left with this fond memory of seeing her up close—but she glanced at him quickly, contemptuously, before turning back to admire her chosen hero. Karna hurried away, humiliated all over again. By the time he got to his chariot, his jaw was set, his eyes were narrow, his lips were pursed. Too hot for him, was she? Fit to be driven around, never ridden, by a driver's son? One day, Karna swore, one day . . . The driver's son drove his own chariot home, envisioning that proud woman sobbing, stripped naked, thrown to the ground. *One day*, swore Karna, *I'll make it happen. And I'll make her husband watch.*

SEQUENCE 7

A TENTATIVE DETENTE

Arjuna brings Panchali home—but an unwitting command of his mother's changes the marriage of one and one into an unorthodox marriage of five and one.

At an invitation to Hastinapur, they return there, cautiously. To reconcile the two sets of cousins, blind king Dhritarashtra offers to partition the kingdom. The only catch is that the Pandavas will get a densely forested, undeveloped, worthless region. Taking Krishna's advice, they accept the offer and build a city to rival Hastinapur: Indraprastha.

Narada, a wandering celestial sage (and notorious mischief-maker, frequently seeding discord and downfall, or showing up in time to advance a plot), visits Indraprastha. He urges the Pandavas to take a collective vow regarding how they will share Panchali. Arjuna transgresses that vow by accident and has to fulfil that vow by going into exile.

His adventures in exile see him fathering sons on a serpent-woman and a warrior-princess. He ends up meeting Krishna, who sets up a marriage between his half-sister and Arjuna. This is yet another way the two men are related, strengthening their bond.

Characters Who Will Show Up Again:

One new, minor character (Arjuna's son by the warrior-princess) will find his way to Kurukshetra to fight alongside his father, but in general, fewer and fewer characters get introduced from here on out. The main cast is set at this point.

SARGA 20

DIVIDING INFINITY BY FIVE

The poor Brahmins attending the swayamvara had to be quartered in the slums. They begged a roof from other beggars. A poor potter had put up Kunti and her sons during their stay in Panchala.

Clay flecked her simple, widow-white cotton. To help out her host, she arranged the pitchers in his shop. She was busy at this when Yudhishtir and the twins arrived to tell her Arjuna had won Panchali.

They looked happy, and they kept saying how happy they were for the couple, how happy Arjuna was, how happy his bride. Yudhishtir grew unexpectedly eloquent, describing Panchali. To Kunti's surprise, and then to her growing unease, the twins, too, jumped in with metaphors and similes, like three court poets trying to out-praise the same queen. Black lotuses, dreamless sleep, the hummingbird's pupil, Parvati, the bare shoulder of night—Kunti had never heard her sons speak this way of anything, much less a woman's appearance! The trance broke every so often and one of the three, abashed, would rush to say, 'Which is why our brother's so lucky!' or 'She'll make a wonderful sister-in-law!'

Kunti feared Panchali's beauty for that hour before Arjuna brought her home. Nervous, she tidied her host's hut while he poured and shaped in his adjoining workshop. After a while, she watched him at his work. As long as that potter's wheel kept turning, she thought, the five fingers of each hand could press together as one and shape the pot. The wheel of dharma worked the same way. Wet clay would spin to a misshapen mess, should a potter flare his fingers and try to grasp the clay, possess it . . . The curves of the clay could be cupped, touched, but never seized. The potter shaped the clay without clutching it all to himself. The clay was no less his for that. Did a pitcher, once purchased, cease to be the potter's? Possession could have the simultaneity of perspectives, the cyclicity of desire.

When Arjuna led Panchali into the potter's workshop—followed by Bheem, who stared at the blue highlights in Panchali's black hair—Kunti had gone inside, to the hut.

'Mother, Mother, we've come home with alms!' called Arjuna with a grin, as he used to after doing beggar's rounds in Ekachakra.

Kunti called back from inside the hut, as *she* always did—'Share equally, boys!'

Arjuna's brothers looked at one another. Kunti had caught them in mid-fantasy. They had all whisked Panchali off to the privacy of their own imaginations.

Panchali herself noticed none of this embarrassment as Kunti stepped out. The fire-born princess was too struck by these five heroes standing in priestly rags, among common clay pots, in this cramped space. What family, really, was she marrying into? In time, their identities would have to come out. Eight Vasus, eleven *Rudras* . . . she could not think of any class of deities that had only five.

'So these are your alms?' Kunti asked. 'What have I said? How will you share her?'

Words were not fungible back then, as they are now. Vows, curses, boons: add to that list, at the top of that list, a mother's command. Kunti couldn't unsay her words, and her sons could not falsify them.

Everything depended on Arjuna's reaction. If he had lashed out, as any man defending his future might (the fantasy *he'd* seen was marriage, not just lovemaking), no doubt things would have turned out differently. In time, Panchali's beauty would have embittered the other Pandavas; their eyes would have smarted with her; their own wives would have tasted like water after pineapple. Arjuna sensed the centrifugal force of her beauty. He brought her to Yudhishtir.

'It's supposed to be that we get married in order.'

'You won her, brother.'

'Eldest to youngest.'

'Bheem already married Hidimba. It's not a strict rule, Arjuna.'

The Pandavas found themselves inching away from Panchali, as they might have from a fire. The potter, focused on his art, kept the wheel turning.

'I want us to do what dharma says we should. You know dharma better than any of us.'

Yudhishtir sighed. 'There's no answer.'

'The dharma is what upholds,' said Kunti, gently, 'and what holds people *together*.'

Silence. The potter's wheel creaked rhythmically in the background. The pot rose between gentle hands, shapely, full and ready to be filled.

If she had not seen Arjuna first, marvelled Panchali, she might have fallen hard for any one of these brothers. Priests were never gallant—but gallant was the word that proposed itself. And why did they all look so familiar? Did she know them from a past life?

'There are kings,' said Kunti quietly, 'who have more than one wife. Prince Rama's father had three. Your own father, Pandu, had two. You yourselves, had you never left the palace and come of age like all the other princes, would have taken more than one wife. And hopefully you will, one day. Other men marry only once. There can be . . . different rules. But it's all dharma.'

Yudhishtir had not been given a command from Kunti, but he knew what she was advising, and so did Arjuna. 'Panchali is to other queens,' Arjuna said, giving permission with a slight nod of his head, 'as a king is to other men.'

'There can be different rules,' said Yudhishtir.

Pink rushed his cheeks and the Pandavas shifted uneasily. Bheem looked at the ground. Nakula cleared his throat, and Sahadev adjusted his tattered shawl.

As for Panchali, she had wandered over to where the potter was working, though she listened closely to everything. When she blew on the clay, her breath baked the clay on the wheel. It needed no kiln. The potter lifted his work from the wheel and handed it to her. It was her first wedding gift.

*

King Drupada sent a messenger to beckon the family to the palace. Cautious after the stadium skirmish, he wanted the marriage finalized with seven rounds of the fire. But first, he wanted to make sure these so-called Brahmins were really Kuru princes. Panchali's brother suggested a ruse.

Footmen escorted Panchali's future in-laws to a courtyard where palace cooks had set up a long buffet with dozens of stations. At the other end of the courtyard, Drupada set out very priestly gifts: palm-leaf sutras, silver cups, freshly potted tulsi plants, red powders, white threads to wear around the chest and small boxes full of saffron pips. Catnip to any Brahmin!

The Pandavas (hungry for centuries) strolled past the buffet stations. Bheem wasn't the only one with a plate in each hand. The five 'Brahmins' ignored the raw spinach leaves, boiled elephant yams, pickled ginger and turmeric bits . . . and instead grabbed slabs of smoked venison. Did they gravitate to the cucumber water or even the lemonade? No, they zeroed in on the rice wine.

Once they finished eating, they strolled about and ignored the priestly paraphernalia. Nakula noticed a pile of weapons in a corner of the courtyard, haphazardly tossed under a tarpaulin, behind a hedge of thornbushes. 'Brothers! Check *these* out!' Except for Arjuna, the Pandavas hadn't handled proper weapons in a long time. Indifferent to the thornbush scrapes, they took up these bows, maces, javelins and whips with smiles and shouts of delight. It sounded like they were meeting old friends again. Kunti wiped a tear from her cheek—how nice to see her boys well fed and playing with their toys again!

Drupada and his son had been watching all this from a hidden window. They entered the courtyard with wide smiles and wide arms. 'Welcome, Queen Kunti! Welcome, sons of Pandu!'

The Pandavas, holding at least two weapons each, did not keep up the disguise any longer. Yudhishtir came forward and joined his hands. With a glance at his brothers and a deep breath, he started explaining—first, who they were, and next, what they had decided in the potter's workshop.

The king had not expected this. His dream groom was Arjuna, and he thought he was getting Arjuna, not Arjuna and four brothers into the bargain. Powerful allies though all five would make, the king had no wish for Panchali to be the object of gossip. There was just no precedent for it, unless you bought the claim that royal women should have as many spouses as royal men, which was absurd. Why absurd? He couldn't say why, it just *was*. If Arjuna's brothers were so worried about Panchali's beauty causing discord, might he suggest a cold bath in the river? Had they really picked up no restraint in their years of impersonating Brahmins? As Guru Drona knew, King Drupada was not an easy man to cross. He grew angrier and angrier as he argued against the fivefold match. The Pandavas insulted him and his daughter even to suggest it.

Fortunately, the first wedding guest showed up just then: Vyasa.

Vyasa's speech was elliptical and clotted when he spoke at his ease, but paradoxically, when he spoke in metre, he was plainspoken, fresh, vigorous and, to a certain degree, rapid. He told Drupada a story in verse of a girl who had prayed Shiva for a husband. Five nights in a row she had prayed, and on the fifth night, Shiva had promised her five husbands in her next life. Panchali was that girl, and this was that life:

> So if you wish your realm to thrive,
> Marry her off to husbands five,
> For if you block Lord Shiva's boon,
> Mudslide and flood will find you soon,
> And neither one nor five will save
> The king and kingdom from their grave.

Vyasa's metrical warning bore all the intimidation of a voice from the sky. Drupada agreed, and scarcely believing his own words, he dictated a new wedding announcement.

Panchali never quite figured out whether her mother-in-law had known what she was doing when she gave that offhand order to share. Share a wife! Not even two brothers, that Panchali or anyone else had heard of, ever tried that, so how could five? Was there precedent in any shastra for it? Kunti told her, privately, that it was for the best. One son with so surpassingly beautiful a wife, the other daughters-in-law invisible, like stars come sunrise—the family's unity would have been done for.

Kunti's unapologetic, instant sense of the upside . . . it set Panchali wondering. Well before the wedding day, and in her mother-in-law's presence, Panchali laid out how she imagined the marriage. It would be not one marriage to five, but five marriages in rotation. Accordingly, she would be five wives, a faceted gem. She would wear a different ring with a different gem to match each brother: Yudhishtir the topaz, Bheem the sapphire, Arjuna the diamond, Nakula the garnet, Sahadev the spinel. To each she would show a different feature of her personality, too. Yudhishtir would converse with a reader of parables and homilies. Personal-record deadlifts would find applause from Bheem's Panchali. Arjuna's version would dance on a terrace with him. Nakula would have someone to taste-test his latest aphrodisiac or entheogen. Horse-taming Sahadev would go riding with his Panchali, and she expected to be taught to leap fences and logs. In the morning, she would soap and rinse yesterday's marriage off her, arriving at today's as clean as fire.

Over the course of a week, Panchali got married to each of the five brothers, from eldest to youngest.

The Pandavas would not know if they had done a dharmic thing or not until much later, when Panchali started giving birth to son after son. Which son was which father's? Not only was that clear at birth, but her sons mirrored the Pandavas' own birth order. Pious Yudhishtir's son came out first, with a pink-stained tilak on his forehead. A chakra birthmark, exact as a tattoo, singled him out as kingly. Next came Bheem's son, a telltale twelve pounds at delivery. He drained both breasts completely at every feeding; a wet nurse rushed over to give him dessert. Arjuna's son came out with a callused left thumb. The identical twins differed only in where their moles were. Nakula's son matched Nakula's constellation, Sahadev's matched Sahadev's.

These signs made it clear that their marriages, though at odds with custom, kept with nature. Panchali didn't marry five men at once; she married once, five times. On her second wedding night, Bheem was astonished to find her a virgin; he imagined his size must have made her bleed a second time. Arjuna puzzled over the same mystery, though, and by the fifth night, Sahadev wondered whether his brothers had kept her intact until she got to him. The youngest (Nakula had beaten him by a few seconds through the bony gate), Sahadev was also the wisest Pandava. With the cool voice of a physician, he asked Panchali frankly about her prior nights. Diagnosis: she had sealed back up by morning. Each husband had been her first.

At the end of that week of weddings, the Pandavas took a day to sleep off the dinners and dancing. Where should they go now? They did not want to live with their father-in-law in Panchala, but they had no palace where they could take their bride. Their survival of the Lac House fire was known throughout Bharata now. The news travelled five times as fast because it rode the scandal of Panchali's five weddings. Was it safe to stay in Panchala? The Kauravas had invaded it once before and knew the terrain now. Was it safe to travel the roads, stay in the forest, retreat to the mountains? Should they just brazen it out and go back to Hastinapur?

While they were still debating, Hastinapur came to them. Their gentle uncle Vidura arrived at the head of a small caravan of carriages and packmules bearing gifts—from Bhishma, from their hundred cousins, from the blind king: peace offerings, wedding gifts, gifts to lure them back to Hastinapur. Or, as Vidura put it: back home.

SARGA 21

PARTITIONS

'It's a new low point,' said Bheem, 'when we can't let our own uncle sit with us in council.'

The five Pandavas sat cross-legged and leaning forward, neglecting the cushions behind them. Krishna, Balarama and King Drupada sat with them—but not Vidura.

'Every council you have when it comes to the Kauravas,' said Krishna, 'might as well be a council of war.'

The two Yadava chiefs, Krishna and Balarama, had joined the Pandavas a few days earlier. Krishna had always been their cousin, Kunti's brother's son, but a slightly distant cousin. The tumultuous politics of Mathura and Dwaraka kept his visits to Hastinapur rare. Now, overnight, he had become their closest advisor—since, even more than Dhristadyumna, Krishna had become their brother-in-law. Krishna alone called Panchali by her earliest name, Krishnaa, and the two impossibly dark-skinned spirit-siblings looked like the same person, seated beside a gender-flipping mirror. Once Panchali stuck Krishna's favorite peacock feather in her own hair. Arjuna (distracted by shelling pistachios) chatted with Krishna for several minutes before he noticed

Krishna was really Krishnaa. It felt natural to include Krishna and Balarama in this tough debate.

'A council of war,' echoed Yudhishtir. 'We can't escape this confrontation any longer. Do you think there is another trap waiting for us? Like the Lac House?'

'Maybe it is best if Panchali stays here, Krishna,' said the new bride's father. 'Just until it is safe.'

'It may well be safe. It's a good sign the Kauravas haven't invaded.'

'You think those hooligans will invade my kingdom again?'

'Let them,' muttered Bheem. 'They couldn't take Panchala without us last time. How will they do it this time, with the five of us defending it?'

'I'm guessing Duryodhan and Karna advocated war,' said Krishna. 'A lightning strike, while you were all still celebrating your weddings. That is their nature. Remember, you were mourned as dead by all of Bharata. They thought they had won.'

'And Dhritarashtra said no?'

'The king probably went back and forth. He indulges his sons. I imagine Vidura and Grandfather Bhishma convinced him not to authorize a strike.'

'And to welcome us back instead? To do what, exactly?' Arjuna shook his head. 'To live in the palace with a hundred Kauravas?'

'And with a beauty like my daughter in tow . . .' Drupada bit his lip. 'A hundred men ogling her every time she steps into the sun! It's a thought to shudder at.'

'I think you should visit the palace, but don't unload these carriages and mules that Vidura has brought. Stride in as paupers, and stride out with a kingdom of your own. What do you say, Yudhishthir?'

'Krishna, how will I do that?'

'By asking.'

'And if our uncle gives in and partitions his kingdom,' Arjuna said, cracking his knuckles, 'but Duryodhan and Karna decide they don't like it? Do we walk in fully armed?'

'Not one Kaurava will dare draw a sword,' said Krishna. 'Not with guests there to witness everything.'

'What guests?'

'Guests you can count on to defend you if the Kauravas get feisty.' Krishna glanced at Balarama—or rather at Balarama's giant shoulders, as round and white as skulls. 'Us.'

*

Five revenants re-entered Hastinapur after a long exile. The city felt its tears had brought the Pandavas back to life. Many citizens had attended a lighting of five symbolic pyres in a barren field outside the city limits. The blind king had permitted it—but sent spies to listen in. Over the next months, Hastinapur had resigned itself to the prospect of a King Duryodhan. Maybe his would mature into a temperament as steady as Yudhishtir's had been.

But here was Yudhishtir himself, alive and waving from a horse! And all his brothers, and the famous Princess Panchali! No one thought it odd or adharmic that she was the wife of all five. If anyone made a comment or joke, angry old matrons swarmed him with insults and impassioned defences of the Pandavas' decision. The gossips themselves quenched the gossip! Seeing the Pandavas again pleased the hearts of every parent who had ever lost a son. If only their own sons could show up years after the accident or sickness, happily married, on white horses! Here was more consolation: Yudhishtir might well be their king after all. Maybe if they danced hard enough in front of their five resurrected hopes, the palace would get the message. So Hastinapur danced and spread marigolds under the horses' hooves. The Pandavas might have been returning from a military triumph. Some of the songs the citizens sang were ballads of welcome. Other songs, fearlessly belted out, mocked the Kauravas. One dated back to the time Hastinapur got the news about the Lac House:

Why did you burn our sandalwood?
Five bars, they cost so dear.
You could've asked us, Agni—
There's a hundred logs right here . . .

The Pandavas were brought to a newly built reception hall and left there for what felt like an hour. Kunti wanted to show Panchali the rest of the palace, but Yudhishtir asked them both to stay back. He did not want Panchali walking among a hundred pairs of Kaurava eyes. Krishna and Balarama waited with them, too. No one spoke. In the silence, a strange metallic hammering started up. The twins murmured to each other how the palace must be getting renovations.

Eventually, a messenger came to fetch Krishna. The Pandavas stood up in alarm, but Krishna, with his dancer's gait winked reassuringly on his way out.

Grandfather Bhishma, chest still muscular beneath his rivering white beard, waited in a hallway. The hammering was louder there. Krishna hurried to touch his feet in reverence. When he rose, he found the ancient Kuru had joined his palms as though in prayer. Bhishma's eyes seemed to say *I know you*. Lovingly, Krishna drew Bhishma's hands apart.

'There is only one reason you've come,' whispered Bhishma. 'War is on its way.'

'Not necessarily,' shrugged Krishna. 'And if it is, I will not fight it for them. I am here to give them a fighting chance.'

'I've done my best to avert a clash between these cousins. Vidura has worked with me. We've pled until our voices went hoarse, as you can hear. Even today, after the Pandavas arrived, the argument started again. Do you hear that hammering? Metal on metal. That's . . . Vidura and I have prevailed on Duryodhan's father. I need you to make sure the Pandavas will take the offer the king makes them. People will be watching, listening. He must not lose face. I want you to find out if they will accept.'

'What's the offer?'

'He will partition the realm. Half the kingdom goes to the Pandavas.'

Krishna was too shrewd to rejoice just yet. 'Which half?'

'The land west of the Yamuna.'

'So, the Khandava Forest.'

Bhishma nodded and bit his lip, waiting for Krishna's reaction.

'A canopy so thick it lets no sun through.' Krishna's voice had gone harsh and grim. 'Forty-nine species of snake, frogs that sweat venom, tattooed tribes that speak no Sanskrit, ornery langurs that bare their teeth and hiss, grinning crocodiles, mosquitoes the size of moths, moths the size of sparrows. No cities, no villages, no roads and the whole place turns to mud and mist every monsoon. Not the kind of place Panchali imagined she'd be starting out her married life.'

'It was all I could negotiate, Krishna. If I were king . . .' He could not finish the sentence. The alternative memories of King Devavrat the First crowded his mind like an orphanage of unborn children.

It pained Krishna to see Bhishma humbled like this, and he regretted his cutting words about the Khandava Forest. He put some cheer into his voice and said, 'That's very generous of King Dhritarashtra. He didn't have to give the Pandavas anything, after all. With one half divided among a hundred sons, and the other half among five? Pandu would be grateful to you. He would embrace you right now.'

Bhishma smiled. 'You think so, Krishna? You think the Pandavas will take the offer? They'll think it's fair?'

'I can ask them.'

'If you tell them to take it, they will.'

'I'm just one voice,' said Krishna humbly, though he suspected the Pandavas, especially Arjuna, treasured his advice more than reason, conscience, instinct. 'But tell me, Grandfather Bhishma, what's that insufferable hammering?'

'If I can please the Pandavas, that will redeem this afternoon. Vidura and I have displeased the Kauravas. One in particular . . .'

To answer Krishna's question, Bhishma walked Krishna to a small courtyard in the palace's south wing. A giant bronze statue of a man stood at the centre of it, nailed to a granite plinth. This statue stood at exactly Bheem's height. Its shoulders were as wide as Bheem's, and the face had a wide-open mouth. *Clang! Clang! Clang!* Prince Duryodhan, shirt off and sweating venom, the flare of his back shining, pounded the statue with a mace. Bronze Bheem's mouth stayed wide open through the onslaught. Grandfather Bhishma thought it a frozen cry of pain; Krishna, who knew Bheem well by now, thought it expressed a wish to be fed. To frenzied Prince Duryodhan, that mouth meant something else: mocking, triumphant laughter.

*

The Pandavas need stonemasons! And woodcutters and carpenters and—citizens!

The call went out, and the call was answered. If not Yudhishtir's subjects in the city, why not Yudhishtir's subjects in the forest? It need not be a forest for long, if they all got to work. They could rough out where the roads would go by walking in their thousands, singing three abreast. Hastinapur filled with chatter.

'Did you hear? The Pandavas have their own kingdom now, and it's just across the Yamuna.'

'Sure, it's a forest *now*, but that just means cheap firewood, come winter.'

'Imagine the city they'll build! All the avenues broad and on a grid, orderly, clean, airy, unlike this chockablock layer-cake ruckus we're trapped in now.'

'Go west! There's a whole new kingdom with a whole new king there, Yudhishtir, who was never dead.'

'Will it be safe?'

'Between Bheem's mace and Arjuna's bow, how could it get any safer?'

'Yudhishtir has declared the hospital will go up before the palace—the twins have put out a call for doctors and nurses to relocate.'

'Do you really want to be here, in Hastinapur, when the blind king dies, and the bully takes over?'

'They say he plans to call himself King Suyodhan the First, but we know the name he's earned for himself. This old chariot Hastinapur is only going to judder for so long, with that Bad Axle between its wheels.'

'Did you hear? They're going to call their capital Indraprastha. Isn't that a beautiful name, honouring the sky?'

'Free and everlasting, big sky country. Go west!'

'All the houses are going to be white to match the clouds. Canals of cool water and lotus ponds will give it the requisite blue.'

'No doubt the sewers will drain better than the ones here, since Hastinapur's date back to the reign of King Shantanu.'

'To the west! There's nothing for us here but Kauravas and cockroaches.'

'Indraprastha will have open-air theatres, gates as huge as Garuda's wings, gardens of plum trees and mango trees and neem trees, and peacocks will be to that city what stray dogs are to this one.'

'The forest around it will keep out invaders and plagues and time and death, and Yudhishtir will raise another Yudhisthir to rule us, and that one yet another, on and on.'

'What are we doing here, friends? The exodus has already started.'

'Someone has to pace out the gardens and dig.'

'There will be work enough for all of us. There will be money and kindness and immortality enough for all of us.'

'The world is beginning again, this late, on the eve of the Kali Yuga, and Indraprastha is where.'

'To the west!'

'To the west!'

'The west!'

*

The city rose to the west just as cumulus-cloudlike as Hastinapur's well-wishers dreamed it would—only faster, given the thousands of energetic people who migrated there. Talent moved in from all the surrounding kingdoms, not just Hastinapur. Krishna and Balarama did not leave the Pandavas until they saw the city stocked and stockaded. Indraprastha was ready to thrive.

And so the Pandavas might have lived, tense neighbours of Hastinapur, sharing a border like a bloodline. But it wasn't to be.

Among the many guests who visited the newly built city, one was the mischief-making, well-travelled sage Narada. Narada always looked a little pink from the solar winds in space. Stories of other civilizations, on the far side of oceans that went on (he claimed) for thousands of yojanas, stories of other galaxies, stories of Patala where souls cried out to get their stories heard, buried to their necks in makara excrement . . . Narada was a storyteller of a different kind than Vyasa or Valmiki. While the two poets told true stories of this world, Narada's stories were always set on other worlds, and no one could tell if he were lying. After all, he had been there, hadn't he?

One other feature of a Narada story: they often had a moral or a point to prove, which made it harder to believe he wasn't making them up. When he met Panchali, he chatted with her about the planet Shukra, Venus, whose fiery veldt (he assured her) held cities of women who looked like her sisters. For the women of Shukra, marrying seven or eight husbands was a common custom. King Drupada's sacrificial fire, no doubt, had opened up a portal between that world and this one. She left her memory there but brought her char-black beauty and her polyandry with her. The hodgepodge of gases on Shukra—nitrogenous patchouli, and the sharp incense-sticks they made of fireproof trees—smelled exactly like the earth's blue lotus, which explained her natural perfume. Panchali, out of politeness, kept her scepticism to herself. But one raised eyebrow revealed her true opinion—and made her look even more beautiful to Narada.

After that chat with Panchali, he made sure to seek out a separate meeting with her five husbands.

'You boys are headed for trouble,' he said, shaking his head, 'if you don't make an arrangement.'

'What do you mean, Narada?'

'I could tell you stories of brothers who fell out over celestial women. I've collected such cautionary tales on every planet from here to Betelgeuse. Usually stories of two brothers. And the lady detonating the discord is a mere apsara, usually—not the black blaze of a Shukran beauty! It's a miracle you five have lasted this long.'

Yudhishtir cleared his throat uneasily. 'We are not rivals,' he said. 'We each take a day to serve as her husband. We rotate. Even if I'm sick or out on a hunting expedition, on my day, she's mine and no one else's.'

'Our system works well, Narada,' Sahadev insisted. Nakula nodded.

'For *now* it does, my dear boy! Have you ever walked in on one of your brothers . . . *with* her?'

The Pandavas flushed and shook their heads. Yudhishtir knew Narada's habit of needling people; he bristled a little but kept his composure around the sage. 'Never, and we hope that never happens. It's a sizeable palace here at Indraprastha, as you can see. We have our own rooms.'

'Oh, but the moment it happens, something deep and ape-like will take over you. That's always how it happens in these stories of brothers sharing a magical woman. It goes along fine until one brother *sees* the other—*sees*, you understand—and a jealous rage overtakes him.'

'We are self-restrained men. We do yoga.'

'As if your yoga will help you in the hour before dawn, when you've just woken up, and your thoughts get out of control! Your rage at that obscene sight will lead to violence months later, maybe years later. The only way to avoid a disaster is to separate for twelve years.'

'It will never come up.'

'But if it does,' said Narada, 'the offending brother, the one who *saw*, ought to go into exile for twelve years. Just to be safe.'

'It won't happen,' said Yudhishtir. 'But if it does, sure, we'll have a cooling-off period.'

'Make it a vow,' said Narada, smiling. 'Make it official.'

'Twelve years of exile?'

'You said it was never going to happen, so you shouldn't mind making it a vow. Or were you . . . lying?'

Yudhishtir could not risk falsifying his own words, so he enjoined all five Pandavas to make that vow. Yet he had misgivings. Shouldn't the vow have made an exception for an accidental glimpse? Too late now. The one who saw would have the ascetic isolation he needed to scrub his memory of what he had seen; the vow was designed, shrewdly, not to punish the intruder but to the nape of the neck, seventeen times. The overkill did not make him feel any better.

The rescued palm-leaf pages of Vyasa's poem had scattered from the rakshasa's hands. Arjuna had to gather them, and he read, almost without intending to, a passage about himself in twelve years of exile from his brothers and wife. In the poem, he stepped into the Ganga and got swept away by an enormous serpent. Arjuna realized Vyasa had been writing the epic of the Kuru line. Given how rapidly he composed, he had already written past the present. His storytelling had lapped time, which was racetrack-circular. Horrific though this foreknowledge was, it comforted him to know that, in Vyasa's version as in reality, he would honour his vow. Arjuna read no more of the poem. The Brahmin to whom he returned the pages was never seen again.

Yudhishtir could not persuade Arjuna to discount the vow and stay back. Arjuna's gaze, his brother argued, had focused only on Panchali, and had never actually seen Yudhishtir, who had been lying on his back—so Arjuna hadn't, technically, seen him *with* her—but Arjuna dared not risk relying on sophistry.

The Gods were watching, after all. They had seen Arjuna enter that weapons room. And they saw him now, strapping on his sandals and shouldering his quiver, setting off, honouring his vow. Arjuna turned his steps to the distant Ganga. He had an appointment with a serpent.

SARGA 22

ARJUNA'S ADVENTURES IN EXILE

The rational thing would have been to avoid rivers entirely. To bathe in lakes or under waterfalls. If, after a daylong sweaty trek, he found no other option, he might trade the dust of the road for the murk of a pond. Or he could just go weeks without bathing at all—didn't ascetics do that all the time? Shiva, plastered in ash, hadn't soaped and rinsed since he entered samadhi. It would have been easy to manage, now that Vyasa's poem had given him warning of the danger. Arjuna did the heroic thing instead. He sought out his fate with fascination and love. He fulfilled the verse like a vow.

Ankle-deep in the cool Ganga, naked and alone, his pulse willed down to forty beats a minute, Arjuna waited. No heron was ever so patient. Hours passed. Sunset, sunrise. He waited.

Close to noon on the second day, something dark ribboned in from the left. There it was.

An almost imperceptible crouch, a flare of his fingers. *It's not your fate anymore*, he told himself, *if you bring it about. It's your choice. However things turn out, you took your future back from the universe.*

That was the code of the hero: love fate.

A whiplash splashdown slapped all that philosophy out of his head. Torso torquing for a gasp of air, the frigid shock of Himalayan runoff, the ridged texture of black serpent scales on his thighs, arms, neck—Arjuna wrestled the solid river of this serpent, but he could not tell where its eyes or mouth were. Muscular coils spiralled over his limbs, but they never squeezed too hard. Somehow he managed to get his head up and breathe whenever he needed to. In fact, the coil around his neck (he had never rid himself of that grip) seemed to tilt him up, let him suck a mouthful, then draw him back down and continue the struggle. The serpent and he fought their way downstream for a yojana until Arjuna, partly out of exhaustion, partly to experiment, let his body go slack.

The serpent steered him towards an island in the middle of the river, the same island where Satyavati, decades ago, had brought her illegitimate son. No one lived there now, though Vyasa's earliest letters lay eternalized in mud. The serpent set Arjuna on the sands. The coils disengaged and shortened until a woman's arms and a woman's legs embraced him.

'Make love to me,' she said, with a lick of his neck. Her tongue had a fork in it.

'I don't even know your name.'

'Ulupi.'

'Why did you try to kill me just now?'

'I wasn't trying to kill you!' she said, visibly hurt. 'I was trying to *ravish* you.'

Arjuna savoured, against his will, the forbidden brush of her limbs. The black serpent scales had vanished to gold skin, but that skin still felt like some cool, non-human surface. Panchali kept her legs hairless, too, with hot wax, but long-limbed Ulupi didn't even have follicles . . .

Arjuna turned his head and extricated himself. 'I'm married.'

'I know, Arjuna. That's why I tried to take you right there on the riverbank. Why did you fight me so hard?'

She rolled on to her back, and now he could see her body in the setting sun. His eyes were so used to Panchali's voluptuous black that Ulupi's bright-skinned, slender body delighted him. It was something new. Without Panchali to contrast, he would never have appreciated Ulupi, for she was almost breastless and hipless. A cobra's hood-diamond tattoo marked the base of her neck.

'You were a serpent just now, when you lunged at me.'

'True.'

'Are you some kind of shape-shifter?'

She looked down at herself. 'You don't like my shape?'

'I . . . didn't say that.'

'You're worried I'm some kind of demoness. I hatched from an egg, ok? Demons spill out live-born from their mothers' wombs, in a gush of blood.' She reached over to stroke, with fascination, his thigh hairs. 'Like men.'

Arjuna looked around uneasily. 'Am I your prisoner on this island?'

'Says the jailer of my heart.'

'I told you, Ulupi. I'm married.'

'What does that have to do with whether or not you make love to me?'

'We men live by something called dharma.'

'I know what dharma is. I'll kill myself if you don't make love to me, and you'll take on the sin for it.'

'First you try to "ravish" me and almost kill me. Now you say you're going to kill yourself? You need to get some religion. You need to study yoga.'

'But I have!' Triple-jointed, sinuous Ulupi sat up and folded her bare legs into an asana not even Shiva could have managed. 'Aum . . . ' she said, crossing her eyes charmingly. 'I also know about karma. The karmic penalty for adultery is *way* less than the one for murder.'

Arjuna, transfixed by her flexibility, folded his arms across his lap. 'Ulupi . . .'

She hiked her right knee behind her own head, tilted her foot inward, and flicked her long, forked tongue back and forth across her great toe. 'Yes?'

Now it was his turn to lunge at her. The ethical calculation had not been what convinced him. Their tongues spiralled together and struggled as their bodies had done in the river. He discovered fangs, parked flat against her palate. When he drew back in alarm, she swung up and moaned into his neck, mouth open, but she was not the one who did the piercing. Soon she rolled him on to his back, and her spine squiggled in sinful waves. With a long hiss, she went white and dry and papery—all her skin, all at once. Contented on the twilit sand, she peeled off her sloughed skin like so many pieces of lacy lingerie. The seductiveness of that undressing overcame his horror, and he skinned her five times that night.

A morning fog descended on the island, so thick he could not see his own hand. This was the same fog that the randy old Brahmin Parasara had conjured to hide his tryst with Satyavati in the ferry boat. It had never really disappeared. It migrated every night to an island in the far west, where all the people were as pale as the late Pandu. When night fell there, the fog came home to the island, where it used to hide Satyavati nursing baby Vyasa, and now hid Arjuna and Ulupi making love.

Arjuna explored the island and found Vyasa's nursery and first schoolroom. The trees were carved with the letters *ka* and *la*, and no other letters. *Kala,* Arjuna realized, meant both *time* and *black,* as in blackout, the consciousness lost for no telling how long. Alarmed, he searched for Ulupi in the fog—and dropped right into a hole in the sand. The shaft took several seconds to hit bottom. There he found a candlelit room. Ulupi was stroking a brown egg tucked into wet sand.

'How long have I been here, Ulupi?'

'Three years.'

'That's longer than I've lived with my own wife.'

'I'm more of a wife to you than she is.'

Arjuna realized he was wearing an elaborate breastplate of bark and a dhoti of some mysterious, resilient webbing. 'Three years? You're sure?'

'Here is our baby to prove it,' she said, kissing the egg.

Arjuna thought back to what he had just experienced, but he got mixed up separating sleep from waking. 'It felt like a night and a morning.'

'Time is special on this island. You know it's where the poet Vyasa was born and raised, right?'

Arjuna nodded.

'The only way he could read everything he wanted to read was if time made an exception.'

'I need to get off this island.'

'Why? A few more nights with me, and your twelve years of exile will be done. We can raise our boy together. Here. Feel him kick.'

The unborn thing sensed its father had laid a hand on its shell. The shell was not as hard as Arjuna expected. More like silk stretched taut. Arjuna stayed in that hole—how long, he had no idea—until the egg hatched a baby boy. This baby was human only from the neck up. His scales alternated two colours; Arjuna's skin had mixed-and-matched with Ulupi's into the copper tiles of that copper-and-black mosaic. Ulupi coiled the newborn's lower half around her forearm and muffled the mewling against her breast.

'I need some air,' Arjuna whispered.

His fingernails, to his shock, had grown very long, and these helped him climb up the shaft into the moonlight. He ran until he splashed, and he splashed until he could throw his arms over his head and swim. Though he wasn't conscious of it, he swam the distance without kicking his legs or windmilling his arms. His whole body just undulated underwater until he stood up on the riverbank. Ulupi, nursing their son, did not follow him. As he trekked inland, he trimmed his overgrown fingernails with his teeth and spat each one off to the side, pale splinters as long as fangs.

*

The days slowed down at the speed of hunger. For many yojanas, he wished he had read more of those rescued palm-leaf pages. Vyasa might have told him where to find his next meal.

Now that he had lived through his fate, he felt free to avoid rivers. What drew him to one was the sound of washerwomen dunking their laundry and slapping sarees and sheets against the rock. Weeks had passed since he had taken off his spiderweb dhoti and bark shirt. The moment he thought of doing it, a spider skittered out of the folds of his dhoti. When (somewhat ungratefully) he slapped at it, the spider got away and ran along the networks it knew so well. Soon he felt sting, sting, sting all along his inner thigh. He whipped off the dhoti. The bark shirt must have gotten some signal between insects, some chemical message of threat, for three hundred and thirty-three termites emerged from tunnels that hieroglyphed the breastplate's inner surface. Arjuna felt the crawling and tore it off.

Now he stood naked, black-bearded, stained with sweat-salt like a castaway sailor—in sight of the washerwomen, who screamed, some with amusement, some with outrage, still others with delight. Arjuna covered himself with his hands and rushed behind some bushes. A young warrior, from the look of his hairless upper lip scarcely in his teens, approached Arjuna with a wet linen sheet. The Pandava wrapped himself as best he could, throwing the excess length over his shoulder. The washerwomen spoke amongst themselves in elegant Sanskrit.

'Please forgive what happened there,' he said, so pale he might have been mistaken for Pandu's son and not Indra's. 'I was . . . I was attacked by insects. I'm terribly embarrassed.'

The women were astonished to hear his Sanskrit, too. They recognized him as a child of the same sun. 'You speak like royalty,' said the young warrior guarding them. 'Where did you learn to conjugate like that?'

'Hastinapur. What kingdom is this?'

'Manaluna.'

'Does King Chitravahana still reign here? I seem to have wandered hundreds of yojanas.'

'He does. Come with me. He likes to meet visitors to our kingdom.'

Arjuna could tell this was a police action, border control—but the youth was so laughable a threat to him, even though Arjuna was unarmed, that he went along. Besides, he figured the king would recognize him (they had last met at the five weddings in Panchala) and give him better clothes than this soaked bedsheet.

'Arjuna!' The king of Manaluna embraced him. 'I see you've met my daughter?'

The youth was really a girl. When she slipped off her helmet, her long hair spilled out with a brief sprinkle of white petals. Just as Panchali smelled of blue lotuses, Chitrangadaa smelled of night-blooming jasmines. Her name was the feminine form of the Gandharva musician-king's. Like that immortal sitarist, she treated the bow as one more stringed instrument, mastered and played for pleasure.

Arjuna got a shave, new clothes and armour, and new weapons, as well as his own room in Manaluna's palace, where he tossed at night recalling the warrior-princess's long black hair. The next morning, he went out to the archery range with Chitrangadaa, where she almost matched his score on three straight occasions. He rated her accuracy and consistency as highly as he did Karna's. Miraculously, she had never grown calluses on her thumbs. Arjuna fell in love when she gripped her bow—bright red nail polish on that small, white-knuckled hand!

At dinner, he shook his head in awe and not a little disbelief. 'May I ask, my dear king, why you've trained your daughter in the arts of war?'

'My great-great-great-grandfather, when he founded Manaluna, made sacrifices to Shiva until he received a boon. He flubbed the wording a bit and asked that "one heir to the throne be born in each generation". He didn't want the dynasty to transfer to another bloodline. You Pandavas and Kauravas, for example, share not one drop of blood with ancient King Shantanu, if you really examine the lineage. Anyway, the wording should have been *at least one* heir. This family has been dealing with that technicality ever since. My great-great-grandfather was an only child. My great-grandfather, my grandfather, my father, myself: the same. And now my own child is an only child, the first daughter born into the family. I've taken measures to make sure she inherits the kingdom, but I need her to know how to fight better than her own generals, or there will be a coup. I know what these military men think when they see a woman on the throne. This way, she can shoot any usurper dead from half a yojana away. She'll be safe when I'm gone.'

Arjuna spent the rest of the week with Chitrangadaa, and he had never had such conversations about the joys of archery before. Here, for the first time, was a girl who loved the same art he did!

'I really don't think they teach archers enough about how to use the wind,' she was saying. 'I toss a little red powder into the air before I go shooting.'

'I do, too!' he gasped. 'I thought I was the only one who knew that trick.'

'I hide some away every Holi.'

'So do I . . .'

'All the archery teachers frame it like, how do you *adjust* for the wind. I say, how do you—'

'*Use* the wind,' they said together.

'It should be a whole class,' she added.

Arjuna laughed. 'We could teach it together.'

That evening, he asked for her hand in marriage. 'I am already married to Panchali, as you know,' he said, 'but a prince can take more than one wife.'

'But not my princess, Arjuna. She can't take a husband. Those are the ancient legal stipulations that pertain here, now that I've made her my "son" for inheritance purposes.'

'So how can she become the mother of her one allotted heir?'

Chitrangadaa's father cleared his throat and fiddled with his sash. 'There's no reason you couldn't help with that side of things.'

Arjuna's good fortune made him dizzy. 'I'd be happy to.'

'Don't jump out naked like the first time you met her, young man. Still, I can't risk turning her over to an infertile man. It's been known to happen—consider your own grandfather, Vichitravirya, who lived seven years with two women and still died without issue. I know you and Panchali haven't had any children yet. Have you ever managed to father a child?'

Arjuna thought back to Ulupi and the egg. 'I have,' he said truthfully. 'The question is, though, is the princess willing?'

Was she ever. It turned out she was an expert at bareback horseriding, too, and wrestling, and sliding the dagger in and out of the sheath. No aspect of her martial or athletic training had been left out. When battling sweetly with his warrior princess, he forgot Panchali's ink-black areolas, constricting with pleasure as her pupils dilated; forgot, too, hyper-extensible Ulupi's overlong torso. Chitrangadaa took him to out-of-the-way caves and abandoned mountain shrines. She rode too recklessly and fast, and when he reproached her, she demanded he ride sidesaddle on her horse, like a wife in skirts, and overcome his fear. He laughed and let her have her way.

Soon enough, she bore Manaluna its one heir, its future king. The morning of the delivery, a thick fog and a grey hair at Arjuna's temple reminded him of kala, of time. He hurried to his unofficial father-in-law. 'How long ago did I arrive here?'

'It will be three years next month. Why do you ask?'

Arjuna stayed long enough to imprint the boy's face on his memory, though the boy's memory was still mostly water, and his father's image didn't set. This was for the best. The king and his ministers warned Arjuna that he had best not get too attached to the boy. To spare his own heart, then, he went to Chitrangadaa, in the rocking chair where she nursed their son.

'Let me guess,' she said. 'You don't want to live here as my pet man.'

'If I can't marry you, if I can't even take you back to Indraprastha, what would I be but a concubine?'

'There are hundreds of concubines in Bharata's palaces, and they're all women. Why is it fine for a woman to live like that, but not for a man?'

'Maybe it will be that way, in some far future. Here, in the world as it is, it isn't any other way but this. And it isn't like I can father another child here. You only get one.'

'You can be a father to this one.'

'I have been here three years. I don't know what time is, but I know it's shredding me.'

'One grey hair, and the famous Kshatriya gets scared?'

'I can conquer an army of men, an army of Gandharvas, an army of Asuras, maybe even an army of Gods. But I can't conquer an army of minutes.'

'I am a Kshatriya, no less than you. Being abandoned by you is nothing to me. Time is my surgeon. Time will tug out this arrow and stitch up my wound.'

'I'm not abandoning you. I am staying faithful to my fate.'

'You know those archery games we played, where I almost matched your score?'

'Of course. Fondly.'

'I let you win.'

*

Arjuna, on the road again, went from temple to temple, saint's cave to saint's cave, sacred pond to sacred pond. The rice was hot, the walnuts fresh and crunchy when he joined the line of beggars and cripples. At those public feasts, he spoke with commoners, 'chaff' as the Kauravas called them, and he learned their woes and ways. They weren't chaff at all, it turned out, but chaff and gold grains mixed together in the shifting sieve of karma. The holy places in Bharata's green-terraced, rainy south offered him a carved and corbeled refuge from time. He stood a foot taller and a shade lighter than the people there, and the women giggled behind their hands at Arjuna—handsome among his own kind, homely among these strangers.

One sacred body of water, known locally as Luck Lake, turned out to be deserted when he got there. No one bathed there, and no one distributed prasad there. The little stone shrine to the Goddess of Luck—he had never heard of her before, but he guessed she was a mask of Lakshmi—looked forlorn with abandonment, just a pile of old marigolds, dry as snake slough.

Still, he was there, and he wanted to thank this Goddess for all the good luck he'd had so far: lucky in love, lucky not to have died of a mosquito bite, lucky to have such a loving family waiting for him to return. So he waded into the pond to say some prayers and got attacked by a crocodile.

Arjuna had wrestled Bheem before and lost; had wrestled whichever Kaurava was closest to hand and won; but that was many years ago. Kshatriyas never fought weaponless, and Drona offered no classes in the sloppy disgraceful art of grappling. This was why he had done such a poor job against Ulupi in her serpent form, and why Arjuna (so graceful with a bow) flopped and flailed against this snaggle-toothed makara. Someone—was it Bheem?—once told him he should punch a crocodile between the eyes. Arjuna did that a few times, and it worked just enough for him to drag the crocodile out of the water and get some purchase on drier ground. The rough, pitted grey-green crocodile skin went smooth and brown, and the crooked crocodile grin shrank to a red mouth. Arjuna was holding a naked apsara in his arms. He gave a shout and dropped her.

She rubbed the bridge of her nose, shameless and unconcerned about the rest of her body. 'That hurt!'

'I would apologize, but you were a crocodile just now.'

'I was also an apsara.'

'Then why did you try to drag me under?'

'I was both things. The crocodile part of me wanted to drag you under and drown you. The apsara part of me wanted you to pull me out so I could get my real body back.'

'Was it a curse that did this to you?'

'What else? Pass a sage on a spring day, and for all his samadhi and detachment, he will try to make love to you, or curse you, or both.'

'Was this Durvasas? I hear he has a temper.'

'It might have been. Every other man's name begins with "D" around here, it seems. All holy men look the same to me anyway, cross-eyed and cross-legged. He said that just as my friends and I had tried to drag him down into the world, we would have to live as crocodiles and drag people into the water.'

'Your friends?'

'Did we know he was meditating beside that lake? We had just finished dance practice on the dark side of the moon, and slipped down here for a quick bath. We pled with him, so he spoke a rider on his curse—that we must prowl this lake until a man of dharma pulled us out. You're that man, I guess. Can you please get my friends out, too?'

'Tell them not to attack me.'

'I can't. Crocodiles don't speak.'

'So they're going to pull me under?'

'You'll have to struggle, just like you did with me.' She stroked Arjuna's arm. 'But you're strong enough.'

Arjuna glanced over at the Goddess's shrine. 'Wish me luck,' he sighed. Splashes, shouts, teeth marks in his calves, but eventually, tears of gratitude: by the time he hauled the fifth apsara out of the water, he was exhausted and bleeding in a dozen places. The five celestial dancers, naked as feral animals, got on all fours and licked his wounds to heal them. Arjuna could not believe his luck. The apsaras, as he could tell from the way their tongues roved to parts of him that were never injured, had not touched a man in months: downright ascetic self-torture to women who lived the apsara lifestyle. Arjuna had five willing women here. Panchali, he reflected, had five husbands. What would be wrong if he took advantage of their gratitude and the deserted area? Why not enjoy his good luck?

Ah, but good luck wasn't the same as fate. Every man loves his good luck, but only a hero loves his fate. Besides, there was something unreal about these females. No moles, no navels . . .

they aroused him as little as statues in a temple. Slipping their arms and wet black hair, he joined his palms and bowed his head to them, and told them to give his regards to Indra. They grabbed hold of his arms and tried to pull him to the grass, but as long as he kept up his namaste, they could not separate those vacuum-sealed palms, much less make his knees buckle. Giving up on him, they each kissed his closed mouth goodbye. The last tried to part his teeth with her tongue, but he shook his head. She laughed and led her friends into the sky. From wind to passing wind and then from cloud to cloud, they leapt on tiptoe, paused and leapt again, carefully, like sisters going stone to stone across a river.

*

Arjuna doubled back to Manaluna out of fondness. Chitrangadaa was already on a horse again. Their son, whom she had named Babhruvahana ('Boo' for short), rode with her, tucked in a tightly wound sling. Arjuna knew the horse she was riding, and the horse knew his whistle. Arjuna held the baby for a while.

'Have you come back to stay?' she asked.

'I came back because I missed you.'

'You can say no to me. I won't get hurt.'

'My fate is somewhere else.'

'Some*one* else.' She ran her fingers through his hair. 'Panchali.'

Chitrangadaa let Arjuna watch, cheek on fist, while she fed their son. She taught him to burp the baby and how to cradle him until he fell asleep. After she nestled him into a bundle of blankets on the grass, her hands and her body were free. Arjuna's reverent fingertip traced the bright pink stretch marks on her side. This, he thought, was so much better than those sterile apsaras. He pulled her flush, but she pulled away.

'The baby will wake up,' she said. 'And someone might see us.'

'You can say no to me. I won't get hurt.'
'No.'

*

Arjuna could have stayed in palaces during his exile. Several capitals had signed treaties of friendship with Indraprastha, even in the all-too-brief time he had lived there. Why make himself beholden to this or that royal family? A secret fondness for the forests made him prefer fasts and pebbles to feasts and pillows.

So when he wandered up Mount Raivataka and heard the gaudy music of a dance, and saw serving men in golden sashes walking around with trays, he almost turned around. The music insisted he investigate. He found the dancers, but he never found the musicians. At the most packed side of the clearing was Krishna, topknot undone and torso bare, shining in the circle of torchlights. The dancers were dancing in a circle around a statue drowned in silks.

Arjuna laughed aloud to see Krishna there. This Yadava party was one royal event he didn't mind joining! Krishna's clan was world-famous for how hard they drank and how hard they danced—Balarama, the best drinker; Krishna, the best dancer. Both brothers were in form.

Krishna must have heard the laugh because he spun like a world until he stood behind Arjuna and shoved him towards the whirlpool of dancers. No bothering with greetings, no time wasted on catching up. The music was never louder than when Krishna shouted in his ear, 'Go! We're dancing for the Goddess! Go!'

'But I don't know the steps, Krishna!'

'You will!'

And he did. All he needed was the full-body relaxation that makes a body float, and Arjuna felt himself borne along on the current. He circled the Goddess clockwise, over and over. Krishna was always close behind him when he glanced back, always just beyond him when he glanced ahead. At last Arjuna understood the stories that *gopis* still told of Krishna in his teenage years—how he multiplied himself during those country dances and danced with all the girls at once.

When Arjuna grew tired, he closed his eyes and kept dancing, and dancing refreshed him like sleep. When he grew hungry, he opened his mouth and sang along to the music, whose lyrics he somehow knew, and the music filled him like food. At last, when he stumbled out of the dance, his ears ringing, Krishna joined him and walked him out of the torchlit cacophony and into the muted music of mountain moonlight.

'Had enough?'

'I think so.'

'It's best to practise dancing on a mountain. The air is thinner here, so your lungs and your blood adapt. When we dance the Nine Nights of the Goddess down at sea level, in Dwaraka, you'll notice you won't get out of breath.'

'So this was just practice?'

'Right! From here I'm taking you home with me. Big festival. All the Yadavas are going to be there, the whole family. You've never seen a party like this one.'

'When is it?'

'Tomorrow night is the first of nine!'

'I feel like I've been dancing for nine nights straight already.'

'Nine nights, Arjuna? You've really lost track of time, my friend!' Krishna gave him a slap on the back and laughed. 'You've been dancing up here for the past three years. Now rest your legs and get some sleep.' Krishna snapped his fingers, and Arjuna heard neither the muted music, nor the ringing in his ears. In that grateful silence, he fell asleep.

When he awoke, he found he had been transported to Dwaraka. A towering Durga, carved of a single massive red topaz, flamed against the night, and he stumbled like a sleepwalker to the edge of the crowd that circled her. One girl, dressed in a pink choli and green *ghagra*, starred with little round mirrors, caught his eye right away. One girl out of hundreds there—how had he fixated on her? She spun and spun and didn't seem to touch the ground. For the first time, he didn't compare her beauty to Panchali's. He didn't think of Panchali at all.

'Krishna,' he whispered. Some instinct told him Krishna was close by and would hear. 'Who is *that*?'

'That girl in the pink and green? Let me go find out for you. Wait for me under the banyan.'

Krishna vanished into the dance, and Arjuna lost sight of his favourite. Though he waited and waited for her to circle past, he couldn't make her out. So he wandered the edge of the open field a while, in search of the banyan tree Krishna referred to. When he closed his eyes and conjured the image of his crush, all awash in red topaz light, he wandered into the hanging roots. Krishna sat atop a branch, swinging his feet.

'So, about that girl,' said Krishna.

'I don't care if she's a commoner. I want to marry her.'

'She's my sister.'

Arjuna held onto a prop root of the banyan tree. 'Krishna, you've been playing with me.'

'My half-sister, technically. Balarama is Subhadra's full brother, by blood—they're both Rohini's children. But she and I are very close. I've been telling her stories about you for years now.' Krishna winked. 'Just not the ones involving snakes and crocodiles.'

Arjuna blushed. How had Krishna found out about his adventures over the past years? 'I am still serious about her. I want to marry her, as long as you don't mind.'

'I would love it and so would she, since she's had a crush on you since she was fourteen. I found her sitting down, with her friends fanning her, because she'd caught a glimpse of you catching a glimpse of her. Our brother Balarama, though, has settled on a different prince as her match. And since he's her full brother and as he's older than me, I have to defer to his choice.'

Arjuna buckled to the ground, instantly forlorn. What he didn't know, and what Krishna was keeping secret, was that Balarama had spent a year in Hastinapur at the blind king's request. Balarama was one of the best mace fighters in all of Bharata; he had learned out in the countryside, during his boyhood, by swinging a giant farmer's plough, and he still preferred that to a conventional mace. He had gone to Hastinapur to train Duryodhan. Since his return, a converted Balarama had made it clear that he wanted Dwaraka allied with the future King Suyodhan I of Hastinapur. Nothing married two kingdoms like a marriage . . .

'Balarama is playing the matchmaker here. All my fellow Yadavas, our whole extended family really—they're excited about this prince. I can't go against them. Neither can she.'

Arjuna nodded and hung his head.

'But *you* can.'

*

Balarama had not expected to like Duryodhan as much as he did. He had only agreed to train the son out of respect for the blind old king, and (to be honest) because he had heard good things about Hastinapur's wine cellars.

Drinking together was how they had bonded: Duryodhan could hold his liquor. The Pandavas were good men, true, but you couldn't sit back and have a drink with the Pandavas. Bheem, with that big body, should have been able to lift a keg and guzzle from the nozzle, but Indraprastha was a dry city. Balarama had to keep his supply stashed away. With the Kauravas, you could keep the bottles on the table and belt out sloppy drinking songs all night.

Enough drinks, and the prince had opened up. He was perfecting his mace skills, he said, because he was going to fight Bheem one day. Duryodhan took Balarama to see the iron statue he'd commissioned, the one he practised on daily. Dints pockmarked every square inch of it.

'Listen, Duryodhan,' Balarama had counselled him. 'You can't focus too much on your brothers. Your brother might be more handsome than you, or a better talker, or have better luck with the girls . . .' Wait, was he speaking of Krishna? He loved Krishna—but it was hard being the brother of a phenomenon. 'Your *cousins*, I mean. The Pandavas. Don't compare yourself! You'll only make yourself unhappy. Uneasy in your skin.' After a great gulp from his bottle, he had clapped Duryodhan on the shoulder. 'My friend, it's a bad draw, getting born in the same family as somebody Godlike. But you'll be lucky in love, too. You will. I'll make it happen.'

Subhadra had no interest in Duryodhan. She had heard as many stories of him as she had heard of Arjuna—all of them from Krishna, so she despised Duryodhan as much as she adored Arjuna. Balarama declared he would set up a swayamvara for his sister—like Panchali's, only instead of a bow, the challenge would involve the mace.

Balarama's temper was not to be risked, so on hearing his idea for the match, Subhadra had not contradicted him. Instead, she had gone straight to Krishna. Even if Arjuna showed up to the swayamvara, a mace-wielding challenge would favour Duryodhan. No doubt Balarama had taught him to stun a beehive, bee by bee by bee—the supreme test of deftness with a mace, beyond Arjuna's skill with that weapon.

'On the morning after the ninth night of the Goddess,' Krishna told Subhadra, 'you'll go to temple with the whole family. When the puja is done, I want you to leave so you're five steps ahead of Balarama. Meanwhile, I'll borrow one of the garlands off the Goddess . . .'

A garland which, on this day after the ninth night, at high noon, he handed to Subhadra. It was the signal: she took off running down the temple steps and ignored her sandals on her way out to the street. Krishna, still on the steps, pointed behind Balarama and shouted, and his brother and many other Yadavas looked over their shoulders. When they turned back to Krishna, he was gone—headed at a sprint for his own chariot, waiting outside the temple. In that chariot stood Prince Arjuna of Hastinapur. Was that Subhadra running up to him? It *was!*

Subhadra threw her garland around Arjuna's neck. Then, to double the scandal, she grabbed the reins of the chariot and gave a shrill, shameless *hiyah!* Years ago, in preparation for this very moment, Krishna had taught his kid sister how to drive a chariot. He made it to the street just as the horses whinnied and galloped off. A few long strides and an assist from Arjuna, and he had joined the eloping couple in the chariot. Balarama and two dozen of Krishna's kinsmen poured into the street, shouting and shaking their fists—but (mysteriously enough) their chariots had been parked two blocks north, and their horses had been unhitched and taken to feed another two blocks north. So the laughing couple and their brother-in-law were well outside Dwaraka before confusion coalesced into a chariot chase.

Krishna told Subhadra to slow the chariot. 'I'm going to hop off here. I'll send for you when it's safe, and we'll have a proper wedding in Dwaraka.'

'How will you get back?'

'There are plenty of Yadava chariots headed this way,' he said. 'I'll stand in the middle of the road and wave my arms to get them to stop, and hitch a ride home with Balarama.'

'Those chariots won't go back to Dwaraka,' said Subhadra. 'Balarama is coming after us.'

'I know how to talk to our hard-drinking brother. I'll talk the Yadavas off the warpath. After all, they can't convince themselves that Arjuna carried you off. You're the one driving the chariot, right?'

After giving the couple a hug, Krishna started back to Dwaraka at a stroll. The chariots of Subhadra's cousins and uncles appeared as a far-off golden dust storm and a rumble that made the horses stomp the tingle from their horseshoes. Subhadra shook the reins and started off towards their first tryst alone. They would wait at a mountainside resort until a carrier pigeon found them with the all-clear. It would be hard, thought Arjuna, admiring Subhadra's profile, not to opt for a 'Gandharva marriage' and notarize it themselves that very night. After all, hadn't he ridden off with her in a chariot, in the grand old Kshatriya style, just as Bhishma had ridden off with the three princesses of Kashi? Might as well go deeper into the archives and marry the way King Dushyant had married Shakuntala, at the very foundation of the line . . . He shook his head of the fantasy. Krishna had entrusted him with Subhadra for the next few days, and he must not violate that trust, not even if Subhadra begged him. Which she might, judging from her free hand's eagerness to squeeze his.

Her profile resolved, as he stared, into a face nearly indistinguishable from Krishna's, adjusted to golden. Between Subhadra's features and Panchali's skin, Arjuna realized, he could have been Krishna's brother-in-law twice over, surrounded by Krishna-lookalikes: vowed already to Krishna's sister in spirit, and now to his sister by blood. That dip in crocodile-patrolled Luck Lake had kept his luck going, but his first stroke of luck had been entering Krishna's good graces. Arjuna sensed his exile finishing out, though he still had three years left in it. No doubt his coming honeymoon would elope with the remaining years. No chariot faster than happiness, no road so short as time. Already he felt this road, the one Subhadra drove on, bending under their wheels east to Indraprastha. They were almost home.

SEQUENCE 8

THE RISE OF THE PANDAVAS

These sections detail how the Pandavas, in spite of being given Hastinapur's worst real estate for their kingdom, assert their dominance.

Arjuna and Krishna clear the densely forested area with fire. The Gods give them gifts—among them, a special bow for Arjuna. Warriors named their weapons in those days; this weapon's name is Gandiva, and while it's not a 'character' per se, it is inseparable from Arjuna henceforth. The Pandavas also seek out and destroy a powerful king, who happens to be Krishna's main rival. (The alliance works to Krishna's benefit, too.)

After that, Yudhishtir sends his four brothers in the four directions: it is a way of projecting power across all points of the compass.

At last, Yudhisthir orders a massive hall built for a ceremonial consecration. He invites kings from all over India ('Bharata') to admire it. Duryodhan experiences it as a marvel and a humiliation. Panchali laughs at him when he mistakes a pool of water for a mirror—a slight he will soon avenge.

Krishna, honoured at the consecration ceremony, gets challenged by an upstart king. The king is actually his nephew. Krishna tolerates one hundred insults from this loudmouth but cuts him off (at the neck) before the hundred-and-first.

SARGA 23

CONTROLLED BURN

Eager though he was to show Subhadra the city of Indraprastha, Arjuna fell silent marvelling and could not point out any of the sights. Empty fields had sprouted towers. Saplings roped to stakes once now gave shade to picnickers. Twelve monsoons had stained the white buildings with smudges of gray and blue, and twelve springs had crowded the public ponds with blue lotuses.

Blue lotuses! The whole city smelled like Panchali, or seemed to—until he got to the palace, where the intensity of her fragrance made him dizzy with yearning, even though Subhadra was right there at his side. He embraced his brothers—*twelve years, you haven't changed, it's like time never touched you*—distractedly, impatiently.

'Where's Panchali?'

His brothers glanced at each other, at Krishna, at Subhadra . . . 'We've been trying to reason with her,' said Bheem, 'but you can't reason with a fire.'

Bheem showed the five fingertip blisters he had gotten when he patted her hand to calm her.

'She's a bit upset about sharing you,' said Yudhishtir. 'Ever since she got the news about your marriage in Dwaraka, she has been stomping in her room, Arjuna, and moping on her bed, and . . . generating heat. That whole wing of the palace is an open oven.'

'Let me talk to her,' said Krishna coolly.

'I wouldn't do that. She's madder at you than she is at Arjuna.'

Bheem nodded. '"Arjuna got lonely," she says, "and Krishna took advantage of it to make an alliance."'

'Fire is pure appetite, fire doesn't know how to share. Krishnaa is only angry with me in the abstract, in my absence. If she met me, she would melt. She is my sister no less than Subhadra, and for all her fire, she'll warm to Subhadra yet. The only way to cool her down is for Subhadra to pay her a visit, alone.'

Arjuna and the Pandavas protested, insisting that Panchali would cool down on her own, eventually—no need to feed her inferno with the object of her jealousy. Krishna took Subhadra to Indraprastha's theatre, where dancers and actors were busy preparing for a play called *The Hundred and Eight Loves of Young Krishna*. At least a dozen young men dressed in dark blue face paint, yellow dhotis and peacock-feather panache rushed past, hurrying to the stage to rehearse the Leela. Not one of them noticed the celebrity they portrayed, intent as they were on the dance to come.

'One hundred and eight loves!' gasped Subhadra, scandalized. 'Is that what you got up to, brother, when you were growing up in Vrindavan?'

'Please, Subhadra, use your common sense. How could I have danced with so many girls at once? Does that sound humanly possible?'

When they got back to the palace, Subhadra wore the get-up of a gopi, her eyes thickly rimmed with kohl. Krishna painted little dots of kohl across the top of her forehead. This was the fashion of cowherd girls when he was a boy, but all that kohl had another purpose.

When Subhadra ventured into the super-heated wing of the palace where Panchali raged, this kohl began to mix with Subhadra's sweat. When she wiped her face, she blackened it. By the time she knelt at Panchali's feet, her face—which already resembled Krishna's—was just as black as his. Panchali saw that dear face and cooled immediately. 'Who are you, young lady?'

'I just herded the cows home to the shed,' said Subhadra, as Krishna had scripted her. 'I came here straight from Vrindavan.'

That clinched it for Panchali: remembering Krishna overwhelmed her with affection, just as he had predicted, and her rage extinguished. A cool wind swept away the heat-shimmers all around her, and when she gathered Subhadra into her arms, she left no blisters, not even a first-degree burn. They emerged arm in arm. Subhadra walked her elder sister into Arjuna's waiting embrace.

*

'I want to see more of the kingdom before I go home to Dwaraka,' said Krishna to Arjuna one morning. 'You'd do well to survey the territory, too, since you're set to review the realm's defences. No better way to do that than by boat, especially on a hot day like this.'

It wasn't all that hot a day—in fact, it looked like it might rain—but Arjuna thought the idea a good one. Krishna insisted on taking a small rowboat, just big enough to fit a lunch and two canteens.

'Think of me as your charioteer,' Krishna said with a wink. The boat slid thirty-three feet every time he pulled the oars. They had gone a few yojanas when Arjuna pointed at the riverbank.

'Look, Krishna! There's a starving, sickly Brahmin resting against a boulder. He's really got the shakes. I can count his ribs from here.'

Krishna wiped his brow. 'And I can feel his fever heat. He must have been bitten by the wrong mosquito. Let's go see if we can help him.'

In no time, the boat had skidded on to the bank of the Yamuna. The Brahmin joined his trembling hands and slowly blinked his eyes—at once bulging and sunken, bloodshot, exhausted and bold.

The stranger raised his hand at Arjuna's proffered canteen. 'I'm hungry, not thirsty. I've come to the Khandava Forest to eat, but I can't eat a thing.'

'You can't forage a single berry in the whole Khandava Forest? I find that hard to believe.'

'Indra won't let me! He chases me out with his rain and lightning. Rain dims my senses and wastes me away. You can see what it's done to me so far.'

'Why does Indra have a problem with you eating?'

'His friend, the monstrous serpent Takshaka, lives in this forest with his serpent brood.'

'Takshaka has nothing to fear from a foraging Brahmin. What kind of Brahmin eats snake meat?'

'I am no Brahmin. I am what Brahmins chant their Sanskrit over.' The stranger raised his hand, and a flame alit on the back of it, tall and proud, like a parakeet crossing over from another dimension. 'My name is Agni.'

Arjuna and Krishna realized they were talking to Panchali's biological father. They joined their hands and bowed.

'Father,' said Arjuna, 'you should have told your sons-in-law you were visiting Indraprastha. You've travelled from so far away, the least we can do is feed you.'

Agni smiled. 'I have come bearing gifts.'

From inside his chest—for his torso, like the rest of him, had given up the pretence of flesh—he drew a metal disc of grey-blue metal, piranha-toothed along the edges, like the blade of a circular saw. This he gave to Krishna.

'This is called a Sudarshan Chakra. It will collapse to a ring on your finger, like so.' Agni showed him. 'Pulse your finger twice, and it will detect the tautening of your tendons, and flare into its blade form. It knows you for its master, and it will sense your enemy, like an attack dog. The chakra will return to you no matter where you send it.'

'How can it do all that? How does it know?'

'It's a metal not found on this planet—a sentient metal, described only in the hidden fifth Veda, the Maya Veda. The only copy of it lies under the Arctic ice, Krishna, and it will be discovered and incinerated at the same time, at the end of time, when Shiva Nataraja dances his dance in a sphere of fire. In that Veda, Brahma shared all the secrets of Maya on all the planets, metals and occult elements that will bring untold power. This is one such metal, mined from a moon of Brihaspati. The chakra thinks. It knows, it feels. It will obey you.'

Krishna slid the ring on to his right hand's index finger, but he held off testing out the chakra. Agni was reaching inside himself for another gift.

'And this is Gandiva. It's made of the same metal. So is the string; the bow won't take any ordinary bowstring, but not to worry, Gandiva's string will never snap or be cut, not even by a direct hit. And here is a quiver of arrows, the same lightweight metal. Together they are a family—bow, bowstring, inexhaustible quiver. Gandiva is just their surname.'

Arjuna took the gifts in hand and peered with puzzlement into the quiver. He turned it upside down.

'Yes, Arjuna, it's empty. As long as you don't glance behind yourself to check, the quiver will always place an arrow in your hand. If you make the mistake of looking before you reach into it—if you fail in that basic faith in your weapon—Gandiva may well take offence and deny you an arrow, no matter how badly you need one.'

'I will never lose faith in you,' Arjuna whispered to his new weapon system. He arranged Gandiva's three parts on the grass, got on his knees and pressed his forehead to the ground.

'And now, at last, for my meal,' said Agni with joy and relief. 'Make sure you don't let my meat get away. Watch over me. Indra can't bear the sound of my chewing.'

Agni somersaulted backwards into the forest, eleven brisk full-body flips before he exploded into napalm droplets. The Khandava Forest swirled into flame for yojanas in every direction. Black smoke chased fleeing cirrus-wisps east-northeast across the sky. Peepal trees held their burning branches in mute appeal to the sky.

Arjuna and Krishna staggered back to the river. Soon, they saw what Agni meant when he warned them about Indra. The sky's mood darkened at this destruction, particularly off in the west. The west sent armadas of storm clouds, armies of raindrops to douse the lifegiving, controlled burn of this forest: to deny the soil Agni's gift of replenishing ash. Even as the west's darkness glowered, Krishna and Arjuna found themselves stampeded by panicking clouded leopards, sun bears, bloodclot-bearded hyenas, wild wolves, gyrfalcons that had just dropped their mice, screaming caracals, squat and poisonous lizards, and an assortment of cobras and kraits. The princes stood in shock for a few moments at this massive assault of the forest's predators. It seemed they blamed Arjuna and Krishna for the forest fire, and they were out for blood.

The two friends had no choice but to start killing. Between the Sudarshan Chakra and Gandiva, they had the weapons for it. Krishna twitched his finger twice, and the ring spun along his finger and flared into the glorious saw-toothed disc. It spun more quickly than any wheel or gear, and the high-pitched whine made Krishna's hair blow to the side. All he had to do was look at the snake that corkscrewed airborne with its mouth open and fangs out. The chakra razored down and returned in less time than it takes a frog's tongue to snatch the fly. Dozens of times a minute, Krishna beheaded the predators attacking him and Arjuna. The forest kept disgorging its most dangerous killers. Krishna's Sudarshan Chakra mowed them all down and mulched them into their ever-growing pyre. Not one wolf got its jaws in his friend.

His steady work freed Arjuna up to fight heaven. Kunti's son handled Gandiva as if he had trained on it for a hundred and eight past lives. Gandiva wanted to prove itself to him, just as he wanted to prove himself to Gandiva. Together, they fired hundreds of arrows into the sky. Not once did Arjuna check if he had an arrow in his quiver. He kept his eyes on the clouds attacking from the west, pouring through a valley of barometric pressure, a climatological Khyber Pass. Arjuna's arrows carried warheads of weapons-grade Sanskrit. They blew the horsemen off their thunder-horses, blew holes in the hulls of those steel-grey rainships. Damaged bombclouds dropped their payloads a dozen yojanas from Agni's feast. Any drops that made it over the Khandava Forest turned pale and steamed skyward in retreat.

Escaping geese and falcons choked on this steam and—their scalded lungs hemorrhaging, their feathers singed black—nosedived into Agni's mouth. Slaughter scaled up as Krishna and Arjuna grew defter with their weapons. When giant muscled figures formed in the clouds, Gandharvas maybe or Yakshas called up to fight for Indra, Krishna sent his chakra into the sky. The cloud-figure, barely formed, could not duck in time and buckled—crisply beheaded. Arjuna lowered Gandiva to hit a jaguar in mid-pounce. The arrow's impact blew the airborne predator back into the fire.

Agni, meanwhile, had built a to-scale model of Indraprastha out of flame and smoke and an infrastructure of wick-black trees. During a lull, while Indra regrouped, Arjuna and Krishna wandered into this unreal city and recognized the streets and buildings, even the palace. Arjuna grew terrified, imagining

Indraprastha sacked one day by barbarians; but Krishna knew both cities, the one of fire and the one of brick, to be equally unreal. The air was hot but not unbearably so. They were being hosted by the fire, after all. At last they reached an unfamiliar Hall of Wonders. It had no corresponding structure in the real Indraprastha. They entered it and found a young man on all fours, choking to death on smoke. They pulled this stranger to safety and revived him with Yamuna water.

They would have asked his name, but Indra rejoined the battle. Now both Krishna and Arjuna had to aim their weapons at the sky. The coughing, tear-blinded stranger watched the two princes fighting fearlessly, silhouetted against the fire. How long did they fight? The stranger lost consciousness and regained it several times. '*Tathastu*!' boomed a voice in the sky. *So be it!*

The sky cleared and the fire went out. Smoke still rose and ashes rustled, but the battle was over—and the victory had gone to the two mortal friends and their two divine weapons.

Arjuna and Krishna turned to the man they had rescued. They studied his appearance with growing alarm.

'What are you,' Arjuna demanded, '*yaksha*, man or demon?'

'My name is Maya, kind sirs. I was meditating in the forest when everything started burning.'

'You didn't answer my question.'

'I am an architect. I've been an architect for four decades. I renovated Brahma's studio, and I built Varuna his underwater desert under the world's largest dome.'

'Yaksha, man or demon?'

Maya looked down and mumbled, 'Demon.'

'I knew it.' Arjuna's hand rose to reach for an arrow, but Krishna touched his wrist just in time.

'Demon may be in his bloodline, but it's not in his nature. If he builds for the Gods, he's godly.'

'I will build for you, too. Out of gratitude. You saved me! Prince, tell me what you want me to build you. Simply wish for it and I'll build it.'

Arjuna was wary of answering this question. He had heard too many fairy tales of wishes twisted in the wording—you ask for immortality, and you end up shrivelling up with old age, all alone, unable to die even though you want to. There was only one shrewd move: defer to the shrewdest person there. 'Krishna, you pick. Tell him what to build me.'

'Maya, what was that hall where we found you? The one built out of fire?'

'It was all forest fire, all a confusion of burning trees. There were no buildings in there, only conflagration.'

'We saw a whole city. We saw Indraprastha.'

'That must have been what was in your mind. If you saw me inside a building you didn't recognize, that was probably the unbuilt hall I had in my imagination. I try to meditate on nothingness but I still get ideas every now and then. The art I love never leaves me alone. That hall was one such idea, assuming that's what you saw. A Hall of Wonders.'

'Build my friend that hall, then. Build it in Indraprastha, out of topaz and ebony—and for all our sakes, make it fireproof.'

SARGA 24

TEARING ALONG THE DOTTED LINE

The hall, like most construction projects, got delayed in the finishing and had monstrous cost overruns. Luckily for the Pandavas, Maya had to foot the bill for his perfectionism. Grateful Gods had paid him well; the architect had several large jewels stashed away to fund his retirement. He sold them off one by one as he fired and re-hired stonemasons, imported rare pink marble and occasionally demolished sections that displeased him. The projected four months became fourteen.

One day, a few months into construction, the wandering sage Narada strolled by the site.

The Pandavas and Krishna were inspecting the progress just then. Arjuna glanced at Krishna. This was the same Narada who had persuaded the Pandavas to take the vow that got Arjuna exiled for twelve years. 'There he is again,' muttered the archer. 'He can't help himself.'

'Doom blooms,' Krishna whispered with a shrug. 'He's the springtime, not the seed.'

Narada embraced the architect. He knew Maya and had seen all the examples of Maya's work around the universe. 'This is your finest work yet! Kama's Maze of Mirrors has nothing on this!'

'My last work,' sighed the demon. 'I only wish it weren't on earth, where buildings and empires blow away so easily.'

'Tell me, Yudhishtir,' said Narada, turning to the Pandavas, 'how are you going to inaugurate this hall? With an Imperial Sacrifice, I assume?'

'That's beyond me,' said Yudhishtir humbly. 'An Imperial Sacrifice? The last one was done by King Rama himself. Bharata has changed since then. All its squabbling kingdoms would never submit to one crown.'

Narada glanced at Krishna. 'The worthiest men aren't always the most ambitious, are they? Scoundrel dreamers beat complaisant saints.' Narada shook his head and strolled on. 'I'm off to Magadha. At least the king there has a vision.'

*

Narada's parting words were a jab at Yudhishtir's reluctance to seek the submission of all his neighbours. But they were also a jab at Krishna. The King of Magadha was Jarasandha, and Jarasandha had kicked Krishna and the Yadavas out of Mathura. For all his charm and agility, savvy and tact, Krishna's military record wasn't perfect. After Krishna had killed his uncle and freed his parents, the slain Kamsa's strongest ally (and father-in-law) had sworn to punish the upstart usurper. Jarasandha had besieged Mathura sixteen times. The wealthy, implacable invader never ran out of armies and siege engines. Mathura, stubbornly bolted, sweated out its typhus. During the seventeenth siege, when the grain-depleted city started hunting cats, Krishna realized he was a curse on Mathura. So he and his Yadava kinsmen fled into the sunset, to Dwaraka by the sea. Jarasandha had not mounted an expedition that far west. Yet.

'Narada is right,' Krishna declared that evening over dinner. 'You should do it. Become the king of kings. Perform the Imperial Sacrifice and make it official.'

Yudhishtir shook his head. 'This is Narada at work again, Krishna, stirring up trouble. Indraprastha has been thriving. Why bully our neighbours into submission? We trade, and we honour each other's borders. That's enough. I don't need to thump my chest like the alpha ape.'

'The time is coming when you're going to lose all of this. And so will I. Didn't you hear what Narada said as he left? Magadha! It's closer to Indraprastha than it is to Dwaraka. King Jarasandha will invade, smash, rename everything. Your kingdom first, then ours.'

'He'd be a fool to attack us. Didn't you and Arjuna just do battle with Indra himself?'

'We chased away some storm clouds, and we had Agni on our side. Jarasandha's armies are literal. There is no poetry in war. I've stood on a city's walls and looked out over those hordes of his, and then looked back and seen my citizens burning their plague dead. Jarasandha will come after you, Yudhishtir.'

'Why me? I've never wronged him. I entertained his ambassador a few weeks ago. We were cordial.'

'You're a king. He's already imprisoned eighty-six kings from across Bharata. He wants to collect one hundred kings and sacrifice them to Shiva. An insane death cult has installed itself in Magadha. They call themselves the Tandava Sangha. Their priests want to accelerate Shiva's awakening so he destroys the universe *before* the long evil age of the Kali Yuga. So they claim it's an act of mercy. They think they're sparing humankind the wars and famines and adharma to come. Murdering a hundred kings is part of the "Awakening". He's getting more powerful every day.'

'Magadha's ambassador warned me about those rumours. The captive kings, the Tandava cult—he denied all of it.'

'Do you think that just because *you* always tell the truth, other people won't tell you lies? You need to send an expedition into Magadha. And you need to do it before it's too late. As early as tomorrow.'

'How could I possibly muster enough troops by then, even if I considered this mad option?'

'Not an expedition of soldiers.' Krishna gave a sidelong glance at Arjuna and Bheem. 'An expedition of *assassins*.'

*

On the way to Magadha, disguised as Brahmins, Krishna told his two companions the story—and the weakness—of Jarasandha.

Half a century ago, Jarasandha's future father had gone into a deep depression. It was the usual trigger: the aging king had fathered no children. He had beheaded a wife every four years because she failed to get pregnant, six in all. It did not occur to him the problem might be with the faucet, not the pail. To double his chances now that he had grey hair, he married twin princesses from Kashi (great grand-nieces of the three princesses Bhishma had carried off long ago). Yet they, too, didn't bear him any children. At last he understood that the wives weren't the problem. He regretted all the beheadings he'd done, and he realized everything he'd accumulated, the great wealth of Magadha, would go to whichever military man managed to slaughter the other military men. His dynasty would be done with! What use all these riches, then? He started giving everything away to friends and strangers, the way suicides do before they hang themselves.

One big gift of cows went to a holy man, and this holy man offered him a boon. The king was so depressed, he couldn't think straight. He had no hope, so he had arrived at a point where he desired nothing but death. The moping king became the first documented instance of someone *declining* a boon. 'I'm all right,' he said to the holy man with a wave of his hand.

'Are you sure, Your Majesty?'

'What's the point in getting more *things*? It's just more to give away. Nothing is worth anything to me. I can't pass anything on to a son.' The king started sobbing into a silk pillow.

The holy man saw a plate of fruit sitting next to the king, and from it, he plucked a mango. He said a *mantram* over the fruit and handed it to Jarasandha's future father. 'Go ahead and have your wife eat this,' said the holy man, 'and she'll bear you a son.'

The king sat up, overjoyed, and by the time he wiped the tears from his eyes, the holy man was gone. The king shouted for his twin wives and fumbled for one of the many knives he kept around in case he worked up the courage to slit his wrists.

'Both of you should really taste this mango,' he said, handing them each a half. The twin queens frowned. The mango tasted like a man's sweat. But the king berated his queens until they ate their halves, and nine months later, they both delivered . . . *halves*. Nature had sliced the mango-sized baby down the middle. The midwives turned the thing cut side up and shrieked in horror at the pillboxes of the vertebrae, the walnut brain in the walnut-shell skull, the bisected baby slug of the penis.

In those days, miscarriages and monstrous births were exposed outdoors. The two halves of the heir to the Magadhan throne were tossed in the jungle. Instead of a scavenger, though, a rakshasi named Jara found the two halves of the baby. 'What a pretty doll,' she sighed, sliding the halves together—and frowning when they wouldn't click. So she got out her needle and thread and sewed the baby together. Rakshasa needlework, like all rakshasa art, comes down to transcendent superiority of technique; and no surgeon for a thousand years could have hitched, hooked up and made whole the two halves as intricately as Jara. When she threw the last stitch in the navel, the baby's eyes flicked open, and he let out a cry.

Jara had smelled baby-smell for so long, leaning in close with her magnifying monocle, that her breasts had filled with milk. She was burping him over her shoulder when her sister showed up. What was that, on the heel of the baby's right foot? Jara had been so intent on the midline that she hadn't noticed the birthmark of a chakra. This was the king's son!

Jara brought the baby to the palace just as the king, exhausted with despair, stroked a *kukri* beside a steaming bathtub. The boy's crying stopped him in time. To honour the rakshasi he named the boy Jarasandha, the one who was *sewn together by Jara*. The boy grew up to be much hardier and more hardhearted than his father. The father's depression had transformed, in the son, into a lust for self-transformation. Jarasandha trained by throwing rocks until his body had itself become rock.

Even so, claimed Krishna, Magadha's statuesque king was not unbreakable. He might be a rock, yes. But he was a rock with a seam down the middle.

*

King Jarasandha sat in the palace courtyard on a tasselled elephant. His priests (ash-smeared priests of the Tandava Sangha, with three black lines tattooed on their foreheads) walked the sacred fire around him. This was an inversion of proper ceremonial form; the fire was supposed to be the still centre of every rite. Krishna, Bheem and Arjuna stood among the Brahmin beggars, none of whom dared to frown. They allowed the twisted ceremony because they had to eat.

King Jarasandha had taken a vow to greet his Brahmin supplicants individually. The intention was to interest them in the Tandava theology. *Find out how you, too, can shorten Nataraja's sleep!* The hungrier they were, the more readily they received the message.

Jarasandha exchanged words with each Brahmin, but he passed by Krishna and the two Pandavas. He dismissed everyone else; the mahout guided the elephant through the gate. Now it was just the four of them. Arjuna marvelled silently at the millipede-leg stitches that bristled down Jarasandha's midline. The seam bisected the point of the king's widow's peak and created a natural part in his hair. His beard hid the seam at philtrum and chin.

Jarasandha stopped and stood eye to eye with Bheem. 'You gentlemen don't look like you need a meal.'

'We're not from around here,' said Krishna. 'We haven't been starved like the Brahmins of Magadha.'

'They would eat well—if only they foreswore all Gods other than the God of Destruction. I am the biggest charitable giver in all of Bharata.'

'If it's conditional, it isn't charity.'

'You're one to preach, Kshatriya.'

Bheem could not stay mum anymore. 'We're Brahmins, God damn it. Do you see any weapons on us?'

'Look at those overly worked-out arms of yours. If you're a rice-and-ghee boy, why do you have battle scars? Why does your friend there have calluses on both thumbs?' He glanced with contempt at Krishna. 'And the dark one, in that absurd yellow dhoti ... What kind of priest keeps a peacock-feather in his topknot?'

Krishna crossed his arms. 'We're closer to Brahmins than those fake priests playing around with the sacrificial fire.'

'That is *our* way of worship. You should know we feed that fire by burning copies of the Vedas in it. We worship by desecrating worship. It's only atrocities that prod Nataraja.'

'Like holding eighty-six kings hostage? And planning a human sacrifice with them?'

'I defeated all eighty-six on the battlefield. I put my sword on each one's throat and drew one drop of blood before I said, 'Live, for now.' They were *grateful*. And I treat them well. I don't house them in a dungeon. They're in a wing of my own palace. I even send them girls every so often. Their appetites are better taken care of here than in the kingdoms I took from them. My jailors do not lock the doors.'

'Human sacrifice is unheard of in Bharata. Shiva will be revolted by it.'

Jarasandha smiled. 'Exactly. Just as he will be revolted when I march my hundred-kingdom army to continents beyond the mountains, beyond the oceans, even. I will devastate Bharata. I will slaughter, enslave, rename entire civilizations. I will make them repeat after me, even if they speak no Sanskrit: 'Tandava now, Tandava now, Tandava now.' You should say it, too. Say it.'

'Never,' muttered Bheem. Krishna and Arjuna echoed him.

'Who are you? Who sent you? Why do you masquerade as harmless, bovine Brahmins—when I can see full well you're trained killers?'

'We've come here on behalf of King Yudhishtir,' said Krishna. 'We've come here to set the kings free.'

'Yudhishtir,' murmured Jarasandha. 'Yes, he's on my list.'

'And you're on *his*.' Bheem punched his palm, barely able to keep himself in check.

'If Yudhishtir sent you,' Jarasandha said, inspecting his would-be assassins, 'you, with the calluses, *you* must be Arjuna. And the big man going to fat—Bheem, I presume? And you, with your black skin . . . Yes, of course! The coward of Mathura.' Jarasandha paced back and forth in front of them. 'No wonder you brought two killers with you. Too afraid to take me on by myself. How do you want to do this? One on one in sequence, or one versus three? Are you hiding daggers or will we wrestle like athletes in a circle?'

'You were right about one thing, Jarasandha. We are Kshatriyas, which means we live by the code.' Krishna stretched, hopped in place a bit, and shook out his arms. 'Pick one of us to wrestle.'

The obvious choice should have been Krishna. He was the slightest of the three options, and his stretches had something dancerly about them. None of his joints cracked. Yet Jarasandha fixated on Bheem. Here was a real challenge—for the first time in his life, a wrestler his equal in bulk. Jarasandha pointed at the wolf's belly. 'You.'

Bheem didn't need much more than that. He lunged. The two giants clashed with a thunderous slap, and soon they were trading headlocks and gut punches. Jarasandha got a good hold on Bheem and threw him into a wall. Bheem shook the bits of masonry out of his hair and charged again. Krishna and Arjuna had to stay on their feet to avoid these periodically airborne wrestlers. When Jarasandha took a fall and had Bheem's knee on his chest, he cried out, 'Kitty! Kitty!' They'd just had the thought *Who's Kitty?* when the ritual elephant charged back into the fray, trumpeting hysterically. This elephant loved Jarasandha, who had nursed her with a bottle. Bheem now found himself between the bruiser of a king and his protective daughter. The trunk batted him aside, but he rolled clear of the elephant's stomp. Kitty would have pursued Bheem further if Arjuna hadn't shown up astride her neck and yanked her ear. Krishna light-footed it up her trunk, shushing her and begging her to stay calm. Neither of them wished to hurt the beast, who didn't know better. Desperately they irked her and cajoled her, anything to distract her from Bheem, who had just absorbed another body blow from Jarasandha.

Oomphs and shouts, walls that collapsed into rockslides, thunderclap spine-cracks called the citizens to their windows. Soon they beheld a runaway elephant with a hero in white rags flapping this way and that from her right ear. Many a Magadhan bas-relief portrayed the vision in decades to come.

That was Arjuna. As for Vrindavan's nimble dancer, he had been thrown off his dance floor. From the debris on the courtyard ground, Krishna picked up a peepal leaf from a tree that Jarasandha had just knocked over. 'Bheem!' Bheem looked his way, and Krishna ripped the leaf along its midvein. Bheem understood and, every time he grappled, he scraped at the stitch with his fingernail.

Scar tissue embedded those threads and knots, but Bheem jabbed and abraded the same area over and over, targeting the breastbone until the sutures started shredding. Pursuing that strategy, he got pummeled and thrown more than once, but his humming skull reduced all its thought to that one goal. Magadha's king was getting exhausted, too. He gave up a few advantages himself. Spinning Jarasandha three times over his head, Bheem tossed him into the air and stuck his thumbs up, side by side. Jarasandha landed on them, impaling his breastbone on Bheem's thumbs. One jerk, and Jarasandha ripped noisily along his seam. The royal heart and bowels pattered on to Bheem's belly and feet. Bheem threw the split peapod of a body to one side.

Arjuna, more dazed than bruised, stumbled in to find Bheem covered in gore and the king dead. Krishna was already thinking ahead to the next step: hijacking Jarasandha's chariot. Five powerful beasts—horse-rhinoceros hybrids, native to Bharata—were waiting for the whip. Krishna took the reins and said, 'I'll be your charioteer.' The sides of the chariot were stocked with new weapons. Krishna steered the chariot to the prison wing where the eighty-six kings were kept—contrary to Jarasandha's claims—in chains. They braced as he swung the side of the chariot directly into the prison wall. Another crash, but a controlled one. Through a cloud of dust, the emaciated kings emerged coughing. The Magadhan cavalry brought horses for these kings to ride: Arjuna shot eighty-six Magadhan captains off their saddles, and eighty-six mounts trotted up to the cheering escapees. Thanks to Bheem's javelins and Arjuna's arrows, a hastily assembled square of guards shattered before Krishna's onrush. They were all back in Indraprastha by evening, rescuers and rescued alike, telling Yudhisthir what happened. Eighty-six kings knelt to kiss their future emperor's great toe.

SARGA 25

GUESTS

Thwarted timelines don't *not* exist. They exist—inside mirrors and dreams. Trapped there, they trouble sleepers. Occasionally, the unrealized world peeks out at night, over a dresser, into a dark and empty bedroom, and whitens a palm against the mirror. At times, too, it scratches and digs and struggles out from under time like a live dog, still whimpering in his owner's arms, dumped unwittingly into a mass grave. King Devavrat's glorious unfulfilled conquests began to deform history soon after the sacrifice, like dark matter warping space and time around it, unseen but all-structuring.

Neither Bhishma nor his grand-nephews knew of this connection, but Prabhasa diffracted, prismatically, into the Pandavas. Yudhishtir, not knowing why, called his brothers to his side one morning and said, 'Go out there and conquer.'

'Whose kingdom?' asked Bheem. He was hoping his brother would answer *Hastinapur*.

'Just . . . conquer. Spread the dharma.' Yudhishtir pointed at each of his brothers in turn. 'North. South. East. West.'

And so four Pandavas rode out to realize the first phase of King Devavrat's thwarted reign: the conquest of Bharata.

Arjuna, dispatched north, tossed a stone into Mirror Lake. A pale arm rose from the water, holding a sword. Arjuna rowed out to it in a humble fisherman's boat, and his army watched as he received it. With it, he marched further north into a desert made entirely of snow. His men lost toes and fingers to the cold, but he kept going. At last he came to the kingdom of the Northern Kurus, where two giants, as big as Bheem and far whiter-skinned than Pandu, stood with arms crossed, their naked torsos indistinguishable from the snow that sprinkled them. In that silence, Arjuna demanded to see their king. The giants told him, in strangely accented but grammatically pure Sanskrit, that no mortal could enter that kingdom. Arjuna showed them the sword and demanded tribute. One of the guards went into the city and returned an hour later. Arjuna stood without shivering the whole time. Finally, the guard returned with a message. The king thanked Arjuna for returning the sword of Uttarakuru, lost since the end of the Satya Yuga. In return, he would refrain from slaying Arjuna and his army in the snow. He would give Yudhishtir nine woolly mammoths. Their backs would be loaded with treasure. But he must remember to shave the mammoths once they crossed the Himalayas or the beasts would die of heat stroke. Arjuna traded the sword for the tribute and returned to Indraprastha.

Sahadev, meanwhile, went west, and he found himself in a real desert. The nomads he found there were dirty and simple, and Sahadev felt pity for them. He built them a shrine in the middle of that desert and stocked it with all the murtis carried by his infantry. The nomads circled the shrine in awe. Sahadev taught them medicine, astronomy and the beauties of the dharma. In return, the chief of the nomads promised him ninety camels, their backs laden with treasure. When the ninety camels showed up, Sahadev went to see what was in the packs. Gold bricks? Emeralds? Neither: just fresh drinking water. That was their treasure. Sahadev returned half the water, taking only what his army needed to get out of the desert. He met many other kings and told them of Yudhishtir's ascendancy, and by the time he got back to Bharata, the camels were loaded with treasures of the solid, shiny kind. But he marched no farther west than the desert.

Nakula marched south, and there he got all the way to Lanka, where King Vibhishan XIV was ruling—a direct descendant of Ravana's brother, whom Rama himself had installed on the throne. Vibhishan XIV welcomed Nakula and agreed to send tribute to Indraprastha. Nakula took advantage of this friendly welcome to ask for a tour of places he had heard about in the Ramayana. The King of Lanka showed him the cracked stone footprints where Hanuman, having leapt off the tip of Kanya Kumari, landed on Lanka. Here was the Grove of No Sorrow, where Sita languished; here was the waterfall where Rama had slain Ravana. Six stones from Rama's original land bridge, each with his name carved into them, had gone to seed six temples. Nakula visited them all. The sixth overlooked the southernmost round of Lanka and the big sea. 'What's beyond there?' asked Nakula. Vibhishan told him the tale of a kingdom composed entirely of islands, scattered over thousands of yojanas, and one massive island of desert and scrub to the south-east, and, if he sailed directly south, one last continent made of snow and ice, where not just the dharma but human beings themselves had never lived, only half-mortal Yakshas who ate the fatty flesh of penguins. Nakula asked Vibhishan for ships to sail there, but Vibhishan told him Lanka did not build ships that could sail that far. He wouldn't even make it to the frozen yojana of solid sea that ringed the island of Dakshinapur. But Vibhishan promised him nine hundred ships, filled with Lankan gold, to sail home, shallow-bottomed so they could make it up the Yamuna. So Nakula ventured no further south.

Bheem crossed the Ganga and turned north and east to a powerful kingdom where men were as numerous as gnats, and their lives just as trivial to their ruler. When their armies saw Bheem block the setting sun, they fled in terror. Several infantrymen suffocated under the unbearable weight of his shadow. Bheem apologized to their emperor and insisted he came to spread the dharma and tell them of Yudhishtir's ascendancy. The emperor offered the king of Indraprastha tribute, just as all the others had: nine thousand men.

Men? Bheem was puzzled. Who had ever heard of men carrying tribute on their backs? Indraprastha was so far away, even mules would have a hard time of it.

No, explained the short and smiling emperor, the *men themselves* were the tribute.

But how, asked Bheem, could he afford to pay so many men a wage and meals? These men would be a drain on him, the opposite of tribute. Even the lowest-born labourers had an atman, a self, that was a piece of Brahman, clicked shut inside a body like the portrait in a locket.

The emperor laughed. In his world, such men could be kept for as long as they lived, then gotten rid of, like goldfish in a bowl. *You are a young civilization yet! Give yourselves time, you will be like us one day.* Bheem shook his head in horror and contemplated conquering this immense kingdom, but he knew he would have to do a tremendous amount of killing, and his soldiers were falling sick in their camps. So he accepted the nine thousand chattel slaves, marched them out of the kingdom—and set them free, settling them in the rainy, many-rivered lands east of the Ganga.

Bheem was the last Pandava to return home. Once he arrived, Yudhishtir assessed the total of his tribute, piled in four treasure houses. He looked over the map of Bharata, which the surveyors who travelled with his brothers' armies had prepared. Looking at Krishna, he asked, 'What do you think? Am I ready?'

Krishna nodded. 'Send out the invitations.'

*

Hastinapur and Indraprastha shared a river border. You would never guess, passing from the older kingdom to the newer one, that Dhritarasthra had saved the richer half for his own sons.

Duryodhan brooded balefully on the ferry. Shanties, weeds, a few rusty fishing boats and a rotten dock on the Kaurava side of the river. On the Pandava side: unloading zones with a line of barges, a boardwalk crowded with strolling couples, a park where a father taught his son to fly a blue kite, a bronze statue of Pandu smiling and waving across the river.

'That statue,' commented his Uncle Shakuni at his ear, 'is really too much. The mockery. The gloating. It was a gift from Krishna, you know.'

'That prosperity came from *us*. Our biggest businesses migrated across the river.'

'They played a shrewd game with tax laws.'

'They didn't have old roads to repair, two hundred temples to fund, pensions for bureaucrats—nothing. We gave them a new world to settle! My cousins used that generosity to hurt us.'

'There's an argument to be made that Indraprastha is yours by right. How is it the other guy's house if he stole every brick from yours?'

It took several trips, but finally all one hundred Kauravas disembarked on Indraprastha's foreign territory. Twenty Kauravas ditched the Imperial Sacrifice entirely to explore the boardwalk. Twenty more followed hooting when the first twenty discovered casinos.

'Gambling dens? Here, in pious Yudhishtir's kingdom?'

'Though he places his faith in the dharma,' commented Shakuni, 'he still loves games of chance.'

At the Great Hall that Maya built, no special reception awaited the Kauravas. They were just one more clan among hundreds in attendance at Yudhishtir's Imperial Sacrifice that afternoon.

The hall was so vast, it didn't feel crowded, not even after the Kauravas poured into it. The brothers, so used to jostling each other endlessly, floated free, marvelling at the colourful fountains, the trees of gold leaf, the titanium nightingales. A painted glass corridor created the illusion of walking through the Saraswati Valley. Duryodhan saw a shining floor made of one large mirror. He stepped on to it—and into it! The 'mirror' rippled in every direction. He was up to his armpits in water.

Laughter—women's laughter—made him jerk his head to look. One level above him, Panchali and her ladies-in-waiting hurried away.

Duryodhan clambered out of the pool and twisted his sash like he was twisting a neck. 'What did they say about me?' he asked Shakuni. 'Did you hear?'

'Shameless, girlish talk,' Shakuni said, turning away with a pained expression. 'Don't make me tell you.'

'What did she say?'

Shakuni took a deep breath. '"The blind man's son is blind."'

The fire-fathered empress-to-be had said no such thing. She hadn't even seen Duryodhan fall in. The women were laughing about something else, some trivial joke. Duryodhan, bowlegged in his dripping, clinging dhoti, carried that laughter in his skull. It made the fifty-foot ceilings echo. So did the splat, squelch, squeak of his sandals. Everyone, he felt, was looking at him.

'They got *everything*,' he rasped. 'Why *everything*, Uncle Shakuni? The fanciest hall, the wealthiest kingdom, the most beautiful woman? The fame, the love?'

'They didn't get everything. They took everything.'

'All they needed was half. Once they got half, they took all. But Panchali—she's married to *all five*. It's unheard of. But people are . . . fine with it.'

'Because it's *them*, Duryodhan. Can you imagine if you and four of your brothers had taken a wife in common?'

'Yudhishtir would have lodged a protest with my father. He would have had philosophers draw up a twenty-page treatise on how it contravened the dharma.'

'They would have called it rape. They would have called it sex slavery.'

'But because it's *them* it's okay.'

'That is Pandava ethics. Not enough there to fill a treatise with! "Anything can be lawful, as long as it's *our* side breaking the law." That's it.'

'And now a Pandava will complete the Imperial Sacrifice.'

'The first since King Rama. The stuff of epics. The presumption of this man . . .'

'And everyone is fine with it.'

'Even you are. You're here, aren't you? Attending his Imperial Sacrifice?'

'What can I do? My father just went along with it. "Who are we to challenge Indraprastha? Be happy for them, Duryodhan." Be happy for the Pandavas. Grandfather Bhishma is here, wearing sacred saffron, greeting guests at Yudhishtir's side. How did they get so much power?'

'I told you, my dear nephew, my dear, wronged nephew. They took it from you.'

Duryodhan stood and covered his face. A puddle gathered at his feet. 'How do I take it *back*, Uncle Shakuni?'

'I have some ideas about that. Let's keep walking.'

Duryodhan nodded and turned and took a step—and stopped short just in time. Another pool of water! This time, he was wise to it. He skirted it warily, lifting his dhoti clear as if some part of it were still dry, baring his unexpectedly slender calves, the wet hairs matted flat. Five guests and then five more strolled past him without breaking their stride. Their jewelled sandals clicked across what turned out to be a mirror. Duryodhan heard Panchali laughing again, up there, in the gallery behind him—but when he swivelled on his heel and looked for her, she was gone. Assuming she had ever been there at all.

Duryodhan did not want to enter the ceremony room until his clothes dried. Bheem, Nakula and Sahadev happened to emerge from the hall, and Duryodhan couldn't get behind a potted palm tree in time. Bheem's booming laughter chased Panchali's from his mind. Yudhishtir emerged and saw what Bheem was pointing at, but he didn't laugh. He embraced the bedraggled and dripping Kaurava, and he ordered servants to fetch his cousin fresh clothes. Soon, Duryodhan wore clothes more splendid than the ones he had arrived in.

'You see how he insults you?' Shakuni asked. 'Dresses you up in gold and silk. Like the prank played on the snoozing pauper—he wakes up and thinks himself a king. I feel bad for you.'

Duryodhan wasn't sure. When he entered the ceremony room, Yudhishtir found him again and told him, with the familiarity of a brother, to help keep the gifts orderly as they piled up. Elsewhere in the hall, Dushasana and other Kauravas were ladling out food and helping out in other ways. Duryodhan, surprised, turned to Shakuni. 'He's treating us like family. He trusts us so much he has us helping out.'

'Treating you like *servants*.'

'The same as Nakula and Sahadev over there, the same as Krishna...' Duryodhan felt confused. 'Bheem is just a bully. But maybe not Yudhishtir.'

'Yudhishtir sees everybody as a servant. That's why he's puffing himself up with this Imperial Sacrifice.' Shakuni pointed at the stacked and cluttered gifts: golden cradles, tasselled swings, murtis, decorative weapons... 'He's got you squatting in front of his goods like a glorified peddlar.'

Maybe putting Duryodhan in charge of receiving gifts wasn't the wisest choice. Within a few minutes, Shakuni didn't have to goad him to rage and jealousy. Witnessing his cousin's wealth grow in real time took care of that. He glowered at the milling guests. His eyes settled on Krishna.

Krishna's task was making sure the Brahmins had what they needed. This kept Krishna from visiting the Kauravas to greet them. Presently he took a break with his dear friend Panchali. Maybe she passed along the story of Duryodhan's dip in the pool. Sitting together in their splendid royal clothes, they resembled a God and a Goddess joking in heaven, heaven where everything, even hell, even heaven, is good for a laugh. Behind those beautiful dark faces, they were just as embodied as anyone else. If they had been omniscient, they would have known Duryodhan's thoughts, and they wouldn't have laughed.

Shakuni circled back to point out a further insult to the Kauravas. Krishna brought Grandfather Bhishma to sit in one of the thrones beside the fire. It was a way of signalling to everyone, Shakuni said, that even the oldest Kuru favoured the Pandava ascendancy.

Not the case at all. Bhishma loved Hastinapur and Indraprastha equally, like a great-grandfather of twins. Two Kuru kingdoms meant twice the Kuru glory.

Everyone took their places, but there was still some time before the ceremony began. Duryodhan joined his brothers in the audience, reduced to anonymity, no special seats. He kept his eyes on Bhishma and Krishna.

*

Their conversation was nothing particularly political. Bhishma asked after Krishna's new wife, Rukmini.

Much as Subhadra had crushed on Arjuna after hearing tales of his heroism, Rukmini crushed on Krishna after hearing rumours of his dancing, wit and good looks. Tales of his rakish teenage years made her think him even more desirable, since desire, like a virus, is something we catch from others. She fantasized about being one of his gopis. Exchanging letters, she had revealed her wish to be spirited away, as Subhadra had been by Arjuna. Not because she thought that particularly romantic. Rather it had become *necessary* that Krishna carry her off—since her family had promised her to another suitor, her brother's friend, King Shishupala of Chedi.

This got a bit awkward for Krishna, since King Shishupala—famed for his swaggermouth and little else—was a blood relative.

Twenty years before, Shishupala had been born with four arms. The extra hands each had a sixth digit. He had a third eye, too, and a third nipple, dead centre. Were these auspicious, Godly signs, the equivalent of a chakra-shaped mole? Shiva had a third eye, and the Gods in the temples were sculpted with two extra arms . . . But never extra arms like *these*: stunted, crooked, veiny, pustule-pocked and jutting out twig-like at odd angles. The third eye bobbed in his skull like a ball compass. The third nipple dribbled blood.

Babies could be exposed after birth in those days, if the parents, grandparents and priests were all in agreement. All except his mother thought the horror was best gotten rid of. The men were still trying to convince her when a voice from the sky settled the issue. All of Shishupala's extra parts would fall away, the voice promised, when his future killer took the baby in his lap.

It was one of the odder prophecies the sky had made of late. How were they supposed to find this surgical assassin-to-be? They kept the prophecy quiet and the baby swaddled.

Uncles and aunts visited in the meantime. Shishupala's mother was Vasudeva's sister: when cousin Krishna visited and took the baby in his lap, the two extra arms snapped off at the sockets. The third nipple grew crusty and peeled off. The third eye sealed at the lids to become a shallow furrow.

Shishupala's mother shared the prophecy with Krishna and begged him not to kill the baby.

'Why would I ever kill my own cousin? Don't believe every voice you hear in the sky. Plenty of showmen can throw their voices.'

'Who knows what might happen, Krishna? What if he offers you some terrible insult and you lose control of your anger?'

Krishna laughed. 'I'm not some hot-tempered Durvasas, and I'm never quick to take offence. I can forgive an insult. I'll go even further, to set your mind at ease. I vow, here and now, to forgive this little fellow a *hundred* insults.'

All these years later, Krishna offered his cousin Shishupala one grave, unforgivable insult: he drove his chariot to the Durga Temple and spirited Rukmini away—not just from her home town of Vidarbha but from her unwanted fiancé.

Bhishma, hearing this story, thought back to the time, in his hot youth, that he had swept into the swayamvara at Kashi. 'You boys, you and Arjuna,' he said, 'you consider yourselves heroes? Bah, in my day, I carried off *three* princesses, like sacks of flour on my back.'

'Every generation is worst than the last,' agreed Krishna. 'We're approaching the Kali Yuga, after all.'

'I think there's a fair bit of talent in this batch. Just look around the fire.'

The ceremony started. Vyasa himself oversaw the ritual. Thirty-three Brahmins recited Rig Vedic hymns in unison. The fire, stroked under the chin by these verses, purred its ninety-nine tails into the air.

Yudhishtir looked out over the assembled crowd. It was a consummation, a scene he would never forget. The dark ones drew his eye like stars against the night: his wife Krishnaa, daughter of Drupada, the poet Krishna Dvaipayana Vyasa, and his best friend Krishna son of Vasudeva. Then his gaze went to his mother, Queen Kunti, beaming at her boys, brittle but luminous in her old age. Grandfather Bhishma was here, and his father's brother, the blind king Dhritarashtra, and the blindfolded Queen Gandhari. His Uncle Vidura was smiling at him. Even Karna and the Kauravas made time to attend—all the past rivalries, he liked to think, forgotten, if not forgiven. Hadn't he forgiven them the Lac House? It was all boyish competitiveness gone overboard. They were men now, they were family. In the front row was his guru, Drona, and his guru's son, Asvatthama, all grown up, still with the weird jewel in his forehead, changing colours with his thoughts. Here was his father-in-law Drupada, his brother-in-law Dhristadyumna. Bheem had sent a carriage for Hidimba; the rakshasi wore delicate earrings and civilized silks, and their son Ghatotkach's bald head glistened under the lights.

All the characters from his story had gathered to watch this consecration, this coronation. And not just the ones who still lived. He liked to think his ancestors, too, were watching this event and smiling: Pandu, his gorgeous and fatal wife Madri, Queen Ambika who shut her eyes and Queen Ambalika who went pale, lovestruck Shantanu and sweet-smelling Satyavati, Kuru their common forefather . . . all the way back to the King Bharata himself. Everyone.

SARGA 26

THE HUNDRED INSULTS

Everyone was going to be here, Krishna knew. He had been on the lookout for Rukmini's jilted fiancé all morning.

Chedi's king had an obnoxious forthrightness, very much at odds with Krishna's suavity and subtlety of speech. Krishna didn't want a scene. Now that Yudhishtir was tossing rice into the fire, now that he touched his right ring fingertip, dipped in Ganga water, to either eyelid, surely the danger had passed? Krishna still couldn't relax. Where was Shishupala? Why wasn't he in the audience?

As if in answer, the double doors swung open and slammed the walls. Twenty feet high and eighteen across, made of solid teak and carved with scenes from the Ramayana, they shivered on their hinges. King Shishupala, scowling with disgust, grabbed an empty chair from the back row, strode up the aisle and set it down next to Vidura. All the guests whose chairs lined the aisle got a whiff of liquor as he passed.

Vyasa, officiating the sacrifice, ignored him. The Brahmins finished a chant and the poet stepped forward to address the audience. 'And now, the king will present gifts to his six chief guests: a guru, a relative, a friend, an ally, someone everyone reveres, and someone everyone loves. As the eldest Kuru here, Bhishma will be the one who decides the order. Tell us, Bhishma: who should receive the first gift? Who is the chief among the chief guests?'

Bhishma had been told in advance that he would be asked this. The vigorous old man had his speech ready. After a throat-clearing that echoed powerfully, he said, 'The one who deserves the first gift ought to be the guest that everyone loves. That is an obvious enough choice. But the truth is that this guest, here with us tonight, has been everything to Yudhishtir, to the Pandavas, and to Indraprastha. He has been their guru—I know what a great guru he is, since I have learned so much about dharma from him, more so than from any theologian. That's not the only reason everyone reveres him. You know what I mean if you've ever seen him on the dance floor!' Laughter. 'This guest has been their friend for years now, present at the founding of this city. Indraprastha has no more loyal ally. We all know he would go to war for Yudhishtir. This guest is a relative, too—Queen Kunti's nephew, and Prince Arjuna's brother-in-law. You have all no doubt guessed the guest by now. I advise Yudhishtir to give all six gifts to the same beloved, revered, loyal, wisest member of this great family. To the best friend the Pandavas have in all the world: Krishna!'

When the raucous applause finally let up, Yudhishtir rose to place a garland on Krishna and fill his lap with jewels, incense and sacred manuscripts. But a crass voice stopped him.

'Oh *please*. Him?'

Bhishma raised his eyebrows. Bheem cracked his knuckles in the shocked silence.

Shishupala toppled his chair when he stood up and swayed. 'That butter-junkie? That upstart crow? Come on, he's not even technically a king. I'm from the same clan as he is. He's my cousin. You ever seen him in the assembly, among the Yadavas? Among his own people? They don't fawn over him like this. They shout him the fuck down when he runs his mouth about dharma and karma and all that. They know him as Vrindavan's stray tomcat, a spreader of genital warts, a cowherd, a coward with sandal-sprayed dust on his calves. That's right, he had to flee Mathura—he was Jarasandha's bitch, that's why he allied with the Pandavas in the first place, to get their help settling the score. Why are you garlanding Balarama's bastard brother? Why honour that amateur flautist, that metre-mangling poetaster, that farmboy still stinking of dung? You've insulted every king here.'

Bheem stood up in outrage at the same time as Bhishma. Bhishma's hand on Bheem's arm managed to restrain the wolf-bellied one. 'You insult Krishna,' said Bheem, 'you're insulting all five of us.'

'Actually, Bheem, I'm insulting Krishna *specifically*. I can get to you in a minute. But when I say wannabe *rishi*, dipshit diplomat, scripture-quoting weasel, iron-kettle-face, sissy dancer in yellow silk, peacock-feather puffboy, hypocrite, self-abnegation-preaching self-aggrandizer, showman shaman, Mathura's regicide, rainstorm foundling, black cloud, black sheep of no one knows which family, lotus-footed pansy, Yadava hillbilly, syphilitic philosophe, Dwaraka's dwarf star, innocent Rukmini's serpent-tongued seducer, Radha's boy toy, butcher of the Khandava Forest, propagandist of the Pandavas, sweet-speaking self-seeker, treaty-breaker, myth-maker of your own damn self, mirror of mayhem and maya, male slut, gigolo yogi, shadowskin, girlyhips with the girly lips, cynical pseudo-*sadhu*—when I say all that, you know *exactly* who I'm insulting.'

All five Pandavas had stood up by now. The crowd murmured and stirred.

'Don't like me calling you out, Krishna? You won't even stand up? Why would you, when you've hypnotized these actual princes into serving as your bodyguard? I've insulted you right here in front of everybody. What are you going to do about it?'

Krishna looked out at the stymied Brahmins and the dimming fire, the hundreds of guests, and finally at Vyasa, who had his eyes shut, the better to memorize all that was being said. 'I'm going to keep doing what I'm doing right now. I'm going to count, Shishupala. You're up to forty-two insults.'

'Is that so? Well, here's some more: cowpiss sipper, Nanda's changeling, udder-squeezing country boy! Dharma's fair-weather friend, holy man with only politics in mind, quack doctor of theology, ladies' man, ladyman, pretty boy, fighter fleetfooted in flight from the fray!' Without realizing it, Shishupala's insults and epithets, his marathon flyting, morphed into what might have been praise, if spoken in a different tone: 'Tornado-wrangler, Kamsa's killer, favourite of all the gopis! Putna's breast-biting cannibal baby!' He shook his head and refocused. 'Con man, slinger of sleaze and slokas, dungbreath, charcoal face, raven wearing a peacock-feather . . .'

Shishupala concentrated on the sight of Krishna and the life of Krishna as he sought more insults. Contempt coaxed him into contemplation. He kept going.

'Leela's illusionist, Guru of Gokula's yokels, sweet talker with dirt in your mouth, revenant avatar, shape-shifter, conjuror doing the great Indian hope trick! Warmonger wordsmith, Yashoda's naughty boy, naughtiest between a married gopi's legs, maker of mischief, blackener of bloodlines, daddy to a dozen backwoods bastards—'

'Only a dozen?' Krishna grinned.

'Don't interrupt me. I'm not done.'

'You're getting there.' Krishna yawned. 'That was seventy-three.'

'Son of a convict, follytheist, so black you're blue, tongue-twister, trickster, godly fraud, intriguer, power-seeker, secret-leaker, dog barking at a mirror, jewel-thief, firestarter, seducer, asp, krait, indigo snake, black mamba, imposter king cobra—'

'Ninety-four.'

'Panchali's lapdog. Arjuna's yes-man. Ascetic with a sweet tooth. Butter-for-brains.'

'Ninety-eight.'

'False prophet.'

'Ninety-nine.'

'False idol.'

An even hundred! Krishna had forgiven them all. Shishupala grinned and kept his peace. Had his mother warned him of the prophecy? No doubt: unlike everyone looking on at Krishna's humiliation, Shishupala knew that only the hundred and *first* insult would prompt a retaliation. To the spectators, it looked like Shishupala had browbeaten Krishna, while Krishna had been too weak to shut him up or strike him silent.

Grandfather Bhishma, who had kept the Pandavas back, could not take this anymore. 'Shishupala! Enough!' His white beard darkened as scattered hairs went black with returning youth. His irises went river-blue, and he found his shoulders swelling, all his rivers of muscle swelling, a flash flood of rage strength. 'Shut your mouth and sit down!'

The foolhardy blatherer turned to Bhishma and pointed a finger right at the ancient Kuru's chest.

'*You?*' shouted Shishupala. 'You think I don't have some choice words for *you*? You think I'll spare you just because you're old? Your boring-ass speech was the reason they're giving him special treatment in the first place. You're nothing but a t—'

He never got the insult out, much less the other ninety-nine epithets he had in store for Bhishma. Krishna raised a finger, as if he had a point to make. The mystery-metal chakra flared and whined atop his finger and ran its errand.

A few queens in the audience screamed, and several kings rubbed their necks uneasily. At a gesture from Arjuna, guardsmen came and hurried the head and body away. The neck had gushed a lot of blood already. The guests lifted their jewelled sandals in revulsion.

Duryodhan and the Kauravas—seated far in the back—got to their feet to see better. Only Shakuni stayed seated, noting everything, rolling his lucky dice between his palms.

Krishna felt terrible that the ceremony had been interrupted on his account. His voice boomed in the hall. Even the five friends who knew him best marvelled at suave and subtle Krishna projecting such a stentorian, commanding voice. Krishna made his announcement in part to distract from the guards, who had returned with mops.

'An insult to someone I love hurts worse than a hundred to me.' Krishna kissed the tip of his index finger gingerly, as though he had pricked himself with a sewing needle. 'I promised Shishupala's mother I'd forgive one hundred of his insults. She didn't know it, but I'd have forgiven him a hundred more. An insult to the great Bhishma, though? To the man who took the fiercest vow of any Kshatriya in history? A man I regard as my grandfather? When it comes to someone I love, I won't even put up with one insult. Not one.'

The assembled guests rose to their feet and clapped. Only the Kauravas joined Shakuni and sat down all at once. The ceremony continued, though the sharp smells of burnt tissue and sawed bone lingered even after Vyasa lit sandalwood incense.

Hours later, when the ritual was done, Krishna and Bhishma did not mention the awkward interruption and the surgical beheading. Bhishma, knowing for sure now what he had always suspected, joined his hands and bowed his head. People, for at least a generation now, had only touched the fierce one's feet; no one had hugged Bhishma for many decades. The last hug he remembered was his father Shantanu's. So Krishna's spontaneous hug brought back many memories for the exiled Vasu. Being held felt like speed; getting enclosed by arms, like liberation. Touching

Krishna's dark skin regressed Bhishma, however briefly, to Prabhasa again. To Light.

*

The Pandavas embraced Krishna one by one and gifted him the chariot they had stolen from Jarasandha's kingdom, repainted and fitted with platinum-spoked wheels. Duryodhan could not bear to witness the send-off. Shakuni at his side, he wandered the hall, admiring, envying, shaking his head.

'I know what I saw. He killed his own cousin in public, in cold blood. And they *love* him for it.'

'Charisma lets him get away with things, Duryodhan.'

'Can you imagine if I killed one of my cousins like that? I'd be a villain, Uncle Shakuni. The world would be writing murder ballads starring Evil Prince Duryodhan. In a generation or two, they'd be painting ten heads on me with horns and handlebar mustaches.'

'Makes you wonder about Ravana, doesn't it? How these stories get told?'

'And that's what's popular. That's what gets praise. Even from Bhishma.'

'Fame is a consensus of fools. You and I know "Emperor Yudhishtir" is just a man with flaws.' Shakuni bit his lip and nodded. 'One flaw in particular. We see the Pandavas and Krishna clearly.'

It was an ill-timed thing to say—because Duryodhan happened to walk straight into an open door painted on a wall. Maya's artistry had pulled off an exquisite *trompe l'oeil* that magnified the hall. 'I want to kill myself,' said Duryodhan, holding his bloody nose and tilting up his head. He heard the laughter again: Panchali's, Bheem's . . . 'I should do it. I can't live like this, Uncle Shakuni. I want to die.'

'Don't you dare talk like that.'

'I'm imagining myself an old man. King of Hastinapur! It'll be a backwater by then. It already *is,* compared to this place. Maybe someone will invade, and I'll have to send across the river for help. A vassal king: me!'

'You'll send for Karna, if you need anyone. Or me. You have allies, my boy!'

Duryodhan barely heard him. 'Born into this strength, this ambition, this bloodline—and forced to be a *vassal* my whole life? How can I live like that? I'm too proud. I have too much self-respect to go on. I want to drop through death like an escape hatch and pop up in another body somewhere. Work my way to the top again. Win through. I can do it.'

'Do you think the king who got murdered today didn't have friends? The king of Shalva saw what happened. He didn't speak up, but he was appalled. And enraged. I had a word with him. We're not the only ones at odds with the new order. The king of Shalva has built an aerial city. The greatest siege machine in history.'

'They've got enough leftovers here to last another yuga. Indraprastha won't fall to a siege.'

'No. But Dwaraka might.'

Duryodhan patted his nose with the rich sash gifted him by Yudhisthir. 'What about the Pandavas? They'll still be wealthier and more powerful than me.'

'But they won't have Krishna, the secret to their wealth and power. He'll be busy with his own city, distracted, drawn away . . . leaving them open, Duryodhan. Leaving them wide open.'

'To what? An invasion?'

'An invitation.'

SEQUENCE 9

THE GAME OF DICE

Envious Duryodhan, egged on by his devious uncle Shakuni, exploits Yudhishtir's known weakness for gambling. Hastinapur builds a rival hall and invites the Pandavas there for a game of dice. Against Vidura's advice (as usual), Yudhishtir decides to go.

Bad move. Shakuni plays on his nephew Duryodhan's behalf. He is a 'skilled' thrower of dice, which can mean anything—good at making his own luck or good at cheating without getting caught.

Yudhishtir loses and keeps losing. He wagers everything he has, including his brothers and Panchali.

Duryodhan, eager to humiliate the Pandavas, has Panchali dragged out in public. His younger brother Dushasana tries to strip her clothes. Krishna, though absent, hears her prayer; miraculously, he renders her clothes of infinite length. But the shame, in front of her five powerless husbands, stings her no less. She will not let the Pandavas forget this.

Quarrels and outrage—but Bhishma and blind king Dhritarashtra, who are present for all of this, do not intervene until after Panchali is shamed. The blind king offers her anything she wants, and she asks to have her husbands set free. But she refuses to ask to get their material losses back; she wants their kingdom to be something they will have to *take* back, by force. Perhaps aware this would entail war, the blind king restores everything to the Pandavas, Indraprastha and all the wealth Yudhishtir lost.

The Pandavas drive off, but a messenger calls them back: one last throw of the dice. Yudhishtir agrees.

Shakuni sets the stakes at thirteen years of exile, with the last year incognito; if they are discovered in that last year, they have to go back into exile for another twelve years. Yudhisthir loses this throw, too.

The Pandavas must go into exile now, as paupers. Each prince vows a specific vengeance; Panchali vows not to tie up her hair until she is avenged. Her hair will serve as a living, growing reproach to her husbands during their exile.

SARGA 27

SKILLED AT A GAME OF CHANCE

If Yudhishtir was so pious, why did he love gambling so much? He wasn't very good at it. 'Best of three' became 'best of five' became 'best of seven' at every coin toss. It was best to let him win at *shatranj* unless you wanted to wait through game after game until he won his wager back. The Pandavas 'gambled' for rock candy, rose petals or, most recently, leftover bolts from the construction of the hall. Nothing of any value, nothing they would feel the loss of. Yudhishtir was always game, and known to propose a game with the prasada almonds still in his mouth.

His virtue was his flaw. Precisely his piety, his sense of an all-pervasive divine, drew him to gambling. He loved games of chance because he did not really believe in chance. Every win or loss was a referendum on his conduct. Victory and defeat, success and failure came from the Gods—hadn't the Upanishads made that clear? The Gods were giving him an attaboy every time he cried 'Heads!' and the coin came up heads; or, if it came up tails, they were signalling their displeasure. Gambling provided Yudhishtir with feedback from an otherwise tight-lipped cosmos. He so desperately wanted to please the Gods.

Vidura brought the invitation. And told him frankly to decline.

'Since it's you bringing the invitation,' insisted Yudhishtir, 'I can trust it's really a friendly gambling match, just like the invitation says it is.'

'I didn't volunteer! I'm here because Dhritarashtra sent me, and Dhritarashtra sent me because Shakuni told him to.'

'If my uncle wants me to play, I really must go. Out of filial piety. The king has been a father to me.'

'Shakuni described Duryodhan to him. "You can't see how pale your son is," he said, "you can't see how he's losing weight."'

'Is my cousin ill? It wasn't the food he ate here, was it?'

'He gorged himself on envy here in Indraprastha. And now he wants you to gamble? You won't be playing for cowrie-shells, I can assure you. Shakuni has agreed to roll the dice on his behalf. Shakuni! The most cunning gambler in Bharata.'

'Is there a rule against that? One man rolling dice for another?'

'"The dice may be thrown by whomever the gambler chooses: / The one who risked the wager wins or loses." That's the verse from the *Dyuta Sutra* they're relying on, the *Game Scripture*. The Asura poet Ushanas, who wrote the *Dyuta Sutra*, lists it as the telltale sign of a cheater. "But if someone is having a friend throw his dice, you can bet / They've schemed together, and will cheat you yet."'

Yudhisthir rubbed his chin. Vidura got the sense he was trying to figure out an excuse to come. 'My uncle has built a new hall, you say? Just like ours? It would be an insult if I didn't visit it. He came to mine, didn't he?'

'You can visit it later. You don't have to gamble there.'

'What if he had sent back that reply, when I invited him to my Imperial Sacrifice? Travelling in his old age for my sake. Visiting the hall—visiting him—it's the least I can do. And if my cousins want to entertain us in their new casino room, what's so wrong with that?'

Vidura rubbed his face in despair. 'Don't do this.'

'A friendly gambling match. Note that, Vidura—"friendly" is their word, not mine. And I do miss Hastinapur! Let me go tell my brothers and Panchali to pack for the trip . . .'

*

The moment they crossed into Hastinapur, Panchali doubled over discreetly with cramping. A bad omen. By the time they arrived at the palace, she was bleeding. A few whispered words to Queen Gandhari, and some chambermaids escorted Panchali to the women's quarters, where she went into isolation. It was a heavier period than usual, so heavy and with so many clots, she wondered if it might be a miscarriage. She traded her clothes for a single bolt of cotton cloth, dyed black to conceal any further drops or stains, which she wrapped around herself. Foetal position, on her side, hugging her torso, she waited out the pain.

So she never got to tour the new hall that Hastinapur had commissioned in response to Indraprastha's. She didn't miss much. The Pandavas nodded and praised what they could tell right away was a tawdry imitation, built with low-grade materials. Hastinapur, already so densely built, offered far less land to build on. This new Kaurava hall had squashed some longstanding slums. Never having seen the real thing, hence unable to identify the knockoff, Dhritarashtra walked the Pandavas from room to room, describing each as it had been described to him by the architect—a Brahmin named Amit, from the Saurashtra Kingdom. No one had heard of him before. Vidura and Bhishma came along, too, helping guide the blind king by the elbow.

At last they arrived in the biggest room of the hall: its casino, crowded with Kauravas. Green velvet circles lay scattered thick as lily-pads. The Kauravas, reclining on cushions, ordering drinks, played games of chance against each other. When the Pandavas arrived, they sent up a cheer. Bheem didn't like that cheer; it had an air of malicious glee. Arjuna stopped short at the threshold, too, sensing a threat so intensely that the hairs on the back of his neck stood up. The twins murmured to each other, full of foreboding; Sahadev was convinced he had heard, smothered under that cheer, the howl of a distant jackal.

Yudhishtir had already flitted to the nearest circle. Duryodhan and Shakuni had waved him over.

'About this,' Yudhishtir was saying. 'I shouldn't gamble.'

'Why not? It's a friendly match.'

'I shouldn't. I mean, look at these heaps of gold coins they're pushing around. I haven't brought anything myself to wager with, either. I'll watch you instead! The master roller.'

'You can wager with words.'

'I shouldn't. Neither words nor coins.'

'One coin, then? Here. I'll give you my lucky one.' Shakuni flipped the coin towards Yudhishtir, who caught it by reflex.

'I don't want this, Shakuni. You can have it back.'

'I gifted it to you! It's yours now.'

'Please, take it back. I . . . I should not gamble today.'

Shakuni sat down and made himself comfortable. One elbow dimpling a cushion, he gestured at the green velvet square on the floor. 'Play me for it.'

The Kauravas left their games to goggle in a crowd. Three chairs were brought over for the blind king, Bhishma and Vidura.

Yudhishtir felt the pressure of so many eyes. He sighed, weakening. 'I should not gamble today, Shakuni.'

'It's such a trivial wager, Yudhishtir! Here. Set down the coin. On my end, I'll wager this cup.' Shakuni drained the cup in one gulp and slammed it on the velvet.

Yudhishtir placed the coin next to it, as gently as if he were placing it on a dead man's eye. He sat down, by reflex, in the lotus asana.

'The King of Cups versus the King of Coins.'

'I should not gamble today.' Yudhishtir shook his head and unfolded his legs to rise.

'Wait! "I *should* not," you keep saying. You don't say, I don't *want* to. Do you *want* to gamble, Yudhishtir?'

'What I want and don't want is irrelevant. I know what I should and should not do, and that is knowledge enough for me to rise. I'm sorry.'

'Wait! Is it true, then, that you *want* to gamble? You aren't committing. Do you or don't you? Tell the truth. You've vowed to tell the truth.'

'I do. I do love games of chance. I do want to gamble. But that won't stop me from rising.'

'Wait! You *are* the emperor of Bharata, aren't you? A king of kings?'

'Yes. I am.'

'Can any man—I exclude the Gods, of course, and your wife—can any *man* keep the emperor from doing what he wants? Honour your vow.'

'No. No man can keep me from doing what I want. Which is why I am going to rise.'

'Which is why you are going to sit down exactly where you are, and roll the dice. You must not tell a lie. You made a vow not to.'

Yudhishtir shook his head, confused.

'No man can stop you from doing what you want. You said it; it's true. You want to gamble. You said that, too, and *that's* true. You are a man, aren't you? If you stop yourself from gambling with us this afternoon, you'll be a liar. A man will have stopped you from doing what you want. The fact that the man is *you* is irrelevant. Honour your vow. Don't make yourself a liar. Play.'

Yudhishtir bit his lip and glanced at his brothers. They could not meet his eyes. Shakuni seemed to have reasoned Yudhishtir into a bind. If only Krishna were here, they thought, Krishna might have exerted some wily logic, or cited some pertinent sloka, but Krishna, indispensible Krishna, Shakuni's sole equal in cunning, was off in Dwaraka, fighting the king of Shalva's airborne city . . .

'Wait,' said Shakuni. 'Before we roll. My cup is worth more than the value of your coin. Do you have a second coin on you? Could you add it to your side of the wager?'

Yudhishtir, whose wealth lay in granaries of sapphires, had only one coin on his person. It turned out he, too, had a lucky coin: the split coin with his father Pandu's profile on it. Vidura had given him one half before he left for the Lac House; Vidura's digging crew had given him the other half. At the foundation of Indraprastha, he had ordered the two halves soldered together. His luck had skyrocketed after that.

Yudhishtir took it out reluctantly and ran his thumb over the needle-thin weld-line. Shakuni smiled, his eyes wide with anticipation. He knew this was the crucial inflection point: could he get Yudhishtir to contribute something of his own? That would hook him.

Yudhishtir, kissing his father's image, set down the coin. Not one glance at Arjuna or Bheem. He had chosen.

'Did you bring your own dice? Or should we fetch you a pair?'

'I brought my own.'

'Of course you did. Because you wanted to gamble.'

Yudhishtir said nothing. His limp wrist dropped the dice, which barely tumbled.

Shakuni rose on to his knees. His fist shook above his head, like Indra getting ready to throw a javelin of lightning. You wouldn't imagine he was playing for two useless coins—one, double-sided, the other damaged and out of circulation. Shakuni knew he could rely on his dice. His mind could control how they landed because he'd had them made from the box-bones of his father's hands.

'I win!'

Duryodhan lunged and gathered close the coins and cup. He handed Shakuni's lucky coin back to him. Then he flipped the coin bearing Pandu's face over to Karna, who snatched it with a swift hand. A page came over to refill the cup, which Duryodhan handed reverently to Shakuni.

'Care for another wager? Let's gamble like men this time, not like schoolboys playing for cowrie-shells. You name it, Duryodhan will match it.'

Yudhishtir, his gambler's appetite awakened with this first taste, rubbed the dice excitedly. His pride was a little offended at this equivalence drawn between himself and Duryodhan. 'I have one granary full of sapphires and another full of diamonds. I have a fleet of twelve thousand war chariots, too, brand new, with retractible side-blades in their axles. Can he match that?'

'You don't have to ask from now on. Hastinapur is his security.'

'We play for this wager and what I lost before it. If I win, I win it *all* back, my coin and yours and the cup and everything.'

'From now on, every wager includes everything before it. Roll!'

They rolled. Shakuni shouted, 'I win!' The Kauravas roared and chattered with joy. Over the noise, Sahadev leaned over and spoke into Yudhishtir's ear. The eldest Pandava did not seem to hear him. He raised his hand to silence the Kauravas.

'Forty thousand head of cattle,' he announced, 'and our riverside docking facilities at Indraprastha, and our solid jasper murti of Ganesha.'

They rolled. Shakuni pointed at his incontrovertible bone dice. 'I win!'

Now that he'd lost, Yudhishtir realized, the baseline stakes were his own lost property. So he had to up the stakes even further. Arjuna and Bheem were shouting in his ears, but the glee of the Kauravas captured his attention. He ignored his brothers.

'Shakuni,' he burst out angrily, 'I know what you're doing. There's no such thing as a "skilled" dice-thrower. It's either random or it's not, and if it's not, it's cheating.'

'Are you calling me a cheater?'

'You're winning *every* roll, Shakuni. Now I know it's considered a great insult to inspect your opponent's dice . . .'

The Kauravas feigned outrage, eyebrows high and mouths open. *Did he? Did he just call out Uncle Shakuni?* Some howled, some gasped dramatically. They were thrilled that this was getting personal.

'These dice,' said Shakuni with great pain in his voice, 'are bone dice. Do you know whose bones these dice are made of, my emperor?'

Yudhishtir and the Pandavas scowled.

'My own late father, now ashes on a mountaintop in Gandhara. In his last will, he bequeathed me a box-bone from the base of either hand. "That my son Shakuni," read the will, "might have them carved into dice, and that with every roll, his father may bring him luck." These dice are precious to me, as you can imagine. No one has ever held them but me—and my late father, technically. He held them his whole life. I hold his hands in mine when I hold these dice.' Shakuni made his chin tremble. 'But if you must inspect them, please do. If only so both my father and I might retain our honour.' Shakuni held the dice out on his palm and looked away.

Yudhishtir leaned forward, but he didn't pick them up, feel the corners, or do a test throw. So inexperienced a gambler wouldn't have recognized loaded dice anyway; and the mystical control Shakuni exercised over those world-historical trapezium-bones had nothing to do with asymmetries of edge or weight.

'Satisfied?'

'Yes.'

'Wager again. You have a lot to win back.'

'The hall where I held the Imperial Sacrifice, built by Maya. The palace at Indraprastha with its whole staff, gardeners, chefs, footmen, everyone.'

They rolled. First Yudhisthir rolled, then Shakuni. 'I win!'

'My kingdom!' Yudhishtir said without a moment's delay, frustrated, baffled, panicking. 'Indraprastha, and everything in it and on it and under it!'

He grabbed the dice and dashed them onto the green velvet. Shakuni took his time. 'I win!'

Yudhishtir, stunned, hung his head. His brothers were talking to him, but he had gone deep into his own thoughts. A revelation: he was being taught a lesson. The Gods were communicating. *Do you see how transient and meaningless all the glory and wealth of the world is? You've lost so much—and how fast! Whoosh, gone! See how it's all chaff? We had to show you!*

'Do you want to keep going?'

'I do.'

'Then keep going, emperor. No one can stop you.'

'I've lost everything! I want to win it all back, but I can't! I don't have anything else to wager, Shakuni!'

'Of course you do,' said Shakuni. 'You have brothers, don't you?'

SARGA 28

RAISING THE STAKES

With every throw of the dice, Yudhishtir had wanted even worse for the dice to be thrown. Chance-enchanted, kismet-mesmerized, his eye tracked them from Shakuni's mysterious hands to the tumbling velvet and from there to a stop. Impossible! He was driven, too, to wager more and more so that his luck *had* to turn—because no man ever lost this much at one sitting, right? The house rules of the cosmic casino would not permit this asymmetric outcome. The God of Probability, who had no hymn in the Vedas but kept chaos honest, would intervene. Oh, but who or what would keep Shakuni honest? The man wouldn't cheat. Not in front of all these witnesses. Watch those hands—what were they doing that defied the odds and the Gods alike? How was dice a game of skill? The next throw would restore balance. No coin landed tails every time. One entry in the Win column and he could breathe out, cash out, get out, and no challenge or wheedling would persuade him to another throw, not even a direct order from Grandfather Bhishma. The next throw, and if not that throw the throw after that, would win him everything back. All he had to do was be willing to lose it—which itself was a test. A test of his faith in probabilities and the goodwill of the

Gods. How pious are you really, Yudhishtir? Do you really believe that the material world, and everything (every*one*) in it, is maya—or was that just talk? Prove it. Risk it. *You have brothers, don't you? Transcend your attachments to possessions and loved ones. Show the Gods you are above it all. Go all in.*

'Stop! All of you, stop!'

Vidura had stood up and clapped his hands, silencing the Kauravas and halting the match. The humble chamberlain, the elderly son of Vyasa and a maid, had never shown such aggression before, and the Kauravas, who had known him all their lives, were amused at it. Vidura himself seemed taken aback at his own passion, and promptly he retreated to his usual—whispering in King Dhritarashtra's ear.

Duryodhan didn't like this. 'Hey! Chamberlain! What are you saying over there?'

'I am serving your father, as I always have.'

'What's he saying, Dad?'

'Son, give us a moment, will you?'

'I want to know what poison he's pouring in your ear! Say it out loud, Vidura!'

Vidura ignored the prince and whispered to the blind king again.

'Are you telling him to have me killed? The way you did the day I was born?'

Vidura went pale and silent. The blind king flinched as though struck.

'You thought I didn't know that story? I've been carrying that knowledge my whole life. Let's air it out now, shall we? Vidura said I was going to lead to disaster for this bloodline, for this dynasty! But now look. I'm the richest man in Bharata. I'm the king of Indraprastha, and one day, when I'm Hastinapur's king as well, Vidura, I'll have reunited the kingdom Dad partitioned on your advice. And the first thing I plan to do is retire *you*. What were you telling him? Were you advising that he have me killed? My own father? In front of my brothers? Were you telling him to authorize an arrow in my back?'

Grandfather Bhishma had his eyes on Arjuna and Bheem. The two fearsome Pandavas were taking advantage of this distraction. Eye contact, quick flicks of the gaze to each of the exits, subtle military hand signals—Bhishma could see them planning. What if they sealed the hall and slaughtered their cousins? Wouldn't that play out *precisely* what had been foretold at Duryodhan's birth? *Oh Gods,* thought Bhishma, *it's happening before my eyes! How can I stop this?*

'Those were the omens, yes,' said Duryodhan's father. 'I should have known that wouldn't stay a secret. I never for a moment thought of hurting you. You were my first baby boy, Suyodhan. My first . . .'

'And now I'm first in every way. I'm a winner.'

'I'm proud of you, boy. But maybe you should go easy on your cousin.'

'I will, Dad. I'm going to give him the chance to win it all back. One throw. What do you say?'

Dhritarashtra nodded.

'So, Yudhishtir,' said Shakuni, 'which brother will you wager first?'

'Nakula. I love him more than Indraprastha.'

Nakula, staring emptily ahead of himself, rose and took a step, placing himself between the Pandavas and Shakuni. 'I hope, for both our sakes, brother, that I bring good luck.'

Pious Yudhishtir closed his eyes and moved his lips as he shook the dice in his hand. No God heard his prayer.

Shakuni kept his mind squarely off heaven and rolled. 'I win!'

'Sahadev,' Yudhishtir said immediately. 'He's the wisest of us. One word of his wisdom is worth everything that has gone before.'

Sahadev was weeping. 'Then why didn't you listen to me today?'

'You should have spoken up.'

'I have been shouting in your ear, brother. You praise my wisdom, but you weren't wise enough to want my wisdom when I offered it.'

'What did you advise me?'

'Stop playing.'

'It's too late now. I have to keep playing to get it all back. The Gods are showing me how to lose everything before they give it all back. So I value this. It's all a lesson. A test.'

Sahadev shook his head. Yudhishtir had been shaking the dice in his fist the whole time they spoke. He threw, and then Shakuni threw. 'I win!'

'Arjuna,' murmured Yudhishtir. 'I still have Arjuna. The best archer Drona ever taught. Everything I've lost, Arjuna could reconquer, single-handedly.'

Arjuna stood. 'If I'm yours to wager, brother, I'm yours to command.' He glanced meaningfully at the Gandiva, which, softly and just for a moment, thrummed and glowed.

Yudhishtir shook his head. 'I can win it back without bloodshed,' he murmured—but his faith in the explanation he'd given Sahadev was clearly fading. Still more quietly, he confessed to Arjuna, intimately: 'You deserve better than this.'

They rolled the dice again, and the outcome was no different. 'I win!' said Shakuni. 'You still have one more brother left.'

'Bheem. I wager him against everything I've lost so far. Look at his arms. He could win it all back.'

The Kauravas grew noisy at the prospect of dressing Bheem up in the livery of a palace footman. They would have to have a special uniform made! Already the Kauravas were riffing on further ways to humiliate the giant: they would dress him like a performing monkey one day, like a dancing-girl the next.

'I need to stay a free man,' said Bheem, glancing meaningfully at the mace parked on the floor behind him. 'If I'm free, I can win everything back for you *right now*.'

The eldest Pandava looked mournfully at his brother, standing straight though the mockery of his cousins. 'You deserve better than me,' he whispered.

'Roll the dice, Yudhishtir!'

They rolled.

'I win again!'

Bheem lumbered over to where his brothers stood with hanging heads. The hooting, guffawing Kauravas flung winecups and sandals at his vast back. He was too stunned to feel any of it.

'What do you have left to wager, my kingdomless king?'

A faint smile came over Yudhishtir's face. *Yes*, he thought, *this is the ultimate message I'm being sent: sacrifice all, and all shall be returned to you.* He nodded. *How poetic, how apt, that I should win it all back this way . . .* 'I wager myself.'

He kissed the dice and rolled. Thanks to his faith in the Gods and his ancestors, he was certain of sixes. But he didn't get them. This time, the ears that heard Shakuni's 'I win!' didn't belong to him. The face that blanched, head that dropped, body that froze were parts of an object that belonged to Prince Duryodhan.

'This is going to lead to war,' said Vidura, his head in his hands. 'The prophecy is fulfilling itself, moment to moment. Why do we pretend we're powerless? Bhishma? You, at least, *you* speak up!'

'We have to keep them from war,' Bhishma nodded. 'But I have sworn my oath to the man who sits on the throne of Hastinapur. I'm loyal to him. Dhritarashtra?'

'Listen,' said Dhritarashtra. 'Shakuni's voice has taken on a conciliatory tone. Let us give these young men time to work things out. We must not interfere. Us and our old-fashioned ideas.'

Vidura shook his head in anguish and disbelief. There was only one old-fashioned idea that mattered to him, and that was the idea of dharma. If only Bhishma had sworn his oath to an idea instead of a throne!

'You can still win it back,' said Shakuni. 'There is one last thing left to you, one last treasure you brought with you from Indraprastha.'

Yudhishtir searched his memory, but he was too flustered. He touched the jewel that lay on his chest. 'Do you mean this jewel? It's precious. It swirled to the surface of the ocean when the Gods and Demons churned it. But it's not worth enough to stake against myself, much less all I've lost this afternoon.'

'No, not that. That necklace comes with the slave, just as the collar comes with the dog. Think, Yudhishtir.'

'I can't think of anything I still have.' He spread his palms. 'I don't even have myself.'

Shakuni looked back at the Kauravas, and at Duryodhan. Everyone was quiet because they, too, couldn't figure out where Shakuni was going with this. 'It's a treasure worth you, your brothers, Indraprastha, Bharata itself, and everything on it and under it. Wager this, and if you win, you win everything back. Even the coins and the cup.'

'What do you mean?'

'Panchali, the blue lotus of Panchala. Krishnaa.' He savoured that last syllable. 'Wager your wife.'

Yudhishtir swallowed and made eye contact with his brothers. They had flushed red, and blood vessels began popping in Bheem's eyes until the whites of his eyes went all one red. Blood trickled from his ears and dribbled from his earlobes. Six Kauravas, fearing what the Pandavas might do, skittered over to their abandoned weapons. The cousins carried off Bheem's mace and Arjuna's Gandiva and hid them somewhere.

'I wager Panchali. Against everything.'

A cheer went up from the Kauravas. Karna banged his golden breastplate with joy, and Duryodhan hugged Shakuni, lifting him off the floor.

Bhishma, Vidura and Drona were visibly sweating, but they looked to Dhritarashtra—who relied on his ears and heard only the cheers. The blind king had half-risen from his chair, but not in indignation. 'Has he won?' Dhritarashtra asked, turning his head this way and that. 'Has he won?'

Yudhishtir pressed the dice to his shut eyelids. The one-dot side faced out: square eyeballs with narcotized pupils. His meditation complete, he shook the dice with renewed vigor. Opening his palm, he threw Panchali away, just as he had thrown away everything else.

Shakuni winked at Duryodhan. Without even bothering to look how the dice landed, he said, 'I win.'

When the cheering died down, Duryodhan swaggered over to Vidura. 'All right, chamberlain! Go fetch our newest serving girl! I want that little black bitch to sweep the floors here first. Then she can go explore her new living arrangement in the servants' quarters.'

'You're suicidal,' hissed Vidura. 'Always have been. Only you're taking all your brothers with you. What kind of dimwitted elk goes up and nips the ears of five panthers and a pantheress? I'd say you're trapped by your own jealousy, but no, you *are* the trap, and you've snapped shut on your own brothers. Give it all back!'

'Shut your mouth. You've never wanted to see me succeed. Where's that architect? You!'

He pointed at the mediocre architect who had vied with Maya and built the fateful hall. The architect shuffled forward, his hands together, his eyes on the floor. 'Yes, Prince Duryodhan?'

'Go to the women's quarters and tell Panchali her presence is required by her master. Don't look at the Pandavas! Or this sniveling cowardly chamberlain. I'm in charge of everything.'

The architect, in a panic at being thrust into this drama, hurried to the palace with a dry mouth and sweaty armpits.

Panchali spoke to him through a closed door. 'What's that you say? Yudhishtir's been gambling?'

'And losing. Losing big! He has lost you to Duryodhan.'

'My husband bet *me*? Why would he do that?'

'Because he had nothing left to wager.'

'How about himself?'

'He lost all his brothers. And himself as well.'

'Go ask him. Did he lose himself first, or me?'

'I was there, Queen Panchali. I—'

'Go ask him!'

She was giving herself time to think. But it ended up being time to weep. In the hall, Duryodhan snarled at the architect and sent him back. 'She can ask her questions in person, damn it! Her master wants her *here*.'

The architect went back. He feared Duryodhan's fiery temper and Panchali's fiery heat. His bowels wanted to evacuate, but not as badly as he himself wanted to evacuate from Hastinapur. At Panchali's door again, stammering, he told her of Duryodhan's demand. It so happened that another messenger arrived, this one from Yudhishtir, who had noticed his charioteer in the crowd and had beckoned him over. Heckles and whoops chased the trusted charioteer as he ran after the architect.

'My queen,' he said, kneeling before the door as if it were the woman.

'Nivedana, is that you? Is what this man is saying true?'

'It is, my queen. Your husband sends word to come and stand beside King Dhritarashtra's chair. A pillar will conceal you. No one will harm you if you stay close to the king.'

Panchali, her fire banked, shuffled in her ungainly garment to that place in the Hall. Dhritarashtra turned his head a degree, and though he smelled the telltale blue lotus, he did not acknowledge her.

'Get out here!' shouted Duryodhan. 'You! Architect! Tell her to get out and stand in front of her master!' He looked at Bheem, as motionless as the statue of Bheem that Duryodhan practised the mace against, and at Arjuna, anxiously picking the calluses on his thumbs.

The architect found Panchali crouched and glaring at him from behind the pillar. He could not decide whom it was less dangerous to offend. 'Sir? You want me to tell her to . . . what?'

By the mere laws of probability, at least *one* Kaurava out of the hundred had to turn out a good man. That one good man was Vikarna. He hadn't always been disaffected with Duryodhan and the ninety-eight-strong brotherhood. What triggered his interest in dharma was the simple accident of his name. When Duryodhan adopted Karna as an honorary Kaurava, Karna became a sensation. Vikarna heard his name everywhere—or thought he did. It always turned out to be Karna, Karna, Karna his brothers were calling over, greeting, cheering on. Vikarna felt replaced. Karna, the new golden boy, was the sun; Vikarna, the midday moon, dissolved and disappeared. That invisibility gave him detachment from his brothers; he could see them from the outside, as the Pandavas saw them. The same emotion that made Duryodhan do wrong—jealousy—made Vikarna do right.

'Brothers,' said the gentle Vikarna. 'We're making a mistake here. Or committing a sin, I should say. It's bad enough that we've brought her out here wearing that one cotton cloth. We all know what that signifies. That's a violation, right there. We're out of line. But that question she asked. Was she really his to wager? Is nobody going to answer that? It's a fair point. In my opinion, he was wagering something that didn't belong to him. She was never "won".'

Duryodhan's face twisted in disbelief and disgust at this betrayal. Kunti's first, secret son stood up and slapped his upper arms to draw attention to himself: Karna, outshining Vikarna yet again. 'Vikarna, sit down and shut up. Is it any surprise she's wearing one scrap of cloth? I'm surprised she's wearing anything, the whore. Listen. Everybody knows she was won by Arjuna, right? At the swayamvara in Panchala? He took her back to meet his family and a few hours later, all five Pandavas showed up at the palace. Just told her father they were *all* going to marry her. Vikarna wants to ask fair questions? Here's a fair question. What happened in that hour? I can guess. I think she let them each have a go. She's a nymphomaniac, is what I think. Are we really going to debate the finer points of who belonged to whom, who wagered what when? I mean, she's basically public property.'

Duryodhan clapped his hands. 'Well said! Well said!'

Vikarna looked appealingly at the elders, but far from getting support, King Dhritarashtra chided him. 'Vikarna, didn't you witness how the Pandavas respected their eldest brother? Learn from your cousins.'

'That's right, Vikarna, you little shit. Respect me. What's your number in the birth order, anyway? You're in the seventies, if I remember.'

'Seventy-two,' murmured Vikarna.

'Right. So wait until you grow a little more hair on your chin before you flap your lips at me. Where's Dushasana?'

The second-born Kaurava strode to the eldest's side. 'Yes, my emperor?' he said with a grin. He savored applying Yudhishtir's former title to Duryodhan.

'See that slut over there? Behind the pillar?'

'I certainly do.'

'I own that. Drag it over here. Drop it at my feet. I want to inspect my new piece.'

SARGA 29

A TEMPLE IS SACKED

If only she hadn't come here—if her first cramps had hit an hour earlier, while she was still on the other side of the river—where was Queen Gandhari? A woman would help her. A woman would not let this happen on her watch, her blindfolded watch. Where was she? Dushasana was playing a game with her, trying to step on the edge of her single drape of cloth, so that her escape itself would strip her and he could chase her naked. She knew what he was doing. She could hear his breathy, vulgar insults. *I don't mind that you're bleeding, pussycat, I like making a mess.* Panchali screamed for Queen Gandhari as she scrambled towards the women's quarters. Her hopes rose as she saw their lavender and gold sarees. Desperately she reached out a hand to each gawking illiterate sister-wife and concubine in those sticky-sweet-smelling halls, but one after another, the Kaurava women shuffled into their rooms and locked their doors. Dushasana, they knew, had a heavy hand. Besides, they were pleased to see the snobbish Pandava princess get humbled. Maybe a splash of acid or a broken nose would drop her beauty a dozen ranks. Maybe their husbands could be persuaded to shave her head—that blue-black hip-length hair of hers would make a gorgeous wig.

Dushasana loved the chase and even prolonged it for a few minutes. He loved that Duryodhan had done him the honour of picking him to dishonour her. The cotton cloth kept slipping her shoulder and tripping her up. Serving girls never ran from him; they went stiff as corpses, or they trembled and cried from start to sweaty finish. They never gave him the leopard's delight of following his prey. If it were just him and Panchali right now, if they weren't expected back in the hall—oh, what an arrow might have pierced this black doe! Dushasana liked seeing her in a panic like this. So much hype had surrounded the princess of Panchala! They claimed she chewed and swallowed fire, claimed she had put blisters on Bheem's fingertips once when she was sulking. Didn't seem so Goddess-like now, did she? No, she was just a sobbing maid, like so many others that had submitted to the Kaurava princes as they came of age.

Dushasana made a decisive grab. Her whole body snapped away, like a flame from wind. This happened twice. Dushasana noticed how her long hair, still wet from a recent bath, trailed her movement with a slow swinging motion, very sensual. That was what he grabbed the third time. And he got a thick, ropelike handful of black hair to jerk her around by. It was cool in his hand.

Dushasana wished the corridor back to the hall had been longer. When he tugged, she leaned forward so her head was level with his waist. When he yanked, she shrieked and lost her footing and he got to slide her a few feet, dislodging the robe a little further. He was already the first Kaurava to touch her; he would *love* to be the first to see her, by accident. A peek. Or, who knew? A preview? It depended on Duryodhan's mood.

When Dushasana got her back to the hall, the Kauravas ran to him and formed a semicircle. Duryodhan made sure the Pandavas had a clear view. The Kauravas chattered about her face and figure, but her shrieks could be heard over the noise, since

Dushasana swung her hair left and right with sweeping excursions of his arm, as though he were slapping her face.

Vidura clutched Dhritarashtra's enormous arm. 'Don't you hear her screams, my king? Don't you hear her?'

Dhritarashtra turned the other way. 'Bhishma, from this chair of mine, I hear a sea bird. Do you?'

From this chair: wherever the king sat was the throne. It was a reminder. Bhishma gritted his teeth.

'What is a sea bird doing this far inland, Bhishma? Is that an albatross that someone shot? Listen to it crying.'

Of the three elders present, so far only Vidura's face had crushed with emotion, only Vidura had spoken up. Grandfather Bhishma of the Fearsome Vow and the blind king Dhritarashtra: these two oh-so-respected figures looked on with the effaced, expressionless faces of Easter Island monoliths, observing the changeless sea. Hadn't Bhishma, in his day, barrelled gorilla-like among the quarrelling cousins and scattered them? In an instant he used to resolve whatever spat had gotten their blood up. But they were children then, and he, though not a young man, had been younger then. They were grown men now, autonomous, taught what they ought to and ought not to do. How long was he supposed to referee the rivalry? They had to work things out on their own, he told himself. Maybe he had stunted their ability to do so when he intervened. Maybe this dice game was ultimately his own fault. Still, when adharma was this obvious—even then, to hesitate? Why? Everything begins with a vow. His fame began with a vow, and so would his shame. Bhishma could not risk defying the blind king who sat on Hastinapur's throne. *From my chair,* Dhritarashtra had been careful to say. For that had been the letter of Bhishma's Fearsome Vow: allegiance to the throne, and by implication, whoever sat on it. Until Dhritarashtra spoke up, Bhishma could not speak up.

So, why didn't Dhritarashtra? Because Pandu had been born with eyes that worked, and he hadn't; because Pandu's sons were beloved, and his weren't; because Duryodhan was winning, and the poor child needed a boost to his self-esteem, since he was always so down on himself, comparing himself to the Pandavas. All of those reasons played into it but he acknowledged none of them, not consciously. He preferred to think of it as fate. Fate had him in its predatory jaws, and his passivity was the slackness of prey lifted off the ground. Sometimes the predator's jaws cracked the spine. The bloody length of fur draped itself over the spiky jaw, paralysed. That was how the blind king felt, sitting in his chair, savouring the joyful cheers and applause of his sons. He knew it was wrong of his sons to rejoice; he knew it was wrong of him to rejoice that they rejoiced. *Note that*, he thought. *I do not rejoice at what is happening. I rejoice at their reaction to it. It's not the same thing.* Fate was deciding how he felt. Was the dice game the prelude to disaster? To total war? Maybe so, but his sons were so happy right now. Obscure and infinitely ramifying vectors of karma had brought the Kuru dynasty to this point. He was fascinated to discover, moment by moment, what fate had decided. Could he really say this was unfair? Maybe fate would give everything back to Yudhishtir. The blind king was curious to know how things would turn out on their own, without his interference. Listen: the girl had gone quiet. Listen: his boys were cheering and clapping and whistling. Wasn't it healthy for them to win for once? 'An albatross, Bhishma. Astonishing. This far inland.'

'When your mother shut her eyes,' said Bhishma gravely, 'she blessed you never to have to see this day.'

*

Panchali, broken into ragdoll passivity, lay on the floor where Dushasana had flung her.

Bheem turned on Yudhishtir. 'You're responsible for this! You and your gambling habit! Gambled us into slavery. Gambled with *her*. You like rolling the dice, do you? I ought to rip your fucking arms off.'

'Bheem!' said Arjuna.

'No! Really! I'm going to rip his arms out and cauterize the sockets with a torch so he never rolls any goddamned dice again in his life. Sahadev! Grab me that torch off the wall!'

'Bheem! No!' Arjuna flung himself between towering, cross-eyed Bheem and seated, slack Yudhisthir. 'We can't turn on each other. Not now. Not ever.'

Yudhishtir himself said nothing, and neither did the Kauravas. They just watched the scene. How satisfying to see the other branch of the family fall apart so sloppily! Panchali on the ground, hair and clothes in a mess, looking like a whore who just woke up. Bheem, throwing a tantrum and threatening Yudhisthir; Arjuna, arms out, trying to hold him back! Were those tears falling from Yudhishtir's eyes? Yes—big, womanish tears! The twins hugged each other. (This was how, when they were three years old, side by side in bed, they soothed themselves to sleep.) What a tableau! Paint *that* on the wall of this casino room.

Duryodhan gave Dushasana the nod. 'It'll be a few weeks before we pass her along to our younger brothers. Might as well whet their eyes.'

Dushasana circled her a few times, sizing her up, his fingers twitching. Then he shook Panchali by the shoulders. She screamed.

'Slave girl!' he shouted. 'You liked five, you'll *love* a hundred. Now let's see what you've got under there.'

Panchali's eyes flicked in terror here and there about the semicircle of onlookers. 'Don't you dare.'

'Who's going to stop us? Your husbands?'

'This is the lowest point of your famous Kuru dynasty! All those prophecies of your extinction—you deserve it! Dragging me out here. A hundred grown men tormenting one woman. What degenerate in-laws I have! What kind of family did I marry into?'

Karna put his pinkies to his lips and whistled and Duryodhan guffawed—but the rest of the Kauravas stayed quiet. Some had gone quiet from lust, and some from foreboding.

Panchali crawled towards Bhishma's feet. 'You, the elders of the family—you're all ok with this? You, Grandfather Bhishma? With the blood of a river Goddess in you?'

'I want reconciliation,' said Bhishma carefully, 'not warfare. I want this to resolve without things going too far. So the question is uncertain.' He glanced at Dhritarashtra's frown. 'I can't answer the question about whether you were won fairly or not. But what I can say, to all these Kurus here, is that . . . aren't we all Kurus? One blood, one lineage? Remember who you are, my sons.'

Dushasana had no patience with old-fashioned platitudes. He grabbed the free end of her wrap and pulled. Panchali fell on to her side. The passive spool of her body spun one full circle, then another. Dushasana, expecting to see her nakedness any moment, lusting to be the first to see her up close, pulled one more time. And pulled again.

And kept pulling. As a kite-flyer during the Uttarayan festival, in honour of the sun's going north after the winter solstice, high on a city's terrace feels the wind slacken and a stranger's powdered-glass-laced kite string descending on to his, and has to draw his kite in hurriedly, pulling the string fist over fist, his wingspan opening and closing, opening and closing as the coarse string piles in loops and tangles on his shoes: that's how Dushasana pulled at Panchali's modest cloth. There was more and still more, one continuous bolt of cloth eternally self-weaving, like the grace of Panchali's dark-skinned God invoked in her agony and shame. The name she whispered over her joined hands sounded very like her own. Seeker and giver, infinite mercy and finite pain, atman and Brahman, identical.

How long did he keep at it? Several Kauravas lost interest and left for pee breaks, and when they got back he was still pulling. At last, drenched in sweat, Dushasana fell back panting on to the small mountain of cloth behind him. Panchali, still on the ground, pulled the closest bit over her shoulder, and her connection to the pile slipped away. Crawling away from Dushasana on all fours, she glared at her five powerless, humiliated husbands.

*

Eye contact with the indignantly trembling Panchali broke a dam in Bheem. He let out a roar. The Kauravas staggered back, unsettled by the miracle that seemed a cosmic reproach, and now by Bheem's belated awakening. 'All my ancestors, all the Gods and Goddesses, all the Kshatriyas the world over, listen up: may I be shut out of heaven, may I never meet my ancestors, if I don't crack this sinner's chest! One day, I will drink Dushasana's blood in battle! Remember it! That's a vow!'

Many other princes and courtiers were present in the hall, though the hundred Kauravas had made the most noise until then. Now a few of those Kauravas, and several of the courtiers, started grumbling and calling things out—but not in favour of Duryodhan's aggression, much less his father's complacency. The blind king heard all this, and the sides of his mouth began to sag.

'It's locked in,' groaned Vidura. 'He said *in battle*.'

The king murmured, 'Nothing is set yet.'

Panchali saw the king's expression change. She hurried over to him. The hall went quiet, expecting her to reproach him—but her instincts served her well. 'I should have done this earlier, but I got distracted. King Dhritarashtra, Grandfather Bhishma, I am so happy to see you again.' She bowed and touched their feet— humiliating them while escaping reproach. The opinion of the crowd shifted further, with scattered applause and at least a dozen Kauravas murmuring their way over to Vikarna.

Bheem sensed the shift, too, and he pointed at Yudhishtir. 'You've always had the right to give me orders, and slave or free man, you still do. I forgive you everything. Just authorize me. I can take care of this right now. With my bare hands.'

Vidura and Bhishma got out of their chairs. 'Hold off, Bheem, please!' cried Bhishma. 'There is still a way out. There must be.'

Karna, sensing the shift, walked over to Panchali. He was the same height and breadth as Arjuna, so similar in shape that her eyes, briefly, confused them. 'You're a shrewd girl, aren't you? Make the best of this.' In spite of all the terrible things he had called her, in spite of his hateful tone of voice, his wistful eyes betrayed his heart. 'Pick a new bull for yourself and shack up. There's plenty who would have you, maybe marry you. You won't even have to make the bed afterwards.'

Panchali did not answer him. She turned, instead, to Dhritarashtra and the other elders. The blind king had turned his head from her voice; Bhishma, bound by his loyalty, could not meet her eyes.

'Once upon a time,' she said quietly, 'my husbands wouldn't let the wind touch me. Now the son of a driver can say anything to me and any man at all can pull my hair and throw me around like a sack of sand. That's what it is to be a queen among the Kurus. I never saw this at my father's house in Panchala. The world knows now how you treat women here in Hastinapur.'

'What's that? Panchali, we treat women royally here!' Duryodhan sat down and pulled his dhoti up to bare his muscular, hairy thigh. He gave it a couple of loud slaps with a cupped hand. 'Come sit on your throne, my queen!'

The Kauravas, still in thrall to their eldest brother, burst into laughter. But it stopped short when Bheem, tapping into raw, primate rage, pummelled his own chest, ape-like. 'I'll snap that thigh one day! Snap it like a twig! I'll see the bone poke through the skin! I'll see you dragging your broken thighbone, Duryodhan! That's a vow! That's a vow!'

Bheem's voice made everyone's bones hum. Dhritarashtra felt it, too—no turning his head away from this. Fearing for Duryodhan's life, the blind king rose from his chair.

'Duryodhan,' he said gently, 'you've behaved very impolitely today. There's an etiquette for treating guests. We don't raise our voices. You know that.' He turned towards the scent of blue lotuses. 'Panchali, forgive me. You can ask Vidura and Bhishma. My poor blind eyes confused me. I thought someone had shot an albatross. "What's a sea bird doing out here?" I kept asking. But now I realize what I was hearing. You haven't had a pleasant visit. Ask me for a boon. Anything, my dear.'

It was best he could not see the disappointment and disgust with which Panchali eyed him. 'I want Yudhishtir set free. He must be his own man again.'

'It's done. Ask me another.'

'I want Bheem, Arjuna, Nakula, and Sahadev all set free as well. The five Pandavas and I should be allowed to leave Hastinapur right now—with all our belongings. Chariots and weapons included.'

'Done. Ask me a third boon.'

'I don't want a third.'

'You could ask for everything to be returned.' (At this Duryodhan cried out petulantly, *Dad!*) 'Take my third boon and simply ask for everything to be returned, down to the cup and the coins. Go ahead. Do it.'

'My husbands stood by and watched what happened here. They don't deserve to have everything returned to them yet. Certainly not through *my* intervention. You can keep your third boon. All I want are my husbands. Armed and free to make war.' Her flamethrower gaze swept the room. 'On *everyone* who deserves it.'

SARGA 30

THE KILLING VOWS

Whether Panchali had intended it or not, she put fear into the Kuru elders. Vidura and Bhishma did not have to counsel the man on the throne. The blind king ordered his sons to stay back and himself walked the Pandavas out to their chariots. Wringing his hands nervously, he said to Yudhishtir, confidentially, 'We both know my Suyodhan has a big mouth. He's always been that way! A virtuous man like you, Yudhishtir, you'll remember the good and let the bad behaviour slide. You have to be tolerant. You're the eldest of all, you know. He's your kid brother! Indulge his tantrums. I let things go for a bit because I didn't want to stop you boys from working things out. I was always going to return everything to you. Which is what I'm doing right now. It doesn't matter that Panchali refused the boon. Everything that was yours when you arrived, is yours now that you're leaving. I give it all back.'

Yudhishtir hugged the blind king and began to weep against his shoulder. 'Uncle Dhritarashtra! I knew it! I knew it! I always had faith!'

'Yes, yes, faith in your good karma. Faith in the Gods, my boy. It's always been your nature.'

'I had to be taught a lesson. "The world is illusory." They always teach us that. Now I know. I've *experienced* it. I know it for the mirage it is.' Yudhishtir kissed his uncle's hands. 'Thank you. Losing and regaining everything—all in an afternoon—it's been a mystical experience. I've learned so much today!'

Bheem, fists at his sides, looked like he might batter Yudhishtir, or Dhritarashtra, or both. Arjuna extended his arm across Bheem's chest, a firm safety brace. Yudhishtir finished up his tearful farewell and mounted his chariot.

The Pandavas drove off towards Indraprastha. Panchali, angry at Yudhishtir, rode with Arjuna, but she didn't say anything to Arjuna, either. All five of her husbands had stood by like eunuchs. She could not imagine sleeping on the same cot with any of her husbands. Reproaches? Browbeating? Shaming? Now was not the time—not because they didn't deserve it, but because she felt too nauseous and exhausted. She was grateful for her condition. Cramps and spotting would ensure nights of solitude. Touch them? She didn't even want to look at them, not even Arjuna. Their faces reminded her of how they looked at her in that game room, when she appealed to them in vain. Their passivity would never not puzzle her. They had no answer when she asked them why they had not done anything. At the time, and ever after, it puzzled them, too.

Yudhishtir averted his focus from that part of the day. Instead he smiled and nodded his head at the fields. What a lesson in transience! But he must make it up to Panchali and his brothers. When he got home, he decided, he would make a vow: this day would be the last day he would ever gamble. He would swear off it entirely! No backsliding!

He had already composed the words of the future vow in his head when a fast horse thundered up the road behind them.

'A message!' shouted the rider, waving a palm leaf. 'An urgent message from Hastinapur!'

The chariots halted. Nakula asked Sahadev, 'Did we leave something behind? Do you have your sword, brother?'

The messenger read, 'Dearest Yudhishtir, Bheem, Arjuna, Nakula, Sahadev and fire-born Panchali: King Dhritarashtra requests your presence in Hastinapur for a friendly game of dice.'

The Pandavas looked at each other, confused. 'There is some mistake. We received that message this morning. The chamberlain, Prince Vidura, delivered it himself.'

'I know about your gambling match this afternoon. This was handed to me by the king after you left.' Just that morning, he would have addressed the emperor of Bharata with downcast eyes. Now the messenger, unimpressed, turned his horse towards Hastinapur. 'What do you want me to tell the king? Are you coming or not? They're all waiting for you in the hall.'

The Pandavas, at any other time, would have taken offence at being talked to this way. Bheem in particular would have lifted the fellow off his horse, one hand under the jawbone. Their confusion at the request, and their recent humiliation, primed them to endure this insolence. Panchali's steady gaze, too, pinned them in their places and flustered them. She was suppressing her own contempt for the fathers of her children.

'It's an order from King Dhritarashtra,' said Yudhishtir apologetically. 'I have to go there to see what he wants. You can go back to Indraprastha without me.'

'The letter is addressed to all of you,' said the messenger.

The Pandavas nodded.

'We should all go,' said Panchali, 'if only to keep Yudhishtir from gambling us all away again.'

'I'm obligated to honour that invitation,' said Yudhishtir bitterly. 'I never sought out any dice games. I know my weakness, okay? I learned my lesson. I'm in control now.'

They turned their chariots and headed back to Hastinapur, back to the gambling room, back to Shakuni.

*

Dushasana had eavesdropped on his father's farewell gift to the Pandavas. 'Duryodhan! Duryodhan!'—sprinting into the gambling hall, where the Kauravas were debating Panchali's decision to decline the third boon. Was it shrewdness to force a war or vengeance to punish her husbands? But if vengeance, why inflict poverty on herself? Whatever the case, now was the time for war, before the Pandavas could take their grievance to neighbouring kingdoms. Strip Indraprastha, Shakuni was saying, and turn it into war material. Seize their armies and chariots and behead all the officers to obviate conflicts of loyalty. And then hunt the five brothers throughout Bharata. No doubt they were escaping to Panchala, to shelter with Panchali's father. Spies would have to be recruited.

'Dad just gave it all back, Duryodhan! Everything we won today! Go out there and ask him!'

King Dhritarashtra walked into a mobbing from his own sons. They all spoke at once, but he clapped his giant hands to silence them. 'Where is Duryodhan?'

'Right here.'

'What you heard is true. I gave it all back, for the good of the Kuru family. Yudhishtir has already forgiven you. Everything has gone back to the way it was.'

'You didn't *see* what the other Pandavas were doing, Dad!' (Neither had Duryodhan, but he had a habit of taking advantage of his father's blindness.) 'Nakula and Sahadev, frowning like yakshas, slid the light along their blades. Arjuna tested that empty quiver of his, conjuring arrow after arrow out of nothing. Every third arrow, he would squint one eye and hold it out, pointed at you.'

'And Bheem?' Dushasana joined in. 'While you were talking, he scowled at the back of your head. Stretched his torso like a wrestler. Do you think Panchali will let them rest? She'll goad them all night until they go mad with shame and rage. There may be an attack as early as tomorrow.'

The blind king felt his way to the palace steps and sat down. 'I see more than you realize, my dear boy. Nakula and Sahadev shuffled their feet in the dust, I heard it. I heard Bheem, his bloodlust cooled at last, dab his nosebleed and his trickling ears. I heard Arjuna whisper to Panchali and wipe the tears off her cheeks.'

Duryodhan did not acknowledge he had lied. 'How could you give it all back, Dad? How could you rob your own sons?'

'I am keeping you boys from all-out war.'

'The only way to do that,' said Shakuni, 'is one last throw of the dice.'

'Yes! Call the Pandavas back! If you invite him, he'll come. One last throw—Dushasana, run to the stables! Tell them we need the fastest horse and the skinniest jockey. We can get them in time.'

'I can't let you play for the girl again. You won't, will you, my boy? That was too much.'

'We won't play for people, or cattle, or chariots, or land,' said Shakuni softly, taking a seat at Dhritarashtra's elbow. 'There's a Pauper's Wager described in the Dyuta Sutra, for penniless men who still want to gamble. Whoever loses, goes into exile.'

'How long?'

'Twelve years in the forest, wearing antelope-skins, like Rama and Lakshman and Sita. A thirteenth year in a city, any city—but not as royalty, as commoners, incognito. If they're discovered? Into the forest for twelve more years.'

Dhritarashtra nodded. 'The Pandavas—twenty-five years from now—why, they would be in their sixties, wouldn't they?'

'Old men don't start wars.'

Dhritrarashtra nodded, even though Shakuni's little dictum was quite false, since it has always been old men who start wars (and young men who die in them). The blind king had just dictated the message, and was reading over the palm-leaf letters with lightly dancing fingertips, when he turned to his blindfolded wife's approach. Gandhari's thin body moved so quietly, only her husband could hear her footsteps. 'Yes, my dear?'

'Boys,' she said sternly, 'go inside. All of you.'

The Kauravas filed inside without a word.

'Dushasana, you little eavesdropper, that includes you.'

Emerging from the bushes, flushed at her preternatural ability to sense him, he hurried inside behind his brothers.

'Shakuni?'

Shakuni cleared his throat, pocketed his lucky dice, and joined the Kauravas. Gandhari sat down next to the blind king.

'Don't indulge our boys in this,' she said. 'Their voices have deepened, but they haven't grown up.'

'They won't be happy unless I give in, Gandhari.'

'You remember the prophecy at Duryodhan's birth.'

'If the line has to go extinct, how am I supposed to prevent it? Everything I do is the wrong thing. Real heroes love their fate. I never won battles like Pandu when I was young, I was never heroic like that. But I can learn to love what's coming. And if, in the process, I can make my boys happy for a spell? It's the least I can do.'

He kissed her forehead just above the blindfold and got to his feet. When the Kauravas heard him call for the messenger, they sent up a cheer.

*

Panchali refused to enter the hall at all. Hugging her knees, she sat on the floor of Arjuna's chariot. Her finger traced the sleek lines of the Gandiva. A fierce wish for rebirth as a warrior in her next life made her long for death.

Inside, Yudhishtir's brothers looked around the gambling hall where they had suffered such intense emotions. They couldn't believe they were standing there again so soon. They had hoped never to set foot in the cursed place again. And now Shakuni was describing some convoluted wager involving exile and disguise?

'I don't mind playing for those stakes,' said Yudhishtir. His brothers were immediately at his side, pulling at his arms, but he stared into Shakuni's eyes. 'There's one condition, though, before I accept your challenge.'

'Yes?'

'I roll with your dice, and you roll with mine.'

'Agreed.' Shakuni produced his dice with a flourish and savoured Yudhishtir's sudden uneasiness.

Shakuni took Yudhishtir's dice and laid them on his eyelids, just as Yudhishtir had, then turned to the Kauravas. They burst out laughing, and laughed even harder when Shakuni clasped the dice between flattened palms and murmured a breathless *Hari Aum Hari Aum Hari Aum!*

'Enough,' said Yudhishtir. 'Let's play.'

Shakuni did not bother taking a seat. It was only one roll, after all. He knelt by the green velvet where he had won earlier that afternoon.

Yudhishtir went pale, realizing what he was risking. 'No!' He pointed to another green velvet circle, at random. 'That one!'

'It wasn't the velvet, and it wasn't the dice,' said Shakuni contemptuously. 'It was the player. It is always the player. But have it your way.'

They knelt opposite each other. Yudhishtir studied the bone dice warm with Shakuni's hand heat. A sudden inspiration made him count the dots on all the sides—but the dice were correctly marked. Would they obey chance, or would dead King Subala's bones favour his son Shakuni? Bah, they weren't sentient, *couldn't* be sentient. That was superstition. But the greatest gamblers believed in superstition, didn't they? Chance wasn't the only law at work in the universe, or the gambling hall. Astrology, fate and divine will fought it out with chance. Yudhishtir had a horrifying vision of divine will being just one force among many, sometimes victorious, sometimes overwhelmed.

'Wait, Shakuni . . . Let's trade.'

Shakuni gave an incredulous snort and exchanged dice again. 'Now?'

'Now.'

*

The antelope-skins were fetched from a nearby temple, where five ascetics found themselves switched into princely attire. Both sets of men found the new clothes itchy and unnatural. Panchali's antelope-skin was cleaner and more comfortable. It came from the costume-closet of the palace's theatre, where it had last been donned by Sita.

Many of the Kauravas hung back, afraid to come near these predators in the wild. Tiger-skins would have better suited the pacing Pandavas. But once Dushasana danced around Bheem and Bheem did nothing, the others couldn't resist. They ventured closer and closer. 'You can stay back with us!' 'Your husbands gambled at dice and lost their balls, Panchali!' 'It'll be a long thirteen years!' 'They're leather effigies of men now—pick a real man like me!' 'Nah, pick me, baby!' 'Hell, pick *five* of us!'

The actress Sita who wore that forest dress first also braided jasmine flowers into her hair. Panchali let down her bun and mussed it into tangles that hung over her face.

'Oh, she wants a little something for the road! Let down that hair, pretty lady!'

'This is what your wives will look like,' she hissed at the Kauravas, 'when fourteen years from now they wail over your dead bodies. I won't tie my hair up until I hear that music. That's a vow.'

Duryodhan crept up behind Bheem, holding his arms away from his sides and turning his feet out slightly. His brothers laughed at how well he mimicked Bheem's body-builder's gait.

'Have your fun while you can. I'll be breaking those legs soon enough. Like I vowed.'

'Shut your mouth, fat ass,' snarled Dushasana. 'Your vows don't mean shit. You've got years of nuts and grass to eat. We'll see how big you are when you get back.'

'I won't be hungry, I'll be *thirsty* when I get back. And you're going to give me a drink. Like I vowed.'

Dushasana scoffed and spat at Bheem's feet. 'Drink that.'

Bheem saw Karna following Panchali. 'Oy! Karna!'

'What do you want, loser?'

'I've reserved Duryodhan and Dushasana. But you're reserved for Arjuna.'

Sahadev, who like his twin had covered his body in mud and dust, heard this and cast his eyes around the crowd. When he saw the man he wanted, he slipped through the crowd of Kauravas and stood in front of him. 'Shakuni,' he said.

'Yes?'

'You're the one I'm going to seek out in battle.'

'You? You're a doctor. Go grind up some herbs and don't make threats to a mountain warrior like me.'

'I won't do it with herbs, no, though I do know some poisons that would torture you for a week. The old Kshatriya way, Shakuni. Steel.'

'All I did was throw the dice for someone else. I wasn't even playing.'

'Just threw the dice, did you?' Sahadev's eyes narrowed. 'I will cut off those dice-throwing hands of yours and pin you to the dirt until you bleed out through your wrists. Remember my saying this. Because it's a vow.'

Sahadev, leaving this image with the man he hated, turned on his heel and returned to his brothers. Where was Yudhishtir in all this? He walked several paces ahead of his family, his eyes covered with his right hand. Some said he did that because he feared his rage would burn any Kaurava he looked at. More likely he was hiding tears. Vidura walked with him, promising to bring Kunti from Indraprastha to live in his house. The Kauravas would scuttle into Indraprastha's many palaces like hermit crabs into abandoned shells, said Vidura. There was no stopping that. It would all be Hastinapur soon.

When the road grew rough and it was time to part ways, Vidura hugged each of the Pandavas. He paused to memorize their faces. Before Panchali, he bowed to touch her feet, insisting on showing her reverence after so many insults. The remaining Kauravas tried their best to ruin the moment by shouting loud, fake-tearful goodbyes. Arjuna grabbed a handful of sand off the roadside and let it spill, very slowly, from his hand. He pointed at the grains as they fell. 'That's how many arrows,' he said grimly. 'That's how many.' He flung the last of it at their feet, and more than a few skipped back.

The five Pandavas and Panchali turned their backs on Hastinapur and proceeded into the forest. Panchali's voice spiralled tremulously into the sky, and the Kauravas fell silent—and stayed silent, the whole walk back to the palace, because Panchali's husbands joined her in a slow, deep, increasingly confident chorus. Bheem kept time by tapping his mace against his thigh. They were singing the Kauravas a dirge.